ANGUISH

WITH ACTIONS COME CONSEQUENCES

ANGUISH

WITH ACTIONS COME CONSEQUENCES

BOOK 1

written by

R.I.S.K

LAGRANGE GEORGIA

Dedicated to Family and Friends.
Especially the very friendship that inspired this story.
Thank you, Leila

Contents

Prologue

She sat staring at her room and the bare bones that were left- the bed and the shelves. Everything else had been packed away and taken to her new home. Then, she heard and felt her mother at the bedroom door. "Do I have to go?" She found herself asking even though she knew the answer.

"Yes, now that your father has passed, there is no one to look after you while I'm gone."

"Can't you just become a normal mother?"

There was laughter as her mother wrapped her into a hug, her sweet sassafras scent infused with a light spray of jasmine draped her warmly. "Darling, you know I love you. But I have to work, and I have a job to do. I can't stay with you because no one else can do my job."

Kalea looked into her mother's green eyes, confused. "I still don't understand, Mom. You fly planes." Her mother looked into her daughter's green eyes. Staring lovingly down at her. The small wrinkles around her mouth grew as she gave a small encouraging smile.

"You will understand, sweetheart. The Wings will help you understand; You are no longer a normal little girl. Perhaps you never have been."

Kalea felt as if she was going to cry. She hugged her mother, burying her face into her chest and holding on to her for dear life. "What can the Wings teach me that you can't?"

"They will help you fulfill your destiny. Haven't you felt the call?" Her mother asked. Kalea heard the words come from her curly hair as her mother held onto her. Kalea muffled words drifted upward…. "If you mean an upset stomach and strange dreams, a call."

Her mother laughed and ruffled her hair as she pulled back from her daughter to look at her. Kalea was slightly shorter than her, but her mother knew that would be very different the next time they met.

"Kalea dear…" she said as she swallowed back a sob, "you are destined for greatness, and know that I will always be proud of you no matter where I am in the universe."

Kalea looked at her mother and sighed with acceptance. "I guess it's time for me to meet the rest of my new family." Her mother nodded as they walked hand in hand out of the house and past the for-sale sign to a small two-door run-down Jeep with the last of her stuff.

Her mother started the engine and pulled the car out of the driveway leaving the small greenhouse behind with its lush pastures and small barn. They had sold most of the horses; the only two remaining were at her mother's new home.

Her father had passed away almost a month ago; he withered away and died from 'natural' reasons. Still, it was hard on Kalea as she had no control over things moving into motion.

Kalea looked out the window and let out a small breath to release her inner conflict. She watched as trees and familiar landscapes flashed by. *How had things gotten so crazy,* she thought, looking away from the window to stare at her mother driving with her window down, which blew her red-brown hair, and her sunglasses gleamed. Her mother, who often was away for long periods, had left the child-raising to Kalea's father.

For 14 years, Kalea saw her mother on major holidays and during long school vacations. Two weeks in the summer, she and her father would fly out and meet her mother at some historical or tropical place. Other than that, Kalea and the horses stayed on the move, never staying in a house or state for more than a year or two. Then last year, her dad fell ill, and they stayed in the small greenhouse for the start of Kalea's freshman year in high school. There she met the girl who was now her legal sister. A shiver went down Kalea's spine as she remembered when she first met Valerie. Valerie sat next to her in the lunchroom and smiled, the connection was instant, and they became fast friends. Thinking back, Kalea found their instant connection odd. Valerie was in Kalea's second block and was consistently swarmed by people and seemed to be quite popular. Still, somehow, she extended Kalea into her life. Little had Kalea known that this friendship would lead to a new life she was heading toward.

Kalea blinked back a tear she didn't know she had shed, remembering when her dad was clearly not going to recover, her mother took some vacation time and came home. Her Mother stood with Kalea as she said her goodbyes and arranged the small service at the end of his life where his one living relative, a great uncle, had come to pay his respects. Other than him, her mother, the preacher, and herself, not another soul had attended the service. But then Valerie and her mother met them at the graveyard with flowers and kind words.

Kalea tried to keep her tears at bay as she recalled the days that followed her father's death. It had been wonderful to have her mother home, even if it was a sad time. She found it comforting to have someone who shared the mourning. Kal, in her mind, fantasized that it would last forever. However, when she arrived home from school, she found Valerie's mother in the kitchen with her mother and was told she would move in with her best friend and her family.

Kalea's mind returned to the present, and she felt the pressure of her hand being squeezed. Kalea looked at her mother and noticed she was also crying. She pulled Kalea into a one-armed hug. "We are almost there. Are you ready?" Kalea nodded, and her mother made the final turn onto an all-familiar road leading to Kalea's new home.

Valerie and her mother met them on big gray horses at the end of the long dirt driveway. While leading them, they conversed and laughed together while riding toward the house. Valerie's father met them in the front yard of the little yellow and brown house, along with Valerie's younger brother Koda and her older sister Arcy.

They helped Kalea settle in the small room she would share with Valerie. The room was almost unrecognizable from what Kalea remembered from her visits. It was no longer a mess with clothes and stuff thrown around but artfully organized, in half with two beds, small dressers under them, and a desk in the middle with a computer.

"Valerie gave you the window. She felt it would give you some privacy until you warm up into the family." Her new guardian said with a smile.

Kalea then looked at Valerie's side of the room; the walls were covered with horse posters, ribbons, and photographs. It was a giant collage compressed into a small space. She looked at her side and noticed that Valerie had made the bed under the red-draped window with Kalea's favorite bedspread. However, seeing her sheets under the freshly painted walls made Kalea melancholy for home. She was unsure of what she felt as she glanced at the equally pressed bed that belonged to her roommate.

"There is an account on the computer for you. The password is 'wolf-girl,' one-word lowercase, but feel free to change it when you log on." Valerie announced, walking into the room from the barn covered in hay. "If you ever want to go out and ride, there are several horses to choose from." She continued toward Kalea only to pull her over to the shared part of the room.

"Feel free to add your own pizazz to the walls. All your framed art and stuff are waiting for your direction to decorate your side of the room. Once you're done with that, you and I, your mother, and the family are all going to lunch. You may want some alone time when we get home if you need it."

Kalea smiled and nodded, and with her mother and Mr. Wing, she got her room set up in no time, adding her flair to the once bare walls. Soon she was laughing with her new family and carrying on like she always did when she visited.

But unfortunately, reality didn't hit till after lunch. Kalea cried to her mother, pleading for her not to go, only to get the same hair ruffle and a kiss on the head. After her mother left, Kalea sat in her new room alone, feeling very small in the world.

CHAPTER 1

The Bigger Picture

The moon rose on a cool winter night as two friends walked out of their warm house in search of adventure. Instead, they walked a well-worn path toward disaster. Except for the crescent moon still low on the horizon and the light glow of the early evening stars, it was a dark night. The bare trees groaned and swayed in the light breeze adding to the night sounds of crickets and bullfrogs. An occasional owl echoed around the party of two as they walked the rocky driveway. A bat flew low overhead, and the smaller girl gave a frightened screech and grabbed her friend's arm.

"I should have told you that I am afraid of the dark," Kalea whispered, her eyes darting around, looking for something. The taller girl, Valerie, laughed and continued to walk the path down the hill to the dark shadows where the barn was in daylight hours.

Besides the slight crunching of the gravel underfoot, they walked in silence again. Breathing the chill, clean air, one girl grinned while the other shook. "It is not the dark you should be afraid of," Valerie stated, finally stopping and taking a deep whiff of air. The moon slowly rose higher, casting deep and darkening shadows on the path ahead.

"I know it's the things that come out a night," Kalea replied through chattering teeth. "I should have grabbed a coat," she stated, moving closer to Valerie and wondering why she had been dragged outside before supper. However, Valerie ignored her remark and seemed unaffected by the cold as she started to walk, casting her eyes about as if expecting danger. Kalea clung harder to Valerie's arm, looking around herself.

Valerie laughed and stopped walking. Kalea could just make out her friend's thin face in the glimmer of the light from the moon. Kalea felt a tiny bit of relief as they walked out of the thick shadows cast by a clump of trees into a moonlit part of the path.

Kalea noticed the calculating look in Valerie's eyes as her friend looked deep into the shadow between them and the barn.

Valerie smiled as she began to pull Kalea further down the path. Kalea received a delayed thought to her last spoken words as Valerie said, "Do Not worry about those things. I will protect you."

Something started to happen as they walked into the shadow of the trees. At first, Kalea did not pick up on it, but as Valerie's body became tense, Kalea noticed that the night sounds had changed. The crickets and the bullfrogs had stopped their song as if disturbed by someone other than them. A low howl and distant rumble like thunder rolling in took its place. As they walked closer to the barn, suddenly, a cloud covered the moon, making it almost pitch black. Kalea grabbed her friend's arm harder as a peal of short non-human laughter seemed to surround them, and yet Valerie continued to walk at her steady pace.

The stars started to go out, and the rustle of the dead leaves came from somewhere up ahead. Kalea noticed as one howl died away; another was quick to start louder than before. Then, the previous laughter resonated, but it felt so close this time she could imagine its breath on the back of her neck. Kalea felt like her whole body had gone colder, and not just from the air temperature.

Valerie stopped momentarily, seeming a little unsure as Kalea looked up at her hopefully. "We are turning around now, right?" She asked. Valerie did not answer in words, but Kalea could tell Valerie was staring out into the darkness, her expression hard and determined as she simply took a step forward, pulling her along. Again, she heard the howl and rumble. But this time, it was clearer, like distant thunder, and it shook the air around them. Not looking away from where they were going, Valerie finally spoke using Kalea's nickname.

"Kal, I haven't been completely honest with you." She revealed with a disclaimer, "If dung hits the fan and we are put in a dangerous situation, I promise to explain."

Immediately, the sound of a ghostly laugh appeared to shimmer in the air around them. A little light peaked through the dark cloud above the girls. Kal nodded, still holding her death grip on Valerie's arm, and asked, "So, who's trying to get us?"

"They are evil creatures who are not to be trusted. You see, some creatures can appear to be human but are not... you know what I mean?" Valerie said as she looked down at her friend, doubting her decision to take a walk, but it was the only way to talk privately. At least, she had thought it was.

Valerie caught herself looking around, knowing they were being watched; she did not know by who or how many. The plan she had so delicately worked out in her head months ago seemed like it was all falling apart.

Valerie closed her eyes, using her mind's eye to review how she would tell Kalea the truth about everything before things got crazy. She looked down at her friend and thought, *it's like taking off a band-aid; you have to do it quickly and as painlessly as possible*; Valerie then felt herself relax again, and despite her arm going numb from Kalea's death grip, she smiled.

They made it to the barns. The large tin buildings stood empty in the cool, clear night, apart from the hunting barn cats and the dozing chickens in their coop. Kal, who had felt her friend relax, had started to settle down. She looked around while shadows flew overhead and small outlines of bats glimmered on the ground. Then it seemed like all the light disappeared, evaporating into the night, snuffed out like a wick. Kalea gave a slight squeal, clinging to her friend's arm; her heart pounded in her chest like a racehorse.

"Will you stop that? You'll let them know you're afraid," Valerie snapped as Kalea clung to her arm. Then, looking around herself and inhaling through the nose, "They can smell fear?" Valerie increased her pace, which left her dragging Kalea behind roughly. She had to get to the meeting place. The point where she had delicately planned and set aside for the last barrier to be broken. The place where Kalea could finally realize what there was to know.

Valerie dragged Kalea past the wash racks, where she cooled her horses down in summer. They stood like tall open shadows, their chains clinking with the slight wind. Valerie silently cursed as she guided Kal over an uneven rut in the path, causing Kal to trip, almost making them fall. "What was that?"

Kal asked, her voice trembling. "Just a rut in the driveway my dad hasn't fixed yet," Valerie whispered back as she took another breath. Yes, everything was in place. The thought brought a smile back to her face. The cloud coverage parted, allowing some moonlight to shine down on the spot Valerie needed to reach. Kalea started crying when the clouds closed, enveloping the path into darkness again.

Valerie forced herself not to roll her eyes as she hadn't planned on Kalea being afraid of the dark. *This could completely traumatize her,* Valerie thought, looking down at her friend; *it's not too late to turn back,* she thought; Valerie then took another breath. *I have to enlighten her... and this is the only way.* Finally, letting her feelings get the best of her, Valerie spoke her frustration aloud, "Can you please relax?" she said as they continued walking.

They were just a few steps away from the spot where she was going to rip the figurative band-aid from Kalea's mind. Valerie licked her lips and thought as she took the last steps, *go big or go home.* Taking the final step to where she knew all hell was about to break loose, she stopped and said, "They are here."

"Who's them?" Kalea found herself asking, her voice shaky.

"We are them," hissed a voice from behind. Kalea wanted to bolt, but her hands clung to her friend, who stood firm.

"Aren't we supposed to run away from hissing voices?" Kalea cried as Valerie turned to face the voice. That is when Kalea stared at her friend, unsure what she saw, as her friend had changed. Valerie's normally calm brown eyes had turned a bright green, her blond hair was now black with green highlights, and the most disturbing thing was she smiled at the demon.

"Okay, now you are starting to freak me out," Kalea whimpered, staring at her friend like a deer caught in headlights. She saw by the tiny flicker of a smile and the slight wink of that shining eye that this was still Valerie as she knew her. A sense of strange calm settled over her, and Kalea tightened the hold on her friend's arm; even if this was as bad as she thought it was, Valerie did say she would protect her.

"So, we meet again, Holjus," Valerie greeted. Kalea gulped as the hissing voice made itself known, and her friend's voice had changed from quiet and sweet to a powerful, commanding tone.

"Yes, we do, Valerie. Now prepare..."

Holjus was cut short by a whinny and a blast of light. Suddenly, a painted stallion appeared between him and the girls.

"Don't you finish that statement," the stallion commanded sternly, turning into a handsome young man.

"Sallisfer," Valerie muttered what sounded like a curse under her breath. And at that exact moment, Kalea's mouth fell open, and her jaw dropped like it nearly hit the ground.

"Wow!" Kalea exclaimed.

"Shhh, Kal," Valerie whispered, looking down at her friend with an irritated glance.

"So, the great manly man to the rescue of two, beautiful, if not fierce looking...young..." Holjus looked around Sallisfer at the two girls, "Okay, I take that back; one is fierce, the other is helpless."

Kalea let go of Valerie's arm and stepped forward, "No one calls me helpless," she said angrily. Not noticing her sweet voice had grown as deep and powerful as her friend's.

"I didn't mean you," Holjus said with a grin, pointing to Valerie.

"Oh, really?" Valerie said, crossing her arms with a grin on her face, "I've been practicing since the last time we met."

"Ooooh, I'm so...." he was again cut short by Valerie snapping her fingers. Kal watched in amazement when he shimmered and turned into a bubble.

"Okay, I still need more practice," Valerie grumbled, her shoulders drooping in disappointment, but Kalea could tell that inwardly Valerie was laughing.

It seemed like some crazy practical joke as Kalea inspected the bubble that was a demon. The bubble fascinated Kalea, its perfect dark spherical shape hovering a few inches off the ground, seeming too heavy to go higher. "How did you do this?" Kalea asked, her finger just inches from the bubble. "I wouldn't touch it." Sallisfer hissed, eyeing Valerie with suspicion. "What if I do this?" Kalea proclaimed, feeling like her old self and acting like it was typical for her best friend to do magic, as she touched the black, disturbingly warm surface of the bubble.

Valerie burst into laughter as she watched Kal poke at the bubble. Seeing that although the plan didn't go as planned, the use of magic, this big, had truly opened her friend's mind at last. The relief that the plan worked made Valerie laugh harder.

Kalea started to laugh as Sallisfer tried to keep Valerie from falling. Valerie was now laughing so hard tears were streaming down her face. Sallisfer sighed deeply and shook his head, and looked at Kal.

"I do not believe we have been properly introduced," Sallisfer said. Extending his free hand to Kal, who took it timidly, "I am Sallisfer King."

"I'm Kalea Breese, but please call me Kal." She answered back, and he gave her a stunning smile.

"Kal, it is," he nodded, shaking her hand, "and we call this one Knucklehead most of the time."

"Knucklehead!" Valerie took offense, pulling herself back together and giving him a glare. Kal saw a very dark shadow cross Valerie's face, and a silent exchange passed between her and Sallisfer, who had turned pale and gulped, suddenly turning himself into a small black puppy. Kal stared at him, trying not to blink in fear of missing something that could explain what she was seeing.

"You wouldn't hurt a mere helpless puppy, would you?" Kal asked as Sallisfer gave Valerie the puppy face.

A dark shadow crossed Valerie's face with an evil smile, then with an "Oh. well..." as she seemed to let it all go. Suddenly she was the Valerie that Kal had met at school. Kal watched as Valerie got down to her knees and patted Sallisfer's head.

"Thanks for coming to our rescue, even though I had it all under control," Valerie stated as she watched them.

Sallisfer's puppy face seemed to smile, and he shimmered as his form started to change. Soon he had shifted into a purring cat. Kal squealed; she didn't care that this cat had been a dog, a man, and even a horse as she pulled him into her arms and squeezed him. Sallisfer's eyes bulged out like one of those novelty toys whose eyes popped out when you squeezed them.

Valerie stared for a minute; her jaw slacked, and her eyes widened. "That's new," she murmured. Then, with a smile, she stood, brushed off her clothes, and gave Kal a wink as she looked them over. "You do make a good couple. I mean, cut a few years off, and you two would be perfect."

Kal grinned, pulled the unwilling Sallisfer up, and kissed him on the top of the head, "Oh really, thank you," Kal laughed as she continued to cuddle with the reluctant Sallisfer, who finally hissed and clawed out of her hold and ran behind Valerie. Valerie gave a small chuckle at Sallisfer's dirty look as he tried to regain some dignity as he shimmered back into his human form.

Kal laughed and pointed at his hair which was a mess. Sticking up were black, blue, and green spikes where she had kissed him. It looked like a cowlick. Sallisfer grumbled as he tried unsuccessfully to put his hair back in order. Before Kal could comprehend what happened, Valerie sighed; reaching into thin air, she pulled out a comb and mirror, handing it to Sallisfer with a tired look in her now-green eyes.

He gave her a small, almost hidden smile, and when he made the comb and mirror disappear, he brushed against her. If Kal had not been paying attention, it could have passed as an accident or even unnoticed as a small trickle of light went from his arm to Valerie's as they turned simultaneously to look at the black bubble still floating in the air.

"What should we do with you, mister?" Valerie asked with a smile.

Sallisfer smiled, "I thought we could put him behind the fence with the rest of them." Kal gave a mantel shake as the hair on her back restarted to stand up on end; fear crept into her heart again as she looked around, "The rest?" Sallisfer nodded absently, still looking at the bubble. Kal gave a terrified squeak as she grabbed his arm, "I don't like demons." She whispered as Sallisfer tried to pry her off him with an irritated groan.

"Yes, about a hundred of them are in that old pool behind my grandfather's house," Valerie explained with a knowing wink at her. Kal shivered and clinched harder onto Sallisfer's already numbing arm.

"What if I keep him like a fish and feed him to my brother?" Valerie suggested. The bubble squealed and started wiggling. Valerie smiled, "I think he likes the idea."

"Wa dw nw," came a distorted answer from the wiggling bubble.

"What was that again?" Valerie and Kal said together, leaning closer to the bubble.

"I....do....not," it exclaimed loud and clear.

Valerie smiled, popped the bubble with a simple wrist flick, and with a thump and a whine, Holjus landed on the ground.

"My tail," he whined, holding his black pointed tail in his hands, "I think it's broken." He tried to flex it but winced.

"That's your problem," Valerie laughed with an evil smile growing on her face, but her eyes still darted around, looking for more of the demons as she felt their eyes on her. She licked her lips while she looked down at the demon who struggled to stand. "I have a little question," she almost whispered. Holjus looked up at her with his red eyes.

"Why did you call yourself them?" Kal blurred out suddenly. Valerie, Sallisfer, and Holjus looked at her with questioning eyes.

"I don't know. I felt like it." Holjus shrugged. Kal couldn't tell if he was relieved by her blurt or annoyed. When he finally stood up, his legs were a little shaky.

"You know, you don't seem like a demon," Kal observed, "at least the ones I pictured in my head from all the stories my mother told me."

Holjus's eyes filled quickly with suppressed sorrow, but he laughed, "Books can be misleading."

Valerie took that moment and grabbed Holjus, throwing him into the air so fast that Kal had no time to grasp where she had found the strength. Holjus must have weighed more than she did, at least how he was built. "Go back to the darkness whence you came," she almost shouted. The darkness deepened, and then Holjus was gone. Kal sighed disappointedly, "Now look what you did; you scared the hottie away," she almost whined.

Sallisfer looked down at her, "It's better that way."

"And why is it better that way?"

"Because Demons and Earth children have always been enemies since the war," Valerie justified. "Always, and forevermore."

"Why?"

"I don't know. It's some sort of punishment," Valerie growled, her green eyes lighting in anger.

"Wow. You really don't believe in making your own destiny, do you?"

"My destiny is laid out before me. I will have to face that demon on my 16th birthday."

Kal rolled her eyes. "Stubborn, crazy person who abducted my friend," she muttered under her breath, glaring at Valerie before leaning her head on Sallisfer's arm.

"One question. When am I gonna wake up?" Kal asked.

Sallisfer looked at her, confused. "What are you talking about?"

"I'm dreaming, aren't I?" Kal retorted, irritated.

"How am I supposed to know? I suspect that if you're here, and nothing unexplainable happened, then you're not dreaming."

"Unexplainable? Everything I've seen is unexplainable!"

"Then you're dreaming!" he said.

"Now that's rude!" Valerie interjected, "You shouldn't lie to a girl, Sal! You know that!"

"She started it." Sallisfer pointed.

"I don't care. I'm going to finish it. Let's all go to bed. I'm tired," Valerie stated.

"How can you sleep in times like this?" Kal asked.

"I don't know. You're the one dreaming!" Sallisfer laughed. "Come on now, and I'll walk you two up to the house."

"Why, thank you, Sallisfer," Valerie replied sarcastically. "You're just too kind."

"Be nice to him." Kal glared at her friend, "He's just worried about your well-being."

"Yeah, right," Valerie stated.

Kal looked at Valerie, "Well, it's better than my other idea."

Valerie, shaking her head in denial of Kal's idea, "Do I want to ask?" She questioned.

"Go ahead!" Kal said with a grin.

"What is the other idea?" Valerie asked dryly.

A smile grew on Kal's face, and she glanced up at Sallisfer. "Sallisfer likes you!"

"ME?!" Valerie choked out squeakily and coughed as if something had gone down the wrong pipe.

"HER?!" Sallisfer said as he reached over and patted Valerie on the back as she looked at him skeptically.

"Or not," Kal spoke, watching them with fresh, newfound doubt.

The rest of the walk was silent until they got near the house.

"When will I see you again?" Kal asked. Sallisfer looked down at Kal with irritation.

"I'll see you, but you won't see me."

"Oh... Why?" she inquired.

"Don't ask, Kal... Please don't." Valerie muttered, and Kal looked over at her with burning curiosity in her eyes.

"What?"

"I'm not telling you." Sallisfer agreed quickly as Kal's eyes turned to him.

"Let's just say I turn into something unexpected."

"Fine." Kal pouted, hugging him around his waist. Sallisfer looked at Valerie with pleading eyes, but only met a smug smile from her.

"Did you do this to her?" Sallisfer questioned with a mild grimace.

"I'm not that advanced! I only helped her along a little bit." Sallisfer sighed and muttered something under his breath, but whatever he said didn't get Kal off his waist.

"You can't undo it," Valerie said with a smile as she ran ahead.

"I hate her," Sallisfer said, dragging Kal with him as he stared at Valerie's back.

"Valerie, what are you doing without your jacket?" Her mother shouted when they came into view of the small yellow house. Valerie rolled her eyes.

"I don't need a jacket, Mom."

"You're gonna get sick!"

"No, I'm not."

"Don't sass me, young lady!"

"Yes, Mom," Valerie muttered, sighing as she stepped back into the house. Kal squeezed the air out of Sallisfer before letting go and followed Valerie inside.

Ms. Wing then spotted Sallisfer and smiled.

"Would you like to stay for dinner, Sallisfer?" Ms. Wing asked.

"Okay...?" He replied, "Thank you, I think."

"Valerie! Go clean the veggies!"

"Yes, ma'am." Came the ensuing grumble, "Horse food."

"Haven't we already talked about being rude, Valerie?"

"Yes, ma'am," Valerie stated, although she was getting really irritated.

Sallisfer smiled, walked into the warm house, and was swept into the activity. Kal paused as someone turned on the radio and grinned as her song came on. She immediately began to sing and dance. Sallisfer shook his head as he watched her. He did have to admit she sang well, and she could dance. But immediately after he realized what he had thought, he shook the thought clear across the room. *I'd rather get run over.* He thought venomously. Kal grinned as the song ended, a little out of breath, but she began to sing again as the next song came on. She pulled Sallisfer into it, and he obliged.

"I'm running away." Kal began, and Sallisfer followed up. When the song was over, they were both out of breath and laughing. Valerie rolled her eyes and stomped over to the radio.

"End of the show..." She muttered as she switched the channel.

"STRONG!" She grinned and pushed Sallisfer and Kal out of the way.

Kal grinned, "And she calls me crazy..."

"How many times have I told you? No magic in the house!" Ms. Wing yelled from down the hall in the bathroom.

"Hey! I wasn't doing anything!" Valerie protested, reaching to turn off the radio when she saw her hands. Valerie stared at them for a moment, her hand hovering over the radio that started to smoke. Sallisfer walked over and snatched her wrist, "Earth children aren't supposed to do that." He growled.

"But..." Valerie stated, bewildered.

"What is it?" Kal asked, watching the green and red glow fade from Valerie's hands.

"It's fire," Sallisfer said, his eyes never leaving Valerie's, which had a guilty startled look.

"Fire?" Kal asked, "Why can't Valerie do fire?"

"Only demons and chosen dragons control fire!" Valerie's voice shook as she pulled her eyes from Sallisfer's and looked at Kal.

"Exactly," Sallisfer replied.

"But... How?" Valerie muttered, snatching her hand back and looking at her hands with apprehension.

"I don't know, but it's not good."

Valerie looked up at him, and Kal saw something cross between them silently, but before she could even react to it, the moment was over, and Valerie smirked and simply replied, "Then that explains it. I'm not good."

Sallisfer sighed and sat back down next to Kal with a worried look in his clear blue eyes. Kal took his hand, and he looked at Kal with a small smile.

"We're in big trouble, aren't we?"

"We? You're only a half-blood," Sallisfer said, a slight and sudden disgust in his voice.

Kal's innocence shattered in the blink of an eye. Her eyes flashed, and her hair faded to white.

"A half-blood... Hah. Teach me. See how much I know. Don't get judgmental."

"Fine, then. I'll see how long you last."

"Fine." She turned to leave but paused as she heard the door open. There stood Valerie's sister, but she too had changed since that morning when her mother had dropped her off with the Wings.

"I've missed something, haven't I?" Arcy asked, her 'faerie' wings folded down.

"We both have," replied a deep, rough voice. A Dwarf stepped out from behind Arcy, his long golden-red beard tucked into his belt. He looked around at all of them and shook his head when he saw Kal's large eyes. He walked over, took Kal's limp hand, and bowed slightly, "I am Talys Connor Jones. It is nice to meet the newest daughter of the Wing Family. You must be Kalea."

Kal nodded, "Please call me Kal." And she saw him smile.

"Nice to meet you, Kal. This must be quite a shock for you. I am sure my dear sister-in-law did not mention any of this to you as she was supposed to. I hope you forgive her; you have been all she could talk about since you two met in August, and your mother probably told you very little about your heritage. She is a very busy time lord." Talys spoke calmly to Kal, and she felt reassured that this was real and everything would be okay.

"It is nice to meet you too, Talys, and thank you." Kal smiled; he smiled back and kissed her head like the big brother she had always wanted.

"Dinner!" Came the call from the kitchen, and Kal almost immediately forgot where she was from the smell of the meat. She sat beside Valerie, pulling Sallisfer next to her on the other side.

"So, you forgive me?" Sallisfer asked hopefully.

"No."

"Please?" he asked.

"Fine. Your mistake," smiling Kal leaned on his arm, cuddling.

He sighed but accepted it grudgingly. Valerie grinned at him across Kal's head. Her look clearly said, 'You know you like her.' Sallisfer's return look gave nothing away, but he leaned his head closer to Kal's cuddling back.

"Is that love, Sally?" Valerie's sister, Arcy, gasped, her rainbow-colored wings flickering out with excitement. "Do I actually get to 'chat' with someone?" Arcy said with an evil look on her face.

Kal glared at Arcy as she snuggled closer to Sallisfer, "No chats." She grumbled, clinging to Sallisfer's arm. "No hurting. He's mine."

Arcy laughed and glanced at Valerie, who had her arms crossed and watched with a distasteful look. "And how old are you?" Arcy asked Kal. "As your older sister, it is my job to be protective and nosey."

"Fourteen. Almost fifteen." Kal stated a little crossly.

Arcy's smile widened so you could see her perfect teeth. "And what grade?"

"Ninth. Happy now?" Kal stared at the plates of perfectly grilled steaks placed on the table. The Wing's had cooked her favorite meal.

Arcy shook her head. "No, as your older sister, I must inform you that he is much too old for you. He is seventeen, in eleventh grade, and also a geek," Arcy stated as she sat beside her husband.

"I don't care! You're just jealous." Kal stuck her tongue out at Arcy.

"I am far older than both of you. So, I am not jealous." Arcy retorted. "And besides. I've got a Dwarf!" She kissed her husband's hairy cheek and, in return, stuck her tongue out at Kal.

"I'm older than all of you." Mr. Wing said, irritated, "So stop talking and start eating."

Kal grinned and piled her plate full of steaks. Sallisfer shook his head and took the carrots and other vegetables, making himself a salad.

Valerie glanced over, glaring at his plate. "Horse food." She muttered, taking a few tomato chunks, cucumber slices, and a steak.

CHAPTER 2

Lesson One, Fairies Love Chocolate

After a delicious dinner, everyone was dozing and making light talk. Valerie's dad, Kal's new legal guardian, was catching Kal up on the routines around the house and some of the magic allowed in the home. And as they were still chatting, Arcy stood up abruptly. "Who's got chocolate? I smell chocolate!"

"Oooh, great." Valerie groaned, "Who brought chocolate into this house?"

"Oops." Kal pulled out a white chocolate candy bar and immediately had Valerie and Arcy staring at her with big puppy-dog eyes.

"Go fetch." Kal threw the candy bar, and Arcy was on it in a nano-second, tearing the wrapper open and stuffing it into her mouth before Valerie could get near her.

"MINE!" Arcy stated.

Valerie stared at the rest of it hungrily, "Can I have just a little bit? Please?"

"NO! MINE!" Arcy repeated selfishly.

Valerie sighed, crestfallen. "Fine." She pouted, "I'm only your sister... What do I matter?"

"Fine. Here." Arcy tossed the wrapper at Valerie. "Lick the remnants off."

Valerie followed that order. Kal just shook her head. "I'll remember that. I can get away with anything if I have white chocolate." She muttered.

"Yup! With us, you can!" Valerie replied.

Arcy looked up from her still position, her pupils dilated. Her body began to vibrate, and her wings flickered and fluttered.

"SUGAR HIGH!!" Valerie yelled, flicking her hand at the door. It burst open, and Arcy almost literally tore it from its hinges as she flew outside. Valerie repeated the gesture, and the door closed. The next thing they heard was a high-pitched scream. Talys sighed. "Not again..." He stood and walked out the door while Valerie and Kal snuck to the window. The only thing they saw was Arcy tangled in the tree limbs of an old oak, shivering so hard the whole tree was vibrating.

Then, with a massive crack, the tree began to tilt and fall. The high-pitched scream again came, but Arcy untangled herself and zoomed off into the night, a rainbow dot zipping and spinning crazily in the air.

Valerie laughed, "My sister can be eccentric sometimes. But it is the joys of being a fairy, very easily excited, and always happy until they are not... one should never make a fairy mad."

"What happens when they get mad?" Kal wondered. Mr. Wing answered her internal thought.

"Let's just say fairies over-exaggerate their emotions." Mr. Wing said, "Can be very dangerous depending on their powers."

"How is Arcy a fairy? Are you a fairy, Valerie?"

Valerie smiled, "I am part fairy. My grandmother was a fairy born, and Arcy's dad was the fairy king. Making her more fairy than anything, she has limited shifting abilities passed down through our grandfather. She is known as an earth fairy because she has a closer tie to the earth because of our grandfather, who was a brown warlock. A true Earth Child."

Kal thought it over, "What am I?"

"Other than a half-blood?" Sallisfer shrugged, "We aren't sure; your power is just surfacing. Your mother is a powerful past time lord, your grandfather was a shifter and a decent brown warlock, and your grandmother was a blue sorceress with extraordinary power. So, we can assume that somewhere in your line is another time lord because of your mother's power. Her level is matched by her mother, your grandmother."

"How do you know so much about me and my family history? I never met my grandparents." Kal had assumed they had died when her mother was younger and felt hurt as she turned to look back out the window at the old cedar tree lit by the glow of the porch light.

A light hand landed on Kal's shoulder, "They were good people. Your grandfather was my master when I was just a girl. Your mother and I never really became close because she was learning time travel from Master Wood and was a few years older than me." Ms. Wing's voice was soft and full of sympathy.

"Are they still alive?"

"Master Scott and his wife retired years ago into the human world. I am not sure; they haven't contacted the magic realm in over sixteen years."

Kal gave a sigh of disappointment. She couldn't help but feel a little less strange in this new realm. She had ties in it. Her mother had been born to magic parents; this magic stuff wasn't some strange phenomenal thing that happened to her; it was meant and in her genes. It made her feel a little stronger, just a tad more confident, and definitely happier about herself,

"Well, I got to be off, or my mom will start to worry," Sallisfer said, breaking the silence and interrupting Kal's thoughts. She looked over at him as he got up from the ashen-colored sofa. "Promise I'll see you Monday." He added when Kal's eye landed on him with suspicion.

"No. You could see me, but I wouldn't see you. Talk to me, not see me." Kal replied, smirking as Valerie laughed.

"She's got you, there, Sallisfer."

"Oh, shut up." He muttered, glaring at Valerie before turning the scowl to Kal.

"Fine."

"Wait... promise!" Kal commanded.

"I promise. Happy now?" He growled.

"Yup!" She chirped, hopping up and kissing his cheek.

"Awww... Classic love. Let me get a barf-bag 'cause I'm gonna be sick." Valerie muttered.

Mr. and Ms. Wing laughed lightly, "Well, you be safe on your way home. Unfortunately, Sallisfer traveling alone these days is not as safe as it used to be. Remember the protection spell I taught you." Mr. Wing said, patting him on the shoulder.

"I will. Thank you for supper."

"You are always welcome at my table, Master Sallisfer." Mr. Wing beamed, and Sallisfer gave a respectful bow.

"Again, thank you."

"Please give your mother my regards," Ms. Wing smiled, "Good night."

Kal could tell that the Wings accepted Sallisfer like a second son. Then it occurred to her that she hadn't seen Koda since lunch and that he hadn't been present at supper. As Sallisfer gave his final goodbyes, Kal asked, "Where is Koda?" Mr. and Ms. Wing exchanged looks and then looked at their daughter, who looked rather sheepish.

"I am here..." Came a tiny voice, and all of them looked down to see Valerie's little brother, who was literally about an inch or two tall.

"Oh... I forgot all about you!" Valerie said with a smile.

Kal leaned down, "Wow.... you shrunk."

His tiny finger pointed to Valerie. "She did this to me!"

"I did not!" Valerie acted offended, scoffing at the notion.

Sallisfer sighed and pinched the air right above Valerie's brother's head. Then, as he pulled his fingers upward, Valerie's brother grew into his regular size.

"Aww... you had to grow him? He was less annoying when he was an inch tall!" Valerie whined. Koda brushed himself off and glanced around.

"Where are those steaks? I'm starving! I haven't had anything to eat since lunch."

"That's your fault! You should have never gotten on my bad side!"

Ms. Wing shook her head and looked as if this was an everyday occurrence in their household. She walked to the kitchen, pulled out a plate she had saved for Koda, and placed it in the microwave. Mr. Wing eyed his daughter and looked from Sallisfer to Koda.

"What did you do?" Mr. Wing asked.

"But I didn't do anything!"

A fire flickered on Valerie's fingertips. "Do you want to test that?" Her green eyes seemed like a veil for the fire that blazed behind them, and Sallisfer quickly shook her before Mr. Wing saw anything.

"Snap out of it! Don't let it consume you! It'll turn you into one of them!" He whispered harshly into Valerie's ear, glancing at Mr. Wing, afraid he might have seen something. He placed his hand on Valerie's shoulder and guided her to the door motioning for Kal to follow him out of earshot.

Valerie shook her head, and the fires were put out. "Don't let what consume me?" She asked, with confusion in her normal brown eyes.

"You're not supposed to be able to do that!"

"Do what?"

"Create fire!" Sallisfer whispered sternly in aggravation.

"I can't create fire! Demons do that!"

Sallisfer sighed, and Kal saw yet another silent exchange between Valerie and him. Then he turned to Kal, irritation on his face. "I gotta go, but I would greatly appreciate it if you would keep an eye on her."

"Alright, Sallisfer." Kal nodded seriously. Sallisfer nodded back with a smile. He turned on his heel, went out the door, and shifted into a paint horse, galloping into the night.

Kal sighed deeply, watching after him, "He's so hot," she muttered as she walked back and closed the door.

"Ya, ya, that's what they all say." Valerie laughed, guiding Kal down the hall.

"What, you know someone cuter?"

Valerie just smiled, a gleam in her green eyes, "I may know a guy that is so cute; all the girls literally fall head over heels for him."

They reached their room, and Valerie was about to close the door when Ms. Wing appeared in the doorway of Koda's room, directly across the hall. "Make sure you take care of Blaze!" her mother reminded.

"I will, Mom," Valerie said over her shoulder as she looked into the small cage on her bookshelf.

"Can I help you?" Kal asked, looking inside the terrarium where what appeared to be a green lizard of some sort.

"Blaze is a baby dragon." Valerie smiled at Kal's large eyes.

"What does he eat? Is he a fire-breather?"

Valerie laughed again, "We have no idea what kind of dragon he is. His mother was an earth dragon, and we are unsure what his father was. Dragons only breed every super blue blood moon, which happens every one-hundred-fifty years." Valerie opened a small refrigerator that sat at the foot of her bed and pulled out a variety of greens, presorted, and washed in tubs labeled with days of the week. "He seems to be a vegetarian," she added, placing the greens into a bowl located in the cage. "It is just that simple."

Kal looked on in awe as Valerie refilled the water bowl. "Would you like to hold him?"

Kal nodded, and Valerie reached into the terrarium and gently picked up Blaze. "He can be a little skittish with new people, but since he thinks he is a human…socializing won't hurt."

"How long have you had him?" Kal asked, allowing Blaze to crawl on her arm; his green scales gleamed, and she could make out small bumps on his sides where his wings should be.

"He had just hatched the day his mother…well, you know… So, I found him and adopted him. Dragons are going extinct as their air space gets clogged, and land becomes harder to inhabit as humans, Earth Children, and demons take over the lands. There were not many dragons, to begin with. Now there are very few. So, I couldn't let him die."

"How big was he as a newborn?"

Valerie laughed and pulled a photo album from the shelf above the terrarium. She flipped a few pages and showed Kal a photo of a little green lizard no bigger than her hand. "He was 2 inches and weighed less than 1 pound."

Kal looked at the photo and then at Blaze.

Valerie laughed, "I had to put a rock in his water bowl to keep him from drowning. I am glad we are past that. Most dragons kept in captivity die before their first birthday. We now have safe havens for them if anyone finds one motherless."

"How big is he now?" Kal asked as she admired the green scaled and golden eyes, wondering why she had not noticed him when she had visited.

"He is two years old, smaller than wild two-year-olds at 11 inches and 5 pounds." Blaze stuck his tongue at Kal tickling her arm.

"I had a pet snake once," Kal said, handing Blaze back to Valerie, who gave him a rub and put him in his habitat to eat.

"What kind?" Valerie asked, giving Kal a squirt of hand sanitizer.

"A garter snake. It was a gift from my dad on my tenth birthday." Kal recalled smiling, "It was so little when I got him. He had grown quite a bit before Mom came home a year later. She wasn't pleased and rehomed him."

"Did you ever think he could have been more than a garter snake?" Valerie asked tentatively.

"Some magical creatures, like dragons," she pointed to Blaze, "look like normal everyday common animals when they are young."

"What could he have been?" Kal asked, looking at Valerie, realizing that the tone Valerie was using sounded like Valerie might know something that she didn't.

"He could have been a serpent… a Scitalis perhaps?"

"A What???"

"A Scitalis… they stupefy their pray and eat humans at full grown. They are dull in color at birth, but as they age, they become marvelously beautiful and use their beauty to slow down and capture their prey."

"You seem to know a lot about mythical creatures."

"Magical creatures, Mythical implies they do not exist."

"Ok, *magical* creatures, and about my pet garter snake."

"Well, I am just guessing as to why your mother might have removed a harmless garter snake. If she saw that it was a potentially dangerous magical creature."

Kal scoffed, "How would a magical creature end up in my home?"

"Many, by accident, end up being sold to pet stores and companies by illegal traders. We have a group of people who go out and try to rescue as many as possible, but some fall through the cracks. When it does happen, if it is dangerous, it usually ends up on the news for killing humans, and we must modify the news and memories. For example, a young griffin killed a family last year; they thought they had rescued a stray dog."

Kal looked at her blankly, then shook her head. A knock sounded at the door, and Mr. Wing stuck his head in.

"Time to get ready for bed," he smiled. "I will come back and check on you two in a few."

Valerie smiled; getting up and grabbing her nightclothes, she headed to the bathroom, leaving Kal to get changed by herself.

When Valerie returned, Kal went to the bathroom to finish up. She was a little shaky and stared at herself for a long time. Kal missed her home, her dad, and most of all, her mother. It was hard to remember that she lived here now and that this was her family and home. This was now her life, this crazy mess of magic and magical animals, shifters, and demons. Her head spun; what had her mother left her to? Why hadn't she shared this world with her daughter? Kal looked down at her toothbrush; her mother could apparently do magic, and she hadn't shared that knowledge. Kal apparently could do magic, but she wasn't sure of herself. She looked so typical compared to the others, normal and not magical.

When Kal returned to the bedroom, Mr. Wing was tucking Valerie in and talking to her in hushed tones in a language Kal did not know. Finally, Valerie said something back, and Mr. Wing nodded, leaned down, and kissed her head. Then, he turned to Kal, gave her a hug, and kissed the top of her head.

"Have a good night." He said, "Sweet dreams." He watched as Kal crawled into bed.

Kal froze as she pulled the covers over her. She looked over at her new roommate and legal sister and at her new legal guardian.

"Is everything okay?" Valerie asked, eyeing her.

Kal's eyes got huge, and she gulped a significant bit of air. "I am not dreaming, am I?" she asked.

Valerie smiled. "Nope, your life just got a bit more interesting." Mr. Wing said, and he turned off the light.

CHAPTER 3

Secrets

The following day Valerie woke up with a start. There was someone in her room. She sat up and looked around groggy; then she saw the occupied bed and sighed. "I am going to have to get used to this." She smiled at herself as she watched Kal sleeping. Settling back under her warm covers, she closed her eyes again, only to be woken a few moments later by her mother walking down the hall to the kitchen.

She heard her mother make coffee and sit at the table with her cup. Valerie knew it would be time for her to get up once that cup was empty. It was the joys of being a Ranch kid. Sleeping in on the weekends was until there was enough light to see outside with a stifled groan. Valerie stretched and tried not to fall back to sleep. A moment later, it wasn't her mother who woke her back up but a light touch inside her mind.

"Did you not sleep well?" Sallisfer's voice was full of concern and was edged with sleep.

"I am not used to sharing my room." Valerie transmitted back to him with a yawn, looking back over to the bed where Kal slept. The Sun was almost up, and the first rays were starting to shine through the curtain.

"I felt you start but never felt fear or pain, so I figured that was the case. Did I help some?"

Valerie suppressed a smile. She wondered what had caused her to pass out so deeply, *"I should have known."*

Sallisfer's laughter came to her as Valerie sat up and tossed the covers off, revealing the black sweatpants she slept in. She swung her legs over the bed and tucked her feet into the waiting slippers. She could hear her mother getting up from the table; her mother would head back to her own room to get dressed, and along the way, she would stop by her and Kal's room to wake her. Valerie met her mother at the bedroom door, clothes in hand; her mother smiled and kissed her forehead before heading into her room.

Valerie slipped into the bathroom to change and take care of business; she felt in her mind that Sallisfer had turned an invisible blind eye and was giving her space to prepare for the day.

When he felt it was okay, he asked, *"What is the plan for today?"* Valerie gave a mental shrug as she brushed her teeth, thinking over what she had to do before thinking of what to do with Kal. Then mentally informed Sallisfer of her thoughts.

"Talk to Headmaster. He should be at Starlight. He mentioned having something to do there this morning. Perhaps he will have time to decide what we can disclose to her about our realm. Valerie suggested as she walked to the kitchen to grab a cup of sweet tea and a muffin.

"Do not forget your meds," Sallisfer said as Valerie turned to put on her boots. Valerie sighed and grabbed her bottle of multivitamins, her iron pill, and two flax seeds. She hated the fact that she was not strong enough on her own to keep her body healthy. Valerie was literally the only immortal to get ill with a simple cold. The headmaster figured it was because her body was so focused on not exploding with power; that sickness could easily slip in and weaken her.

Sallisfer felt her mood, *"On your sixteenth birthday, Valerie, your body should balance out when you reach your full power."*

"Maybe... maybe not." Valerie sighed, finally putting on her boots, hoodie, and coat before heading out the door to the barn.

Valerie was getting on her second mount of the day when Kal walked down to the barn bundled in a fur-lined heavy coat with the hood pulled up like an Eskimo. "Good morning, Kal." Valerie smiled at her from atop the black Friesian mare, who pawed the ground in irritation.

"Good morning, beautiful," Kal said while looking at the horse. "And you too, Valerie." Then, reaching a gloved hand to rub the mare's nose, she asked, "What is his name?"

"She is called Willow," Valerie informed her, rubbing the mare's neck and smiling at Kal. "I am usually out a few hours on different horses. There are two on the left-hand side of the barn you can ride if you want. However, they will go out when I get back with Willow in an hour."

Kal nodded. "Thank you," she said, watching Valerie leave the barn area across a strip of grass between the barns and go across the road to the workout arenas.

Kal walked into the barn and saw Ms. Wing brushing down a young Dun, "Good morning, sweetheart," Ms. Wing said, turning to her with a smile. Then, wanting Kal to feel more at home and a part of the family, she continued with her morning greeting. "I see you have found your way to the barn. Did you find breakfast okay? Dad wasn't sure what you would eat?"

Kal nodded, dismissing the term dad spoken by Ms. Wing. "Yes, I did, and thank you. Mr. Wing told me you were down here."

Ms. Wing nodded, "Yes, Valerie and I spend most of the weekends in the barn."

"Why are all these horses in?" Kal asked, walking down the row of full stalls. "Surely Valerie isn't going to ride all of these today?"

Ms. Wing laughed. "No, she has a show with Willow and is training with the Cavalry today."

"The Cavalry?"

"Yes, she is carrying on a tradition set down by her grandparents. You are welcome to watch it, I'm sure. The Warriors will be here soon to get their mounts ready. The Ranch has always been the home of the Cavalry horses, and in times of war, the warriors will stay in the barracks in the back of the hayshed."

Kal stared at Ms. Wing, "Is this little guy a part of it?"

Ms. Wing laughed, "No, this is Comet. He is my mount when I ride with Valerie. He and I are like her squire. He was born a grumpy old man." She affectionately patted the Dun and returned to brushing him clean of dry mud on his fetlocks. Kal walked over to the two horses on the left, who had their heads hanging out of the stalls.

One was the horse the Wings had bought from her mother, a dark bay paint named Aragon. The other was a red mare Kal knew as Raz, which was the first horse Kal had met when she first arrived on the farm as a guest. Kal patted each horse's nose and then decided to brush them both, not sure if she was ready or not to ride.

Kal had just started on Raz when the first trucks arrived, and the barn began to fill with people. Kal peered over the stall door as men and women began placing gear on bare stall doors or racks beside the stall. They got out horses, both big and sturdy and small and lighter. They began to prepare the horses by brushing them down; by this time, Ms. Wing was grooming the big gray mare Valerie had ridden yesterday. "Valerie is late getting back. I hope she is alright?" Ms. Wing was saying to a slim woman with dark red hair and eyes so blue that Kal could see them from her stall.

"I am sure she is okay. Do you know if she took her cell phone?"

Ms. Wing shook her head, "I didn't think to ask, I sent a text, but she didn't answer."

The girl thought for a moment, "Have you called Master Sallisfer?"

Ms. Wing shook her head, "Valerie said he had a meeting with the headmaster this morning."

"I will call her Madam Wing." A young man said. He pulled the last strip of navy-blue cloth tight around his big bay's leg and fastened the Velcro. He stood and examined his work, placing two fingers between the wrap and the leg to ensure it was not too tight before pulling out his phone.

He pushed a button, and Kal realized he kept Valerie on speed dial. The rest of the warriors continued to get ready. Then when he shook his head and left a voice message, they all seemed to go on the hustle to prepare. Kal found herself throwing a saddle on Raz's back and buckling on a helmet as Ms. Wing mounted the big gray.

Valerie finally came into view with a dreamy look and a sweet smile on her face. She looked at them with surprise, "What is going on?" Valerie asked, "Am I that late?"

Yes, and you didn't answer your cell." Ms. Wing said, eyeing her daughter up and down.

"I didn't hear the phone go off. I apologize for worrying everyone. Let me change and take care of Willow, and then we will start."

"I will take care of Willow. Take the warriors and Kal out." Ms. Wing said as she dismounted.

When Valerie's feet hit the ground, she was suddenly dressed in black armor. Kal stared at Valerie, wondering how she had changed so quickly. *Wasn't she just wearing riding britches and a T-shirt?* Kal thought as she watched Valerie exchange reins with her mother. Ms. Wing grabbed Valerie's wrist and stared at her daughter's unwavering gaze. "How did your ride go on Willow?"

"Willow was perfect, and I remembered my test that I will be riding in a few weeks at Three Points."

Ms. Wing nodded, looked over at Willow, who showed signs of a proper arena workout, and handed the reins of the gray mare to Valerie while taking Willow's.

"Master Phillip will meet you at the field."

"Thank you, Mother," Valerie said, smiling and swinging her legs upward onto the gray mare.

"Move out," she ordered.

Kal found herself between the guy who had called Valerie and the redhead woman from the stable. They were dressed in matching silver armor with gleaming helmets. "I am Walker Johnson," the man said, reaching a hand to her while guiding his horse with his legs." Kal took his hand. "Kal."

"I am Tema Johnson. Nice to meet you, Kal. Welcome to the Cavalry." The girl said, reaching over when Walker finished his introduction and shaking Kal's hand.

"Thank you…. I guess."

Tema laughed lightly and beamed an impressive smile, "It isn't as scary as it seems. It is just a drill to prepare for war. We meet up twice a week normally."

"I am not joining the Cavalry…that I know of."

Walker laughed, nudging his horse in front of Kal. Tema fell back behind her as they rode towards the dam that led to the fields beyond the lake. Kal sighed as she was herded down to the practice fields. There the warriors spread out, and Kal could see practice dummies, old haystacks, and a single man standing in gleaming gold armor with his arms crossed with a stern look. "You are late!" he boomed.

Valerie started apologizing, "Sorry, Master Phillip, I lost…" but his one look in her direction, Valerie shut her mouth and bowed her head in submission.

"Twice the practice, you better all be perfect, or you will be severely punished."

The man boomed then his eyes fell on Kal, who lost her breath at the sight of the white eyes and bright red lips. He was pale, and his skin looked like leather stuck tight to his bones showing hollow cheeks.

"Master Phillip, this is Kalea Breese. She is now my legal sister and has just started learning about our ways." Valerie said, riding her gray mare over to Kal with a reassuring smile. Master Phillip looked at Kal on Raz and then moved so fast that Kal didn't have time to blink when she noticed he stood beside her and her mount.

"You may join the warmup if you and that mule can keep up." He smiled, showing wooden teeth and black gums.

"Thank you, Sir." Kal tried to smile back as she nudged Raz into a trot to the end of the line behind the already-moving warriors. It wasn't long till she was swept into the commotion following the simple commands given by Master Phillip's booming voice. Then they split up the light and heavy Cavalry into two sections. Kal saw Valerie galloping around the heavy Cavalry, shouting with her sword in the air. Then the light Cavalry moved into a formation independently, with Tema at the lead. She and all the other first row of riders guided their light steeds with their legs and flew ahead of the second row with arrows flying at a neck, breaking pace.

Kal gulped as the next rows released a piercing war cry, with their blades raised in the air. Kal struggled to control Raz as she burst into a gallop with them. It was absolutely terrifying as the practice dummies suddenly erupted into life. Valerie was suddenly at Kal's side handing her a sword with a wink as she kicked her gray to leap ahead of Kal and behead the attacking dummy.

Kal soon found a rhythm with the others, at least until a mounted dummy knocked her off, and she fell into the mud. Raz reared and ran off. The mounted dummy's horse's legs started forward as if to trample Kal. But before she could react, Walker, who had the look of also being thrown off his mount, jumped in front of Kal with a snarl that made Kal's skin crawl. With the force of a man twice his size, he chopped the sandbag horse in half and then took on the rider in hand-to-hand combat.

Kal winced as she stood looking around at the chaos; it looked like half the Calvary were on their horses while the others were on foot. Their horses had left them in the mud. Kal watched as Master Phillip moved at incredible speeds around the field, observing, booming orders, and fixing his students. Suddenly he was by Kal's side, he grabbed her arm, and they were on the outskirts, where the horses, including Raz, were all standing around a fresh hay roll. A few had broken reins, and some had minor injuries, and as Kal stumbled over to them, she could tell that all the horses looked perfectly happy and at ease.

Just as quickly as the mock battle had started, it ended. The field cleared, and Master Phillip was helping the fallen back to their feet. Kal watched as those on foot walked forward tiredly to claim their mounts —Valerie and those still mounted dismounted and led their tired steeds toward the hay. Master Philip met them, handing out water bottles and helping untack and cool off the horses.

"Good job Kalea." Master Philip rumbled, helping Kal place her saddle with the others on the back of the hay trailer. "Not bad for a first-timer."

Kal couldn't help but beam, "I do hope I never have to do that again, Sir," she admitted stroking Raz's sweaty neck.

"We all hope we never have to do this in real life," Tema replied, coming up beside Kal. "However, it looks like our skills will be needed sooner rather than later."

"What do you mean?"

"We are headed to war, and this time it will be the war to end all wars," Tema said. "Especially with the finding of the chosen one, war is on our horizon." She then turned away from Kal and walked her bay over to the trough, allowing him to drink some water.

When all the horses were cooled off, the warriors started their walk to the barn, where Ms. Wing waited with a tall, slender balding man and a short, plump woman with graying black hair. The tall, slender man was the ranch's veterinarian, Dr. Robert Finnegan, while the woman was the ranch's nurse Mrs. Beverly Harris. The two of them got straight to work inspecting each horse and rider.

As soon as the vet cleared the horses safe to put in the stall, riders placed a sheet on them. "What is that?" Kal asked Walker as she watched him buckle the straps of the white sheet on Raz. "This?" Walker asked, "This is a cooler sheet; it protects the wet horse from chills as they dry."

"I didn't know they needed these?" Kal asked as she put Raz back in her stall. Walker laughed. "We mostly use them in the winter after a hard workout like today."

After tending to the horses, Walker and Kal walked down the aisle-way between the stalls until they reached the lounge and sat beside the heater. There, Master Phillip went over the morning ride while Ms. Wing handed out bowls of hot soup and cider for lunch.

Kal ate and listened to the lecture but didn't really hear or taste any-thing. She felt small in the room, filled with muscular men and women who appeared way older than herself. Kal searched the crowd for Valerie and found her sitting at the front, nodding at what Master Philip was saying, looking deep in thought, her food forgotten in her lap.

At the end of the lecture, the warriors filed out of the room and went to their horses. Kal watched as they expertly removed the cooler and replaced it with a different one. Kal walked over to Raz and found Ms. Wing taking off the cooler. "Can you hand me her blanket?" Ms. Wing asked, pointing to a thick green cloth that hung on the stall wall. Kal pulled it down, and one of the long straps got caught on the other side. Ms. Wing reached over and popped the metal fastener loose. Kal handed it to her, and Ms. Wing tossed it over Raz's back and started fastening it. By now, most horses were being turned out with their riders laughing and talking together as they walked. Valerie waited with the gray, and Ms. Wing handed Kal the lead rope, and Kal led Raz out of the stall and down the hill to the pasture.

When they returned from the pasture, Kal saw each warrior stopping at the tractor to get their saddles out of the hay trailer. Valerie handed the saddle used by Kal to her as she gathered hers, and they walked back into the lounge. There were now metal stands set up by the stools. Kal placed her saddle on one of the stands and accepted the sponge and leather soap handed to her. When they all got settled, Valerie spoke.

"I want everyone to meet Kalea Breese and take a moment to introduce yourselves. She was not raised in our world and needs to know who she can rely on." Valerie pointed to a dark-haired boy sitting to her right, "Kris, you go first."

Kris smiled, "I am Kristofer King. I am a trooper in the light Cavalry." The list went on as everyone told her their name and rank while poor Kal tried to process matching names to faces. There were over two hundred of them, and before long, Kal gave up and just nodded and smiled.

By the end of the day, Kal was beyond exhausted. After her shower, she collapsed on her bed and was asleep before Valerie entered their room. Kal felt like she had just fallen asleep when she awakened to a light tap on the window. Sitting up and listening, it came again. She went and poked Valerie in the next bed. Valerie sighed and opened her eyes.

"What?" Valerie groaned.

"Listen," Kal whispered. The tap came again, and Valerie sighed.

"I'll take care of it." She got up, pulled on her long coat, and disappeared down the hall. Kal heard the door open and close, and she peeked out the window. Her eyes grew huge as she saw who was outside with Valerie.

"Holjus?" Kal whispered in disbelief as she watched the moon's light reflecting off a pair of red and green eyes. Holjus stood outside the shadow of the cedar tree. *What is he doing out there?* Kal thought. Her breath fogged the window as she pressed closer, torn between screaming for help or seeing what fight was about to happen. Then she watched in horror as the moon showed them touching hands palm to palm. Their non-blinking eyes stared so intensely into one another she doubted they would take notice of anything around them. Then in a single heartbeat, Holjus swept Valerie up and kissed her on the lips.

Kal slid away from the window and pulled the blankets up to her chin, "No way," she whispered, "I really must be dreaming." She pinched herself and blinked, "I wish I was." Kal looked at the clock, then back outside. There was no sign of Valerie or Holjus.

Torn Kal took a deep breath and stabilized her breathing. *I will give her a few…* she thought. Then, looking at the clock, she closed her eyes. *A few moments more…*Just as Kal was about to get up to awaken the Wings, Valerie came back smiling. Kal looked at her, "Is it gone?" she asked.

"Yes, it's gone," Valerie said, a smile on her face. Her cheeks looked a bit flushed, and she was giddy with excitement.

CHAPTER 4

Monday Morning

The next morning was a school day, and both girls were trying to decide what to wear. "So... What does Sallisfer turn into?" Kal asked, and not for the first time that morning.

"I've told you- I'm not telling you!" Valerie growled. Kal realized Valerie was not a morning person when it came to going to school. She was sluggish and irritable, and Kal felt like Valerie would slip up and tell her if she pushed hard enough.

"Why not tell me?"

"You'll see when you see," Valerie yawned. "Besides...You ignored what Arcy said the other night, so I won't tell you."

"Oh, c'mon! We're best friends! Pleeease?" Kal begged.

"Alright, then, I'll give you a hint. I feel sorry for poor George."

Kal stared at her. "Who is George, and what's he got to do with anything?"

"That's for me to know and you to find out," Valerie replied.

Kal realizing her plan didn't work, continued to beg Valerie all the more. "Please, tell me, Valerie? Please..."

"He's at school. That's all the info I'm gonna give you." But Kal was not one to give up... so the questions didn't stop.

All that day up to lunch, Kal searched for him and questioned Valerie. They had second and third classes together, which meant they shared lunch. Valerie was getting rather annoyed, and Kal knew that if she pressed a little more, Valerie just might blurt it out, so she asked another yes, no-question. "... Is he with the popular?"

"For Heaven's sake, no!" Valerie almost laughed as she sat down with her salad and baked potato covered with cheese. Kal had packed her lunch that morning; she never trusted the school cafeteria food.

"So, what is he?"

"He isn't popular as most of them are demons and human followers. People tend to be idle, dark, and moody. Besides us, Earth Children tend to be nerdier, arts and crafty, musical inclined, actors, and drama seekers. Most do not play sports or have an interest in sports, and humans prefer sporty people."

Kal thought about Valerie's statement for a moment, "So demons are not musical?"

Valerie laughed. "I didn't say that. Some really good bands are demons. Even the earth children listen to them, and I think demons secretly like our bands."

"Are there any sports that Earth Children play?"

"Yes, as I said, most of them dislike sports, but that doesn't mean all. And besides, a lot of our kind watch sports mainly here in the south, just like anybody."

Kal nodded and looked around the cafeteria again, wondering how many kids she saw were humans, demons, and magical. Valerie seemed to sense what she was looking for and placed her hand on Kal's. Kal felt a slight tickle go up her arm and looked around again. She saw a mist around several students, including Valerie, when she turned to look at her best friend. "Is this how you know who is a friend or who is a foe?"

Valerie looked at her questionably and removed her hand, "Anyone can be friend or foe."

"I saw non-fog with non-fog mostly and fog with fog and blur with blur," Kal stated.

Valerie laughed, "I cannot help that natural segregation happens. You can be friends with anyone you want as long as it isn't a demon. I happen to have human friends too."

Kal looked at her and almost blew her secret with a smart comment about Holjus. She was glad when something caught Valerie's eye over her shoulder. Kal turned to look at the geek walking toward them with a bowl haircut, with giant glasses. He looked like a white Steve Urkel, plaid polo shirt tucked into flood pants pulled to his belly button, held with neon-colored suspenders, and his feet adorned with white Jordan tennis shoes. He sat beside Kal nervously, looking over at Valerie with worry and then at his salad tray.

"George... What do you think you're doing?" Valerie growled, glaring at him.

"I'm sitting down." His voice was high-pitched and not at all manly. Kal felt appalled by him and tried to scoot away, eyeing Valerie for a sign.

"Not over here, you're not!" Valerie said, looking away from him.

"Fine, then. Kal, c'mon." George said, standing up, hunched back, and taking his tray to an empty table.

"What? How do you know my name?" Kal looked at George suspiciously.

"Kal... remember what Arcy said? He's a GEEK! Remember this morning when I said, I'm sorry for poor GEORGE! Put two and two together." Valerie snarled, her eyes flashing. Kal immediately jumped up and followed George, whom she knew was Sallisfer, no thanks to Valerie's outrage.

"George is my first name." Sallisfer smiled when they sat down, "It is also my father's name…. I am a junior." Kal nodded as pieces of his story clicked into place as she ate her meatball sandwich.

"Why the geek look?"

Sallisfer looked away from her and put a fork full of salad in his mouth. "Do you have news?" he asked around his mouthful.

"Oh, yeah, I have scary news," Kal stated while she nodded. She shivered as she took a bite of her sandwich-making Sallisfer wait as he had changed the subject by jumping to business. After gaining the nerve to talk, Kal apprehensively reported her news to Sallisfer.

"Last night, Holjus came to our house, and Valerie met him outside. I saw them touch hands and then.... and then.... they kissed." Kal looked at Sallisfer only to notice his eyes widening and his slack jaw dropping open.

"Does she know you saw her?" Sallisfer whispered, after overcoming the surprise from Kal, as he looked across to Valerie, now joined by a few other kids.

"She doesn't know I know yet."

"That's good... she might have killed you if she knew you'd seen that." Sallisfer took another bite of his salad as if he had just said something unpretentious.

"Kill me... Kill me?" Kal whispered, "Kill me?"

"I just don't understand." Sallisfer sighed, rubbing the arch of his nose under his glasses and ignoring Kal's comment. "Why him?" He asked, staring over Kal's shoulder at Valerie, who was laughing.

Kal realized the human friends Valerie talked about were among those who filled the table she had vacated. Valerie had a knack for attracting trouble, Kal assumed, looking back at Sallisfer, who was now looking at her.

"That match is to the death!" He stated matter-of-factly, taking another bite of salad deep in thought.

"To the death?!" Kal almost yelled, dumbfounded. "This is even worse than I thought," Kal muttered, then looked at Sallisfer with worry.

"What are we going to do?"

Sallisfer took a moment to answer, chewing his salad with a look of mulling it all in his head. He eyed Kal in a way that made her feel like she was being weighed and measured for worth, making her uncomfortable. She continued to eat her sandwich, hoping she didn't look as unworthy as she felt.

"First, we have to find out how far their fling has gone," Sallisfer stated, suddenly breaking the silence.

Kal looked at him in disbelief, remembering his kill statement, and blurted out her worst fear. "Great, let me guess, I have to do that?"

"Pretty much. Sorry." Sallisfer revealed, not sounding very remorseful at all. Instead, he simply took another bite of his salad as if what they were discussing was as simple as the weather and not a Romeo and Juliet story that made Kal feel like Mercutio.

"Yeah. I'm *not* looking forward to this." She mused, packing away her sandwich, opening her water, and taking a sip to calm herself.

Suddenly Sallisfer jumped in his seat, his face aglow with glee, and gave an excited squeak making Kal jump and slosh water all over herself as he burst out excitedly, "Or we could interrogate Holjus."

Kal stared at him as he practically shook with excitement in his seat. "We can scare him into telling us how long they have been seeing each other, and that way, Valerie never has to know.

"I bet...," Sallisfer nervously motioned his fingers together with a scary glint in his eyes. "I bet I can keep it from her." Kal then pointed over to the popular table.

"Do you know what he looks like disguised as a human?" Sallisfer's smile almost faded, but he then smirked.

"No... but Valerie knows." He said, looking over at Valerie.

Kal looked over and saw Valerie glance at the popular table often and casually as if she were just looking at the clock on the wall. Kal and Sallisfer then turned their eyes and watched the popular table. They noticed one of the guys doing the same but in Valerie's direction near the teacher's table. If one wasn't watching closely, it would have appeared that he was on the lookout for his friends and would tell them if a teacher was coming, and the secret smile that he and Valerie shared would go unnoticed.

"That one." He pointed at a demon wearing a white t-shirt and dark, baggy jeans with chains. Kal nodded, "Do you want me to get him?" Kal asked, preparing to prove herself once and for all. "I don't think that'd be a good idea. We'll have to catch him in the halls."

Sallisfer sighed and picked up his tray to take it to the trash can. Kal gathered her trash as well. As they walked together through the cafeteria, Kal could feel the odd looks she got while she walked next to this silly little guy. She silently vowed to get Valerie for not preparing her for his shocking appearance.

"Alright..." Kal agreed when they were back at the table. Then a thought occurred to her. "What if we can't break them up?"

Sallisfer sighed and rubbed the arch of his nose under his glasses, "Then we must keep it our secret. You see, Kal, I needed you to find out about the two of them. I knew Valerie had been keeping something from me." Again, he sighed, and this time he put his glasses on the table, and Kal could see the blue flare under the brown illusion.

"Valerie and I, well..." he trailed off and said, "We have been friends for a *long* time, and I knew something was up. But I did not know what it was, how it began, and where it was all coming from. I had seen small changes in her power level and subtle new talents that were not there before."

He smiled at her and said, "Thank you, Kal; once I know more about... her relationship. I believe I can get past Valerie's defenses, and all will become clear."

His eyes went misty for a moment, "If we cannot end it... I fear it will be up to us to protect them." Kal looked down at her hands; she felt so small and insecure, but she tried to hide it as she voiced her inner fear. "What would happen if they were exposed?"

"Disaster and darkness that even Heaven cannot stop." She looked at him a little confused and was going to ask what he meant when Sallisfer said with another one of his startled, exciting jumps.

"I have the plan." He put his hand on hers, and she suddenly felt braver as he leaned over the table.

"This is what we are going to do," he whispered. His breath was sweet, even though he had just eaten, making Kal wonder in the back of her mind what her breath smelled like.

"What?" she asked, berating herself for not listening as Sallisfer squinted at her and let out a frustrated breath.

"I am going to shift when we get to the first set of doors by the bathroom." He said slowly, "No one should see me. I can be pretty invisible when I want to be." He looked at her for a sign of her understanding him. Kal nodded, feeling even more ashamed that she had not listened to him the first time, as he changed his tone. He recanted his thoughts to her like he was talking to a child, not an equal.

"I will fly ahead and hide in the broom closet that Mr. Ebb never locks. Once there, I will wait for Holjus. I need you to separate him from his friends, so they don't notice him leaving…." Sallisfer looked again at Kal, who looked back at him wide-eyed.

"How am I?" she blurted, her face growing hot at Sallisfer's smile just as the bell rang.

"Showtime." Sallisfer purred as they watched Valerie purposely pass Holjus, both of them glancing at each other and smiling secretly.

"I think it goes pretty far," Kal idly observed, glancing over at Sallisfer.

"We'll see about that…" he had his hands balled in a fist. Kal worked her free hand to open one of his fists. Their hands clasped together; she squeezed, and he squeezed back as he looked down at her with a smile that made her insides twist in glee.

The two of them watched as Holjus threw away his tray. Then, as he walked by the table with a few of his friends, they pushed in close to him, losing Valerie in the push of the crowd. By the bathrooms, Kal realized that Sallisfer had vanished, and she knew it was now or never. She pulled out her half-empty water bottle and unscrewed the top. She took a deep breath and fell onto Holjus, showering him with water.

In the pushing crowd of students and teachers everywhere, Holjus told his friends to go on and that he would meet up with them a bit later.

As he turned back toward the restroom, Kal stood before him, blubbering apologies. Then, unexpectedly they were yanked inside a broom closet by a tug on their collars.

"Hey! Next time be more careful! My shirt could have ripped." Kal growled and was met by a genuine Sallisfer smile. Holjus sat on the floor, still trying to figure things out.

"Why did you kidnap me?" He asked, then recognizing Sallisfer, fear flashed over his features. "I didn't do anything."

"You sure about that?" Sallisfer answered, turning to Holjus with a smirk. Kal came up to stand next to him.

"How long have you been seeing each other?" She whispered, glaring at Holjus in what she hoped was a fearsome fire.

"What do you mean? Seeing who?" He asked, feigning confusion.

"You know who!" Sallisfer answered with a growl, grabbing Holjus's collar and holding him threateningly. Holjus's eyes searched desperately for a way out, and he was highly distressed when he found no hole. Finally, he hung his head and answered, not looking at Sallisfer in the eyes.

"A month... maybe more." He muttered.

Sallisfer threw Holjus to the ground and growled with rage. "A month! Maybe more? Tell me when you started hissing your nasty little lies in her ear! Tell me!"

Kal placed a calming hand on Sallisfer's shaking shoulder before crouching next to Holjus. "You know you shouldn't be doing this... That fight on her 16th birthday is a fight to the death! How can you forget what you have done? How can she? Because of this, there is a high probability that both of you will pay for the consequences."

"Do you think I'm that stupid?!" He yelled, jumping up, pain in his red eyes, with fire on his fingers, "Valerie and I share that day! We both share the 26th; we were chosen to fight each other. We have been training for this our whole lives!" Holjus turned away from Kal and headed to the door. "However, love and death seem to be connected," Holjus muttered. Sallisfer grabbed him again and flung him down.

"Connected, you two feel connected?" Sallisfer almost screamed, "You are stupid... how can a demon feel connected to an earth child?" Holjus growled and attempted to fight back, but it was feeble. Kal almost wondered if Holjus was holding back as he seemed to allow Sallisfer to throw him on the ground again.

"If you do not call off this relationship, I will have no choice but to kill you myself." Sallisfer growled, "I will not have demon filth ruin all we have accomplished."

"You accomplished?" Holjus spat back. "Ruin everything?" he laughed. "I don't think you need any help in that department, I know."

For a time, fear flashed in Sallisfer's eyes and was replaced with rage faster than what should have been possible. He was on to Holjus, one hand wrapped around his neck, the other holding a shining dagger.

"Spy," Sallisfer hissed. "You are nothing but a spy."

Holjus seemed to smile. "Keep telling yourself that, ponyboy. Besides, you can't kill me; you would start a war you could not finish." Sallisfer threw Holjus down in disgust. Kal sighed, stepping in between them, trying to act brave "I don't think you're stupid, Holjus...and...."

Just then, the door burst open, and Valerie stood in the doorway. "What are you doing? You're late for class!" She glared at the three of them, green eyes laced with fire. All illusions were gone as she radiated with power. Sallisfer stepped between Valerie and Kal, who was kneeling next to Holjus; he also sparked with energy. Kal glared at Holjus and whispered, placing all the venom in her voice as she could while being quiet enough to where only he could hear her.

"See what you are doing to her, demon! You are turning her into one of your own kind, slowly! Take care to rethink your decision." She stood, mustering as much courage as possible, and took Sallisfer's hand in hers. It was as if she had hit a switch. All the heated power that had been in the closet was gone. Everyone looked almost normal. Sallisfer was back in geek form, and Valerie looked like the girl Kal had first met months ago. They walked out into the main hall and made a few more steps when a sob of anguish washed over them. It took all of Kal's power not to run back to Valerie and beg for forgiveness as they heard her fall to her knees. Finally, Sallisfer stopped, and Kal silently pleaded that he would continue. She pulled gently on his hand, hoping beyond hope that he would take the hint, but he looked back. Holjus had a tear streaming down his face, but he took Valerie into his arms and held her, talking in her ear.

Kal pulled again, "Remember," she pleaded in a whisper, but it was too late Sallisfer let go of her hand and walked back and tore them apart.

"Didn't we tell you to stop this nonsense?" He yelled, anger hot in his voice as he kicked Holjus hard on the ground while pulling Valerie to her feet.

"This has got to end," he yelled, but he received a fireball in the gut from Valerie, who looked almost to be entirely in flames. "It's not his fault; it's mine. I'm the one that started it. He was nice enough to see that I needed someone to comfort me!" She screamed. Valerie ran down the hall towards the front door, the fire going out just as quickly as it had started, her sobs trailing behind with a smell of magnolia and pine.

Holjus glared at Sallisfer as he pulled himself upright, stretching to his full height. Holjus showed he was uninjured after their exchange as he put on a leather vest that seemed to appear from out of nowhere, and stalked off to his classroom, knowing he couldn't go after Valerie.

Kal walked quickly over to Sallisfer, worried and concerned.

"Are you alright?" She asked, checking the burn.

"I'll be fine...see?" His skin slowly began to heal, and Kal smiled.

"Alright..." She nodded at him, "I guess I'll see you around..."

"Yeah... and now you'll actually see me, at least."

Kal laughed. "That's a good point." She hugged him and walked down the hall to her classroom, humming her song. Sallisfer shook his head and walked down the hallway to his class, not knowing if it would be fitting if he walked out and talked to Valerie. But, reaching out with his mind toward Valerie, he felt sorrow and pain. He rubbed his stomach and shook his head. He didn't want another burn to repair.

As he walked to his classroom, he felt eyes on him. He looked over to see his cousin walking toward him with concern. "What is going on?" he asked in a distant voice. "I feel a lot of power."

"It is going to be fine. But, we must allow Valerie some time to cool off."

His cousin, Kris, didn't answer. Instead, he looked at Sallisfer and down the hallway to the front doors. "She is going home." He said at last. "Is it wise to send her home?"

"Don't go after her just yet. Tomorrow you can talk to her," Sallisfer advised.

"Is there a lesson today?" Kris asked.

"No," Sallisfer confirmed.

"What about the new girl?"

"Kal, Well, we have already started her informal training," Sallisfer stated.

His cousin nodded and returned to his classroom with one last look down the hall to the door. Sallisfer held in his breath of relief. He didn't need too many people to know what Valerie could do or confirm suspicions.

Sallisfer went back to class and waited for the day to end. Then, as a massive headache set in, he found himself sitting outside in his car during class time. He let his mind rest with his eyes closed, "I must stay here for Kal." He kept telling himself over and over. Finally, the pain diminished, and he was able to go back to class.

CHAPTER 5

Valerie VS. Fire

Valerie sat on the curb and called her mother, telling her she didn't feel good. Although, it wasn't the exact truth. She felt sick to her stomach because her mental and emotional health was disturbed. The repeated action of hurting Sallisfer and her loss of control allowed the fire to consume her, and now she was trying to fight it off in a losing battle.

Tears flooded her eyes as she thought of last night by the beautiful lake. Everything had felt perfect as she and Holjus surveyed the stars glittering in the night sky above their heads. Valerie felt pulled apart, she wanted to listen to her heart, but she knew that she would suffer the consequences of the decision.

Her mother pulled up, and she got into the front seat of the big Ford truck. Her mother smiled at her with concern and drove off down the street toward home. The ride was quiet. Ms. Wing didn't say a word as her daughter cried in the seat beside her. Ms. Wing had learned long ago that if her daughter didn't want to talk about it, not to press the matter. So, she only placed a calming hand on her daughter's knee to retract it quickly. "You are burning up," Ms. Wing burst out despite herself.

Valerie pulled her knees into her body and wrapped her arms around them. Her tears steamed off her red cheeks. Ms. Wing reached into the backseat and got a towel, which Valerie took with a grateful look as she wiped her face. When they arrived home, Ms. Wing helped Valerie into a cool tub of water for a bath.

"I would ask if I can take you to the doctor, but I already know the answer." Ms. Wing said, watching Valerie remove her burning clothes from her body. "Are you going to tell me this is a Hand thing?"

Valerie didn't answer as she stepped into the tub. The water started to boil, but her cheeks' redness began to disappear as she sank into the water up to her neck. "I can't tell you anything," she finally stated, "and I would appreciate it if you didn't share this with anyone." Ms. Wing saw the pleading look in her daughter's green eyes. She looked like Ms. Wing's clone but acted so much like her father.

Nevertheless, the fact that Valerie was revealing her weakness showed a part of herself was inside her daughter, which comforted Ms. Wing's heart. "Mom," Valerie cried, her eyes flashing red momentarily, and she began to shake. Ms. Wing quickly grabbed her daughter's hand. "I am here. You can count on me."

Ms. Wing refreshed the water and got Valerie a glass of chocolate milk. Soon Valerie's temperature was almost normal, and Ms. Wing helped her dress and crawl into bed. "When you are up to it, perhaps you should visit the barn. It will help you focus on your path." Valerie looked at her mother and listened to her words of advice. She nodded with gratitude in her eyes. "I will have your mare waiting," Ms. Wing stated.

Valerie rested for a bit and then did her homework. Once she could stand without falling, she went out for a ride on her gray mare, Sorrow. Valerie brushed and tacked her and then pulled herself into the saddle. When they were on the trail, Valerie told her everything that had happened that day. Sorrow listened to every word and even stopped to nose her on the leg as she broke into tears again.

"I don't know what I should do, girl?" Valerie cried. The mare looked at Valerie with light in her eyes, then took off in a gallop down the path. All at once, they were flying down the pathway. Valerie gave a hoop and let go of the reins throwing her arms into the air. Her problems were left far behind them.

They came to a stop, and Sorrow tossed her head and looked at Valerie, seeming to smile as her rider laughed. Then, Valerie wrapped her arms around Sorrow's neck. "Thank you," she breathed. The mare nodded, and they turned to the path homeward.

Kal was pacing back and forth at the barn while Sallisfer munched on some hay nearby. His paint coat glinted in the sun as Kal had labored on it while they waited for Valerie to return.

"What if she's seeing him?" she asked. Sallisfer picked up his ears, looked up from his meal, and glared at her as he chewed.

"I don't think Sorrow will let her," he said, turning into himself again and walking over to her. "Besides, she was pretty hurt from the ordeal. I think she just needs some space to figure it out."

"Sorrow?" Kal asked, puzzled, "Why name a horse that?"

Sallisfer shrugged, "I don't know," he emitted, "But she's the best one to tell your problems to, and she'll keep them a secret. She wouldn't tell a soul. I'm certain she knew about Valerie's crush on Holjus long before they decided to go out."

Just then, Kal saw Valerie and Sorrow on top of the hill. As they approached, they heard Valerie's laughter and saw her smile. Kal and Sallisfer both breathed a sigh of relief.

She waved at them and dismounted. "We saw a doe playing by Willow Spring!" She called as she took the reins over Sorrow's head and led her into the barn.

"I think she's better now," Kal said with a smile as they followed her into the barn.

"Yes, I have to agree," Sallisfer said with a smile. When they entered the barn, Valerie was already starting to untack. She pulled the bridle off Sorrow's head. Sorrow started to rub her large gray head on Valerie's back, using it as a scratching post and a napkin leaving gray hair and green slobber on Valerie's black shirt.

"That looks painful," Kal muttered.

Valerie laughed. "No, it is quite delightful. But unfortunately, Sorrow has a bad habit of injuring her eyes when allowed to scratch on something other than a body." Sallisfer nodded, and when Valerie had placed the halter on Sorrow's head, Sallisfer hugged Valerie.

"I forgive you," he said calmly before letting her go. Valerie nodded, looking as if she was about to cry. Kal coughed and then asked, "Shall we help you untack?" Valerie nodded and smiled thankfully at her. As they helped Valerie untack and pull a sheet over Sorrow, Kal really looked at the gray horse. "Is this the one you rode yesterday?"

"Yes. Sorrow is my cavalry mount and war buddy. She and I have already seen one civil war together, and I don't know how many demon scuffles." Valerie patted Sorrow's neck as she turned her out.

"A civil war?" Kal asked, looking suspicious, "scuffles?"

"Yes," Sallisfer and Valerie replied simultaneously; Kal scratched her head with disbelief.

"I have an idea; what if we find our animal totem," Kal said, changing the subject as she remembered something Mr. Wing had said about the importance of knowing her animal totem.

"Find? You don't know?" Sallisfer asked, confused. Valerie nudged him hard in the ribs.

"I think that's a good idea," Valerie said, ignoring Sallisfer's outcry of pain. "I think I could use advice from mine."

"Okay...I guess," Sallisfer said with a shrug rubbing his ribs, still looking confused.

They walked into the pasture and up the hill to the meadow. They sat cross-legged in a circle and listened as Kal read from a small pocket-size book Mr. Wing had loaned her.

"We'll go first. You keep an eye out in case of trouble," Valerie expressed to Sallisfer, he nodded, and the two girls closed their eyes. After a little while, they both sighed and lay down.

Sallisfer watched their faces; he saw Kal's peace and calm, and Valerie's face was in total delight. But, then, he heard a little whimper from Kal as he watched her- Kal's face was full of fright, she took a deep breath, and her face relaxed again.

Kal woke first, well, not really woke, but came back to herself. She sat up, looked at him, and then at Valerie, still in the state.

"What did you see?" Sallisfer asked in a whisper, his eyes looking at her but also past her.

"I saw a wolf," Kal said with a sigh. They looked over at Valerie, who started to stir.

"Cool," Valerie said, sitting up with a smile, "That was really cool."

"What did you see?" Kal asked.

"I saw a huge and beautiful gray horse. I got up, and it swept me off my feet, and we went for a gallop. It spoke to me about the universe and showed me how to control the fire inside me," Valerie said with a smile. She jumped up, glanced at Sallisfer, then dashed to the woods without a second thought.

Kal sighed and looked at Sallisfer, confused. He shrugged with a smile that told Kal he knew what Valerie saw, yet she didn't understand how. "I guess it's my turn," he said with a sigh. He lay down and closed his eyes.

Kal watched over Sallisfer; at first, he just laid there breathing, then his breathing evened out, almost like he was sleeping. She crawled over to him and looked down at his perfect face. He looked so much better without those big round glasses and the bowl haircut. His uneven ragged black, blue, and green hair was much more fitting.

He twitched his face and slightly hissed, making her jump back from him. Then, he rolled his head in the grass and opened and closed his hands, smiling slyly.

When Sallisfer opened his eyes, she saw the pupils were oval, and then they became round again, "That was cool." He said, "I hadn't communed with my totem in a while. Thank you for the opportunity."

"What is your animal totem? Is it a horse like Valerie?"

Sallisfer looked at her for a moment, with an answer on his lips that died there and was replaced with a slow nod, "Yes, yes, my animal totem is a paint horse with blue eyes." He answered with a grin.

"What did you talk about?"

"Nothing out of the ordinary, the weather and stuff."

Kal looked at him, and before she could say anything, he tackled her, and they rolled playfully down the hill, laughing. At the bottom of the hill, Kal had forgotten her suspicions as he started to tickle her sides.

"Stop, stop," Kal objected breathlessly. Finally, he stopped, picked her up, and danced around in the grass. Music trickled through the air, a sweet melody.

Sallisfer stopped and bowed. "May I have this dance?" Kal smiled and curtsied, realizing she was suddenly in a skirt over her blue jeans. It was a little long for her and was a dark royal blue. Again, Sallisfer smiled, and she had a feeling he had something to do with the sudden appearance of the accessory.

"Yes," her smile turned into a grin as she took Sallisfer's hand, the music grew louder, and Kal let Sallisfer draw her closer to him. He took her right hand in his left hand and placed his right hand on her shoulder blade, and Kal smiled at him.

"Put your other hand on my shoulder." Kal blushed and did as she was told; it was a little hard because she was so much shorter than Sallisfer.

Sallisfer guided her slightly to the right of him, and he started to Waltz with her guiding her feet to the right places. She tripped over his feet some, but he never complained.

CHAPTER 6

Disturbed Night

Valerie didn't come home till right before dinner. When she burst into the little house, she was out of breath and covered in mud and grime. But nevertheless, she smiled at them as she pulled off her boots.

"Where have you been, young lady?" her mother asked, hands on her hips, standing in front of the stove where she had been stirring a pot of soup.

"I went to see Mr. Wheedle down by the swamp," Valerie gasped with a smile.

"Who?" Kal asked.

"Why didn't you tell me first?" Valerie's mother asked, still glaring at her daughter, moving the soup from the stove to the hot pads at the middle of the table and serving each bowl.

I didn't have time. I'm hungry," Valerie said as she started towards the table.

"You can't eat at my table like that," her mother snapped, "You go and get a shower right now!"

"Yes, ma'am," Valerie said, running to the bathroom and showering. Ms. Wing smiled after her daughter and returned to serving the five bowls while Koda set out the spoons and napkins.

"Kal, will you get everyone a cup?" she asked. Kal nodded.

"How many?" Kal asked as she went to the cabinet to get everyone a cup.

"Well, Arcy and Talys only come over once a week for a family meal… so," she looked at Sallisfer, who was lounging on the sofa leafing through a big blue and green book. She sighed and said, "six, dear." Kal nodded, filling the cups with ice from the ice maker and pouring tea into each.

"Who is Mr. Wheedle?" Kal asked again as casually as possible, walking into the living area and handing Sallisfer a cup.

Sallisfer laughed as he took a cup from her and smiled one of those dazzling smiles at her. "Mr. Wheedle is an old shifter who teaches all his students discipline," he explained. "He is kind of a hermit who lives in the swamp not far from here. He hasn't taken on a student in this decade, but I am glad he had it in his heart to take on Valerie… now how to fit seeing him into her already busy day…." Sallisfer shrugged. "I am sure we can figure it out."

When Valerie emerged from the shower, all clean, Ms. Wing smiled at her. "So, do we wait for your father? He hasn't called me all day?"

Sallisfer said, "Since Valerie was sick, he informed me that he would not be home till 9." Mrs. Wing glared at him but sighed.

"Well, have a seat. It is all ready."

"How do you know when your dad will be home?" Kal blurted out.

"He is a government official and must report to Valerie and Sallisfer, who then reports to the headmaster." Ms. Wing informed her, just a tad bit annoyed.

Kal looked at Valerie and Sallisfer, confused, and was about to ask why government officials had to report to them, but Ms. Wing said, "So when do you report back to Mr. Wheedle?"

"I go once a week, at least twice a month," Valerie said.

"Will you take Kalea with you to meet him at least once to a lesson? She should at least know where he is and who he is," Ms. Wing said, smiling at her daughter, and again Kal felt like Ms. Wing knew more than she let on.

"Of course, mother. I can take her to my next lesson. I have to inform the headmaster." Valerie said, "That way, I can arrange it around my work."

"Speaking of which, when are you going back to work? I know you took time off from work to help Kalea. I expect you will put in extra time on the ranch. The weather is supposed to grow quite cold before spring hits."

Valerie choked on her tea "Mother, I…I will put in the time on the ranch, but will I return to work when the headmaster tells me to."

Ms. Wing nodded. "I will hold you to that. And when he does inform you of a job, please call me." Ms. Wing gave Valerie a look only a mother could provide, and Valerie nodded with a silent yes.

"Now, how was school?" Ms. Wing asked.

"It was school…." Koda sighed. "When do I go to the other school?"

"Tomorrow." Ms. Wing sighed with a laugh. "I was there all day today preparing for the new arrivals. The school must have grown an extra story to make accommodations. How many new ones do you think we will have?"

Valerie took on a thoughtful look and looked at Sallisfer, who had the same look. "Well…" she made a funny face and seemed to be silently calculating something. "Each older master will have to have two students, and all the younger Masters will have one student each."

"Alex will be graduating, so I will get a new pupil, and Valerie will get a pupil…." Sallisfer said. Kal looked at them, even more confused.

"You will have two pupils?" Ms. Wing looked at Valerie, her eyebrow raised. "Or has your pupil graduated?"

"I will have two," Valerie said. Ms. Wing shook her head with a sad look in her eyes.

"When will graduation be?"

"I don't know," Valerie said. She stood from her chair and smiled. "Thank you for supper. It was wonderful." She rinsed her bowl, and with her cup, she placed it in the dishwasher. Then Valerie kissed her mother's head.

"I will take care of the barn." She smiled, walked to the door, and put on her hoodie and boots.

"I will see you tomorrow," she said to Sallisfer and was out the door.

Ms. Wing smiled. They finished supper, cleaned the kitchen, put everything away, and then got ready for bed. "Go get a shower, Koda," Ms. Wing instructed as she glanced at Sallisfer, then wiped the table clean and started to unload the clothes from the dryer onto it.

Kal walked up to Sallisfer and whispered into his ear. "Will you stay around and watch for Holjus?"

Sallisfer nodded slightly and looked at Ms. Wing, who was watching them with interest from the table where she was now folding clean clothes. "I must be off now," he said with a smile, which she returned.

"Be safe; stop and remind Valerie to give Fancy her night meds."

"I will. Thank you for supper." He said.

"You are always welcome." Ms. Wing said, "Good night."

"Good night," he said, then looked down at Kal and gave her a small peck on her head. Then, he walked out, changed into his horse form, and galloped off, but Kal knew he would be back.

Before Koda finished showering, Ms. Wing called Kal to the table, "I am not sure I approve of your relationship with Sallisfer. You haven't known him very long."

"I feel. like I have known him a lifetime." Although Kal admitted, "He may be a little white and nerdy, but he isn't that bad."

Ms. Wing laughed. "People, especially Valerie and Sallisfer, are well known for hiding secrets… But unfortunately, it is part of the job."

"What job do they have?" Kal asked, her curiosity from the early conversation at the table finally boiling over.

Ms. Wing was silent for a while as she sorted out the clean clothes, "They are servants…" she paused again with a sigh to gather her thoughts and continued. "They are servants to the headmaster. They are his ears, his eyes, and his voice. He makes the law. They enforce the law."

Kal swallowed. "That doesn't make them bad people."

Ms. Wing smiled and laughed slightly. "No, but it creates rifts when you are not in the circle."

***

Kal thought over what Ms. Wing had said, wondering if she was part of that circle. Before she could ask another question, Koda came out of the restroom, and it was Kal's turn for a shower.

Kal stepped into the bathroom and showered, all the while her brain continuing to turn over the words that Ms. Wing had said. Finally, she got out of the shower. Then looking at herself in the mirror, she freaked out. Her hair was white, and her eyes, which usually were a light shade of hazel, were bright blue and glowed with light and power. She flexed her fingers, and blue sparks flickered into life.

"I can do magic!" She whispered and screamed to herself with excitement. She made more sparks flash down her arms. Kal looked at the curtain she had left open after her shower. "Close," she flicked her wrist, and the curtain flapped once but did not close. "I guess that is why I have to learn how to do this," she said to herself quietly.

Kal watched her hair and eyes return to normal. Not having any control, she knew it would come again. But when? She wondered as she left the bathroom, passing Valerie, who smiled at her knowingly as she entered.

Later that evening, Kal walked into their room to find Valerie sitting on her bed reading.

Valerie looked up from the book and smiled. "Do you know anything of your past?" she asked, closing the thick leather-bound book in her lap.

"Only the small tidbits I've picked up on or have been explained, like the part about my grandparents."

"It is such a shame your mother hid you for so long and compressed your power; you could be a master by now. But your mother did have her reasons, I guess."

"What do you mean compressed my power?" Kal asked, looking up from trying to read the title of Valerie's book.

Kal thought her power had just surfaced, as Valerie's mother had tried to explain at supper the night before. Valerie sighed, placed her book on her bed, stood with a groan, stretched tall, and walked over to her shelf. She opened her red oak jewelry case, pulled out a small silver box, and handed it to Kal with guilty eyes. "I only took them for your own good. If we hadn't met…" Valerie licked her lips, trying to get her thoughts together.

"Kal… you have potential to be powerful… and with that power comes…. well, responsibility."

Kal looked at her friend, confused, and Valerie wiggled uncomfortably. "As you know, power tends to reach its full potential at 16, right?"

Kal nodded, and Valerie again wiggled uncomfortably. "When power blooms, as we like to call it…it can do two things to an unprepared person. It can explode or vanish. In either case, it would have killed you."

Kal took the box with shaking hands. "I had to protect you. You understand?" Valerie asked. Kal's hands continued to shake as she opened it. Inside the box was everything she had lost; pair of earrings, a broach, a jade necklace with a cool pendant of an owl, a ring, an anklet, a baby pacifier, a pair of baby socks, and even a cool belt buckle with a tiger on it.

Anger flashed up in Kal as she touched the items she had treasured the most and was devastated when she lost them. "They were gifts from my mother! You had no right to take them!" she fumed.

Valerie looked down at the floor, "Try on the ring, then try to pull on your power," she almost whispered. Kal did so, and suddenly she felt weak and ordinary. She pulled the ring off quickly and threw it as if it had just bit her, the same ring she had slept in and shown off. It was one of the few gifts her mother had given her. Tears fell as she whimpered, but only for the moment to escalate into a sobbing fit.

"Why?" she asked. Valerie sighed, sat beside her, and pulled her into a one-arm hug.

"I do not know. Perhaps your mom saw what happened to me and feared for you. She had told everyone she had lost her baby, yet here you are." She gave Kal a squeeze, "We knew you had been born, or we believed we knew. But we did not know to whom, and when there was no sign of you or your great power, things got a little fiery around the magic realm. People almost lost hope."

Kal looked at her friend, blinking her tears away, "You talk as if I am important." Valerie laughed and gave her friend a tissue from the box on the bedside table. "Kal, you are more important than you know."

"How do you know?"

Valerie pulled up her pant leg and rolled down her sock. There on her ankle was a birthmark, half of a butterfly wing. Kal pulled up her pant leg and revealed her own birthmark, it was on the same ankle, and it was the other half. "You also have another birthmark on your back left shoulder blade. It looks just like the one I have on my chest, below my right breast. These marks are just part of your destiny."

Kal nodded in silence. She stood up, retrieved the ring, and placed it back in the box. She considered throwing the box away, forgetting the items, and placing them all in the past. Then as she looked down at the box of treasured memories, she reconsidered. She put the box on a shelf below the window to keep it safe, feeling that the things within could be useful one day.

"Thank you." Kal whispered, looking out the window before turning back to Valerie, "I'm sorry I got into your business."

Valerie smiled, "I am sorry I got into yours. But just as I took away your jewels, you only did what you felt best with Holjus. As well as Sallisfer talking you into it." Valerie laughed, "I should have known he would eventually find out. If it wasn't for you interfering, the fire might have run away with me… it still could, but at least Sallisfer knows so he can help."

"Does he help often?"

"Too often. You see, we share everything; we are good friends. Sometimes too good of friends, but we have to work together, which involves complete honesty and openness in our line of work. But we are trying to be less open with one another, not out of trust issues, but out of respect for others." She smiled, "We speak more in words now because it's polite to speak the language around you."

Kal nodded, a little confused, but before she could ask, Valerie stood and went to the door; she looked back at Kal. "More will become known tomorrow. I have to explain some stuff to Koda, too, so it's better to say it once than twice." Valerie slipped out to the hall, and Kal heard her close the bathroom door.

Kal walked over to Valerie's bed to look at the book, but it had vanished. In its place, as if Valerie had predicted Kal's motive, was a small hardback book with gold lettering "The History of Earth Children, written by Fredrick Jones and illustrations by Harper Williamson." Kal picked up the book, walked to her bed, and slid under the covers.

"Good night, Kal." Kal jumped. She had just read and reread about the first known magic users and hadn't heard Valerie come back into the room. Kal looked at Valerie, who went to her bed and pulled up the covers. Kal watched the light fade, and Kal placed the book down and laid back onto her pillows, with her mind racing. "Good night, Valerie," she managed to say, as she had much to think about.

Kal was still thinking about what she had learned, putting the pieces together, when she felt Valerie get up and walk out of the room, only to return to get a jacket. Kal sighed, slid out of bed, and watched as Valerie met Holjus. They did the same thing as the night before; except they didn't kiss. Instead, Valerie just fell into Holjus' arms, and he held her close. Kal watched from the window wishing she could hear what was being said without being detected.

***

Outside, Valerie felt hot tears sliding down her cheeks as Holjus held her close to his chest. Through his leather jacket, she heard the steady beating of his heart; it seemed to beat in time with hers.

"Let's run away together." Holjus whispered into her hair, "We can make a quick escape…. No one could find us."

Valerie laughed, and she looked up at him. "If only we could." He wiped her tears away and cupped her chin with his hand.

"I see him in your eyes." He said, "Can't he leave us alone?"

Valerie closed her eyes and opened them Holjus smiled. "Tell him -thank you." He kissed her forehead, and she leaned back into his embrace.

"I'm going to miss you," she whimpered.

"I'm going to miss you too," Holjus whispered.

They stood there for a moment, maybe two, "Where would we go if we ran away?" Valerie asked. "I can stop time… not forever, but I could," Valerie stated.

It was Holjus' time to laugh. "If only we would be alone," he said. "I guess that is why we must…" Before he finished, Holjus pulled away from her and looked into her eyes.

"I can do magic," he confessed. "I don't know how much I can tell my brother?"

Clearing his throat as if something was caught…and with a sigh, he continued talking… "this new power I have that I shouldn't have."

He stopped talking again as if deep in thought for a moment and continued his thoughts aloud. "And then if he finds out…," the words got caught in Holjus's throat as he looked at her. He had the most immense urge to take her into his arms and fly away.

She sighed and stroked his tears away. "I guess it is for the better than…" Not speaking the unthinkable.… "isn't it?"

He gave a slow, reluctant nod. He saw the pain in her eyes as part of her heart was breaking. He didn't want to do that to her. He kissed her slowly, hoping to put enough feeling into the kiss to stop the breaking. He loved her, and he wanted her to know before they separated. She kissed him lightly back and then looked down at her feet.

"I'm…" she trailed off as he pulled her close and kissed her again, putting as much feeling as he could in the kiss. Her arms wrapped around him, and she kissed him back with the same feeling. A low growl could be heard under the porch, and they parted.

"Don't be," he said, stroking her face lightly, wishing he could stop the tears and hating that they still had a chaperone.

"I…" she couldn't finish her sentence as another growl issued out from under the porch. Valerie hugged him and whispered "I love you" in his ear, then turned and left. Stopping as she reached the door, she looked back at him, he smiled weakly, and she smiled back.

Valerie opened the door and stepped inside; she stood in the living room at the door, her body shaking with silent tears. She sat down on the couch and buried her head in her hands. Valerie made a choice not to follow her heart. It wasn't a choice she made lightly, as the pain ripped her inside and out. But it didn't hurt as bad as a broken heart because Valerie knew Holjus still loved her. She heard him whisper, "I love you, Valerie," when she was at the door. Valerie loved that demon. For some reason, she had fallen for the one she couldn't have.

Outside, Holjus sighed, gazing longingly at the door; his red eyes were full of pain and sadness. Holjus flapped his leathery wings and flew into the air without looking back. Sallisfer watched as Holjus flew away into the dark. He listened for a while, and as soon as he was sure the demon was far enough away, he stepped out of his hiding place.

Sallisfer felt Valerie's pain in the back of his head and began to wonder if he had done the right thing. Was he doing what was right for them or what he thought was right for himself? If he had been in Holjus's shoes, what would he do? What could he do? Sallisfer shook his head. This was the right thing; he shifted back into his horse form, but before he could gallop home, he felt Valerie's anger; as the pain faded. Fearing for Kal, he stopped and shifted back. He walked to the door and found Valerie waiting for him.

He reached out to Valerie, who turned away from him. He walked over and wrapped his arms around her. "I am sorry," he said, "But it will be easier for you to kill him in a few months. You have to win. Another death is something we cannot afford."

Valerie leaned her head on his shoulder and looked at him, "I still don't think I could kill him."

"Would you rather die at his hands?"

"No. but…"

Sallisfer sighed, "The longer you two stay away from each other, the easier the pain will get…" a thought occurred to him that would put a dent into that idea; he spun Valerie around and looked into her green eyes. "Did he… did you give?" He simultaneously felt a blush and a spike of anger, but it all faded when she shook her head.

"We never crossed the boundary. Holjus hasn't even seen me without my clothes on." Sallisfer felt a smile forming on his face, which he quickly schooled into surprise.

"So, you are still?"

"As promised to my dad, I shall wait until I'm 18."

Sallisfer sighed and pulled Valerie into a hug, "Do you want help going to sleep?" He asked, feeling the conflicted thoughts and feelings inside of Valerie.

"Yes."

Sallisfer suppressed another smile and kissed her forehead, sending tiny calming sparks that calmed and quieted her mind at once. He guided her to the bedroom door and felt Kal was still awake. He cursed mentally and sent Valerie in first, waiting outside as he heard Valerie walk into the room and crawl back into bed. She sobbed silently.

As soon as Kal's eyes were closed, Sallisfer entered the room and slid up against Valerie, who clung to him like a rock in a raging sea. He sent calming thoughts, and Valerie started to fall asleep. Sallisfer was about to wiggle out from under Valerie when the door to the bedroom opened, and there stood Mr. Wing. Sallisfer was caught; he stared at Mr. Wing with eyes like a deer caught in headlights.

Mr. Wing shook his head and motioned for Sallisfer to get out of bed. Sallisfer slid his feet into his boots on the side of Valerie's bed. He tiptoed to the door looking back to make sure neither girl woke.

In the living room, Mr. Wing looked to Sallisfer, waiting for an explanation, "She couldn't sleep."

Mr. Wing rubbed his tired eyes as he got a glass of ice water, "So you decided to cuddle with her? Why not send her to sleep while you are at home?"

"I tried, sir. She was too restless."

Mr. Wing looked at Sallisfer again and sighed. "I am glad, however, to see you two are getting along again. I was starting to worry something had come between you. You two must work together…. Just not in my house and her bed."

"Yes, sir."

"Go home to your own bed. Be extra careful. The closer we get to the full moon, the more demons will be out."

"Yes, sir," Sallisfer walked to the door, and as soon as he was out in the open, he shifted back into a horse and galloped home, thinking of all the things he had to tell Kal in the morning.

Mr. Wing walked back to the girl's room. He walked to Valerie's bed and pulled the cover back over her shoulders. In the dim light of the hall, he could tell that she had been crying, and he wondered what had made her so upset that Sallisfer broke the rules to comfort her. It wasn't like them to break household rules. On days when Valerie's power spiked or emotions ran high, it wasn't uncommon to wake up and not have Valerie in her bed with just a note.

Mr. Wing looked over at the other bed. He guessed it had to do with Kalea. A girl; he had allowed into his home, a girl who had no idea how important she was to the livelihood of Earth Children. The sight of Kalea had both delighted him and saddened him. He looked away from Kalea and back at Valerie; he knew just as Valerie what Kalea's appearance meant. The unfortunate fact, Valerie's life was coming to an end sooner than anyone had expected.

Perhaps, Mr. Wing thought as he stroked the hair out of Valerie's face, *that was the reason for the upset and the rule-breaking. They didn't want to leave Kal alone just yet.* Mr. Wing stood and walked out of the room, his personal emotions surfacing as he walked to the bathroom to prepare for bed.

CHAPTER 7

Tuesday Morning

"**G**irls, time to wake up!" Valerie's mother called, opening the door and allowing the hallway's light to shine into their room. Kal groaned, sat up, and looked at Valerie, who growled and rolled over. Kal stretched and walked to Valerie's bed.

"Valerie, time to get up." Kal poked her lightly as she walked to turn on the light.

"I don't wanna go to school," Valerie said as she sat looking at her friend. Her eyes were red and puffy, and she had a bad case of bedhead.

"Why not?" Kal asked cautiously.

Valerie stared at her driving daggers with her eyes before she rolled over. "Because."

Kal watched Valerie for a moment. "Why?"

Valerie sat up. Her eyes flashed dangerously, making Kal step back. "I just don't!" She snarled before taking a deep breath, closing her eyes, and letting it out slowly.

As Valerie swung her legs over the side of the bed, Kal gathered her stuff to go into the bathroom. Koda ran in and jumped on Valerie's mattress. "Is it true today is the day?" he asked, jumping up and down, making Valerie laugh and grab him in a warm hug.

"Yes, today is the day." She said, "You will ride the bus to my school today and meet me to get on the bus. Mom already put a note in your book bag to inform your school that today from this moment on, you will be a bus rider instead of a car rider." Koda squealed in delight and ran off to his room.

"What was that about?" Kal asked.

"Sometimes Koda has to ride the bus to our school to ride home. Now he will do it every day." Valerie said with a shrug.

"I just hope the bullies leave him alone." Kal walked to the bathroom, prepared for the day, then went to the kitchen and fixed her lunch. When she was done, Valerie was nearly ready and was pulling her long hair into its standard ponytail.

"How do you look so normal?" Kal asked as she glanced at her reflection on the TV screen; her hair was still white, and she had a slight glow of blue in her eyes. Valerie laughed, pulled a coat off the hook, and handed it to Kal.

"It isn't a power suppresser," she laughed as Kal eyed it suspiciously "it is more like a power hider… it already has the illusion charm on it."

Kal put it on and walked to the bus stop with Koda. They watched Koda get on his bus, and then they waited for theirs. Kal observed people passing by as they dealt with the inclement weather, and then she noticed Valerie.

"How do you stay so warm?" Kal chatted as she huddled in the coat while Valerie appeared calm and warm.

"One day, I will take you to the peeks of Kangchenjunga, the Mountain of the Dragon Princess. That is cold." Valerie said, "This is just annoying."

Kal stared at her and was about to ask how Valerie had gotten to Kangchenjunga when the bus pulled up. They boarded and found their seats after greeting good morning to the always grumpy older man who was their bus driver.

Kal looked out the window as the bus got on its way, and the small yellow farmhouse faded from view. It was quite an adjustment for Kal to ride the bus to school. Her dad had always driven her, saying that buses were too dangerous. She looked around the silent bus full of dozing kids and was startled to see that she could identify the humans, demons, and other earth children. She looked in awe and didn't miss Valerie's slight smile, "You are learning quickly," she whispered, "You are naturally talented."

"So, what happened… why is this happening?" Kal asked.

"There are many doors in one's mind… as your power surfaces, it opens more doors and abilities." Valerie smiled.

Kal smiled too, and then she made another note, as Valerie looked only out the window and didn't even glance over at the demons who sat just two seats over in the other row. Kal saw the demons take notice of them, and one smiled a pointed tooth grin at her.

The bus stopped again, letting on two human boys with long blond hair and soft blue eyes. The older one looked around the bus; his eyes landed on Valerie. They exchanged a smile that made Kal wonder how many boyfriends Valerie needed. Kal looked away again and saw the demon was still watching her, his smile even more gruesome, making Kal shiver involuntarily.

"What is it, Kal?" Valerie whispered, looking at her friend, concerned.

"Nothing," Kal mumbled, not wanting to start something.

The bus stopped again, and two more demons got on, making Kal uncomfortable; even though she knew they had survived the bus ride on Monday, she hadn't realized how many demons road with them. She counted a total of eight earth children scattered in their seats. Most were snoozing and not caring what the demons did. The twenty or so humans also had no care in the world as they stared out into the darkness at the ever-growing population of houses flashing by the windows as they grew steadily closer to school.

Kal tried to relax; *just act normal*, she told herself repeatedly. *They don't know, you know. You look just as normal as they do.* She looked at one from the corner of her eye and saw that one of the demons across from her said something that made the others laugh, and Valerie turned and glared at him.

The demon smiled. "Good morning, my girl Valerie." He said, making Kal jump at the name. She looked at Valerie for confirmation that they looked normal, but Valerie just winked at her.

"Good morning, Ivor. What did you say to our dear friend Keir?" She asked in an overly sweet-pitched voice, tinged with annoyance.

Ivor smirked and nudged his buddy, who said, "We were making bets on how long you will last in the pig pen. I said maybe an hour, but Keir thinks you won't last but 30 seconds."

Valerie snorted, which made the humans look at them, and the other students on the bus erupted in whispers. It took a few breaths, but Valerie's grin did not waver as she pulled herself together. "30 seconds…. an hour…. Damn, place your money in will he last to the afternoon. You know the rules, having killed your earth child in November. Give a show, show the effort, and give them time to show their loved ones they did their best," Valerie grinned.

When Kal looked at the demons, this time, she did it in awe. They were 16 and had already killed their assigned earth child. She swallowed and looked back at Valerie. They had committed legal murder; some poor kids were not here today because of them. Valerie discussed it like it was all trivial. Keir leaned forward in his seat, his face hard and very menacing "You think you are so daunting. You haven't seen your worst nightmare yet. Holjus is going to tear you to pieces. Your own Mama ain't gonna know who you are."

Valerie rolled her eyes and gave another laugh, "You think you can intimidate me? You might as well start saying your goodbyes and getting on your man Holjus's good side if you want to be in his will. Because he won't be around much longer." Valerie smiled, her eyes shining with such hatred, and Kal could feel the air go cold around her that it took all her willpower not to shiver.

"I doubt that," the demon jeered.

"You know, I think you and your gang are a little too sure of yourselves." Valerie taunted.

The bus stopped, and a few more humans got on. Kal sat weirdly, wishing she had the window seat to escape the demons now exchanging insults with Valerie. Valerie and the demons were popping off insults faster than Kal could formulate what they said and witty responses, yet Valerie never missed a beat. The demon flashed his teeth at her, and the other demons laughed.

"You won't be laughing for long." Valerie sneered. "You and your gang will find yourself written into lore." Her eyes lit a brief flash of bright green, the demons laughed and sent their red eyes aglow, and panic erupted on the bus.

Valerie grinned, jumping over Kal, "That was smart." She grabbed Keir and hit him square in the nose. The fight distracted the humans from the panic of seeing demons. Keir yelled and swung, but Valerie was already back in her seat, and the punch hit one of the human boy's cheeks. The boy let out a rebel yell and hit the demon back.

Both human and earth child kids were going after the demons.

The whole bus was a chaotic frenzy, with Valerie sitting, in the middle of it all, smiling, while Kal just stared at the mess.

The bus driver yelled and pulled over to the side of the road. Kal watched as the bus driver stomped down the aisle, breaking up fights as he went.

Suddenly a stern calmness took over his face as he reached Keir and the human. "What is this nonsense?" the bus driver yelled.

"They were jive' n a girl, sir." The human replied, rubbing blood from his split lip.

"Is this true?" The bus driver asked, looking down at the other kid, whose pouring nose had blood all over the place.

"No sir," he said, rather funny.

The bus driver turned to the human and glared at him. "What girl got teased?" he asked.

"I did, sir," Valerie said softly, sniffling. The bus driver looked at her, and his stern face softened as he saw she had tears sliding down her face.

"Are you okay?" he asked, laying his hand on her shoulder. He only knew Valerie as a good girl and kind.

"Yes, sir. Thank you, sir," she said, looking up at him with her big brown eyes. He smiled and turned back to the boys.

"You get three days off the bus," he told the human boy and his brother.

"But you, the bus driver turned to look at Keir; I am writing you up for two months' suspension off the bus," he said.

He shook his head, walked to the front of the bus, lowered his sun visor, pulled a roll of paper towels from the compartment, and then walked to Keir.

"You can use the entire roll," he said sternly, handing him the roll. Keir accepted it with a stated thanks.

The human boy looked over at Valerie; she smiled weakly, and he smiled back.

"What an exciting morning." He said with a laugh to Valerie, who laughed back softly.

"Who is your friend?" he asked as he nodded to Kal, held out his hand, and stated his name. "I am Josh Bowing."

Kal took his hand, "Kal," she said, simply not knowing what she should say and wondering how Valerie knew him.

"Nice to meet you, Kal." He smiled, then he released her hand and looked at Valerie.

"Next time you want to exchange insults with those jerks, warn me. My Mama isn't going to like that she has to drive me to school for three days."

"I'll let Mama know; she may drive us all for a while. You know she won't mind, and thank you."

"No problem. You know I never mind lending a hand. But damn, Valerie, it is only 7 in the morning." He laughed.

Kal observed Valerie and the human Josh talking. Retreating from their conversation, she let out a breath as she turned her head, looking at the landscape blur through the glass as they traveled. Kal pulled out her old MP3 player, and listening to the music, she became oblivious.

The bus pulled into the high school, and the students filed out. Kal watched as Valerie walked past the demons without a sideways glance as they walked into the school.

Josh trotted up to Valerie and Kal, giving them a nod; he stated, "Remember to let me know if your mama can take me to school," he said.

"I will, and thanks again," Valerie stated as he nodded, then walked off, leaving the girls to talk.

"How do you know him again?" Kal asked Valerie.

"My grandfather has been friends with their family since he found himself in Georgia. They raise cattle and other things. We buy our meat to supply food for the military from local farmers, such as the Bowings. It keeps pricing low for transportation."

Kal nodded thoughtfully, and the conversation moved to different things. Finally, they met up with Sallisfer and his friend, Kris, who was also a shifter. With recognition, Kal looked at Kris and stated, "You mean Kristopher King, the trooper from Sunday?" Kal asked as she looked closer at his face. Kris had bright blue hair and brown eyes, quite contrasting to the black hair and blue eyes she had met at the barn.

"You remembered." He said, falling into step beside Valerie while Sallisfer walked flanking Kal. They talked about what had happened on the bus and laughed jointly at the reasoning.

Holjus observed them, trying to control the anger that came with jealousy. He waited in the hall where the students entered the school from the bus terminal; as he had done since the first time, he and Valerie had purposely found run-in points. He had forgotten or tried to ignore Valerie, saying goodbye to him the night before, as it felt like a bad dream he could not wake up from. It was painful thinking about the truth in the word goodbye, and the nagging feeling of never being able to hold her hand in his again and relish the feeling of being whole.

"Hey man," one of the other demons said, walking over to him and jarring him out of his thoughts.

"Hey, Miltiades," Holjus said, pulling himself away from Valerie and looking at the demon walking beside him.

Miltiades was slightly taller than Holjus with a broader build. His dark hair hung long and unwashed. Tiny black hairs where he hadn't shaved covered his chin. Holjus could smell blood on his company's breath. "Did you have a good hunt last night?" he asked Miltiades.

"Oh ya, you know I did," Miltiades said with a smile, looking down with his dark black eyes that had a tinge of redness.

"That's good to hear," Holjus lied as they walked down the hall.

"Did you go out?" Miltiades asked.

"Yes, it was a good hunting moon." But, again, Holjus lied, hoping the other wouldn't pick up on it. Then Keir and Ivor met up with them, and Holjus did a double take as Keir's nose was still red and swollen with a slight crookedness.

"What happened to you?" Holjus asked, his tone stern and disapproving.

"Valerie decided to make a statement on my face," Keir hissed, his voice still a little pitchy in his nose.

"She tried to kill us," Ivor agreed with a nod, "We were minding our own business as you ordered us to, but she attacked us."

"Started a whole battle right there on the bus, even had the humans joining in. If it hadn't been for your birthday, I would have killed her right there and then." Keir said.

"Did anyone other than you," Holjus looked around as they walked to the lunchroom for breakfast and to await the morning bell, "Get hurt," he asked.

Keir looked down at his feet, his face going hot. "No... just a scrawny human boy, but I think Valerie healed him."

"I think she and that human have something going on," Ivor spoke.

"The way they looked at each other was disgusting."

A few older Earth Children heading in from the student parking lot passed them without much of a sideways glance, but the sight of them made Holjus's companions hiss. Miltiades walked close to Holjus so no one could overhear. "You know what I saw; that was extremely weird?"

"What?" Holjus asked, getting worried.

"I saw a shapeshifter down by the red rivers on our side of town, and he looked to be looking for something or someone early this morning."

"Who was it?"

"I don't know; it shifted as soon as I landed."

"Did you see its hair?"

"It was tri-color, I believe."

"Sallisfer!" Holjus hissed and glared over at the lunchroom table where the four sat. "That medaling fool has been trying to map out our rivers. King Krishna will not be pleased his guards are not keeping unwanted visitors out."

As if feeling his eyes on her, Valerie turned her head and glared back. He caught his breath and blinked at her, confused, before remembering he was being watched. "The ugly scum," he spat out to his companion, "all of them."

"It won't be long till you show all of the earth scum that we are better by defeating that filth of a leader." Miltiades spat back. Holjus suppressed a shudder and nodded as more of his kind met and walked with him to a table.

"Yes, I will rid the earth of that maggot. I will kill her and kill her again till she rises no more." He heard such venom in his voice that it scared him. His companions laughed and patted him on the back.

"We look forward to the show. August can't get here fast enough." Miltiades said with grunts of agreement from the others. Holjus swallowed a hard lump in his throat. How could he be part of this? He didn't want to hurt people, at least not Valerie. How could he get out of this? No ideas came to him, and he realized the others were talking.

"What?" he asked, "I blacked out imagining the world run by demons." His companions roared with laughter, guiding him to a table where a tray awaited him. He smiled at Nikephoros, who was the one who had acquired the tray for him when he had waited for Valerie's bus to arrive. As he sat down at his table, and started to talk with more of his 'friends,' he noticed that Valerie's eyes were on him; he tried to ignore how they bore into his back.

"Hmm, what is she looking at?" Nikephoros sneered, looking over at Valerie, who quickly looked away.

"I say we give her some trouble today. Don't you, lads?" Miltiades smiled as the others nodded, "We need to send a message that she can't scares us."

"Why don't we go after the bus?" Nikephoros smiled, "I heard it is going out today. They have new recruits."

Miltiades and the others looked at Holjus, who repressed a sigh calculating in his head how to get out of it and finding none.

"I will send a message to my brother. The King must approve such an outward fight; as you know, he is preparing for war; this may be the start."

The thought of war elated his fellow demons as they hooted and laughed around him. Holjus pulled out his phone and texted his brother the question. He hoped his brother would disapprove of such a bold move, but when he got the go-ahead, he felt the waffle he was eating turn to ash.

He swallowed hard, trying not to gag as he tried to put excitement into his voice.

"We have the go-ahead." he smiled. The bell rang, and he stood with the others. Nikephoros took his tray to the trash can, and Miltiades walked once again beside him while the others joked and play-fought in front.

Holjus saw Valerie peek at him, and he saw her sigh, and it softened her eyes. She gave him a love sign under the table, and he nodded and understood her as he walked away, feeling a little more confident about himself.

CHAPTER 8

Lesson Two of the Magic Realm

The last bell was about to ring. Valerie pulled her heavy book bag on her back and walked to the classroom where the other kids in her nutrition class gathered. Only three others were earth children, eight were humans, not including the teacher, and the rest were demons. She didn't know why demons cared about nutrition, but they all seemed determined and delighted to be the best in this class.

The bell rang, and they all burst out into the hall. Valerie walked as fast as she could. She even put a spell on her feet to help her walk faster. Demons looked at her, and so did the Earth Children, but she didn't care. A gang of bullies had formed, and they picked on little children, like her brother, and no one picked on her brother but her.

She sped through the lunchroom, out the doors, and down the sidewalk. The gang saw her coming, and they all started to laugh.

"Sister to the rescue!" one said.

She saw Holjus in the group and shot him a deadly glare before she sent them tumbling into the wall with the wave of her hand.

"If my brother is hurt in any way, you will not see the light of day, or the moon, again," she warned and walked off in search of her brother.

She couldn't find him anywhere, and she was forced to cast the spell of fetch. She looked around, but no one was paying attention to her, so she cast the spell. It brought her brother to her. He was under the spell of paralysis, a cheap demon trick. Valerie sighed, knowing that reducing the spell's effects was the only possible solution at the moment. Unfortunately, she was not able to rid him of it. Pulling her brother along by the arm to the bus, as it would take two to break this spell. Kal got on the bus and slid into the spot opposite Valerie and her still-paralyzed brother.

"What happened to him?" she asked.

"The gang got a hold of him, and only two can get rid of his issue," Valerie grunted.

"Can I help?" Kal piped up. She felt excited at the prospect of doing magic.

"Ya, as much as he can move." Valerie sarcastically stated as she huddled deep into her hoodie, looking morose.

"Come on, let me help. Tell me what I have to do." Kal put her hand on Valerie's arm and shook her pleadingly. "Come on!" Kal begged.

At first, Valerie did not respond, but Kal had seen the look many times from Valerie and knew what it meant. She was calculating. Valerie looked at her, and her facial expression changed.

"Fine," she said, finally consenting.

"Hold your hand out, palm out," Valerie instructed. Kal did so. Valerie touched each finger counterclockwise. She then sent a tiny spark to Kal's hand, which lit up Kal's sparks on her hand.

"Now open your mind. You don't know it, but you got a natural shield on your thoughts." Kal closed her eyes, "Your shield is still up. Imagine two big oak wood doors with long brass handles and an old fashion keyhole.

"I can see the doors." Kal gasped at the heavy set of doors in her mind's eye.

"Good; now unlock the door and push them open."

"I can't," she said, staring at the doors. "They are stuck."

"That is only your fear." Valerie said, "Let go of your fear."

"I don't know if I can." The words came out as a whisper as Kal stared at her internal doors that stood so impressive and intimidating.

"You got this far; just try."

Kal took a deep breath and opened the doors. A massive rush of freedom flooded her mind, and an intense fear came. A squeeze on her hand, held open by Valerie, gave her the courage to know without words that it would be okay. Kal let her consciousness slip out a little, which was met by another, Valerie.

They lightly touched, and Valerie sent her instructions with no words. At first, they came as images too fast for Kal to understand. Valerie's experienced mind was not used to a person who had no idea what the hand positions or required spoken words meant.

Realizing her mistake, Valerie flooded Kal with overwhelming apologetic feelings. She slowed down her instructions, placing meaning behind the actions and explaining the words and the power of proper pronunciation. When they parted, Kal felt like she had performed the spell before.

Letting her mind close, Kal felt confident as she placed her hands on Koda's shoulder and head while Valerie placed her hand on the other shoulder and forehead. Then, on an understanding of the third count, Valerie, and Kal uttered the words to reverse the curse and broke the spell. Instantly after the last spoken word, Koda came back to himself, looking around, somewhat confused. Valerie laughed and hugged him.

"What?" he asked, looking at her. Valerie smiled and kissed him on the cheek. The buses had already filed out and were headed down the road. They pulled up at the middle school, and Valerie got up.

"What are you doing?" Kal asked.

"Just follow me," Valerie said, grabbing Kal and Koda by the wrist and pulling them off the bus and down the line of buses. Finally, they stopped in front of one of the buses. Valerie held up her palm, and the door opened.

"Good afternoon, Valerie," the bus driver said with a smile.

"Good afternoon Mr. West," Valerie said with a smile.

"I see you got two newey's," Mr. West said with a grin at Kal and Koda.

"I hope you have their library cards," he said.

"I do," Valerie said, leading them to aisle nine on the bus. It had a large enough seat to accommodate all three of them. She allowed them to sit first, then sat outside next to the center aisle. She reached into her black leather purse and pulled out her wallet. She pulled out two white cards. "This one is yours, Koda, and here is yours, Kalea," Valerie said with a smile. Kal growled; she didn't like her first name at all.

"What are these?" Koda asked, looking at his card; it only had his name and a picture.

"These are your library and student I.D. cards to enter the sorceress school. They will be replaced, but if you do not have this card, you will not be able to walk into the doors." Valerie said with a smile as other kids came on from all ages and grades. "Every person on this bus are earth children."

"Hey, Val!" A voice called cheerfully.

"Hey Diana," Valerie called, "I see you have your brother too."

"Yep, he's my newey."

"I got two," Valerie bragged, pointing to Kal and Koda with pride.

"No fair, you're going to get to the top before any of us do," Diana said with a half-hearted pout.

"It's not my fault," Valerie said with a grin. Soon the bus was filling up. Sallisfer and Kris got on as well.

"So that's where the card went. I was going to get the card, but Noooo, you got it," Sallisfer said, sitting behind them and eyeing the white card in Kal's hand. Kal saw that Kris had another young boy with him, and they sat next to Sallisfer. The young boy looked just like Kris but younger and almost the same height.

"Yes, I got it, but I got something else too," Valerie said, pulling out another card and handing it to him. Sallisfer's eyes went huge, and he looked at her.

"Is this for me?" he breathed, looking astonished and a bit frazzled.

"Yes."

"Thank you, and I got you a surprise too." Sallisfer dug into his pocket and pulled out a piece of paper. "I took the liberty of signing you to the next level in training."

He handed her a piece of crumpled paper, and she took it, unfolded it, read it, and then looked at him with the same look he gave her when she handed him the card.

"Tha...thank you," she breathed.

"No problem. In fact, I have to say it was easier to sign you up and get you that than it was for you to sign me up and get your way with me teaching Kal."

"You are teaching me?" Kal asked.

"Yes," Valerie said with a smile, "That's why I came to lunch so late."

"Oh."

The bus pulled out of the middle school and headed down the road. "So, are you teaching Koda?" Kris asked.

"No way, I am going to teach a girl this time. No offense Kris, you are a great student, but I am tired of the Male ego," Valerie said, looking at him like he was crazy.

"You teach Kris?" Kal asked wide-eyed.

"Ya," Kris said with an exacerbated sigh, "She has been my master," he used his fingers for quotations and rolled his eyes, receiving a playful punch in the arm from Valerie. "Ow," he laughed. "Valerie is a great teacher and has taught me for almost two years." He finished sweetly, receiving yet another playful punch.

"I am a fabulous teacher, and you will receive your master stars soon." Valerie cuffed with a wink at Kal.

"So, then he will be a master? Shouldn't he already be a master? How long do you have to be a student?" Kal asked. Then as Valerie was about to answer, Kal had another thought.

"Isn't Kris older than you?" Kal finally spoke.

Valerie laughed her ringing belly laugh that Kal always found so lovely and genuine.

"Yes, Kris is the same age as Sal." She nodded to Sallisfer, who screwed up his face in distaste, making Kal laugh.

"But age doesn't matter. It's whenever your powers surface; remember, Mom told you that. You are one year younger than me, but you are just beginning the art. I am a Master, thus a teacher." She nodded to Kris. "Kris is my fourth student since becoming a master, and I will take on another student since he will earn his low master rank soon."

"A Master?" Kal asked.

"Once you finish all the beginning classes, normally two years. You gain low master status," Valerie stated.

"Then, as a master, you take on tutoring and start refining yourself. I am a five-star master, but I am still refining; besides, the learning never stops."

Valerie smiled. "Older masters sign up to help the new masters, and new masters teach the young students. Occasionally an old master will take on a young student. However, after my father retired from teaching and started to handle the political side of things, no other older masters have taken up the challenge." Valerie shrugged.

Kal considered what Valerie said and nodded as it all made sense; she looked around, then asked, "What does your mother do?"

"Mom?" Valerie asked, confused. "Mom is well…mom, the keeper of the Ranch and the Cavalry. She is also an accountant for extra income. Occasionally, she does extra work at the school and the castle." Valerie smiled, giving Koda a hug, who groaned.

Sallisfer laughed and said something that received a smart comment from Valerie. However, Kal was no longer paying attention to them as she looked around the bus. She noticed that the earth children showed themselves as they traveled farther away from the human school. Kal gazed in awe, seeing the various diversities of styles and looks. As soon as the bus turned onto a dirt road, the earth children transformed even more.

They would become engulfed in a puff of smoke, and they were entirely changed as it cleared. The younger siblings or newcomers like herself stared inquisitively, and it appeared they were the only ones who wore regular clothes. Kal turned and looked over at Valerie and gazed in astonishment.

Valerie now wore a red halter top tied at her hip and her hip-huger blue jeans; she had a tattoo on her shoulder of a gray horse head. Curiosity made Kal look deeper; the horse's eye caught her attention. She looked into the green eye of the horses and saw an orange tiger cub looking at her with a cocked head. She looked into its eyes and saw a red dragon, and she saw something beyond that, but Valerie's hand covered it fast.

"You looked into my spirit and the shifting I can do…." Valerie said with a half-hearted glare. "What do you think?"

Kal looked at her and shrugged. She was still curious about what was beyond the dragon but decided she was better off not knowing. She looked at Sallisfer. He, too, had changed. He wore a red muscle shirt and baggy blue jeans.

Sallisfer also had a tattoo; it was of a painted horse. Kal looked into its green-blue eyes and saw a silver owl looking at her. She looked back at the owl and saw past it, seeing a green snake. Instantly, she was interested in its red eyes, and then all at once, there was a white glow, and she could see what appeared to be an angel or perhaps just a white X-wing. As she started to stare harder, a hand slapped over it, and Valerie grabbed her shoulder and shook her, glaring at Sallisfer.

"Sorry, I didn't mean to let her go farther than the owl, but she skipped all the way to it," Sallisfer grinned.

"Ya right," Valerie growled, looking at Kal as if she was looking for symptoms that Kal might fall sick.

"When will I get a tattoo?" Kal asked, trying to see Valerie's again.

"You have already started to develop it. It starts like a dark mark that develops as your power starts to show." Valerie pulled up Kal's long sleeve and showed Kal a dark mark of something resembling a dog or a wolverine. "As you learn more about your abilities, you will discover you can shift into different animals or things depending on your power level."

Kal nodded and stared at her mark. How had she not seen this mark in the shower… Kal looked at Valerie, about to ask if it had shown itself on the bus because of all the power. Her question died on her lips as she looked at Valerie, whose eyes went unfocused as if she were seeing something no one else could.

"What…what's wrong?" Koda stammered.

Kal and Sallisfer shrugged, but Kris gasped, and they looked at him, "Demons," he said, "I saw them. They are waiting for us at the end of this road," Kris said.

"How do you know that?" Kal asked.

"Because I got a natural foresight," Kris stated, as a matter of fact.

"Oh, you do?" Kal asked, looking at Valerie. "Do you go like that?"

Kris shrugged. "I have never seen myself. Just the future."

"She has a natural animal connection," Sallisfer said, staring hard at Valerie as if trying to see what Valerie saw. "I think that's what she's doing."

"Mom has it too… it is creepy," Koda said. "But I didn't know you could have a connection to animals away from the animal." He looked out into the woods beside the road. "Mom always seems to have to be near or touching it."

"Cool!" Kal said, looking out the window to see what animal was out there.

"Normally not cool. It can kill the animal depending on how long the connection lasts…and yes, most animal connections have to be close up, but Valerie is gifted. She can sense animals and understand them up to four miles unless it is in water. Water can carry sound faster so she can hear them farther away." Sallisfer continued to look at Valerie with piercing eyes.

"That has to be maddening."

Kal realized, looking at Valerie now, wondering how she kept all the noises at bay. "Is it all animals or just mammals?" she asked, seeing an ant on the windowsill.

"All animals, but land dwelling is Mom's specialty," Koda said as he watched the same ant.

Then Valerie gasped and then spoke in a still, eerie, calm voice. "They plan on stopping us before we get to the school." Valerie slowly rose from her seat, and Sallisfer caught her arm.

"How many?" he asked, staring at her hard, and Kal saw a silent interchange. "Oh," he said, letting her go, and Valerie walked to the front of the bus and talked to the bus driver. Finally, the bus stopped after pulling over onto the grass. Valerie walked back toward her seat.

"Sallisfer, Kris, Diana, Frank, and Judith, come with me," she ordered. "Rayla, Zviadi, and Jones patrol the perimeter and keep the bus safe from those who may suspect something is up and slip by us." Then, looking over the rest of the bus, she took a breath, "Jay and June," Valerie smiled as her eyes landed upon them. The two red-headed kids looked at her and grinned, "My little speeders," she said. And they stood up. Kal immediately noticed that they wore a blue halter top and a muscle top. They were extraordinarily muscular and maybe two years younger than she but about the same height. "I need one of you to warn the school and one to stay with the perimeter crew. An open communication link with the school will make life much easier."

Kal watched as the two children she decided were twins -were grinning wide, wild grins, and they followed Valerie out of the bus.

Valerie's team shifted quickly into various swift-footed animals, while Rayla's team seemed to vanish into the woods.

Jay hugged his sister as they shot into the air. Jay morphed into a peregrine falcon and vanished into the sky. His sister became a mara bird and bounded into the underbrush, leaving Kal staring at them from the window. Kal ran off the bus after them. "What can I do to help?" Valerie shook her head and nuzzled her towards the bus door, "I do not want to stay. I want to help." Sallisfer nodded and pushed Kal closer to the bus door again, with a look of hold on a moment. Kal saw an exchange pass between Valerie and Sallisfer. Valerie sighed, nodded, and galloped off, leading the others and leaving Kal and Sallisfer still in horse form. Kal pulled herself onto his bare back and held onto his long brown mane.

"I don't know about this," she said, suddenly doubting herself as they took off in a gallop. Kal grabbed Sallisfer's mane hard and gripped him with her legs. They came to a trot and then to a walk. Valerie shifted into a mountain lion, and soon all but Sallisfer and Kal followed. Sallisfer remained a horse, and the others traveled the path. Valerie looked at Sallisfer, he nodded, and she nodded back and continued traveling the path. Sallisfer looked at Kal, and she slipped off. He shifted back into his usual form.

"The plan is that they will do the first strike. Valerie said you and I are to wait until she needs us."

"So, what do I need to do?" Kal asked.

"Nothing, we are to wait."

"But I can do something, can't I," Kal asked, not just a little confused.

"You are not trained in the art yet. It isn't your fault. Once you get to the school, you will be measured for a bracelet or anklet of your choice that will help you and the other first years learn to master the art of mind speaking."

"Is it like opening the doors? Valerie already showed me how to do that."

Sallisfer smiled, "Not the doors, more like a window. It isn't large enough for pictures or detailed instructions. More like words and feelings."

"It seems like you and Valerie don't ever close that window," Kal stated matter-of-factly.

Sallisfer moved as he felt uncomfortable by her statement.

"The link between Val and I…well, it is different and more than a little open. However, Val has discovered ways to make her mind more cluttered, which is like a wall for me, making it harder to speak freely telepathically." He gasped and looked unfocused for a moment. He looked as if he was ready to run into battle, but his body relaxed, and he looked back at Kal, "Would you like to get closer?" Kal nodded, "I am going to teach you how to shift. We are going out of order in your lessons, but you must learn as needs arrive. Think back to your animal totem; this is usually the first animal you can turn into and is the easiest to master."

Kal closed her eyes and pictured what she wanted to be. She called softly in her mind and saw that the wolf responded quicker than it had the day before. Kalea reached out and embraced the wolf and felt her body change. It hurt as muscles stretched and her body elongated. A cry penetrated her lips, neither human nor animal. Kal felt her eyes water, lashing out violently on the ground. Her whole body rippled from human to wolf.

Sallisfer seeing and sensing her insecurity, called out to her. "Kal, you must trust yourself. You must let go of the human form, tuck it into your heart, and hold it there." Kal thrashed, and Sallisfer was forced to place a shield up as he heard demons closing in on them. "Kal, I have to go. I will be close, but unwanted visitors are approaching. You are almost there…remember, trust."

"But…" Kal protested in a painful whisper as she felt hair flood all over her body. Sallisfer kissed her lightly on the top of her head and looked into her eyes.

"I trust you," he said, shifting into a tiger and bounding off. Kal stared, dazed but pulled herself together. She could now hear the demons and smell their rank scent in the air as she began to trust herself.

Once she felt the tingling sensation stop, she stood, shaking, on four legs. She moved her head side to side, pricked her ears, wagged her tail, and thought *I did it.* She was a wolf, a shifter. She laid down on her belly and moved as quietly as possible through the underbrush toward the loudest part of the fighting.

Sallisfer was at Valerie's side, who appeared to be wounded as blood flowed freely from a cut on her arm, yet she fought on. There was so much power ringing through the field that it crackled and popped in the air around the demons.

"Retreat!" the demon leader shouted; even though he had eighteen demons against five earth children, he couldn't endure being sorely outnumbered by their power.

"Run…Run demon fools…Run…I'll get you all someday," Valerie snarled.

Holjus was among the demons retreating. He had no idea that Valerie had so much power in her, he looked at her, and she smiled at him, but it wasn't an evil grin. No, it was the Valerie he knew, smile, light, and beautiful. But he now knew what she was capable of, and he would never underestimate her or her friends again.

As the demons retreated, Valerie surveyed the woods. She felt she had missed something when suddenly Kal was dragged out in a net. A trio of demons had snuck up on the distracted wolf. "No," Sallisfer whispered as Valerie's rage, -filled him for leaving Kal unaccompanied.

The retreating demons stopped and turned back, ready for a second fight as the thrashing Kal tried to escape.

"Who is behind the fur?" laughed the leader nodding at the head of the trio. He raised his hand to strike out in flames.

"No," Valerie breathed as she quickly rushed to where Kal thrashed to escape the inevitable slaughter of an attack. Before anyone could stop her, Valerie had reached Kalea's location, grabbed the demon's wrist, and averted the flame by twisting his arm. He looked at her bewildered. Fire flew around the demon trio and Valerie. Sallisfer and the other earth children flew into action, grabbing Kal and retreating to the bus.

"We cannot just leave her," Kal protested. In shock, she had shifted back to herself.

At the bus, everyone could see the flames and the curl of thick black smoke. Before they boarded the bus, Diana grabbed Sallisfer's arm, "Did Master Valerie perform fire?" Sallisfer looked at the small group at a loss. Then, Valerie landed with Holjus, and everyone stiffened as if ready to fight.

Valerie and Holjus looked at the bus full of earth children and at those gathered, ready to spring into action. Valerie licked her lips and took Holjus's hand; she locked eyes with Sallisfer and Kal. "I can't do this without y'all," she said Sallisfer swallowed and nodded. He took Kal's hand and then Valerie's other hand.

Holjus nodded to Sallisfer with an almost gloating expression on his face. Kal felt her hand grow hot as Valerie and Holjus said in unison, "With our powers combined, make the intruders forget."

All at once, red and green sparks flew from their fingertips and fell on the gawking earth children.

Kal watched as the Sparks rained around her and Sallisfer. She saw the knowing smile again as Valerie and Holjus separated. "We can't do this alone." Valerie smiled.

Sallisfer sighed hopelessly and cast a dagger-like glare at Holjus. He let go of Kal's hand and took Valerie's. "No more secrets between us?" He asked; staring into Valerie's eyes, she nodded.

He took a deep breath and closed his eyes, adding a blue spark around the dazed onlookers. "You better get a move on," Sallisfer growled at Holjus, who took off into the woods.

As the sparks vanished, Kal stared as Valerie picked up where she had left off. "Nice work, people. Let's get to the Academy." They all boarded the bus with laughter and jokes as if they had just finished some game.

Kal felt a hand in hers, and she looked over to Sallisfer. He smiled at her. "Let's start your formal training. You will be a master in no time, love."

Kal smiled and allowed herself to be pulled back onto the bus, and soon they were traveling onto a large parking lot in front of a massive brick building. The outside looked different from any academy Kal had ever seen. It had large chimneys and so many windows it was hard to count them all in the gleam of the hazy early evening light. As soon as the bus stopped, they all got off, including the older magic welders and the masters, leaving all but Sallisfer and Valerie.

Valerie briefed the newey's on what was about to happen. "You are going to go through a classing, power course. Have any of you seen the new hero movie?" Valerie asked. Many of them raised their hands. "Good, this is kind of like that, but you will not pick a sidekick and hero." Many of the kids laughed, and Valerie smiled.

"Okay, you will all be escorted to rooms A and B. There you will be measured and receive a physical, assessing your health socially, mentally, emotionally, and characteristically. You will be asked about your favorite number, color, animal totem, and other important confidential information. Some of you may get interviewed by your parents," she winked at a few new boys who smiled nervously. "When someone asks about your race, please indicate whether you are full-blooded or half-blooded," Valerie said as she looked at Sallisfer questioningly. "I think that's all, right, Master Sallisfer?"

Sallisfer nodded, then stood beside Valerie on the pavement and called out, "I need the new boys to line up in front of me!" So, the boys got into a line and followed Sallisfer into the building.

A woman came out of the building and quickly ran over to Valerie. Kal watched as the woman bowed before walking up to her.

"You're being called to see the Headmaster, Master Valerie," the woman said, holding out a parchment marked with the headmaster's seal.

"Thank you, Dona. Can you take the new girls over for me?" Valerie asked, taking the parchment from her.

"It will be an honor," Dona said with another bow before turning to the group of girls.

"Follow me!" she called, leading them into the building. Kal looked over her shoulder in time to see Valerie disappear into thin air.

"I wonder where she's going?" Kal said with a shrug before following the others into a long hallway.

The inner building was amazing, and many children stopped to admire their surroundings.

"This part of the building is over ten thousand years old," Dona said with a smile, looking at them. "If you look on the walls, you will see some of the most famous Earth Children."

Kal looked at many portraits and photos, but the newest one caught her attention; it was of Valerie and Sallisfer.

Valerie sat on a stool in a light green skirt and blouse. Sallisfer stood behind her, wearing a light blue tuxedo. She looked closely and saw that Sallisfer's hand was on Valerie's shoulder.

She looked closer and felt herself being drawn into the picture. Then she saw the light, a tunnel that drew her in, and she landed with a thump in a room with a camera crew.

"What the hell?" Kal asked, looking around, puzzled. She jumped when she heard Sallisfer's voice behind her. She turned and realized he could not see her as he walked to the door.

"Ah, there you are Val!" Sallisfer's voice rang out as Valerie walked in.

"I feel so weird. I can't believe I let you talk me into this," Valerie said, looking down at herself.

"You look beautiful," Sallisfer smiled. Rage rushed through Kal as she was forced to view this outrage.

"You're just saying that," Valerie glared, crossing her arms.

"Am not."

"Are too."

"Your turn in the spotlight," one of the cameramen said.

"I don't think I can do this," Valerie said. Then, Kal saw Valerie shaking with fear for the first time since they had met.

"Yes, you can," Sallisfer said, reaching out a hand to her. Valerie hesitated and then took it.

"We'll do it together," he assured her with a smile. Valerie smiled back. The cameraman organized them.

"What a lovely couple you two make," the man said with a smile. "I guess that's why you do such a good job as partners."

"Ya, I guess," Sallisfer said, looking down at the frightened Valerie with a smile.

"I can't," Valerie said, trying to get up.

"You can," Sallisfer said, placing his hand on her shoulder. "Just smile."

With a flash, it was over, and Valerie jumped up, nearly running to the door. Sallisfer caught hold of her arm.

"Now, Val, they're expecting us to show up at the ball," he said. Valerie growled.

"I don't dance," she said. Sallisfer rolled his eyes.

"You have used that excuse since you were four." He laughed, kissing her gently on the lips. "And I always say, don't worry, I'll lead," Sallisfer said with a grin.

"I was worried you'd say that."

Kal followed them into a long, torch-lit hall. "This is definitely not the school," she said, looking around. Then, she heard music and followed them into a giant ballroom.

Sallisfer walked over to the musicians and asked for a song, and they nodded.

Suddenly the ballroom became more spacious. People moved to the walls as Sallisfer and Valerie took the floor.

"You had to draw attention to us, didn't you," Valerie whispered harshly as the music began to play.

"Yep," Sallisfer said with a grin. "It's tradition."

"I am so going to kill you; I should have left you to die in the hands of the Gray King, but no, I had to save your sorry, Mister Instincts," Valerie said as Sallisfer led her through the movements of the dance.

"You will never let me forget that will you?"

"No."

"I was sorely afraid of that," Sallisfer whispered as he bent ever so toward Valerie's ear in an intimate gesture, so she could only hear his spoken words. Valerie smiled a little at the gesture.

Kal was getting angrier by the moment and not just slightly envious of what she was witnessing. Her thoughts were running rapidly, with one thought repeatedly resonating in her mind... WHAT THE HELL AM I WITNESSING HERE? Knowing they could not hear her, she was held captive as if in a trance, unable to stop what she was watching... the shock, horror, and disgust of the next scene before her.

"You know you have a problem. You are way too stiff." Sallisfer said as the other dancers joined in.

"It's not my fault," Valerie complained.

"No, it's not; it's mine. I need to show you a way to relax." Sallisfer said with a grin.

"Why do I get the feeling I'm not going to like this," Valerie said with a sigh as Sallisfer twirled her under his arm.

Kal noticed that no one watching knew the two of them were talking. Kalea observed their lips were not moving and that only she could hear the private conversation they were sharing in their minds.

"Oh, I think you will," Sallisfer whispered, bringing her close to him and then bringing her out again in the process of the dance.

"I can't take any more of this!" Kal growled in frustration. Suddenly the scene changed, and the dance was over.

"I am never going to dance again," Valerie said, panting. Sallisfer smiled and handed her a glass of water. Valerie thanked him and took a sip.

Kal noticed that the party was ending, and people were approaching Valerie and Sallisfer paying them respect. With only a few people left, Sallisfer took Valerie by the arm.

"Well, time for your lesson, that is, if you're not as tired as you look," Sallisfer said with a sheepish grin.

"We might as well get it over with," Valerie said. Sallisfer wrapped his arm around her waist, and they disappeared. Kal was pulled along with them.

They arrived in a room with a canopy bed and beautiful quilts hung on the walls. An ancient-looking desk was in a corner piled high with papers and books. A beautiful, full-length mirror with a gold frame hung on the wall beside a wardrobe engraved with horses and angels.

"I need a change of clothes," Valerie said, walking up to the wardrobe.

"I think you look fine," Sallisfer said, sitting on the bed.

"Well, I don't feel fine," Valerie said, disappearing into a wall and coming back in a cloth shirt tied behind her neck and mid-back, with a nice pair of flare pants.

Sallisfer's jaw dropped considerably. "Men are so easy to flatter," Valerie said with a shake of her head.

"Women, medicine for a man's soul," Sallisfer said with a dreamy look in his eyes.

Kal nearly blew her top. "Are you two seriously like this… this…." Her words failed her with the indignation of possibly being played the fool with their denial.

Kalea continued watching as an inner force within would or did not allow her to take her eyes off them. The more she observed, the more she thought and swore she would make them both pay. How could they have lied to her? Kal had seen the connection between Valerie and Sallisfer the first day she saw them together, but they both denied it. Watching them now, Kal knew they had more than dated, which hurt.

Sallisfer stood up, and the lights went dim. He slipped out of his shirt, letting it drop to the floor as he walked up to Valerie, who smiled at him.

It was like watching a movie, as Kal observed.

Sallisfer organized himself on the floor, and Valerie positioned herself in front of him. Sallisfer grinned, placing his hand on her bare back. Valerie immediately stiffened from his touch, and Sallisfer shook his head.

"You have to relax," Sallisfer whispered in her ear with a slight hiss.

Valerie's eyes rolled to the back of her head. Sallisfer was obviously pleased with himself as he placed his other hand on her back, and Valerie stiffened a little more.

"You tell me not to go off my Instincts, yet you can't go off yours," Sallisfer said.

"Your Instincts nearly got us killed," Valerie said, her eyes unfocused.

"They led me to you, didn't they?"

"And I will lead you to your doom," Valerie smiled.

"At least I'll be doomed with you."

"Whatever," Kal said, anger flashing.

"Now relax. I'll start this shhhow." Sallisfer said, and Valerie sighed and allowed her body to relax.

Sallisfer grinned and sent blue-green sparks of magic winding their way around and into Valerie. She gasped and started to stiffen.

"Relaxsss," Sallisfer hissed, sending more sparks. Valerie rolled her head. *"Just enjoy."*

Kal watched fury washing over her in huge uncontrollable waves.

Valerie turned around and faced Sallisfer, looking into his eyes. She placed her hand on his chest and sent sparks as well.

Sallisfer gasped, and Valerie giggled. *"Relax, Sally,"* she said, wrapping her legs around him.

"I think I can manage that," he said. *Valerie giggled as he clasped her and held her closer and closer, acting like they were about to kiss. Then they smiled and started laughing and holding one another.*

"I can't wait till we are 18." Then, *Sallisfer whispered,* *"I plan on showing you just how I feel for you."*

"We will have to wait till after the wedding. You know my dad will kill us both by trying to kill you, especially if we betray his trust.

Sallisfer smiled, kissing Valerie's neck, *"It may be worth dying for."*

"I can't take ANY MORE!!" Kal shouted, and she was standing back at the school, looking at the picture.

"Master Valerie and Master Sallisfer, Sorceress of the year 2005 and today," a girl said.

"This way, ladies," Dona said. Kal sighed, her anger simmering a little. "They have some explaining to do," she said as she followed the crowd farther down the hall.

She heard shouting in a room they passed. "What do you mean?!" she heard.

"You know exactly what I mean, Mister. I need the supplies now!" Valerie said.

"Yes, Ma'am," Kal heard a strange male voice confirm.

"Thank you," Valerie stated as she rushed out with a handbag. Sallisfer walked out of another room with a bundle. Kal stopped and slipped behind a table holding a vase of flowers.

"I got it," Sallisfer whispered, holding up the bundle, and Valerie smiled.

"I got the other stuff we'll need to go on this insane, yet we knew it was a coming trip," Valerie said, opening the bag and allowing Sallisfer to look into it.

His eyes widened in awe. "That is so cool. Can I have the blue ones?" he asked.

"Na Da', you always get the blue ones, and I get stuck with the green ones," Valerie said.

"Meet you at midnight then," Sallisfer said with a nod, "I'll leave it in the normal place."

Valerie nodded, and they clapped fists with a sound like thunder.

"They're going down," they said together, as sparks flew into the air as they hit, and the other hand swooped down and clapped.

"Together, we will wipe them off the face of the earth," they said as one, eyes flashed in anger. Then they parted and disappeared.

Surprised by the tremendous emotions, a wave of unrighteous anger gripped Kal's mind with an overwhelming sense of sadness that tortured her as if it choked the breath from her being, but she couldn't let it show. Instead, she took a deep breath to calm down and looked at the emptiness of their departure. *Answers would be given soon enough,* Kalea thought to herself.

She hurried up the hall and found the others being organized into rooms. She was rushed into a room which she paced restlessly. "Will you stop that?" Valerie asked, stepping into the room from thin air.

"No, I will not. Can we get this over with?" Kal said, glaring at her.

"Scared, I understand, completely, but that's not why I'm here. I'm here to take you to the Find room," Valerie said with a smile.

"The...where?" Kal asked, completely lost, her anger forgotten for a moment.

"The Find room is where you get interviewed by supernatural people who determine your fate. If I were you, I would be totally wowed out, but it is kind of scary, discovering, then knowing your path in life," Valerie said with a weak smile.

Kal looked at her friend seeing her so different than ever but somehow the same. "Well, come on. The weird ones hate waiting," Valerie said, waving her arm and grasping Kal's wrist, pulling her in.

They arrived in an old torched-lit room with five older women looking at them.

The air was eerie and smothering as they stared at Kalea inquisitively. Not one of them moved. Their eyes were fixated on Kal as if nothing else was more important. Time seemed to stand still as they waited to give what they knew the instant she appeared before them.

They began to speak one after the other, quickly revealing their thoughts.

"She's the chosen one," one said, looking at Kal with old eyes.

"She's the one that will wipe the enemy out," another one said.

"You found her Valsherkama Wings of the forest," the third one said.

Kal looked at Valerie. She was standing with her eyes aglow.

"I said I would, didn't I," she said.

"Ah yes, you did, you with the path of uncertainty," the fourth one spoke.

Valerie smiled. "My path is clear old ones. You just don't want to see it."

"You are powerful, you are strong, and you are wicked. But, unlike your friend here, she is strong, powerful, but good," the fifth one stated.

Valerie smiled a dark humorless smile at the woman that made Kal uneasy. "You all created me this way," she said, taking Kal's hand. It was cold, and Kal almost snatched her hand away. "You perfectly bred your way to the ultimate leader, knowing that if you got me...the forgotten one... you would be prepared for war." Valerie lifted Kal's hand clasped in hers. "Once you had me, you knew the Told one wouldn't be far behind. The one you created for peace." Valerie smiled at Kal.

"Yes, I found her. Now, what do you have to say for yourselves." The room grew even more smothering, to the point of suffocation. Then suddenly, Kal found herself standing dazed in the previous room. The old woman's last words were ringing in her ears: "Yes, Wicked one, you have found the chosen."

What had those older women said? She was the chosen one, and Valerie is wicked? She was still puzzling it over in her mind when the door burst open, and a tall, tough-looking man was standing outside the doorway. "Choosing time, get a move on," he roughly said as he walked away.

Kal walked out of the room and found the other children in a line, girls in one and boys in the other.

"Move! You don't want to keep the masters waiting!" The man shouted. Their pace increased to double time, and they were herded into a massive room. Two lines were drawn; the girls stood on one line and the boys on the other.

The room was long, almost like a massive hallway. Large windows on one side showed the sunset-painted sky. Above their heads hung large crystal chandeliers that made the checkered floor shine. Large marble white pillars rose eight in a line on either side. Shadows hid what might have been doors, and Kal was very tempted to go and see what was behind those doors. Instead, the large man with a cough-like sound dragged Kal's attention back to him. He stood in the middle of two lines where the checkered flooring was covered with a blood-red carpet. The man pointed, and the girls stood on one side of the carpet and the boys on the other.

Kal gazed at the line of boys trying to see Koda, hoping he didn't feel as plain as she did. That is when she noticed the space between the lines was massive. Three people could walk shoulder to shoulder with a horse on either side and still have room to turn safely.

The children burst into chatter as soon as the man left. One of the girls standing next to Kal looked over at her.

"I am so nervous. I hope I get a good teacher; my older sister got the fourth leading teacher. My sister said the teacher is the greatest and most patient teacher ever. So, I hope I get her," the girl said.

"Who are you hoping to get?" the girl on Kal's other side asked.

"I don't know," Kal said.

"I hope I get Master Sallisfer. He is so fine." Kal looked at the girl in total shock.

"He won't train a Half-blood like us," the other girl sighed. "Besides, you know the stories, Hillary; he's taken by some mysterious but powerful girl that Master Valerie pulled from the middle of nowhere," the other girl snapped.

"I wouldn't say she's from the middle of nowhere," Arcy said. The three girls turned and looked at her. "No, I would have to say she came from somewhere." Arcy smiled at Kal with a wink.

"Master Arcy," Hillary said with a bow.

"Shouldn't you be with the other masters?" Kal asked.

"I know, I should, but I like to take a peek at the future," Arcy said with a smile. "I best be off. Shh, I was never here." With that last spoken word, she was gone.

"Silence!" shouted the man again. All was silent as everyone looked to see a line of Masters marching in. At the lead was Talys. He walked in the middle of the Newey's lines.

"Good evening, children," he called.

"Good evening, Master Talys," they all said.

"You all are about to go through what I call a teacher-student choosing. When you are chosen, you will receive a necklace that may look like this." Master Talys held up a glittering jeweled necklace; it was of an eagle flying, and it clutched a sea blue marble or stone in its talons.

"This will be your room key, your teacher's grading post, and your hall pass!" he continued.

"Now, ladies and gentlemen, I present the greatest, most extraordinary, and deadliest teacher to ever set foot into this school marked in time."

With a flash of light, Valerie stood at the head of the lines. Koda's widened eyes of shock, confusion, and disbelief enlightened Kal's questions about Koda's knowledge that his sister, Valerie, was considered deadly.

Valerie walked up the line, hands clasped behind her back as she walked up and down the line, looking at each person in turn. Finally, she stopped and looked at Hillary and then at the other girl named Ava. She then smiled at Kal and walked on.

"Did you see that? She looked at me." Hillary said with a smile.

"Ya, I saw it," Kal said as her anger rose again. Valerie returned and looked at Ava, walking up to her. She smiled.

"Name, please," Valerie said nicely.

"My name? My name is....is...is... Avalon Krasen," Ava stuttered.

"Well, Miss Krason, I am going to be your teacher. You may call me Master or Miss Wings," Valerie said, holding her hand. Ava shook it, and a necklace formed in her hand when they separated.

"Wear it with pride, for you are one of the true fairies," Valerie said with a slight bow. Ava bowed in kind and looked at her new necklace in wonder. It was a sky-blue stone held up by a beautifully carved fairy that stood on her tiptoes.

"Wow," Hillary said with a sigh.

"Cheer up, friend. You still might be chosen by Master Sallisfer," Ava said with a smile, pulling her new necklace over her head.

"I give you the mastermind of Heaven, Master Sallisfer!" Talys announced as Sallisfer walked forward, and in a bolt of light, he was standing in front of Kal, holding a shining, glowing necklace.

He smiled, and she took it from him, and then he was gone.

"Behold the lovely lady Arcy!" Talys said.

"Oh, Talys," Arcy said, flipping her hair, walking forward, and looking at the students.

Kal looked down at her necklace; it was of a wolf sitting and howling at the stone, which was blue but near clear.

"Wow, you're so lucky," Hillary said with envy.

"Ya, I guess," Kal said. She had the feeling she was stepping into something that was beyond her imagination.

"You do know what this means, right?" Ava asked, with an excited glint in her eyes.

"No...?" Kal stated, shaking her head.

"The Hands both chose a half-blood to teach. So, we," Ava said giddy, "Are going in the history books!" Kal blinked, even more confused than ever.

CHAPTER 9

The Master's Play Cards

After The Choosing, students were all filed into a cafeteria. Students chatted about what they expected in this new and wild school. Kal glanced at the teacher's table. Valerie sat with a half-eaten steak, and Sallisfer was talking to her with a stern expression.

Kal slipped closer and heard Sallisfer scolding Valerie.

"You really must eat," he said.

"I'm not hungry," Valerie said.

"I am not going to have my partner die of starvation and lack of awareness because she refuses to eat," Sallisfer said.

"I'm not going to die of starvation or lack of awareness. I can assure you of that," Valerie said with a smile.

"Whatever, now tell me what's on your mind," Sallisfer said, his eyes aglow.

"It's what the aged ones said," Valerie said.

"I know. I saw what the necklace was. Kalea is the chosen one, no doubt about that," Sallisfer said with a sigh.

"Headmaster says it's up to us to protect her," Valerie said.

"That's not going to be an easy task."

"No, but together we will prevail," Valerie stated as she stared at her plate.

"Yes, together," Sallisfer said. "Now eat. We have company."

They both looked at Kal. "Join us," Valerie said.

"Yes, have a seat," Sallisfer flicked his hand, and a chair flew from one of the nearby tables and pulled her up to the table. A plate was put in front of Kal with two substantial juicy steaks.

"Eat," Sallisfer said, glaring at Valerie, who sighed, picked up her fork, and started eating, but she had only gotten two bites when Kal looked up from her empty tray.

"Are you going to finish that?" she asked.

"Yes," Sallisfer answered for Valerie. "She will finish it herself, or I'll force it down her throat."

Valerie glared at Sallisfer but continued eating.

"Newey's, if you will follow me!" shouted Talys when all was done.

"Where are we going now?" Kal asked.

"Oh, the real young ones go with their parents. Mom already took Koda home. She wasn't happy that I wasn't coming home any time soon. The older ones like you, Ava, and the others of age…will be assigned a room and will have a chance to set up your space today or set up a time with their parents to come back another day."

"A room?" Kal asked.

"Ya, each student gets a safe place to practice magic or rest after a long day's work. Magic takes a lot of energy, and having your own room gives you a place to recover. We also have a medical wing. It is like a boarding school. Children from nonmagical families often stay here permanently, the bus taking them back to normal school. Others choose to stay here besides holidays. Some masters even live here."

A master laughed, "I do." He was a brutish-looking man with brown hair cut high and tight. He had a long scar on his face from his chin to his ear. His eyes radiated with magic that swirled in blue and green sparks.

Kal sighed. "Well, I guess I'll go," she said when she saw the room was emptying of the normally dressed children leaving only the halter tops and tank tops. Soon those started to get up and go.

"You can stay, Kal. We, masters, are going to play a game." Valerie said with a grin.

The other master smiled back. "A game? it's no game; it's the future!" He and Sallisfer said, pulling out a deck of cards from his pocket. Valerie pulled out three six-sided dice that changed colors.

Other masters walked up, each holding a deck of cards and dice. "Kal, these are some of our masters. This guy, she pointed to the man with the scar.

"This guy is Uncle Pike Rogers; he is super cool and likes to hang with us babies," she laughed. Uncle Pike shook Kal's hand and grinned.

"This is Master Raū Masashi and his best friend and partner, Master Tommy Lee." She pointed to a small, wired-haired man with broad shoulders and glasses and a tall, muscular man with a buzz cut and piercing black eyes.

"You wouldn't happen to be related to that Cavalry girl?" Kal asked suddenly. Master Lee smiled, and Valerie looked impressed.

"Tema is my older sister." Master Lee nodded. "She chose action over teaching." He laughed.

"These two are Master Asier Olmos and Master Kanna Kimura." Valerie nodded to two beautiful, strong women who nodded with encouragement at Kal, who nodded back, feeling much smaller than usual.

"And Over here, we have Master Jia Zheng and his partner Master Adam Zviadi."

Kal looked over at the pair, who winked at her in unison, shuffling their cards.

"This is my good friend Master Jiahao Xun…" she trailed off and looked around. "Where is Master Kallisto?

Master Jiahao smiled. "She has retired for the night. Her daughter is in labor."

Valerie grinned. "That is wonderful news. Ligria is going to be a wonderful mother. Do you know if they have chosen a name for the little miracle?"

Master Jiahao shook his long black hair. "No, not that I know of. Like any child born to this world, the name shall come when they first meet."

"These nice people are Master Zavion Okafor and his partner and wife, Master Khyle Okafor. Their youngest daughter is due in what…"

she smiled at the couple. The man was stoutly built with a long red beard and a clean-shaven head, and his wife, who was clearly expecting, was slightly taller with beautiful dark curly hair and green eyes.

"Next month." The woman Master Khyle smiled. "And I wanted to thank you for allowing me to take the season off from teaching."

Valerie smiled. "You need to focus on your little ones. How is little Valerie?" Valerie smiled, and the lady beamed.

"She will be two in a few weeks. Will you come to the party?"

Valerie nodded and said, "Yes. Of course."

She then pointed to familiar faces who were on the bus, "Master Diana Garza and the set of twins, Master Jay and Master June Amala, also like to play in our little group."

Valerie continued, "There are other Masters, but some go home. Others retire to their rooms or play in other groups. So, this game is only really suitable for, like," she did a quick head count, "twenty team pairs."

"Ready to go down?" asked Master Masashi when Valerie was done.

"No, you and Master Lee should be ready to go down because my trio is going to bring you down," Valerie said with a wicked smile that made Master Masashi back up a step.

Kal glanced over at Sallisfer with unease. "How do I play?" She whispered for only him to hear.

"Just follow our lead," he said, looking at her. He had a dark smile on his face, "We are so going to kick butt." He said rather anxiously.

Kal sat down between Valerie and Sallisfer. She looked at the cards that Sallisfer had handed her.

One was a gray griffin, and another was a knight in golden armor. She also had a small green dragon, a pale unicorn, a big black horse standing by a cherry tree, a small, sparkling fairy, a sea serpent, and a red-bearded Dwarf.

She glanced over at Sallisfer's hand and smirked. She had cooler-looking cards. She then glanced over at Valerie's and nearly erupted into laughter. All she saw were goblins, ogres, and other unsavory creatures.

Kal paid extra attention as they brought out the dice. "Are you going to roll?" Valerie asked Sallisfer.

"You can, you can start our victory," Sallisfer said. Valerie nodded and rolled her dice. They hit the table along with the others, and they were all sixes. Talys, who had suddenly appeared at the table, picked one up, looked at it, and then looked at Valerie.

"It was a lucky roll," he said, handing her back the dice. "Pick your opponent."

"I pick The Bachelor Duo," Valerie said with a laugh. Master Masashi smiled and laid three of his cards out in front of him on the table. Valerie did the same.

Then they flipped the middle one up, and Kal examined the pictures. Masashi's eyes grew huge. She looked down at the cards as Valerie's basilisk confronted his white wizard.

They rolled, and Kal saw Master Lee praying as sweat rolled down his partner's face.

As soon as the dice hit the table, Sallisfer and Valerie grinned.

"Your dead," they said as one, their eyes lighting.

The card figures floated off the cards, and the white wizard died and fell back into his card. "Wow," Kal said in wonder as the basilisk slithered back to its card.

"Next," Valerie said, swiping the wizard and adding it to her deck. Masashi flipped the next card over to reveal a red dragon. Valerie's smile disappeared, and she glared at Masashi as she flipped her card over. It was a bay paint horse with bright blue eyes. Masashi's jaw drooped as Sallisfer's laid a card next to the bay paint. It was of a black witch.

"Partners stick together," Sallisfer said as he picked up his dice, and she picked up hers. Sing sighed and picked up his. They rolled.

"I can't do anything to help?" Kal asked with a sigh.

"I think we may need it; place the unicorn down," Sallisfer said as the cards' characters floated off, and the battle was on.

Kal placed the unicorn down, picked up the dice she had been given, and rolled. It was a six, four, and seven. The unicorn sprang into action and added its presence with the two characters fighting the dragon. Lee placed down a Black fairy and rolled; it, too, came into the fight. Valerie added a goblin, and Sallisfer added a White witch.

"Add your black horse," Sallisfer said. So, Kal did, and it, too, joined in.

Soon all the players were fighting, and the cards gained, lost, and then gained again.

Kal noticed that Valerie, Sallisfer, and her, when added, were winning, tearing the other masters apart. "I need backup," Valerie said as a fierce Dark dragon was pinning her bay paint horse.

"Add the fairy," Sallisfer said, laying down a green cougar and rolling. She placed the fairy and rolled. Their cards went to assist Valerie; she was saved but was severely wounded.

Sallisfer held his head and groaned. "I feel sick," he said as the horse stumbled to its card.

"You're not the only one," Valerie said as the Black witch was struck down.

Kal tilted her head, and Valerie looked ready to pass out. Sallisfer sighed, placed the black witch back in his deck, and shuffled it. He laid the black witch back out, and Valerie was back in the game.

"Sorry about that," Valerie said with a smile.

"Okay...can anyone tell me what just went on?" Kal said, looking at Sallisfer, who was still holding his head and groaning.

Valerie grabbed the paint horse card and started shuffling it in her deck, and Sallisfer smiled.

"Thanks," he said.

"No problem. Now, let's end this and look what comes out of it, for we have a deadline, remember," Valerie said, laying out all her cards and rolling the dice. All the cards came to life, and the other players were defeated in one easy strike.

"Deadline?" Kal asked, looking at Sallisfer. She remembered them talking about midnight.

"Yes, we won't be at school tomorrow, but we will meet you here in the evening.

"I will. But Sally will probably be in bed still. He can sleep for days if no one gets him up," Valerie said.

"No, I won't," Sallisfer said with a humph.

"Ya right."

"Okay, where are you going?" Kal asked.

"That's classified... Sorry." Sallisfer answered, and Kal sighed.

"Yeah…You never tell me anything." She muttered, glaring at Sallisfer. "Like you and Valerie's past history."

Valerie's eyes widened. "I'm gonna go... and get some soda!" She called over her shoulder as she sped away. Sallisfer was stuck looking at a very angry Kal.

"And how do you know that?" He asked hesitantly. He felt very small when she glared at him.

"Let's just say—"

"Uhm... Guys... you'd better see this." Valerie said, and both Sallisfer and Kal got up to see Valerie crouching over the dice she had rolled when she got up.

"Well, that's a good sign!" He replied.

"What do dice flipped onto the three, five, and two sides matter?" Kal asked, still extremely irritated and staying well clear of Sallisfer for spite.

"It means that all will go well tonight!" Valerie replied with a smile.

Kal, too angry to care, stalked out of the mess hall. Sallisfer ran after her, still trying to think of how to explain the situation.

"Look..." he growled, pulling her around to glare at him before continuing, "It's been a while. Things change."

She pushed his hand off her shoulder, glaring at him with venom. "Are you sure things have changed, Master Sallisfer?"

"If I could tell you, I would... But it's classified! I can't go around telling people classified information!" He yelled, wanting her to understand. But unfortunately, she was too deep in her anger to want to stop.

"Yes... I'm just people. I'm no one important! I have never been." She growled.

"Yes, you are! You're more important than you think, and you'll see that one day."

She wasn't listening. She was running out the door. Valerie watched the wolf race out of the front door, fully knowing it was Kal but figuring she could run out her anger.

"And besides, we have a deadline," Valerie added, muttering, to herself, as Sallisfer appeared, staring out into the forest.

"Come on, Sal... We have a mission to complete!" She said.

"But—"

"She needs a breather, Sal! She is confused, which makes her angry. Let her run her anger out." Valerie cut him off, looking at him sternly.

"Fine. But if you had told Kal the truth in the first place when you were supposed to, maybe we wouldn't have this problem."

He glared at Valerie, glancing over at the forest's edge more than once.

Valerie snarled, "So! You think I was going to walk over to a girl who has never seen magic in her life and say, Hi, I'm Valerie Doom. You are the chosen one. You have great power that I need to defeat and end the war. Would you please come with me?" She rolled her eyes and went toward the tree line stopping at a particular tree. "I don't think that would have worked." As she drew near, blue eyes vanished into the undergrowth.

"Well, you could have tried! You didn't even give her a chance!"

"You know what, Sal! If you didn't screw up in the first place, maybe things would be slightly different!"

"HOW!" Sallisfer yelled as Valerie shifted into a mountain lion, digging her claws into the tree bark and climbing up to a long bag in the limbs. "You would still be sneaking off with Holjus. You would still be loving him, not me! And HELL, you would still be unhappy."

"Sal..." Valerie stopped and took a deep breath. "Look, I'm sorry. Maybe you're right. I should have been more open to Kal and even you. But you know the past can't be changed without severe repercussions." Sallisfer nodded with a sigh.

"I just want to be happy, Val."

"I know. But you and Kal are just not going to end well. You know that."

"No, I still think we have a chance... I'm not giving up on her as I did you."

Valerie laughed. "Catch!" Sallisfer ducked. A long saber narrowly missed his head and pierced the brick wall.

"Oops…" Another saber dropped to the ground, sinking up to the hilt. Valerie jumped down, shifting back into her human form as she fell. She pulled the sword out of the dirt and wiped it clean on her sleeve. She looked at Sallisfer and grinned. Black clothing now replaced her other clothes. She received a growl as Sallisfer tugged on his sword.

Valerie laughed and walked over, slipping the first saber thrown out of the brick as if it were butter.

"Show off!" He muttered, snatching his sword back.

"No… it's called a lady's touch. I don't think you have it." Valerie replied with a grin, "… In fact… I can assure you!"

Sallisfer growled, and he shifted into a massive red dragon. Valerie rolled her eyes, walked over, and carefully got on his back.

"Settled yet?" Sallisfer asked, looking at her with a massive blue eye.

"Yes, I am," Valerie said with a slight grimace.

"I hope you've been practicing."

"I have a little," Sallisfer said with a smile flapping his wings and taking off.

"You know, you are really uncomfortable," Valerie said.

"Well, if you don't want to ride, you can always walk," Sallisfer said, rolling over.

Valerie screamed and held onto one of his spikes. Sallisfer laughed and swung his head around to look at her.

"I think I'll ride," Valerie said weakly with big eyes. Again, Sallisfer's laughter shook the night.

Kal followed them, running as fast as she could underneath them, always keeping her eyes on the sky, thinking of how nice it would be if Valerie fell.

She followed for a while till she was weary and fell to her side huffing. She then curled up and fell asleep, only to dream of tearing them apart.

CHAPTER 10

A Near Encounter with Death

Kal woke with a start. She noticed her surroundings, and nothing looked familiar. She sniffed the air, and only a faint scent of Valerie and Sallisfer remained.

"So, they haven't come home yet," she said, her emotional turmoil still boiling anger in her veins.

Kal looked up at the early morning sky and howled, letting all of her anger out as she did so. Then she got up and started walking, letting her senses guide her back to the school. Upon her arrival, she found Diana pacing back and forth.

"Kal!" she shouted, with delight on her face. "We were growing worried!"

"About me?" Kal asked.

"Of course, silly!" She replied, opening the door for Kal, who padded past her and shifted back into her human form.

"You're one of us; besides, someone has to look after you with Master Sallisfer and Master Valerie being away."

"What do you mean?" Kal asked, looking at her. "Do you think I can't handle myself?"

"Heavens, no, I understand your confidence, but you're a new one, and you don't fully know how to protect yourself," Diana said with a smile.

"I can too!" Kal growled.

I know you think that, but it's not true. No time to argue; you must get clean and ready for school."

Kal glared at her but did not press the issue.

"Did you know about Master Sallisfer and Valerie dating?"

"Yes, it was common knowledge," Diana said with a sad smile.

"Can you tell me about it?" Kal asked, hoping.

"It was a business relationship…. You know, one that comes from working with someone so much." Diana assured.

Kal glanced sideways at her, "So they weren't really in love?"

"I don't know if I can answer that… they seemed like they loved each other one moment, and then they were trying to kill each other in the next." Diana laughed a little and ran a hand through her short dark hair. Then, she stopped and looked a Kal, "I guess they had and still have a love-hate relationship… more like siblings, but since they aren't related… it just didn't work."

Kal saw that Diana was telling her the truth as she knew it, so she sighed, frustrated, "How long ago was that picture in the entrance taken?" she asked.

"Last Spring. The headmaster wanted an updated picture of the Hands." Diana admitted with a grimace.

"Can you tell me where they went?" She questioned as they started walking again.

"No, I don't even know the whole business behind the quest. The clearance comes with rank." She showed Kal the three stars on her cuff. "I know where they went but not what they will do. I am, however, on standby with Master Lee, who knows the whole scheme if something goes awry."

"So…can Master Lee tell me what is going on?" Kal asked sternly.

"Why do you want to know so much? You are just getting into this world… the average newey falls into line and builds up from there."

"I guess because I am not average. I want to know everything." Kal felt hot tears in her eyes, and she willed herself not to cry. "Most 'newey' kids grew up with magic. I did not even know it was a thing till now. I want to know how I am linked to this whole... this whole... thing," she gestured in frustration. "If you can't give me clearance to know what the H is going on, then direct me to someone who can," she stated rather loudly.

Diana stared at her. Kal was surprised as she became aware of herself. They were surrounded by people staring who quickly adverted their eyes and returned to doing what they were doing before the outburst of her thoughts to Diana.

"I can't give you clearance; hell, the Hands can't even give you clearance. Only the Headmaster can give you what you want, and no one outside the Hands has seen him in a century. So, you need to accept that there is more to this whole plan than anyone can know. But do understand that you are important."

"Ya, I bet," Kal stated matter-of-factly.

"Don't act so depressed. It's almost been two years since they sort-a dated, if you can call it that way."

"Ya, and you're going to tell me things change, aren't you?" Kal growled.

"Yes, I was. And you would be a fool not to listen to that." Diana said, opening a door that led into a huge bathroom.

"I'll leave you here, gesturing toward the bathroom. When you're done, call me, and I'll have Arcy take you to Karterway." Diana said.

"Last spring wasn't that long ago," Kal grumbled, and then she stopped and looked at Diana's sad brown eyes. "Thanks." She said, suddenly feeling bad for pouring her anger on her.

Kal showered, dressed, and headed to school. In the first block, she sat next to the empty seat Valerie usually occupied. It was so quiet since she had no one to talk to. At lunch, Kalea barely ate, even though Valerie's father had fixed her rainy-day tomato soup. The rest of the day went by in a blur, and before Kal knew it, the school day had ended, and she was boarding the Sorceress's bus. It buzzed with excitement and news.

"Hey Kal," Ava said, sitting down beside her.

"Hey, Ava," Kal said.

"Have you heard the new rumor?" Hillary asked, sitting down beside them both.

"Which one? Ava said. "The one about the chosen one, or when my teacher and her teacher took on an entire army. Then there's one that states that Master Sallisfer nearly died of a broken heart?" Ava stated.

"The one that said that he nearly died of a broken heart! Who do you think did it? I want to give her a piece of my mind?" Hillary said with a growl.

"He nearly died of a broken heart?" Kal asked with bewilderment, gaining stares from the two girls. "When did you hear that?"

"This afternoon from my older sister, she's a nurse. She texted me at lunch. Here you can read it. I saved it." Ava said, handing Kal her cell phone.

Hey Sis!

Hey, what's up?

You will never guess who I had as a patient an hour ago!

Who?

Master Sallisfer, that's who.

Oh, what was wrong with him? Is he Okay now?

Yes, he's okay, he just needs rest, but when he came in, we diagnosed him with severe heartbreak-nearly killed him.

Who did it? I am going to rip her soul out!!!!!!!!!!

I don't know, but Master Valerie refused to see him!

Do you think…?

```
No! I don't think they are back together. She
was the one who gave him to us and told us
that we either make him well or put him in
an insane institution. However, she did seem
rather mad, and she was muttering to herself
about having a talk about how he is sensi-
tive. Then she laughed, and only to say no, she
would have to figure it out alone! And then she
teleported somewhere. Don't ask where. I hav-
en't a clue.
```

Kal had a split second to school her features into an innocent surprise.

"Who could do something like that!" She growled, anger in her voice but guilt wracking her heart. She knew she had done it.

"I don't know, but she should know better, whoever she is! A shifter that suffers from a broken heart could really die!" Hillary said, with her eyes bright with excitement. Kal turned away from the conversation as the girls moved on to other gossip topics.

She stared out of the window, watching the scenery half-heartedly. She had never meant to hurt Sallisfer, let alone kill him!

Before she knew where the time had gone, the school filled her whole vision. She found that she was fearful of seeing Sallisfer.

The students were led to the back of the school and out to the training field. Kal and Koda walked together, sharing a lighthearted argument.

"Nuh-uh!"

"Uh-huh!"

"Nuh-uh!"

Valerie flew toward them with extreme enthusiasm, shouting a greeting.

"Hi Koda! Hi Kal! How was school? Got homework? What'd ya do?" And all of this was in one breath. Kal stared at her as she passed, hardly slowing down to ask those three questions.

Koda sighed. "Caffeine high..." He muttered. "Be careful."

Just then, Valerie made another pass. "I'll be your teacher today! Sally has orders not to get out of bed! Yup, yup! Now I have two... wait.

THREE students!" She stopped running but had unstoppable shivering, with fiddling and shuffling following afterward.

"Today—Today, you get your books!" She, Koda, and Kal teleported to the library, and Valerie giggled. "Pick one, anyone! Plenty to go around! I'll be outside!" And with a flash, she disappeared.

"I think we have a free day today," Kal muttered, still trying to understand what Valerie had said. With another flash, Kris and Ava were standing beside Koda and Kal.

"Books? Wait a minute, and we have to do bookwork?" Ava complained. Kris sighed.

"Yes, we have to do bookwork. We've already been through this."

"No, we haven't, future boy," Ava snapped.

"Well, anyways, I'm here to help you two ladies find your books. Koda, your teacher, will be here in a moment to help you." Kris said with a smile.

"You have Valerie as a teacher too?" Ava asked.

"Yes, I've had her for about two years now," Kris said.

"Cool, can you help me with the test? I really hate bookwork?" Ava said with an innocent grin.

"I can be your tutor, sure, but normally we aren't in the same class. My lessons are from noon to six, and yours are in the evening." Kris said, sitting on a large carpet next to the hearth.

"Is she like that often?" Ava asked.

"No, only when she's been out on some classified mission. And those are only about one every month." Kris said.

"Are you helping them find their books or chatting?" A small wrinkled man asked, walking up to them.

"I'm chatting," Kris said with a grin.

"Well, you need to show them how to find their books." The old man said.

"Will do," Kris said, looking at Kal and Ava. "Open your mind, and follow the singing. It will lead you to the spell book that is right for you."

Kal and Ava sat cross-legged on the carpet and opened their minds. Kal opened her eyes with a slight gasp. She immediately stood up and wandered through the shelves. The voice grew steadily and louder until she finally stood before a midnight-blue, leather-bound book with silver trim. She reached out a hesitant finger and stroked the spine before pulling it out. The weight of it felt... right.

She walked to the front desk and laid the book on the counter in the presence of the old librarian.

"So that's the book, eh?" He asked, looking at the cover before looking at her with a smile. "So, it is true... you're the chosen one."

He wrote her name down on the front of the book and handed it back to her. "Take care of her... She's a good book."

Ava came up behind Kal with her book, a green leather cover embroidered with gold. She placed it on the desk, and the older man began to take care of her.

The door opened and closed, and a tall thin man walked in. The man had a thin face lined with long brown hair. He looked around, and his bright blue eyes landed on Kal, holding her book close to her chest.

"There you are," the man said, his voice light. "I've been looking all over for you." The man walked toward her, but Kris and the old man stepped in front of Kal protectively.

"What do you think you're doing?" the man asked, a smile on his thin red lips.

"You have no right to be here, Tarhunna," the old man said, looking up at the man.

"On the contrary old man, I have every right to be here. I have a student to teach."

"Only Master Sallisfer and Master Valerie are allowed to teach her," Kris said.

"Now, now, boy, weren't you just teaching her?"

"No, I wasn't. Kal had already been taught how to open her mind."

"Ah, such young drama," the man said, swiping his hand, which sent Kris flying in the air, and he landed hard on the old stone floor.

Ava shrieked and ran towards him, but the man smiled, and the ground fell under her feet.

"Help me," Kal whimpered. Turning into a wolf.

"Yes, my student, I will help you," the man said, walking up to her.

Kal growled, and the man rolled his eyes.

"TARHUNNA DEON! We are so going to KILL YOU!" Shouted a joined voice.

Sallisfer and Valerie stood side by side, staring at the man, eye to eye.

"I have only come to claim what is mine by right," the man said calmly.

"YOURS!!!!! Yours by RIGHT!!!! We won the war fair and square!" The joined voices shouted.

"I am so lost right now," Kal said. "I have no freaken clue what's going on."

Valerie and Sallisfer turned and looked at her. "We'll tell you later, we swear," they said before looking back at Tarhunna. Kal watched as a war was fought in the once-quiet solitude of the library.

"It's going to take forever to get this place cleaned up," the old man sighed, shaking his head.

Valerie and Sallisfer banged Tarhunna into one shelf, then another. Then they somehow were the ones getting beaten.

Kal couldn't believe what she saw. Valerie and Sallisfer moved and fought as one and even breathed as one. Irritation flowed over her, but then, just as quickly as the battle began, it ended.

"Be gone," they said, and, in a flash, Tarhunna was no more than a playing card.

"Interesting," Kal said, tilting her head. They looked at her, grinning, then walked to where Kris lay motionless.

"Heal that of a brave soul," the voices said with a hand on Kris and a hand on Ava. At once, Kris moaned and moved and then opened his eyes.

"Master?" he asked.

"It's Okay now, you're safe, we all are," the voices said; then they stepped back, and their glowing eyes were replaced with normal ones.

They held their heads in shaking hands. Then, finally, chairs pulled up, and they sat down with a sigh of relief.

"Remind us next time not to mess around with caffeine. It really throws us off," Valerie said.

"We will," Sallisfer said. Then they looked at each other in surprise.

"We never talked like this before, have we?" Valerie asked.

"Us don't know," Sallisfer said, eyes wide.

"Nice... Really nice how you leave me out of it with the whole 'we' and 'us' thing. I'm gonna go kill something now." Kal growled, turning away.

"We can't help it," Valerie said.

"Us need help," Sallisfer said.

The old man sighed, shaking his head. He snapped his fingers, drawing Kal's attention.

She saw a glowing line between the two of them. The librarian walked to his desk and pulled out a thick green book with tattered binding. "You two haven't merged in a while, eh?" He laughed. "How often have we told you to stay in practice so this kind of stuff won't happen again?" He returned to them and sighed as they looked at him with pleading eyes.

"Ready?" he asked; they nodded, and the old man knocked their heads together just slightly. The line was gone with a yelp from Valerie and a groan from Sallisfer. The man laughed again and gave Kal a wide tooth smile.

"These two are like a machine; you must keep them oiled."

"Can I....hey, I said I," Valerie said, jumping up.

"Kal listens, we have asked to give you clearance, isn't that..." Sallisfer was cut off by a growl, and Kal turned and walked off.

Sallisfer sighed and got up. "Hey, what do I have to lose?" he mumbled to himself. He transformed into an English Mastiff and tackled Kal.

"Hey, look at their first fight!" Valerie said with a grin.

"I need a bag of popcorn. GO KAL! Beat him down!" Valerie shouted, slurping a cola.

Kal twisted as she recovered from Sallisfer's weight, snarling and snapping. Sallisfer leaped back, play-growling. Kal laughed and jumped on him, both falling with a thump. She nipped him and rolled onto her feet, wagging her tail as he got up. She pranced around him, just out of his reach, and then ran off, teasing him into chasing her. Again, she laughed and turned sharply into the maze of shelves, Sallisfer on her heels. She jumped forward, twisting to face Sallisfer in the process. He bowled into her with a grunt, and both rolled. Kal leaped to her paws and sat on him, pinning him to the ground.

He shifted back into his human form, glaring at her half-heartedly. "You're kind of stopping my ability to breathe." He muttered, and Kal got off him long enough to change positions. She now lay on his stomach, watching him with a wolf's equivalent to a grin.

"How's that?" She asked, laying her head on her paws.

"Not much better." He replied in a strangled voice.

She sighed but stood up. Sallisfer immediately restarted the play-fight, hugging Kal around the throat and pulling her toward the floor. Kal grinned and lifted her head as much as she could, dragging him back out of the shelves when he didn't let go.

Valerie got a puzzled look on her face. "Did I miss something?" She asked, then burst out laughing. Kal smirked and sidestepped, laying down on top of Sallisfer so that Valerie could only see the top half of his chest and head.

"Am I forgiven?" Sallisfer asked, peering up at Kal with pleading blue eyes. Kal sighed and started to lick his face happily, oblivious to his protests.

"I think I'm gonna be sick," Valerie muttered, looking slightly green. Sallisfer finally fell silent, understanding that Kal would stop when she wanted to and no amount of pushing or wriggling would free him.

"At least cut the pleasure line..." Valerie muttered, feeling Sallisfer's irritation but also his total delight. Her face got a little bit greener.

"Call it payback." Sallisfer retorted.

"Oh, shut up..." Valerie growled, but Sallisfer disappeared under Kal's head, who was nearly bursting with laughter.

Arcy rushed into the library and then paused with a look of bewilderment. She heard a muffled plea for help, and she saw Valerie sitting in a chair eating popcorn and drinking cola, and Kal was in her wolf form, laying on top of... something.

"Could anyone explain what is going on?" She asked.

"Well... the fact of this is... those two need a room." Valerie pointed at Kal, who raised her head to allow Sallisfer to breathe.

"Can you just get off of me, please?" He asked.

"No," Kal replied, earning a groan from Valerie.

"Is this a bad time? Cause I can come back!" Arcy said hurriedly.

"What is it?" Valerie asked, trying to ignore Kal licking Sallisfer's face again as she stood, taking the parchment from Arcy. The headmaster was not seen by anyone but the Hands; however, he sent messages to the front desk whenever he needed their presence.

"The headmaster wishes to see you two. But if it's a bad time, I can tell him," Arcy said.

Valerie groaned. "Again...We were just there this afternoon. And Sally has been resting... I mean, we just woke..." she rolled her eyes. "Well, fully anyway," she complained.

Arcy nodded to the scroll in her hand and said, "That's what the message said. You know I wouldn't have come if it didn't."

"Fine. Kal, I'll bring him back soon. Can you please get off him for at least an hour?"

"So, is all forgiven?" Sallisfer asked again.

"Yes." Kal smiled as she shifted back into her normal self. Sallisfer beamed and pulled her into a hug.

"This…" she moved her arm around in a wild gesture of the whole room, which was silent with many more eyes than Kal had originally thought staring at them. "I'll see if I can get you two a room when I return!" Valerie said as she shook her head, looking at them pathetically.

Kal blushed, and Sallisfer smiled at her, his blue eyes beamed with an overly warm feeling that showered Kal with confidence.

"Mmmm, Na, we can just use my room," Sallisfer said with a grin, kissing Kal on both cheeks.

"That's fine with me. "Valerie sighed as she grabbed Sallisfer's arm. "I just need him for a little while to see what the 'headmaster' wants," Valerie said, rolling her eyes.

"Come on, let's go."

Kal sighed, reluctant to look away from those eyes, but she let go slowly and felt Sallisfer release her just as slowly. Then as soon as their bodies were no longer touching, Sallisfer disappeared in a flash of light that still left Kal a little dazed.

CHAPTER 11

Clearance

Valerie and Sallisfer walked down a long narrow hallway. The stone walls were lit by burning torches. The was no echo as their booted footsteps were cushioned by a thick carpet. They walked side by side, neither talking, yet completely in step with one another as they faced two tall doublewide doors.

They did not break their stride as they approached the doors. Neither of them reached for a handle to open the blocked view of the room behind it. However, the doors opened upon their command or from the one within who knew of their presence.

"Ah, there you are," The headmaster said, looking up from his writing. "I was beginning to wonder what you two were up to."

"Sorry, Sir. We came as fast as we could," they said, with their eyes lit.

"I heard about the commotion in the library." The Headmaster eyed them, "All okay?"

Valerie smiled and placed the playing card on his desk. "Ah…" the headmaster sighed, taking the card and licking his lips as he looked it over. "There's going to be quite a few people unhappy with this?"

"Would you rather we kill him, Sir?" Valerie asked, her voice dark, and her smile had turned wicked.

"No, no…" the headmaster sighed, placing the card face down and shaking his head.

"He will get his trial."

Valerie rolled her eyes as Sallisfer placed a hand on hers. The scowl diminished from her lips, and her eyes lost some of the darkness hidden within from a few moments before.

"I have what you requested," the headmaster said with a smile returning to his face as he rolled up the parchment he had been writing on when they entered. "A bit of an unorthodox method, but I understand the reasoning. If only she had been brought up in our realm." The headmaster sighed as he sealed the scroll and handed it to them.

Sallisfer took it, and Valerie bowed. "Thank you, Sir. Anything we need to do to make it up to you?" They asked in one voice.

The headmaster smiled at them. "I see getting Tarhunna has made you two start working together again. I thought you two had forgotten how to be civil to one another."

Valerie and Sallisfer glanced at each other, "Is there anything else, Sir?" They asked.

"No, all I ask is your service, and that's all I need." The headmaster smiled. "Go make a fabulous Hand out of Kalea."

"Thank you, Sir. We will do our best." They turned as one heading toward the door.

"One more thing, you two." The headmaster said, making them turn to face him once again. "I want to see more of this…no more I and Me, only us. You two are a team."

"Yes, Sir." They spoke in unison.

"You are dismissed," he said with a nod, and they exited the room.

They walked the hall to a set of stairs and stopped. A feeling of understanding fell between them as they looked at each other. The strength of their magic tapered off. They consciously uncharged their magic to give it a rest. Valerie looked over at Sallisfer, and he felt her clasped hand trembling within his.

"I never want to repeat those words again," Valerie said, holding her head with her other hand as they descended the stairs.

"If...you and I... can avoid it, I agree," Sallisfer said. He touched her head with his, and she felt the pain leave. She smiled at him gratefully.

"He is right...." Sallisfer sighed as they started to walk again. "That we are out of practice."

"How else are we to create some barrier between us?" Valerie sighed. "I mean, a wall is a wall and merging." She looked at him; her green eyes shined with tears. Sallisfer stopped and pulled her into a hug, and kissed the top of her head.

"We will figure it out," he sighed. "We have to."

They stood there for a moment or two, then, with a single sigh, as they took the final steps to the landing. "Let's get this to Kal." Sallisfer held up the scroll.

"This isn't going to be easy." Valerie mused, "I mean do we have to tell her *Everything?*"

"No, it isn't going to be easy... but it needs to happen. After all, Kal is the chosen one." Sallisfer reassured Valerie, making his voice sound stronger than his inner mixed emotions.

"Yes...the chosen one." Valerie sighed as she took Sallisfer's hand and guided him the long way around. Without them quite realizing it, they had stopped talking out loud for fear of someone overhearing. "The next set of Hands must be prepared, and she... well, Kalea is at a disadvantage."

Thinking about the next set of hands after pondering over Kal's disadvantage, ideas came to Valerie and Sallisfer's minds and were mentally discussed.

"They both are, to be honest...Heaven and Doom are supposed to be training together at the same level of magic... She is a half-blood. The first Half-blood Hand.... how is this going to work?" Sallisfer asked, his mind racing -only to be calmed by the memory of those wild blue eyes that took his breath away.

Valerie rolled her eyes and laughed, slightly amused. "What will we tell her..." she asked, getting his mind back on track.

Sallisfer sighed as he responded, "Everything, I guess...we owe her that." And he shrugged as if to say it was the only way.

Valerie thought about everything and became overwhelmed with a feeling of fear.

"Do we have to tell her everything?" Valerie asked in a squeaky voice of fear.

Sallisfer stopped and looked at Valerie, who had stopped with him right outside the doors to the hall where they could transport. "What parts should I leave out?"

Valerie shrugged, "I don't know…maybe the whole Kris thing?" Sallisfer nodded with recognition in his eyes.

"How are we going to tell her about Kris…" he asked slowly.

A calmness fell over Valerie suddenly, and her eyes took on a misty look.

"He will tell her. Since we have been working out a proper way to tell Kalea, I will slowly arrange it so she can adapt to him and he to her."

Sallisfer watched her eyes clear with her idea, but he had to voice a thought she needed to consider. "Valerie, he has flashbacks."

"I know." Valerie sighed and looked at Sallisfer. He saw a mixture of pain and regret in her eyes and felt it as she spoke, "You know they are meant to be right?"

A coolness washed over Sallisfer as the implications became more apparent. His composure was followed by a rage of jealousy as he thought of those wild blue eyes. His inner thoughts hardened, and his fists clenched. "Over my dead body." The words sliced out of his mouth and mind like a knife.

Valerie winced, "I hope it doesn't come to that." She pushed open the doors, stepping out together, and they transported themselves back to the library.

Just then, Kal saw them and walked up to Sallisfer, she wrapped her arms around him, and he sighed. "I am going to be truly sick," Valerie said, walking off.

"You have to start!" Valerie called to them as she walked into the library to help with the cleanup and left Sallisfer to stare after her.

"Start what?" Kal asked, releasing him.

"We got the contract for you to have clearance," Sallisfer said, showing her the scroll.

"Cool," Kal said, hugging him again.

"Not so much. People are beginning to stare," Sallisfer said, and while holding onto her, he transported them to his room.

Kal looked around; it felt like she had been there before, but she couldn't place it. Sallisfer handed her the scroll as he sat in a chair at the roll-top desk.

"Sign, and I can tell you almost everything," he said, pointing to the line at the end of the very long scroll and pulling up a second chair.

Kal picked up the pen on his desk, and without reading, she signed the contract. Sallisfer looked at her name and then laid it aside.

"Where do I need to start?" he asked.

Kal shrugged, "Why not start at the beginning," she said.

"Beginning? Um...beginning...ah..." Sallisfer thought for a while. Kal watched him as he shifted uncomfortably in his chair.

"I came into my power early. Not as early as Valerie, who was born with power, but by two years old, I could wield magic."

Sallisfer sighed and licked his lips. "I started school here at the same time I started regular school at five."

He laughed. "That is when I first met Valerie. She was four years old and arguing with her father in the hall when I arrived with my parents at the choosing."

"Did you know you two would be destined to work together?" Kal asked, eyeing him Sallisfer shook his head.

"Yes and No. My parents had been preparing me for months before I met my Master that I could be teamed up with someone."

"Could be?" Kal asked.

Sallisfer swallowed. "Well, it was just a hunch that I would be Heaven...." He cleared his throat. "Anyway, the old Hands died a few months after the choosing, and Valerie and I were named."

"Named?" Kal asked, confused.

"Ya...I am the Hand of Heaven, and Valerie is the Hand of Doom." Sallisfer said, "That is who and what we are."

"What are hands?" Kal asked.

"The Hands of Doom and Heaven," Sallisfer sighed and scrunched his face in thought. "Um… The Hands are host to an external spirit…." Sallisfer licked his lips again. He could tell Kal was lost, but he continued trying to explain.

"They are the Hands, balancing equality between light and dark powers, heaven, and hell. The Hands are controlled by the headmaster, who owns and commands them. He wields us as if we are attached to his wrist. We can be weapons or peacekeepers." Sallisfer explained.

Kal nodded, although she didn't quite understand it.

"We are scales of good and evil in the world," Sallisfer said slowly.

"So, when did you two become more than friends?" Kal asked.

"Well…ah…ah…" feeling the weight of her question and trying to avoid telling too much. Sallisfer opened a drawer in his desk and pulled out a small book, flipping through the pages to distract himself and align his thoughts to continue.

"I would have to say the day we first combined our strengths and mind…." he trailed off, lost in thought.

Kal waited patiently, wanting to hear more.

"See, the Hands are normally grown up before they are named." Sallisfer explained, "Val and I are the youngest ever named…we did not get much of a childhood."

Feeling uncomfortable about what he was about to say and the implications of what she would have to embrace or could embrace, Sallisfer looked away from Kal and stared at the wall. His eyes took on a distant look that was disturbing, considering his inner struggle.

"Hands normally get married, have kids, and die. So, heaven is naturally attracted to Doom; we are one of the same but in two bodies. Powers of equality are too powerful and unpredictable to be placed into one being."

"What happened then? Why are you not attracted to Val, and she to you?" Kal asked, trying to soak it all in.

"I got in trouble, and she went on a mission alone and got captured, and I couldn't save her. Valerie was heartbroken and beaten; she nearly died.

Sallisfer shuddered a little as he looked at Kal, and his eyes took on a reminiscing look as his mind replayed the past event.

His voice just barely over a whisper, he continued talking, "I almost died too. But for Val, Holjus saved her. I never had a chance. But who cares? She's happy now. I am, too, for that matter. But for a long while, I wasn't. Then I met you, a half-blood, you changed me, and I am internally grateful."

"How would you die?" Kal found herself asking, although she feared the answer.

Sallisfer looked at her pain with his crystal blue eyes. He swallowed and took a breath.

"As a hand, you give up everything you once had, family, friends, and individuality. You become one person, one thought, one body, and worst off, one soul."

Kal felt herself shudder from a sudden chill as the heavy burden he and Valerie shared was revealed. *How could they be just friends if they shared all of that?* She thought as she looked into Sallisfer's eyes. Kalea saw her reflection in them and her own sadness. And as she looked deep into Sallisfer's eyes, she saw Valerie's fiery green eyes looking back at her. Kal swallowed hard as she saw the begging look in them to understand, and Kal realized that Valerie made Sallisfer who he was. They were always in the back of each other's minds. Kal closed her eyes momentarily and looked back into those eyes only to see that Valerie was gone. It was just she and Sallisfer again.

Kal tipped her head back to think through her next question, which unnerved her in ways she did not like. She had to make her thoughts known Sallisfer watched her knowing it was a thought he would not want to address, but it was inevitable with all that he had just disclosed.

"So, you and Valerie are just really good friends, who just happen to share feelings and thoughts, and you leave me out of it?"

Sallisfer shook his head quickly and then nodded slowly, "Not anymore. She's working for a way to break the bond. Her ability to have kept Holjus hidden from me for so long is proof of that, but so far, she can't find anything permanent." Kal nodded but still had to ask the difficult question.

"So, you still love her, and she…she loves you?"

"No, all her love dried up when I let her go on that mission alone. Perhaps our shared love was never meant to be. It is my turn to be happy. You make me happy, Kal."

Kal could see the green had vanished from his blue eyes, "Can you promise me you will love me and allow no dissipation?" Kal asked quietly, hoping for the best, considering how she felt for him and his unavoidable connection with Valerie.

"I can guarantee I won't let anything harm you, including myself. I didn't mean for you to ever think that I would take your heart just because I wanted to hurt it. I love you, Kal, and I hope to show you that one day." He grabbed her and held her close to him.

Kal swallowed the invisible lump in her throat that she didn't know existed and felt a little lighter in mind and body with his confession. She wanted to relish in the ambiance of his thoughts, but she had another issue to deal with.

"So, tell me about the headmaster."

Sallisfer laughed and was happy to have the most challenging part of his explanation complete. Then, thinking about her question, he was pleased to move on to a discussion that did not involve his inner struggle.

"He is the most powerful Earth Child of them all. He is immortal and has ruled the Earth's Children for thousands of years. He has been waiting for a child to be born with the same power or more to become the next headmaster, so he can retire. Normally Headmasters are replaced every two hundred years or so, but the last powerful child that could replace him was murdered in the last human/earth war. So, he has had to wait."

"So, does everyone have different power levels?"

"Yes, they range from the weak, like witches and wizards, the moderate, like the warlocks and enchantress, to high sorcerer and sorceress. Everyone who enters the school is taught by a master around their own ranking."

"So, what am I? Will a sorcerer train me?"

Sallisfer's laugh was low and sexy, and he held her closer to him, "You rank an enchantress, but when your power blooms at your sweet 16. He nibbled her ear, "You will be a sorceress, my love."

Kal allowed him to kiss her neck as she began to purr, "What other things can I shift into?"

"I don't know yet; you will have to build your totem pole and your own portfolio."

"How do I do that?"

"In time, I will teach you. It will not be long."

"How often do you go out for the headmaster?"

"More often than I would like. Last night was a recon mission gone wrong."

"Did you really take on a whole army?"

"Na, it was more like fifty to eighty… maybe. Of course, they were guards, and we did get a lot done despite the little nick in the plan."

"Why are you a nerd at school?"

"Because I got called out in elementary school and exposed my power. As a nerd, you are regularly ignored and expected to be a smart ass."

Kal laughed and kissed Sallisfer's cheek, "I just cannot be seen with someone so poorly dressed. It will blow all that I have worked for at this school."

Sallisfer laughed and hugged Kal tightly, and kissed her lips with a smile. Kal kissed him back and then started a peck war.

Just then, a light knock sounded on the door. Sallisfer sighed and slipped out from under Kal, and opened the door. There stood Dona, "You have a meeting in 10 minutes with the infantry." She said, wiggling uncomfortably.

"I forgot all about it, thank you." He closed the door and turned to Kal, "I have to go to this meeting, as Valerie is in the cavalry. I am in the infantry. Once we have addressed your fighting stances, we will see your placement in the military. I will be back in two hours. Come back then. Dona will be waiting to take you to your room so you can see where you will be staying on the days you need a place of your own." Sallisfer mentioned.

"I have my own room."

"Yes. Every student has their own room." Sallisfer laughed.

"Remember what Val said" Kal nodded and flushed. "Valerie had one at birth because of power surges…." He shivered a little, thinking back.

"Anyhow, you can make it your own; there should be a crew to bring in whatever furniture you want." He kissed her and made his exit with a final thought.

"See you in two hours." And he was gone.

Dona was waiting at the end of the hall. Kal admired the perfect posture of the Hands secretary. Her dark hair with dark blue highlights was pulled into a tight bun on the top of her head, highlighting her thin face. As Kal walked up, she felt the judgmental look from those dark gray eyes. Kal shoved her fears aside and tried to walk as confidently as possible. The look of distaste deepened on the woman's face as she looked Kal over her long red fingernails tapping impatiently on a checkered dress. She was much older than Kal though her age only showed under her gray eyes. Dona was only a tad taller than Kal and wore a pinched expression. "This way," she said, leading Kal to a set of stairs. "Your class is on the fourth level."

Kal watched as Dona glided up the stairs while Kal had to climb the old fashion way. Two sets of stairs later, they were looking at a white door with the gold number 415 burned magically in place. The adjacent rooms were already decorated with names on the doors. But as promised, a crew appeared and bowed when Kalea entered the empty room.

"How can we be of service, Madam?" They said, showing Kal a thick book of furniture and décor.

"So, I can point to any of these things and say I want, and I get it?" Kal was skeptical.

"Yes?" one of the crew members said, smiling.

"For how much?" Kal was staring at the thick book now.

"There is no charge Madam." The crew member assured her.

"Cool." Kal looked through the book and pointed out a king-size four-poster bed, and it appeared. The crew moved it into the spot she wanted. Next, Kal saw a matching dresser set and wardrobe that she chose, and they appeared. After choosing something, she noted that the spot went white in the book. Also, the white spots disappeared after closing the book and opening it again, and the book rearranged itself. She wondered what she had missed by not being the first in line.

Kal got her room set up, and the crew left with a poof. Kal sat on her bed and looked around, satisfied that the room was a reflection statement. "This is the room of Kalea Breese. It just hummed with her personality." Kal walked to the wardrobe and opened the door to see what was inside. Kal screamed and jumped back as a rubber spider the size of a bulldog fell out with a note.

She picked up the note,

Kal, I left you a welcome home gift.

Hope you like it.

Valerie

Kal looked at the spider, "Some welcome home gift." She said, picking up the spider, which turned into a wrapped box with glittery blue spiders. Kal carefully unwrapped the box to reveal some outfits and dresses. There was another note,

The outfits are for you to wear to work out on the field. All first-timers wear white. As you advance, the colors will change depending on you and your needs. You will find 4 white halter tops and light, heavy-duty jeans. Inside the wardrobe are varieties of boots and dress shoes. The dresses are for formal things, dances, promotions, and such. You can also bring clothes from home. Mom can also take you shopping for Academy clothes. Hope you enjoy it.

Love, your best friend,

Valerie

Kal looked at the clothes and smiled as she hung them in the ward-robe and looked at the shoes. She explored the rest of the furniture and then returned to the dresses. She touched the silky fabric and smiled. Why not try them on to see if they fit? In the process, Kal looked at herself in the full gold-etched mirror and smiled.

CHAPTER 12

News from the Enemy Line

Valerie was in the shower at home, trying to block out Sallisfer and his emotions. But unfortunately, she wasn't succeeding as they were too strong.

"Hey," said a voice, and she looked out of the curtain and saw Holjus looking her dead in the face.

Valerie looked around him. "What are you doing here? How long have you been there? How did you get in here?" She asked in a shocked voice.

Holjus smiling ear to ear over the situation, started answering her questions as she looked at him incredulously. "I'm here to give you some information. I've been here long enough and got here by transporting invisibly." Holjus grinned.

Valerie stared at him for a moment, her jaw slightly slacking. "How did you know that the bathroom was the weak point and that I would be in here?" she finally hissed.

Holjus shrugged, paused for a breath, then looked at her curiously. Why is your bathroom the weakest point?" He asked. Valerie looked at him crazily.

Holjus continued dismissing her look. "Your house is well protected, I must admit. I first tried to teleport into your bedroom the shield was too strong. Several times, I tried to get your attention outside the house, but you were not in your room. So, when I reached the roof, it was this spot, and this spot only. I could not move from it, as it was the closest, I could get to your room and the only part of the house with the weakest protection," he sheepishly stated as he looked at her again with focused attention. "So, I transported in, then I saw your clothes..." He nodded to the hanger where she had laid out her night clothes, "And fortunately, I knew you had to be the one in the shower." He smiled at her, and she relaxed her eyes.

"So, what sort of information?" Valerie asked, closing the curtain and continuing to bathe.

"Kal is in grave danger. The demons are after her for revenge, and they want to stop her from wiping them out." Holjus said. Valerie poked her head out again.

"They know she's the chosen one?" she asked, shocked.

"Yes, they know," Holjus said.

"This is going to be more complicated than I thought." Valerie mused.

"I have to lead the revolt, I don't want to, but being one of the eldest and experienced, I have to do it," Holjus said.

"I know." Valerie's voice was just above a whisper as she thought about what Holjus had said.

"What am I to do? This is all so complicated." Holjus rubbed the arch of his nose. With his eyes closed, he could make out the sweet smells from the shower, and his mind wandered for a moment. Then, as the silence lingered, he crept closer to the tub. Just as his hand was about to reach out, Valerie's voice came from within, making Holjus step back in alarm.

"I don't know; I don't know...." Valerie thought hard as she rinsed and then turned off the shower. "I just need to think."

Using a tad of magic, she pulled her towel around her and drew the curtain aside. Then, coming face to face with Holjus, they stared at each other briefly, not blinking and eyes wide. Finally, Holjus gave a slight cough and stepped back, allowing Valerie to step out of the shower.

"What do I do?" Holjus asked again, his red eyes not leaving Valerie's green ones.

"You can start by turning to face the wall," Valerie said. Holjus sighed but obeyed.

Valerie dried herself quickly and got dressed. As she was putting on her shirt, an idea hit her.

"I think you should lead the revolt," she said.

"What?" Holjus sputtered as he spun around in shock, and Valerie covered herself.

"Sorry," he said as she glared at him; he turned around again.

"Men always need to look," Valerie muttered to herself, putting her shirt on to cover herself. "You can look now," she said, drying her hair with her towel.

"So why should I lead the revolt?" he asked as he slowly turned, facing her.

"Because you know you won't win, and Sallisfer and I can feel that, so we can spare your life, but barely," Valerie said, brushing her hair out to help it dry faster.

"So, what are you going to do?" Holjus asked.

"I'll prepare; we have many students ready to move up to master and begin teaching and scouting," Valerie said, smiling at Holjus. "Everything is going to be fine. I know it will be," she said, walking up to him and kissing him.

Valerie transported them from the bathroom to a small cabin. "Where are we?" Holjus asked, looking around the tiny one-room cabin with a small desk, a chair, a small bookshelf overloaded with books, and a ladder to a loft.

"This is my aunt's old cabin that she kept for writing. She hasn't been to Georgia since I can remember. She and Mom had a falling out after my grandfather died." Valerie sat at the desk and unrolled some parchment, "Mom thinks it is still abandoned, but I fixed it up as much as I could to use as my headquarters."

"Where is it?" Holjus asked in aww as Valerie folded open a map and turned on a battery-powered lamp.

"I can't tell you that, Love," Valerie said, her smile fading, and a dangerous look took root in her eyes. "You are still a part of the enemy."

Holjus nodded reluctantly. "I understand."

Valerie took his hand, and Holjus felt himself relax. He looked at the map of the magical kingdom they both inhabited. "The assault will start with the smaller kingdoms, the out-laying lands. These are distractions to pull your troops away from the main castle. Then, I will lead the largest assault starting at the South Wet Lands, working up to the castle."

Valerie wrote on the map with a bright red marker. Holjus could pick out a few symbols that his people had been able to crack, but most were a mystery, and the randomness of the placements baffled him.

"I estimate this attack to take place in three fortnights," Valerie said, bringing out a roller, measuring the distances, and marking a note on the side of the map. "The first two could be a diversion depending on how fast your brother can find the men."

Valerie looked up at Holjus then with concern, "I feel like they haven't told you everything…. Do you think they suspect?"

"What do you mean?" Holjus asked in fear, raising the hair on the back of his neck, and he thought she might be right.

"We must be careful. Our steps must be surprising and as if luck was on our side that we were in the right place at the right time. After you return from hunting, I want you to report to your brother that Kal is weak, and if not killed soon, she will get stronger every day. Place someone to watch her movements and to plan the time."

"You think they are planning to kidnap her?"

"No, but it would save lots of blood if they do…."

"You are willing to sacrifice Kal?"

"To save lives, yes…. War is the last option. Besides, I will be able to save her each time…."

Holjus nodded, feeling a little weak in the knees. He placed his hand on the back of the chair to stabilize himself, "Are you okay?" Valerie asked, turning to look up at him a little better. Holjus knew she saw right through him as she reached up and touched his face.

"When was the last time you fed?" she asked. "Your strength is fading."

Holjus looked away from her, "I haven't hunted since we…since I started…." Valerie held her wrist up to his lips, and he could smell the sweet blood that ran through her; it made him shake his head as he walked to the door.

"You must eat, everyone will know something is wrong if you start falling out, yet you go on hunting trips. You only hunt once every full moon but at your state… you are going to need more than what the full moon revives. Take my essence to get you on your feet again. The extra power in your system is going to sap more strength than you are used to. Maybe having some essence of me rather than just the power will level you out." Holjus looked at Valerie; she was on her feet now, and he could tell there would be no getting out of there without doing what she requested, and he thought it wouldn't hurt to try.

"I don't want to hurt you. What if I can't stop?" The line was as lame as it had sounded in his head, and he blushed.

Valerie laughed, "I doubt you could kill me… besides I have lives left."

"What about Sallisfer?" He countered.

"Sal will understand. I guess you would get some essence of him in my blood as well… that could be interesting." There was a spark in her eyes, and Holjus could smell the sweetness as she walked closer to him.

Holjus shook his head, "Earth Children's blood is a delicacy. We only drink it on special occasions. There are bottles of it with dust on it…yet if we can get fresh…."

Valerie smiled, "So you need today to be a special occasion?"

"Yes." Holjus lied, "Just take me to the woods. I will find something if it is your wish."

"I do not think you can find something. You are fading." Holjus looked at himself and saw she was right. He looked startled as he translucently shimmered. His legs began to buckle, but this time, there was nothing to grab hold of, and he fell. Valerie caught him with unmentionable strength that he could only fantasize about where it came from. She placed her wrist to his lips again, "Just a sip will not hurt you." Holjus gave in to his instincts despite his rational brain sending alarm bells. He bit into her wrist with his sharp fangs and sucked up the sweet, warm liquid that flowed. Then the wound healed, frustrated Holjus tried to bite again, but the wrist was gone. Power flooded his veins. It burned him on the inside- lights flashed before his eyes, and his blood roared in his ears. He felt his mouth open to scream but heard no other sound. Then a pleasant sensation folded over him as cool liquid drops touched his lips. He blinked and saw he was feeding on a young Piasa. The full moon was high in the sky, sending cool light over him and his prey.

He sat up feeling gorged for the first time in months; this would hold him over till the next full moon, perhaps more. How lucky he was to find something so rare to sustain him. The demon flexed his wings, feeling more potent than ever. His ram-like horns gleamed in the moonlight, a stark contrast to his long dark hair. Holjus stood, realizing that his shirt and pants were in tatters. Burn marks and blood stained the ruined white shirt and could be seen on his dark pants. He realized with a start that it must have been quite a fight with the Piasa but had no memory of it. He stood stark still, then turned around faster than the eye could blink, hands lit with fire ready to fight when the most beautiful creature his red eyes had ever seen walked out of the shadows. When he tossed his fire at it, the fire simply bounced off.

"Relax, Holjus, it is me." The creature said; her voice was smooth and laden with power. Holjus felt his arms and body relax; despite himself, the darkness faded as the creature stepped fully into the moonlight. Her clothes were tattered and burned like his, and she had small horns protruding from her dark hair. But, in contrast to his, Valerie's horns were red like the blood dried on his chin from his meal. Her eyes were forest green, and her bare feet made no sound as she walked to him.

"How are you feeling?" She asked, her eyes watching him with concern. Her movements were cautioned as if she expected him to lash out at any moment and attack her again.

"I am fine," he said, at last, flexing his large leathered wings, eyeing her with suspicion. Then she flung her arms around him and kissed him. Everything flooded back to him, the cabin, the blood, her blood on his lips, the burn of its power. Love poured over him and through him. He kissed her back, wrapped his arms tight around her, and held her close to him. "Thank you," he whispered when they parted.

"For what?" Valerie breathed, looking up at him.

"For loving me."

She smiled at him and then rested her head on his shoulder, and he held her closer. They stood in silence for a while then he felt her stiffen, "What is wrong?"

"I must go." Valerie mouthed, looking at him with pain and fear in her eyes.

"I will go with you."

"You can't. You must return and set our plan in motion." Valerie slipped from his arms, "I love you," and she was gone.

Holjus stood there for a moment, rolled his neck, jumped into the sky with a frustrated cry, and let the darkness take him home.

When he arrived at the fortress, he was greeted by his older brother's wife, Lamya; she stood dark and stern, the full image of what the queen of demons should look like. Her short curved white horns sticking out of her auburn hair, her thin pointed wings were held ready for takeoff relaxed when he landed on the draw bridge.

"Brother." She declared with venom in her voice; Lamya had never been a fan of keeping him alive. After Holjus's mother had passed away at his birth, it had become imperative that there be an heir to the throne. But unfortunately, Lamya had yet to give Holjus's brother King Krishna a child making Holjus a threat to her.

Holjus was the third and youngest son of the late king and queen. His older brothers Krishna and Alter were twins. When the late king, Holjus's father, Lord Fausus, had passed away before Holjus was born, the twins fought for succession.

Alter had fled with his followers in disgrace. Holjus had never seen him in person, and as much as Krishna hated him, he wasn't going to allow his youngest brother to fall into his twin's hands and become an ally.

"Lamya, my lady, how are you?" Holjus replied with a small mocking bow.

"I was going to ask you the same thing; you look like you were in a fight. Did you tease a hound again?"

Holjus smiled, "I didn't have you drop me into the pit. So, no, I found a Piasa."

Lamya's eyes widened, and it took her a moment to conceal her fear, "A Piasa," she uttered. "You lie! One hasn't been spotted in these parts for hundreds of years."

"Believe what you will. But I see you have no guards with you tonight. So, you overestimated your safety on this full moon hunting spree."

Lamya looked around with unease, "Be careful, sister," Holjus spat his last word at her, "You never know what might be waiting for you to end your reign of darkness."

Lamya stepped back uncertainly, "You wouldn't."

Holjus just smiled and walked through the open doors. He went to his room, showered, dressed, and headed to see his brother. The plan was going to be placed in motion; only time would tell if it would work.

CHAPTER 13

Moving Too Fast

Kal strolled down the steps from her room slowly. It was just five minutes after the two-hour window Sallisfer had given her earlier that evening. She had tried on every dress in her new wardrobe, and as the silky fabric brushed against her bare ankles, she now doubted her decision. The sun had set, and she had heard lots of commotion in the halls, but now the academy's halls were empty save for her. Her eyes belied her calm face. Fear and unease flashed in her eyes as she turned in the direction of room 219. She closed her eyes and breathed, stuffing her fear into some far-off closet in her mind.

First, she purposely passed his door. Then walked back, and with one last calming breath, she knocked on the door and shivered. The fear returned as his vocalized welcome drifted through the door, but she forced her hand to the knob hesitantly and stepped into Sallisfer's vision.

His eyes widened as they took in the midnight blue, backless halter dress. "Am I supposed to be taking a hint?"

She grinned, went over, plopped down on Sallisfer's lap, and promptly leaned on his shoulder, forcing his response. He rolled his eyes, forcing himself to relax as her thick scent of evergreens and clove both enlightened him and appalled him. He smiled, thinking how lucky he was to finally have her in his lap as he complied with her wishes.

"You aren't demanding, are you?" He asked but only got a prolonged purr as a reply. Finally, he laughed and pulled Kal closer, kissing her neck. After the long run of anger, he was glad to comply.

She buried her head in the crook of his neck, muttering against his skin. He swallowed hard and glanced into her gray-blue eyes. "What did you say?" he shuddered, trying to calm his beating heart.

Kal smiled, feeling his heartbeat. "I'm sorry for being angry at you for so long," she answered. She went to lay her face back down, but Sallisfer's hand turned her face around toward him. She met his eyes and held them, spellbound. The next thing she knew, Sallisfer was kissing her. After a second of recovering, she pushed him back, pressing him hard against the chair.

His confused eyes met blindingly blue ones ringed with gold. Feral admiration flickered in Kal's eyes as she ran a finger down his neck.

Her eyes closed as she leaned close to him, kissing the wild pulse on his neck. The next sensation was pain. Kal's teeth slid through his skin, missing the artery but drawing blood. He felt her stiffen, and then her body flew off him.

He watched in stunned silence as Kal brought a finger to her lips and wiped off his blood. She stared at the red liquid in growing horror.

He felt a worm trickle and looked down, surprised at how fast the blood oozed from the wound. Kal saw the blood, and tears leaped into her eyes. She began backing up, shaking her head as she went. She felt a solid coldness on her back that made her jump away from the sensation when she hit the wall. Then, coming to her senses, she turned and ran out the door; disgust and horror trailed.

Valerie ran as fast as she could, her inner feelings building and compounding the amount of panic she felt, cursing the length of time as she ran down the stairs to get to Sallisfer's room. Wondering why she had not just teleported to his room, she stood in front of Kal, blocking her way.

"You almost killed us," she said, a hurt expression in her green eyes and anger in her stance.

"I..." Kal burst out in tears and fell to the floor in hysterics.

Sallisfer walked up, his face drained of all color, and Valerie shook her head at him. Then, she dropped to her knees and took her friend, her sister, in her arms with a calming sigh.

"Shh now," she whispered, rocking her back and forth on the floor.

"Spend all your time...." Valerie sang lightly and powerfully, lacing each word with a spell till Kal was asleep in her arms before transporting her home to the farm. She laid Kal in bed, pulled the cover over her, and then sent some magic to help her sleep better.

With Kal done, Valerie transported back to the academy and found Sallisfer standing where she had left him.

Valerie led him back to his room, sat him down, and sighed. She didn't like what she saw on his shoulder. She pulled his shirt off and looked at it closer. He had healed it, but it still looked nasty, all bumped up and bruised.

Valerie laid her hand on the spot and took a deep hesitant breath. She wasn't very good at healing magic, destroying and hurting things she could do without a problem, but healing did not come easy.

She closed her eyes and pulled on Sallisfer's knowledge. He was one of the best healers for his age and experience and tried to remember everything she was taught. Then, taking another breath to calm herself and to steady her mind, she drew upon all her remaining strength as tonight had been a long night. Valerie opened her eyes and sent sparks out of her fingers, commanding them to clean up the wound. Then, watching the action, she carefully massaged the shoulder to get his skin smooth.

Sallisfer sighed, and she felt the heat of his skin fill her cool hands and smiled a little. Then, gaining her confidence, she kissed his neck where Kal had bitten. Then the turmoil of his mind hit her, and she gasped in pain and surprise. His body was healed as if nothing had ever happened, but his mind was full of pain and confusion. She sighed and ran her hands down his chest, feeling his strong muscles flex and tremble. Valerie braced herself as her mind was refilled with pain and hurt from his overthinking mind.

Valerie remembered a song and started humming, realizing it had been theirs. She continued to hum as she massaged his shoulders, feeling his mind empty of pain and hurt and, most of all, devoid of all thoughts besides the song she was humming and her touch on his now cool skin. With his mind quiet, she slipped more sparks down his back, making him smile.

With that done, she guided him into bed, removing his shoes and pulling the blanket up to his neck. He sighed and rolled to his side. Valerie then cleaned up the mess of blood on the desk, the chair, and the papers he was working on. Valerie used the spoiled shirt to clean up the blood and then wiped everything off with a disinfecting wipe Sallisfer kept in his drawer. She looked over the soiled papers realizing they were plans for the upcoming Valentine's party; she shook her head.

"Really, your theme is Cupid's Kisses?" Valerie laughed, picking up the papers that were spoiled. She pulled out a new paper, again drew upon her remaining magic, made a magic copy of the plans, and tucked the document into a safe place. "I am always stuck with the janitor job," she grumbled, picking up his spoiled shirt and papers and setting it all on fire.

She felt a twinge in her mind from Sallisfer, but she quickly reassured him. "At least it's good for something," she heard him chuckle, and she smiled. She checked to ensure he was comfortable and kissed him lightly on the forehead before leaving his room and locking the door behind her. She walked down the hallway and sighed, leaning on the wall for support. She was so tired.

She had to get home; Kal needed her to be there when she woke up. Valerie knew, unlike Sallisfer, Kal's mind would not put tonight's actions to rest easily. Valerie tried to use her magic, yet she was too exhausted. A noise behind her made her jump, and a soothing hand took hers.

Kris looked back at her, his stunning blue eyes filled with confusion and hurt, "What happened?" he asked, his voice lower than a whisper.

"Relationship problems. Kal hasn't learned to control her animal side yet." Valerie reassured him.

"But that shouldn't have drained your magic.... what happened?" Kris asked, observing her run-down condition, torn clothes, and bloodied hand.

Valerie sighed and closed her eyes. "I will explain later. But, right now, can you help me get home?"

Kris studied her for a moment; his eyes bore into her then he nodded, "I will take you home." He pulled her into his arms just as her legs failed her. He picked her up as a parent holding a child and transported her home.

Mr. Wing met him at the door, "Kristopher," he greeted, opening the door and looking at Valerie, who smiled weakly.

"Hey, Dad." She whispered.

"What have you been up to?" Mr. Wing asked Valerie as he reached to take his daughter from Kris.

"Thank you for taking me home." Valerie yawned.

"Have a good night." Kris whispered, then with a nod, "Mr. Wing."

Mr. Wing nodded back, and Kris left the same way he came and returned to the academy.

"Care to explain yourself?" Mr. Wing asked, but all he received was a shallow sigh from her. He shook his head as he looked down at his sleeping daughter and carried her to her room. He put her into her bed and tucked her in. He looked at Kal, who was rolling and mumbling restlessly in her sleep.

"What happened?' he whispered, and with a sigh and a shake of his head, he went to his bed.

A short time later, Kal started to cry out in her sleep. Valerie got up, walked to her, and calmed her inner turmoil with more magic as she sat in a chair beside the bed.

Kal woke that morning to find Valerie asleep in an armchair beside her bed. The alarm went off, and Valerie groaned, opening her eyes. They were green, and she looked at the alarm clock, which exploded. She smiled at Kal and got up, rubbing her shoulder as she walked to wake Koda.

"Koda, time to get up, school," Valerie said in a growling voice. Kal could tell she hadn't slept well. "I need some coffee. Kal, you want some?" Valerie asked.

Kal looked at her, shocked, as she pulled herself out of bed. "You don't like coffee," Kal said with a confused look.

"I don't care. I need some, like bad, along with a nice cup of chocolate milk," Valerie said, rolling her stiff shoulders up and around.

Valerie walked into the kitchen, and things started happening on their own. The mugs flew off the shelf, and water began to boil as instant coffee spooned itself into the mug. Kal's lunch box filled itself, and Koda's backpack packed what it needed for the day. Valerie was dressed and, with a yawn, reached out and took the floating hot mug, sat down in Mr. Wings' chair, and took a sip.

Kal stared at the floating mug and splashed a bit on herself when she finally took it out of the air, still in her pajamas. "Where is your mom?"

"Mom had to sleep in the barn for foal watch. But don't worry. I also sent a mug down to her." Valerie smiled. "I told Mom I would ensure this morning ran smoothly until she comes up to see us off to school."

Valerie yawned again, closing her eyes and taking a sip of coffee, "I really want to go back to bed. But, Kal, you need to work on your nightmares. You kept me up all night."

Kal looked around, the house was cleaning itself, and she wondered if Ms. Wing would know that Valerie was doing what Ms. Wing called forbidden magic inside. "If you are tired, why all the magic?"

"This magic is relaxing. Hadn't you heard about how cleaning is a way for you to relax?" Valerie smiled, "I am relaxing."

Just then, Koda came out of the bathroom and sat in front of a cup of Orange Juice and hot cakes. "Thanks, sis. I love when you wake me up."

Kal slipped into the bathroom and smiled. She guessed by Koda's reaction that this was a norm. As Kal exited the bathroom, she heard Valerie talking to Koda in a low whisper.

"Can you help me put a hot patch on this stiff shoulder? I have gym class, and it will get on my nerves all day."

Kal's eyes widened when she saw the red wound on Valerie's shoulder as Koda put the patch on. She immediately remembered what had happened last night, and tears began to flow from her eyes.

Kal gasped, and Valerie quickly pulled at her shirt to cover her shoulder and rushed to Kal. "Back off," Kal streaked, remembering what Valerie had said about almost killing them.

"I won't, you are my friend, and I will not have you hurting." She scooped Kal up in a hug despite Kal's protest and held her firm. "Besides, I'm Doom; whatever happens to me won't necessarily affect him," Valerie said with a smile, trying unsuccessfully to cheer Kal up.

Just then, Valerie's watch started to beep, summoning Koda and their backpacks; she half-carried, half dragged Kal to the bus stop. They quietly rode the bus, Kal sitting as far away as possible from Valerie. She kept repeating the same message repeatedly, even when she knew Kal had stopped hearing her.

When they arrived at the school, Kal rushed ahead, and Valerie had to run past Holjus, without a playful glare, in hot pursuit. "Kal," she breathed when she finally caught up, "Chill out. It isn't as if you did kill us… though I am positive, you will be the death of us…."

"Not helping," Kal growled, trying to outwalk Valerie's long legs.

"I am not good at this… I am not the soft, sentimental type… Kal Stop." The word had so much power in it that the world became nearly motionless around them. It was just Kal and Valerie who glowed fiercely with a mysterious darkness that hummed as she walked toward the stoned Kal.

"Look, Kal, what you did was not the best thing you could have done. But dang, Kal, it happened, and the reality is that the action came with minimal consequences. So, I am stiff and sore, and Sallisfer is now confused and a little intimidated. So what? I have buried the hatchet; why can't you?"

"*I almost killed you two!* What else am I capable of that I don't know about yet?"

Valerie smiled, which enraged Kal. She tried to walk off but couldn't make her legs move in the bubble that Valerie had created around them, "You know where I sleep. You are a member of MY family, MY herd. Do you think I would let a danger to my family, my herd, my way of life into it? We share a room! If you and I were to kill each other, do you think we would be having this conversation now?"

Kal shook her head slowly with a "But."

"Oh, I know what you are capable of… it is up to you to decide how and when you will fulfill your capability.

Now you can avoid Sallisfer for as long as possible, but you cannot, and never can, avoid me. It will be a hell of a lot easier to take you as my student than to let you be Sallisfer's. Of course, you will still have to face him at some point in time… but you and I are friends and sisters first." Valerie stuck out her hand, and Kal shook it.

"Okay." Kal said, "But I will avoid him as long as possible."

"Agreed." Valerie shrugged nonchalantly with a smile now on her face.

The air lightened, and the next moment Kal was walking next to her best friend as if nothing had happened. Kris was now flanking her, trying to talk to her, but Kal had stopped listening, and Valerie quietly shook her head at Kris when he tried to tell Kal that it wasn't her fault. Kal walked in front of them just as the bell rang to head to the first block.

"She is having a moment. She will forgive herself. She has too." Valerie said, giving Kris's hand a squeeze. "Let her cool off."

When they saw Sallisfer in the hall, Kal walked in the other direction, avoiding him. Sallisfer sighed, "Let me know if she changes her mind." He said with a smile and a wink at Valerie, who rolled her eyes, but she, too, smiled.

"What was that about?" Kris asked Sallisfer as he watched Valerie rush to class. Sallisfer smiled and shook his head, and walked on. "Dude, I haven't seen you this happy in years. What is going on?" Kris asked.

"Nothing, except Kal tried to kill me, and Valerie put me back together." Sallisfer's grin was so large, and his mood so light that it seemed he walked on air.

"Really, how did she do that?" Kris asked, eyeing him suspiciously.

"Man, you are as nosey as Grandma." Sallisfer laughed, pushing Kris lightly on the shoulder, who groaned.

"If grandma asks me one more time when I am bringing a girl home… I swear she is stuck in the seventies."

Sallisfer laughed. "Have you seen the way she dresses? She is stuck in the 60s when she was a much younger Sorceress." Kris grinned, and they parted ways in the science hall.

Sallisfer walked into AP Anatomy and Physiology with Mr. C, a former Master who retired into the human world and became a teacher. Mr. C smiled at Sallisfer when he walked into the room. "Good morning, Mr. C," Sallisfer said as he took his seat in the middle of the room and got out his things for class.

"Good morning Mr. King." Mr. C turned back to his board and started to write again. Sallisfer was soon joined by the rest of the students. The class was buzzing as they pulled homework out and placed it in the basket. Sallisfer had just sat down again when he suddenly felt Valerie's presence in his mind.

"Sally," she whispered, showing the book she was supposed to have read, "I forgot to read the chapters. What happened in chapters 5-10 in Lord of the Flies?"

Sallisfer laughed and tried to remember when he was forced to read that book, "I think it is where Ralph rallies the boys...." Sallisfer sent her the information and was caught off guard when Mr. C called his name to explain the muscular system. Sallisfer gave the definition out loud and chided Valerie for getting him distracted in Mr. C's class, who could tell by experience when Sallisfer zoned out. She laughed and sent a mental hug.

Sallisfer sent a hug back with a smile, his heart was light, and he had a song in his head that he had almost forgotten. He found himself humming quietly to himself as he labeled the different muscles on the worksheet.

CHAPTER 14

New Friends and Old

Sallisfer walked into his second block class, AP geometry. His beaming smile created more smiles. His good mood spread to everyone who walked by him, a symptom of being the Hand of Heaven. Valerie told Kal that Sallisfer forgave her and that he had healed cleanly and not to worry. It didn't cheer Kal up, but it helped his mood. He was thinking of devious harmless plans as he, the Hand of Heaven, often did to keep his overactive mind amused.

He saw Holjus in his seat and smiled at him. 'I think it is time to get to know my partner's lover,' he thought, quickly forming a note in his mind as he walked by purposefully. As he walked past Holjus's desk, he laid the note on it before sitting at the desk just behind him. He felt Holjus look at him confused as he unfolded and read the note...

Have you ever wondered what the girls do in PE?
They have it 3rd, and I'm going to check it out. want
to come with me?

Holjus looked at Sallisfer in bewilderment but picked up his pen and wrote back, handing it to him. Sallisfer read it.

Ya, I have. I'm with you!

Sallisfer smiled and nodded, handing him the letter.

Cool, meet you after lunch in 200 hall.

Holjus smiled, handing it back.

See you there! Thanks for adding me in!

Sallisfer nodded, and the conversation ended as they concentrated on their studies.

Valerie was still talking to Kal, trying to convince her that last night's accident was just an accident.

"But I could have..." Kal began once again on her argument as they walked into the gym.

"But you didn't," Valerie said, anger replacing her frustration. "I don't want to hear more about it. We are going to enjoy the rest of the day." She squeezed the bridge of her nose, closing her tired eyes. "You need to exercise this stress out. I am glad we are working out; it will help you clear your mind."

"I'll try," Kal said, taking a deep breath.

Valerie felt Sallisfer's guilt and sadness, but she pushed him away. She didn't want to talk to him at that moment. Instead, she wanted to concentrate her efforts on Kal and continue to help her.

"I need a vacation from life," Valerie said, laying out her mat to stretch.

"Why don't we do a girls' day out this weekend?" Kal asked, going through the pre-workout stretch and finding it was doing wonders for her stressed muscles and mind.

"You know, I think you're onto something," Valerie said with a smile. "Boys are great and everything, but sometimes they're annoying."

"Are you thinking of a certain demanding handsome boy?" Kal said with a grin. Valerie blushed as Kal went into a giggling fit.

"Girls!" the teacher said.

"Yes, ma'am," they said, finishing their stretching, then they moved to the parking lot and started laps. Valerie paired up with another girl who ran at the same pace, and Kal with a few others who walked a lap, then jogged one, walked one, and jogged one. Kal had what the teacher called no endurance, and her exercise regime helped build it up without straining anything. Valerie breezed through exercising from the first time she stepped into the gym. To push her, the teacher had her do more crunches, laps, and weights. Kal was slightly jealous as she smiled at Valerie, who breezed by her on her second lap. Valerie made everything look easy, striding along at an easy lope. Valerie was done first and went into the school to get some water and do her cool-down stretches. Kal pushed herself to run the last two laps and joined Valerie, still breathing hard with stitches in her side.

Sallisfer found himself walking down the hallway from the lunch room with Holjus leading the way. No one challenged him as he made his way to the gym, but a teacher or two gave Holjus a look and a question from time to time. As they got closer to the location, Sallisfer shifted into a small squirrel and headed into the gym. He felt rather than saw Holjus slip in behind him, invisible. The girls came in from the half-mile run outside and were preparing to do a miniature obstacle course. Valerie looked relaxed and wasn't winded from her run Sallisfer smiled, knowing she had done a whole mile as she strolled among the less fit who grudgingly started on the next task. Kal was one of those who didn't look pleased with the exercise. The boys followed them slowly into the gym as they talked, unaware of their presence.

"I don't get why I have to exercise," Kal breathed, trying to stretch out the pain in her ribs and calm her gasps and racing heart.

"The stronger you are, the longer you can produce magic. The easier it will be to wield the magic. Many humans who chose a large fitness path have unlocked the magic hidden in their DNA because they are suddenly healthy and strong enough to use it." Valerie smiled, standing up and doing her final stretch. They walked over to the obstacle course and selected dumbbells.

The boys watched as Kal had one of the smaller 5lb weights she lifted as she went through the ropes and over to the stools and only jumped on the first 3, the ones that were the same height, and then to the jump ropes placing down the weights and doing ten jumps before picking up the weight and jogging back to the start and doing it twice more before moving into the lesson of the day.

Valerie grabbed two 20-pound weights, jumped through the ropes, and did the steps before placing the bells down and jumping 30 over the jump ropes before picking up the weights and running to the start. She did it twice more than grabbing a step she walked to set up for the day's lesson joining Kal.

"Valerie is super fit…." Holjus whispered with awe in his voice. Sallisfer smiled and nodded. "She is fitter than the teacher."

Sallisfer laughed and shifted into a mouse and cast a small spell so he could speak, "She is a ranch kid… there is not much room for weakness."

"I see that." Holjus's voice came from beside him, and Sallisfer imagined the Demon's eyes wide with admiration.

Valerie and Kal started doing crunches on the step as the teacher walked around them, watching their postures and forms.

"One…two…three," they counted, doing crunches on the step. Once they had done 10, they started to do the leg lifts. Making the girls around them giggle as they talked about looking like a peeing dog.

"What if they came here and saw us doing this?" Kal asked, a light blush on her cheeks as someone nearby made the hissing sound like they were peeing.

"I don't know. Sallisfer is a very talented shifter who can transform into animals and things, like this step or something," Valerie said with a shrug as she sat up from doing her twenty. Then, she rolled over and started doing her crunches again.

"What if he is?" Kal asked, sitting up, forgetting what number she was on and looking around wide-eyed.

"Then I'd feel his 'pleasure,' and besides, I hope he should know better than that." Valerie rolled her eyes, looking around as well. She felt glee in her mind but couldn't place it.

"I didn't know he could shift into objects…." Kal asked, patting the step before doing her round two.

"It isn't recommended as objects are very hard to transform back to yourself from…like a bug or insects. Not forbidden but not recommended. Even the strongest shifter can get stuck." Valerie shrugged, and Kal noted she was already on her last round. The teacher had placed down a timer so she could do step planks independently.

"So, if he isn't an object, he could still be small and in the room watching us?" Kal hissed as she gritted her teeth, pushing herself to do another 10.

Valerie scowled at her as she did her plank. "I sure hope he is using his study hour wisely.

"Study hour, is that a thing?" Kal asked.

Valerie laughed. "Sallisfer is too smart for his own good."

"Still don't get it…." Kal whined, making Valerie shake her head; the teacher then coughed at them, and they both smiled cheekily at her and finished up.

After the step exercise, they moved the steps and cooled down with stretches. Just as the bell rang, Valerie helped Kal get up as they left the gym to change into regular clothes. They walk into the locker room to get their stuff.

Valerie hesitated at the door and turned to face the wall. She was sure that they were being stalked. She cast a slight spell that revealed Sallisfer and Holjus in the corner; she sighed and shook her head. "I am very disappointed in you two. Spying, trespassing on my privacy, I am disgusted."

Holjus and Sallisfer looked away from Valerie in shame, a red blush appearing on their cheeks. "There will be hell to pay George Sallisfer King Jr. and Holjus Akakios Melanthios! Mark my words. You two are going to pay. Now be gone with you traitors." She turned and walked away, running into Kal when she entered the room.

"What is it, Valerie?" Kal stopped and handed Valerie her bag, looking at Valerie's angered expression.

"You were right. They were watching us," Valerie said, shaking her head as she quickly took her stuff from Kal and walked out of the room onto the hallway.

Kal followed her, laughing, "You are joking."

"I wish. Why are you finding this amusing? The boys betrayed our trust?"

"I think it is hilarious. First, we talked about it, and now it happened."

"Perhaps it is your time instincts. Then, you may be ready to take classes with the time master."

"The what, master?"

"The Time Master teaches young time lords how to travel through time and hone their abilities. He is the only one who can go forward and backward in time. There is no one like him; all time lords learn from him."

"You can't teach me?"

"No. I am a shifter. I can time travel because of my extra spirit…" Valerie took a breath and lowered her voice. "The Hand of Doom… it can do magic that the host isn't born into." Valerie yawned- "He taught us some things to control the time travel inside of us… but no, alas, I cannot teach you time travel."

"When will I be ready to meet him?"

"He will know… he knows everything."

Kal nodded and linked her arm with Valerie's as they walked up the hall, stopping at Kal's locker and allowing her to exchange books. "I was thinking about my mom's birthday," Valerie mentioned. "We should throw her a party."

Kal looked at her, "What do you have in mind?"

"Do you think we can pull off a surprise party? March is practically around the corner."

Kal laughed as she scratched out January 25th, "I should think we have enough time to pull off a party for your mom." Valerie smiled, and Kal took out her literature book just as the bell rang for a warning, and they parted ways for the fourth block. Valerie cast a protection spell on Kal before heading to her classroom.

CHAPTER 15

Thriving

Kal sat in silence, her mind racing; she took some notes on what the teacher was talking about but not all.

She was suddenly afraid of what today's magic lesson would bring. Valerie had told her everything would be okay, but she didn't believe her. Before she knew it, they were packing up to go home. Kal met Valerie in the hall, and together they walked to the buses.

"Sisters!" Koda shouted, running up behind them, a demon stud looking at them with a smile.

"Oh look, your pathetic sisters are here," he said.

Valerie took Koda's hand and walked to the bus. Unfortunately, another demon got in their way, and soon they were surrounded by them.

"I'm going to clear the path. You get on the bus. Sallisfer will meet you on it, he is in his geek form, and he'll take care of you," Valerie hissed with a heavy sigh. Kal watched as Valerie rolled her neck, suddenly glowing with power as she confronted the demons with an evil smile.

Kal took Koda's hand from Valerie; they both looked at Valerie, who suddenly had a sword in her hand. Valerie charged, and they boarded their first bus as soon as the way was clear. As Valerie had said, Sallisfer sat in the first seat, looking at them with concerned eyes penetrating through his huge glasses.

"Have a seat," he said, getting up and allowing them to take his seat. Then he sat in the one closest to the door, looking at Valerie taking on the demons. She was like a whirlwind. Valerie moved faster than the eye could follow in a blur of darkness. She sliced and cut down demons, their bodies disappearing as they hit the ground. Valerie made her way to the bus, but more demons appeared, cutting her off. Again, Valerie sliced and cut down more of them, but she was overwhelmed. Kal saw that Sallisfer was itching to go out there but stayed only because of her. Valerie was caught from behind, and Sallisfer let out a yell of anguish and jumped up. A hand grabbed and held him in place. Kris suddenly appeared on the bus while no one was looking.

"She will not allow anyone to help," he gasped. He looked awful; Kris's hair was blackened with soot, and his nice clothes were a patchwork of holes, "Trust me, I've tried."

Sallisfer sat, and his eyes never left Valerie's form. He shook all over, sweat dripped down his brow, and his hands clenched so hard that his nails cut into his skin.

Teachers, bus drivers, and police soon arrived. "Valerie, is gonna get caught?" Koda and Kal almost yelled simultaneously, looking at Sallisfer, but he just shook his head, his whole-body relaxing.

"Valerie is out of harm's way," he whispered, pointing over to the girl in police custody; she looked like Valerie, but Kal could tell she wasn't.

"Who is that?" Koda whispered back.

"That is Jane. She is a particular type of shifter. Each hand is always assigned a double. However, ours are the only pair in history that has been used more than once. They always get the Hands out of trouble, especially for school-related stuff and human law." Sallisfer smiled with a shake of his head as the bus pulled away and headed to the middle school.

On the Sorceress's bus, they found Valerie sitting in her regular seat. She was breathing hard, and she had a split lip.

An extended cut ran from her shoulder under her arm and down her left side. Sallisfer looked at it with concern and pain in his blue eyes as Valerie smiled at him weakly.

"I think that's the most fun I've had in days," she said, closing her eyes and trying to slow her breathing without success.

"Can I help?" Sallisfer asked her; as the bus driver was cleaning her wound. She winced and cursed.

"It would help a lot if you could do that connection thing and make her heal as you do Sallisfer." the bus driver said.

"No, I don't want it to heal like him," Valerie said, breath still coming short, and she spat blood everywhere. "I can heal it on my own."

The bus driver looked at her, surprised. "I don't want to merge -must hold my own," Valerie said. Kal, Koda, Kris, and Mr. Wheedle looked at Sallisfer.

"Is she okay, or is blood loss making her go nuts?" Kal asked.

"She has a secret, and I can't get into it. She's afraid of her weak state. But, if we merge, I'll find out," Sallisfer whispered. Banging on the school bus door told them the other students were ready to enter.

"Don't let them see me. I don't have the strength to transport," Valerie said, looking at them with pleading eyes. Sallisfer sighed.

"I'll transport us all to school. It's much safer that way," Sal stated before he turned to Kris. "Stay here and make sure the bus gets to school without problems."

Then Kal and Koda held on to Sallisfer as he transported them to the infirmary.

The nurses gasped as they rushed and took Valerie from them, but she had lost so much blood that Sallisfer was feeling the effects of it.

"Get him into a bed and her into surgery," the primary doctor shouted.

"What happened?" a nurse asked them.

"My sister got into a fight; what does it look like?" Koda said, hands on his hips.

"Your sister?" the nurse asked.

"Yes, my sister, Val is my sister, full-blooded too!" Koda said, irritation in his young voice.

"Is this true?" the woman said, looking at Kal.

"Yes, it's true, masters have a family. They have a life other than that at the school," Kal said.

"Yes, but Hands rarely ever have connections with their family. They rarely have friends outside themselves," the woman said with a smile. "But I see that it is not true with this pair. I wonder what the next pair will be like if we can't stop Master Valerie's death here and now or on her upcoming birthday." The woman seemed worried as she walked them out of the wing.

"I wonder what she was so uptight about," Kal told herself.

"I don't know," Koda said. Just then, Kris ran up to them.

"What is it? Have you seen something?" Kal asked.

"Yes, I have, and I really must talk to Sallisfer once Val is healed. From what I discovered, Valerie was planning to take Sorrow out to meet and fight more demons, and then she was going to meet someone in a huge field," Kris said.

"So, they aren't going to die right now?" Kal asked, relief flowing over her.

"No, not right now, but I saw Nurse Samantha, and she was distraught. She can see the death of someone by looking into their blood. No doubt she's seen Val's and Master Sallisfer's too." Kris said, rushing away to find Sallisfer.

Kris returned a few moments later, looking downcast to find Kal and Koda sitting in the waiting room, "They won't let me see him." Kris sat next to Kal with a heavy sigh.

"What is going on?" Koda asked.

"They have pumped Valerie up with more blood and are giving her iron through an IV. She is all stitched up and is resting." Kris shook his head, "I could only glance at her. She is healing now that she has stopped fighting. She can heal on her own. Just not as good as Sallisfer."

Koda nodded, "She never takes the time." He said, "At least that's what my dad says."

Kris laughed, and soon Kal and Koda joined him. Just then, screams erupted from the medical wing. "Hold still!" shouted someone.

"NO! Why should I!" Valerie could be heard.

"Stop this nonsense!" The doctor shouted. Kal looked at Kris, and they started running to the room where growling could be heard.

They rushed in and found a huge orange tiger, who they knew was Valerie, pinned by a massive white tiger- Sallisfer. Kris took one look and ran to the doctor, who appeared in shock with long claw marks on his shirt but no blood. Kal came to her senses and helped Kris get the doctor out of the room just as Valerie spoke.

"Get off of me, you furball," Valerie shouted.

"Not if you're going to hurt someone. You're allowing the fire to consume you," Sallisfer growled.

"It's too strong!" Valerie said, struggling.

"You're stronger!" Sallisfer yelled.

"No, I am not." Valerie's voice was filled with pain and fear.

"Yes, you are. Now fight it!" Sallisfer ordered, and Valerie closed her eyes, took deep, even breaths, and opened her eyes again.

Kal saw that unspoken words were passing between them and wished she could hear what was being said. Valerie and Sallisfer closed their inner mind eyes, and the people watched the orange tiger eyes close. Valerie and Sallisfer shifted together back into human form. The air around them became a dense fog, and she could no longer see them, but she heard Valerie whisper, "Thank you."

The fog cleared, and Sallisfer stood, helping Valerie stand on shaky legs. Their eyes never left the others as the air stopped shimmering, and their eyes stopped glowing. Then as one, they breathed a single sigh, and Sallisfer let go of her, dropping the eye connection as he did so. Valerie smiled faintly before threatening to fall. Kris came out of nowhere. Kal looked at where Kris stood next to her and when he caught Valerie. She then watched Kris lay Valerie on the bed, looking at Sallisfer questioningly. Sallisfer laughed and walked out of the room with Kris on his heels.

"What happened?" Kal asked.

"I healed her."

"How?" Kris asked, but, Sallisfer just shook his head with a smile.

"I have a lesson to teach," was all Sallisfer would say as he smiled at Koda. "Master Smith is waiting for you in the library. He understands why you are late, but take this note to him anyway." Sallisfer handed Koda a note from the air and smiled, rustling Koda's hair. "She is going to be fine."

Koda nodded, and Sallisfer took his hand, "We will walk with you," he smiled. "We are headed to the field." Koda smiled up at him.

"Thank you," he said. Kal took Koda's other hand and walked out of the hospital wing. Kris was silent as he walked a step behind them, but Kal could feel his eyes on her as they walked down the stairs to the main hall. At the foot of the stairs, Sallisfer let go of Koda's hand while he spoke, "Go now, Koda. Master Smith is waiting." Koda took a deep breath and walked off to the library, holding the letter like a shield in front of him. Sallisfer watched him until he disappeared around the bend and smiled at Kal and Kris. Sallisfer then led them down the hall to a set of large red doors that pushed open to a large field, and saw masters with their students. Ava was watching Hillary's lesson with Master Lee. Ava spotted them as they came onto the field and waved farewell to Hillary as she walked towards Master Sallisfer, Kris, and Kal in her school outfit. Kal then noticed she had forgotten to change. Kris smiled at her and handed her a grocery bag.

"Master Valerie gave this to me this morning. She must have known you would forget to change. The bathroom is back inside, second door on the right."

Kal looked at him wide-eyed as she took the bag and rushed to the bathroom. In the bag, she found loose-fitting blue jeans, a white halter top, and black combat boots from her room. How had Valerie known Kal was at a loss, and why had she given the clothes to Kris? It was so embarrassing.

Kal rushed out of the bathroom, placing the grocery bag on the ground by the door in the field. Sallisfer smiled at her, his blue eyes tracing her form with a hungry look.

That was when Kal saw Kris give Sallisfer a nasty look, his hands in a fist at his side. Kal blinked, and the natural uncaring look was back on Kris's face as he turned away from them, making Sallisfer rip his eyes from Kal and smile at Kris and Ava, "Kris, I'll teach you and Ava today. Master Valerie needs rest!" he said, leading them to an empty part of the field. "We will begin with warm-up stretches."

They began to stretch. "Uhmm, master, I think she might not stay," Kris finally spoke up as they warmed up.

"What do you mean?" Sallisfer asked, looking at him.

"I saw the future. It didn't look good," Kris said.

Sallisfer shook his head. "Can today get any better?" he sighed, sagging his shoulders.

Kal looked at him. "Can I make it better?" she asked.

"You always make my day better," he said with a slight smile. He stood and walked around Ava and Kal, examining them with penetrating eyes.

"Today, I want to test how natural your powers are," Sallisfer explained to Kal and Ava. "Kris and I are going to attack you, and you have to attack back. This tests instincts, as a great deal of your power shows up when you are frightened. It also will show how strong you already are in the art of defending yourself." He looked at Ava, "You took martial arts and boxing classes as an early child. These skills will come in handy. Add your power to the moves you already know. This will show an honest view of your abilities. Kal," he looked at Kal then, "You have the knowledge. It is inside of you…at least instantly. Pull on your instincts and then add your power to them."

Kal nodded, looking at Ava, who looked confident, while Kal was confused. She lined up on the other side of a white chalk line Sallisfer drew on the ground. Kris got Kal because she refused to attack Sallisfer, especially after last night.

The two guys pulled off their shirts and laid them on the grass. Kal saw Hillary's eyes widen as she spied Sallisfer's strong, broad chest from the sidelines. They were prepared to fight the two girls in halter tops and jeans. They awaited side by side, ready to strike.

"Stop, that is so going to teach someone how to get hurt," Valerie said, walking up to Kris and adjusting his arm.

"Keep your chin up and eyes focused," she instructed. "How many times do I have to tell you to protect your core."

Then she walked to Ava and adjusted her body to stand a certain way. "Martial arts and boxing are a strange mix. I suggest you place the balance and grace of the arts on boxing skills. Use the power inside you to flow around your muscles, pulling at them as you move your arms out to strike." Valerie demonstrated this with a quick movement and had Ava try. With a nod, Valerie walked to Kal.

"Kal, you need to focus on the game, not on hurting anyone. Trust me, anything done here will not- cannot hurt anyone. Even a voice fight here cannot hurt a thing," Valerie said, moving Kal's arms like she had done Kris and widening Kal's stance. "Without a strong base, you will fall."

"Now fight. I'll watch."

"Thank you, Master Valerie. You've always been better with students than I am," Sallisfer said. Valerie smirked.

"That's why I have two students, and you have one." He laughed, taking up his pose again.

The fight wasn't long. It was a typical fight; the new ones got their butts kicked by the more experienced.

"Good, now we have a basic understanding of how much is natural," Sallisfer said, catching the towel Valerie threw at him. He wiped his face and the back of his neck.

"Kris, you still need some work, too," Valerie said, throwing him a towel.

Kris grinned and whipped his face and neck. Valerie handed a towel to Ava and Kal, and she beamed at Ava. "I am quite impressed with what you already know. We can sit down in our next lesson to work out your potential. You have quite a bit of power."

Ava smiled, "My sister works with me at home."

"That is good. She is quite a powerful healer and knows quite a bit about how magic flows in and around the body. I believe it is time to learn to call on the fairy power that flows. It will add to the power you already know how to pull. I will let my sister help you with that because I am only 1/3 Fairy, and my fairy powers are minimal compared to yours. Is that alright? She will teach you that lesson tomorrow, and we will meet the following day, Friday, to discuss building your skills."

Ava nodded, "Why don't you cool off and get a sip of water. We will work on core skills today." Valerie turned to Kris, "You are meeting the Master tomorrow, yes?" Kris nodded. "Take Kal to meet him. She will receive her first-time lesson. Now let's work on some core skills. Sally? Do you have a lesson idea for your pupil?"

Sallisfer grounded. "Um… She is to work on core skills too?" Valerie rolled her eyes and sat down. Kris sat next to her.

"Master, are you sure you are up to this?" he whispered as Kal sat beside him.

Valerie looked pale now that Kal was observing her. Valerie's eyes kept changing from green to brown, and she looked drained. "I am fine." She said as Ava sat down, "We will work on breathing exercises first. These focus the mind. Take a deep breath in and breathe out through the nose." Kal watched as Kris and Valerie placed their hands fist to fist in front of them. Kal and Ava did the same, "While breathing," Valerie enlightened them to focus on the power in their body. "It will hum and feel warm. Pull them to the surface and hold them. Sometimes it helps to close your eyes the first time to imagine colored variations, usually your favorite color." Kal closed her eyes and breathing even breaths, she found bright blue spots dancing inside her. Kal pulled on the power and held it at her fingertips.

"Good. Good." Sallisfer said, a smile in his voice. "Now let it go again, power off." Kal did so, "Nice, now pull it up again." Kal pulled the power, and it came faster than her last pull.

"Well done. Now take a moment and release the power. Next, open your eyes and try pulling on the power without focusing on it."

Kal opened her eyes to find Valerie in Sallisfer's lap. She looked asleep, and a blanket was settled on her lap. "Pull on the power."

Kal tried to pull on the power, but anger and jealousy clogged her concentration. Finally, she closed her eyes again and produced the power. Then she opened her eyes and could hold the power at her fingertips.

"You must be able to pull on the power without closing your eyes. Much like shifting into the wolf has become natural. You must become natural in pulling your power at will." Sallisfer clarified, "Try again."

Kal let go of the power and tried to ignore Valerie's peaceful form on Sallisfer's lap and took a breath through her nose and out. Then, she concentrated and pulled on the power. She felt it warm her fingers and smiled. Sallisfer smiled too, but it was the grin on Kris's face that made Kal relax.

Sallisfer had her and Ava let go and power up a few more times; then he stood holding Valerie like a baby in his arms. "Take a moment. Rest, and get some water. These exercises can be very tiring on new minds."

Kal hadn't realized how tired she was till she started to stand, and her legs which had fallen asleep almost failed her. Kris caught her just as fast as he had caught Valerie. He smiled and handed her a water bottle. "She chugged down the entire bottle in one go."

"What is your favorite drink?"

"Root beer," Kal said without thinking.

Kris produced a can out of thin air with a grin. "Mine too."

Kal took the can with a thank you and sat on a bench, looking around. The other masters were still working, yet time didn't seem to show in the field.

"What time is it?" she asked.

"The same time it was when we entered. Time is very different in the field. It moves when the headmaster wishes it to."

"He has the ability to stop time?" Kal started.

"Yes, if he wants to." Kris shrugged.

Kal drank some root beer and found herself recharging with every sip. She looked curiously down at the can and shrugged; she figured things would be explained in due time. They had to.

CHAPTER 16

The Masters and the Students

Sallisfer was getting Kal and Ava back onto the field when a distinguishing deep voice boomed.

"Students!"

Sallisfer stopped and watched a short bald man with a long white beard walking over to him. "Where is Valerie?" he asked, eyeing Sallisfer before he could say anything. Valerie appeared beside him and smiled at the man.

"Master Fisher," Valerie said with a bow.

"Valerie," Master Fisher said with a smile and a bow.

"Need anything, master?" Sallisfer asked, wrapping his arm around Valerie protectively.

"I just wanted to show the next level what they have to achieve." Master Fisher said, grinning at Kal and Kris.

Sallisfer and Valerie looked at each other. "Do you think it's the right time? They don't even know that they are the next level down. Isn't it going a bit fast?" Valerie asked.

"And Valerie requires rest." Sallisfer chimed in with a worried look at Valerie, who scowled back at him.

"We are at War, Master Valerie. Things have to go fast in war," Master Fisher said sternly.

"What, he approved it?" Valerie asked, stumbling backward from Sallisfer as if something had hit her. Sallisfer nodded, looking downcast as he caught a mind full of knowing before she did.

"The demons have committed an act of war. You said so yourself," Master Fisher said.

Kal looked at Sallisfer; he had a smug expression on his face. "Now, we must show them what they must do, now fighting pattern 3," Master Fisher commanded.

"Yes, Sir," Sallisfer said. They took a deep breath and lined up side by side.

"Masters!" Master Fisher shouted.

At once, all the masters were standing on the enemy side. The students gathered around to watch whispers humming in the air as Valerie and Sallisfer faced off two against at least a hundred.

Sallisfer and Valerie smiled as energy buzzed around them. Then, Valerie sang what appeared to be a foreign song to everyone. However, Kal had heard her sing it often to herself, 'perhaps it's a song she wrote herself,' Kal thought as she caught bits and pieces of the lyrics.

"I should be asleep," she quietly sang as she nodded to Sallisfer, who nodded back. "But I am not," she took a step forward, looking dashing as if this was just a stage seen in a musical. "I can't help thinking—Something is wrong," at that, a power bolt shifted its way around the startled Masters.

"Made of confusion and mistakes," Sallisfer chimed in, and the power around them grew slightly, "My mind is a whirl. Dreaming of a falling-out lasting—"

"Sorrow." They sang together with a slight breathless wink, and the power wavered and vanished. The masters were quick to recover, and as soon as Sallisfer seemed to dance to silent music and stepped closer to one or the other, they started their own plan in motion, and soon it was a small civil war, but just as Valerie had said, no blood was spilled. Sure, muscles were pulled, and magic tired the body and mind. Yet, not a single drop of blood was spilled, and not a single gash or bruise was made.

Kal stared in utter bewilderment as Valerie danced and magically wiped out some of the masters with a simple hand wave. Kal wondered just how much power or what sort of trickery was going on. She found herself flat-out flabbergasted as Sallisfer laughed a rumbling, sexy laugh. With a shake of his perfect hair, he got in the middle of the mess, for as Kal had observed, he had been hanging on the outside, keeping anyone who tried to run away busy.

He gave Valerie a knowing wink as she stood by him, "You think you're sooooo good, don't you, sister? Well, let me show you some." Sallisfer rolled his head, and the music seemed to ring in the air, and again he started to sing. It was like a scene in High School Musical but with more creative lyrics, "There's no combination of words—No song that I could sing." He and Valerie moved as a single force, "But I can always try for your black heart. We have dreams," as he sang, he wiped them out.

Kal looked up at Master Fisher. "Do they always sing when they are fighting?" She asked and heard the other students whispering the same question, some of them even laughing.

Master Fisher laughed and nodded. "They do when they need to stay together but not merged. They say it helps them stay in tune with each other." Master Fisher said with a smile.

"Attack pattern sixteen and then twenty-one!" he called.

The mood changed in the songs, from light-hearted to middle saddens. Then they stopped singing and merged, finishing the other masters up.

They stopped as soon as it was done, and the light and energy faded. Valerie fell to the ground laughing. "It's true," Sallisfer said, also laughing.

Students swarmed them with questions and amazement, which they did not seem to hear, still absorbed in their own little world between them.

"You are bad...so bad..." Valerie said. Kal pushed her way toward them.

"What's so funny?" she asked, hands on hips. The crowd around them grew quiet and anxious for another fight.

"He....he...he's so bad," Valerie said, trying to focus. "Come here, and I'll show you why." Kal walked up to Valerie and sat down beside her on the grass. "Now all you have to do is let me show you," Valerie said.

Kal closed her eyes, and an image of Sallisfer came into her mind.

"I feel just like a kid again…" came with the image, then she saw herself with Sallisfer dancing and carrying on, all in a cartoon state.

Kal laughed, too, and smiled up at Sallisfer. "Like I said, it's true," he said, bowing, "Now I must be off. I have a meeting with the headmaster in an hour."

"Remember, lay off the wine," Valerie said, pulling herself together. The crowd parted to allow Sallisfer through then the questions started all over again.

Valerie laughed, stood up, and asked, "Ok, class, can anyone tell me what was just demonstrated?"

A few of the older kids raised their hands. Valerie looked them over and pointed to a boy around Kris's age, "Luke, right?" she asked. He nodded, and Valerie gave a sigh of relief, "Ok, Luke, tell us what Attack pattern three is."

Luke licked his lips, "Attack pattern three is a distraction. It can be intimidating; the goal is the throw the enemy off guard."

"Yes, now why is it important to practice this with other masters and allies?"

"So, they can't be distracted by it. Note the quick recovery done by the other masters." Valerie beamed, and Kal could tell that Luke's Master, Lee, was also beaming.

"Good job, Luke. Now which of you, older students, can tell me the first two attack patterns?"

There was silence, "Um… Master…. You can't really explain it…." Kris spoke up at last.

"Quite right, Kris. Split up into two teams. Newey's gather around." Valerie grabbed Kris and a girl as they walked by. "You two are going to be leader A." Valerie moved toward the other group and nominated another set as leader B.

"Now, before you begin, how do we communicate on the battlefield?" Everyone in the teams raised their hands.

"Kal, open your book to page 5. Then, Ava, open your book to page 10." Kal and Ava looked down to see that their leather-bound books had appeared before them.

Kal sighed and did as she was told.

"Read the first paragraph Kal, and Ava, pick up on the second paragraph after Kal," Valerie instructed.

Kal felt hot as all eyes fell on her, "During team activities, like battles or games, the group becomes a single consciousness. This allows each team to speak in each other's heads and plan as one. However, each person has to hold themselves, and no magic can be transferred between the lines."

"During the link, each player or soldier can coordinate and perform faster and cleaner attacks with less loss. If a person cannot keep the link, some magical devices have been invented to safely enhance such links without damage to the wearer or others. They are also small enough not to be noticed by the enemy and removed," Ava read. Valerie nodded and picked up a tiny bit of dirt off the ground. She called attention to herself and tossed the dirt lased with a spell. At once, there were lines between all the team members; Team A had blue lines between them, and Team B had red lines between them.

"Now, teams commence demonstration!" Valerie called.

Team A faced off against team B, Kris, and the girl faced off, Luke and Alex, and the rest faced off, dividing into smaller groups amongst themselves.

Kal was enthralled as she watched the more experienced students simulate two of the attack patterns and counterattacks. Master Valerie, as Kal was asked to address her friend on the field, called out orders and then explained each movement. She even slowed down the people on the field, so she could point out mistakes or explain why such a move was crucial. It was like watching a live play on stage but having the TV on demand to pause or skip through the scenes.

In the end, all those watching, like Kal, had homework, and those who had done the demonstration were allowed to rest before pairing up with their masters to work on some skill toning.

"Kris, you may take the rest of the evening. You did well." Valerie smiled proudly at her pupil.

"Thank you, master" Kris smiled with a bow.

"Where are you going?" Kal asked, noting how Valerie was slinking off slowly.

"I must be going. I have an appointment with Sorrow to attend to before sunset." Valerie nodded to them and then transported herself to the barn before anyone could ask anything more of her.

CHAPTER 17

Take it or Leave it

Valerie quickly tacked up Sorrow and road off at a fast pace. "I don't know if I like this plan of yours," Sorrow suddenly said. Looking at Valerie, who road nervously, observing her surroundings looking from side to side.

"I know, girl, but I have to do this. It's for Kal, the chosen one," Valerie said, nudging the mare onward.

"But you have to pay for information. So, what are you paying for this?" Sorrow asked, stopping again to look at her.

"I have the payment, don't worry, now hurry it up, or we'll be late."

"Fine."

They continued in silence at a trot and then at a canter. Suddenly there were flames all around them. Sorrow went into cavalry horse mode and felt her rider's weight shift as armor, shield, and weapons appeared. They had ridden right into an ambush. Valerie pushed Sorrow on with her legs, and Sorrow responded, leaping through the flames. Surprisingly, there weren't any demons waiting for them on the other side of the fire, just bodies. Valerie did not push Sorrow forward as she observed her surroundings for several moments, a little confused. *How did this happen,* she thought, as her watch beeped the hour, and she kicked Sorrow into a gallop.

They arrived at a massive field, and a figure in white stood in the middle. Sorrow snorted as they approached.

"I don't like the smell of this guy," Sorrow sighed, stopping and refusing to move further.

"Sorrow, move," Valerie uttered, kicking her. Sorrow walked forward in a fast trot and circled around the figure.

"You are Valerie Wing, am I correct?" The figure spoke, his voice light and powerful at the same time.

"I am, and you are?" Valerie asked. The figure laughed and pulled off his hood. He stood tall, with long blond hair and the darkest depth of blue eyes.

"I am the Oracle of prophecy. I'm here to tell you what you, as the hand of doom and your chosen friend, will face in the future, but I must warn you the price is high for one so young and one so dark," the man purred.

"I am ready to pay," Valerie said, licking her dry lips nervously.

"Very well then:

Black glass holds your death in its hands,
Darkness stares into golden eyes,
But love will fulfill any demands
And Life's story is open to rise.

On your soul, there is a path,
One must choose to go with your soul or mind.
Pick carefully -one will lead you to my wrath,
balance you will never find.

Blood rivers will flow from your veins
mountains will crumble from your screams.
Your hands will loosen from the rain,
dooming your whole team.

Down to the ashes, you will fall
Rising from the heat, she will succeed.

Valerie stared at him, trying to soak it all in. "Take it or leave it?" The man asked.

"I'll take it," Valerie said once the words entered her mind, and she could call them at will.

"Now pay," the man said.

"What do you want?" she asked.

"Your immortality," the man said.

Valerie felt a pull at her heart and the sudden thud at the doors of her mind that held firm to Sallisfer's attacks. She only hesitated for a moment, thinking it was over. *Do I even have forever to live?* She knew the answer was no, at the appearance of the Chosen One. Valerie had spent years searching and denying the prophecy, but here was proof that her life was indeed doomed, and she had also doomed Sallisfer. She reached out with her hand. Perhaps mortality was better. She would pass at her last death and avoid all politics.

"She owes her immortality to me," a wing horse landed on the grass. Valerie only had to look at him to realize he was the legendary Pegasus, the creator of the paths and chaser of the winds. "I settled the debate in her family when her grandfather died. I saved the land from falling into the wrong hands!" Pegasus's reached his head out. "She has to pay me first!"

The oracle laughed, "What does a horse who cannot die have use with immortality? I shall take her immortality she owes me now or take away the prophecy. Suddenly Valerie felt the poem starting to fall out of her mind. "I will pay you with something else, Pegasus. I am sure we can work something out." She reached out to the oracle and nearly met, but a dark form came between them.

"Shadow?" Valerie asked, shocked at the sudden appearance of her 'imaginary friend,' the protector of the childhood spirit and a close friend.

"Hello Val, I am here to pay your price," Shadow said, her black eyes looking at her. Very few people have seen the face of their shadow. Many believe it's just a trick of the light and take it for granted, but a Shadow is what was and what is of a person. It's a reflection of oneself. Valerie had heard and even believed before this time that shadows leave them when they fall into darkness. A shadow is an extension of darkness, where most darkness is feared, but your own shadow never is.

"But you said..." Valerie protested, looking desperately to the oracle to refuse to find some argument that she could support, but Shadow put her finger to her black lips and then turned to the man. "I am going to pay for her."

"That is fine." the man said.

The man and Shadow shook hands, and her friend wilted away, long overdue.

"Goodbye, my friend," Shadow said, waving a hand before disappearing into nothingness. The man turned and vanished. Valerie took a deep unsteady breath, and with one last look at the spot where her friend had vanished, she looked at the wing horse who waited. "I can pay you now," she said. Pegasus shook his head, "Your beauty of a horse has agreed to pay the debt. In a few years, she will become my wife." Before Valerie could respond, Sorrow turned for home and galloped away. They arrived at the barn; Valerie jumped off and quickly untacked, blanketed, and fed Sorrow in silence.

Sallisfer and Kal ran into the barn. "Are you okay?" he asked her.

"Fine," she said, rushing past them and into the tack room to put away her tack.

"I don't think that's true," Kal said, looking up at Sallisfer.

"I know it's not. Something is on her mind..." he closed his eyes and then opened them, looking down at Kal with concern "Guilt," he finished, a tear forming in the corner of his left eye, "and sorrow."

Kal reached up and gently stroked the tear away, he smiled at her, but she knew it was troubling. Valerie was about to walk past them again, but Sallisfer caught her arm. "Tell me, what happened to Shadow?" he commanded.

Valerie swallowed hard. "She...she paid her...her...immortality," she said, her bubble of pride burst, and tears streamed down her face.

"What? What have you done?" Sallisfer asked, anger in his voice as he grabbed Valerie's shoulders and shook her.

Valerie swallowed, "I needed information, and I got way more than I needed, but..." she trailed off and looked at Kal.

"I was doing my duty to the headmaster, our people, and you," Valerie said, looking at Sallisfer in the eyes.

He gasped and let her go, holding his head. "Hold up, slow down, too much to handle," he said.

"Sorry," Valerie muttered, and Sallisfer sighed deeply. He reached out and held Valerie's shoulders once more, this time less violently, and kissed her head.

"Thanks," he whispered.

Sorrow pawed at her door, and Valerie walked over and unlatched it, then walked with the gray mare to the pasture and opened the gate for her.

"Are you okay?" Kal asked.

Sallisfer swallowed, "I'm fine."

"Did someone name Shadow die?" Kal asked, not just a little confused.

Sallisfer shook his head and sat on the barn bench, rubbing his head. "No, Shadow is or…was rather a shadow. She was assigned to Valerie as her protector, what human children call an imaginary friend. I had one as well… but I haven't kept up with her as Val did with Shadow. Shadow became Valerie's shadow… she will have to create her own shadow now, which will take a few weeks to grow."

"Valerie no longer has a shadow?" Kal asked wide-eyed, squinting at Valerie's small figure as she turned Sorrow out at the pasture down the hill.

"She never had one," Sallisfer uttered, watching as Valerie sagged against the gate, looking out across the lake. Kal could tell in the setting sun that what Sallisfer was saying was true. Nothing swept the ground where her shadow had once been.

"Wow. So, what information did you get from Valerie? Who did she talk to? And why is her shadow friend dead… and…?"

"Not right now." Sallisfer suddenly laughed, raising his hand, stopping Kal in her forceful questioning. "It's up to her to share what she has shared with me. I cannot make those decisions. But I can tell you we will pick up the pace on you and Kris's training."

"I have to second that. We have a battle to fight, a war to win, a feud to end, and just between us three..." Valerie trailed off. "Two won't see the end of it either." Valerie put up the halter on the peg by the feed room door.

Kal's eyes went huge, and she looked at Sallisfer. "You know when you're going to fall and how?" she asked.

"No, we only know when, and trust me when I say you'll have to put up with us for longer than you can hope for. Trust me, you'll start getting tired of the fact that we're in the news, we have fans, and we are in a higher rank than you are," Sallisfer said quickly, glaring at Valerie, who just shrugged.

"I'm just getting used to you," Kal protested.

A silent conversation passed between Valerie and Sallisfer, who just smiled and shook his head at Kal as Valerie rolled her eyes. "Trust me, you'll get tired of us." Kal knew they weren't telling her everything but decided not to push her luck.

CHAPTER 18

Threats at Half Mast

Valerie watched Kris on the practice field with Gina, the Master tester. Gina was running Kris through his paces, "You know it will happen soon," said a voice beside her.

"Master, what a surprise," Valerie said clearly, not surprised as her eyes stayed on the test.

"You are going to have to let it happen." Headmaster continued unphased. "I do not understand why you hold him back."

"You know why I am doing what I am doing," Valerie continued. "He is not ready."

There was a sigh of frustration, and the Headmaster wrapped his arm around her. She felt the familiar heat of his skin and the pull of her power and mind, but she did not budge. She did not let him enter and make decisions for her.

Feeling the weight of his frustration and her determination, he stated, "Very well, but if you do not do it soon…." But she cut him off.

"I am slowly releasing his potential… as I am improving the other."

Looking at her incredulously, "You live dangerously. What if this plan of yours doesn't work? What is plan B?"

At that, Valerie did look over at the Headmaster's changing eyes, "What is your plan B?" she asked. "This preposterous plan of yours, taking our people to war. Endangering The Chosen One when she is not ready and creating rifts in the ranks of what holds this realm together."

"I am the Headmaster. I plan on creating a better world for us... and humans," he stated in a commanding tone.

Valerie turned away from the Headmaster, observing the practice field, and spoke. "You live dangerously, Headmaster... You forget you were created by Hands... You can be destroyed by Hands...." At that, Valerie walked to the middle of the field; as the test ended.

She shook Kris's hand, and a slight spark went down her hand into his and was gone. The Headmaster watched in the shadows as he often did, wondering what he would have to do to get this unruly hand under control. He opened his left hand and closed it. The tether was weak and growing weaker by the day. She was just too powerful to control. He opened his right hand and felt the warm glow of heaven's tether, but it was thinner than it should be. It had been sliced in half four months ago, and until it was whole again, he would keep losing the balance of good and evil.

"This war will be the Death of you, Valerie Wing Hand of Doom... and when it is, I will have new hands... weaker hands, and I be able to restore the balance of this planet, realm, and the universe." Tears rose in his eyes as he watched Valerie in the disappearing sunlight. Kalea had joined her, and Valerie was putting the new Master, Kristopher, in charge of teaching the basics. She introduced Gina, and he watched as Valerie transferred some of her power to Kalea, who was only a minor power-level Witch. Valerie was slowly transforming Kal into a sorceress. The Headmaster thought about the day Valerie had announced what she planned to do to him. "I have plenty to spare," she laughed, looking so alive in his office. "Besides, I will get more in August when all my power is accessible." She said as she smiled at him, her face full of glee.

"Yes, 16 is a huge day. I expect a victory supper." He had said, and her smile shifted to one of a grimace and then of malevolence.

"There will certainly be supper." Her vagueness these days baffled The Headmaster. What had happened to the little girl he had watched and raised into this young woman? He saw her at birth, brought before him by the last Hands. Her power was already shining, and she shifted into a baby dragon at his touch. The Headmaster had known she would be powerful, yet he thought if he changed her at a young age, he could mold her into obedience. Watching her now, he knew how wrong he had been.

CHAPTER 19

Land and Dynamics

February came in a blink of an eye for Kal, who wasn't sure where the rest of January had gone. She had learned so much in a short time. Magic was becoming more and more natural to her since Kris had been promoted to low master and was taking over most of Kal's basic lessons. As a result, her lessons were more frequent and lasted long hours in the evening. This left Valerie and Sallisfer free to lead the war preparation.

Although the war had not started, the armies were assembled, the supplies were ready, and high-ranking masters were moving out to the fields to prepare for the coming war. As more masters were leaving the school, more and more new ones came; all the masters had their hands full. The younger masters were taking on three to four students. It wasn't about how many there were but the decreasing number of masters. Older masters, regardless of rank, who were out of school, opted to fight in the war and couldn't teach. Even Master Fisher joined the war, declaring Valerie and Sallisfer done with training. However, he still dropped by to keep their nerves up and skills tested.

Kal sat in the library by the blazing hearth, reading an assigned book about the importance of hiding magic and war from the human world.

"How is it going?" Sallisfer asked, sitting down beside her and making Kal jump. She looked over at him. He looked tired, but he had a bowl of steaming soup. "It is past supper time. When we didn't see you in the cafeteria, we figured you were still working."

Kal smiled, grateful for the break and the food, "I am just having trouble understanding how all of this is hidden from the humans. The world isn't that big... is it?"

Sallisfer smiled, "You are looking at the world as one-dimensional. However, the realm that we are in is composed of several layers." He walked over to the hearth and stood, where a pile of books was artfully arranged and lined with bookends shaped like trees. He ran a thin finger down them and pulled one out. Sallisfer then handed the book to Kal. "Think of the cover of this book as the world. Now open the book."

Kal opened the book and gasped; It was a three-dimensional map. Sallisfer reached into his pocket and pulled out a few colored game pieces. He sat down on the floor again with Kal, "These are the realms layered one on top of another, which is not exactly how it looks. It is more like a funnel, but this way, you can see the layers." He pointed out the folds, "The top layer is now the human realm. It is occupied by the least amount of magic; as you come from the human realm, you slide into the creature realm. This realm is in constant flux with the human realm, which is why so many myths about dragons, fairies, and whatnot exist. Most full moons are where these two meet, and Demons have developed hunting on these nights. They need blood from magical creatures to have enough strength to terrorize the rest of the realms." He laughed and looked at Kal to see if she understood, and she nodded.

"Continue, please. Where are we now?" Kal said.

"The school sits in the Creature Realm, making it easier to get those just learning magic to it. However, it takes lots of energy to travel between the realms. If those with magic but born into a family without it would travel to the other realms prematurely, it could kill them." Kal nodded again, "The Earth Children and Demons mostly reside in the third realm. The greatest amount of magic lives here. This realm is divided between the Earth Children and the Demons." He pointed out several features, "Most demons live south of the realm, but a few have ventured as far east toward the wetlands."

"That is where the first battles are taking place, right?" Kal asked, thinking over what she had overheard at the dinner table the day before.

"Yes," Sallisfer said with a smile. "There is a no man's land between them, with only one building where those seeking to put away their differences go for a good time. This place is also linked to the farm. The field where the teens fight at 16 sits on top of this place. They are both a place of peace." He pointed out the parts of the third layer and then moved to the fourth.

"A fourth layer is a place of good and light; it hovers above the previous layers but sits below them. You have to go down to get up. Finally, the last layer is a place of darkness and hate. It is basically hell, but hell is not a realm; it is a place, just as heaven is a place. These two realms are a holding spot for souls."

Kal stared at him. "To better show you how the realms are intertwined," Sallisfer turned the page, and a funnel-like shape popped out at them. Kal saw the familiar outline of the Ranch at once, and she gazed at it where it sat at the crease of the funnel linking all the realms together.

Sallisfer nodded as realization formed in Kal's eyes. "Yes, the Ranch is on the crack between the realms. This land has been many things before Doctor Molly found it and turned it into his family's home. If he knew that the four hundred acres he bought were going to be so crucial, I don't know…. But, when he expanded and took the responsibility of the peace point, I believe it occurred to him."

Kal stared at the ranch on the map, unnerved. "Do lots of bad things happen there?"

Sallisfer laughed and placed a green peg on the place where the ranch sat.

"I can't remember anything bad happening there because of the crack. It makes moving between the realms easy; sometimes, you don't even know you have done so. Like the field with the practice dummies, it sits here in the magical kingdom, yet you cross a dam beside a man-made lake, and there you are." He placed a white peg at the spot, and Kal could just make out the word Cavalry's Plaza.

"But bad things can happen there because of the crack?"

"Well, yes, bad things can happen anywhere at any place, time, or realm," Sallisfer said, rubbing his neck with his free hand. "I guess what you mean to ask is, how are you protected by the changing of the realms? It is the headmaster, of course, and the power of the Earth family. Brown wizards have a way of protecting their own land, which is hard to overcome." Kal nodded, although she was still a little dumbfounded.

"Can the crack be used for evil?"

"If it falls into the wrong hands, I guess. However, Valerie, as a Brown Sorceress and succeeding apprentice to the land, took care of it falling into the wrong hands."

"How? When?"

"When her grandfather died, he left his land between his four children. It was the wish of his late wife to not choose a successor but to be fair among the children. Well, Dr. Molly left the Ranch part, the calvary, the horses, and the land for the horses, which includes the peace fence, to Ms. Wing because she is the true successor. Ms. Wing was the only one of the four children to have the magic and know how to run the ranch safely and carry on the family traditions. He divided the last of his land among the three eldest children. One had inherited the forest, and Valerie's eldest aunt proved to be a green witch who knew plants and much more than animals. She was happy with her part and built a house on it. Making a deal with Ms. Wing to use the land as needed for the horses as the land had always been used. The second daughter got a house and a portion of the land by the river where her cabin sat. She was a free spirit, and Dr. Molly wanted her to feel like she had a place to call her own if she drifted back this way. The son got a small plot of land and a share of his father's wealth. He had no magical abilities and had to live under close surveillance in case he revealed the magic realm.

Well, you can guess that the second daughter and the son did not like what their father had left them. They devised a plan so nasty that it led to a civil war and nearly wiped out the magic community we know."

Kal stared. "The civil war that you and Valerie fought in?"

"Yes, we were just named Masters. Neither of us knew the horrors of war, just the notion and feeling of it from our past lives. The horror was even more magnified when you fight your own people."

"The man who came in here on my first day," Kal recalled, "the Tarhunna guy, was he a part of the Civil War?"

Sallisfer pulled out the deck of cards he kept on him and revealed the man who had attacked Kal only last month. "Yes, this man, he is or was Valerie's uncle. He was married to the second aunt, Valentina. They threatened to take everything away from the Wings. They turned their life into a hell storm, and each time they recovered, another sledgehammer would fall. That year and the next two were tough, and Valerie's mother almost had to stand alone for most of it because Mr. Wing had to fight and train the defenders. It was the last year he took on a student and a military role. It hasn't kept him more at home, but it has allowed him to be more of a husband and a father."

"How did it all work out? Obviously, y'all won?"

"Valerie got in touch with Pegasus. She pledged herself to him if he would send an army to help turn the tide of the war. It worked, but the war cost us many people, resources, magic, and time to prepare for a greater war... we are at a disadvantage with the one we are about to face."

Kal looked at Sallisfer, "What is this war we are heading into truly about? Why is it even happening? Haven't Demons and Earth Children co-existed for millions of years?"

"Not exactly co-existed, but yes, Demons and Earth Children have lived with each other and accepted one another since the dawning of time."

"Then why have a war?"

"To answer that, you must learn about the prophecy that started the hatred and loathing the demons have for our people. It started when the first humans began to emerge and the fear of any being who carried the magical art."

"So... what is the prophecy? What is it about?"

Sallisfer looked at Kal for a long time, "I am not sure I can give you all the answers you want and need at this time because I am still figuring it all out myself. However, it is about you. You are the chosen one, the awaited one."

Kal stared at him dumbfounded. "I have heard that term used about me since I stepped into this *Realm*. What does it even mean?"

"It means your birth was foretold when the realms split apart, and our people went into hiding."

"How do you know it is me?"

Sallisfer reached over and touched the necklace Kal wore now around her neck always, it was warm against her chest, and his cold hand magnified its warmth, making it feel hot and seem to hum.

"The wolf," she whispered as if she had always known.

"Yes," Sallisfer breathed, taking the book with his free hand and placing it on the floor beside Kal. "The demons will fall to their knees. When the wolf who once lived arrives again, they will submit, alive, and the wolf will erase them from time."

"When this necklace was crafted, it was the only one like it. It was crafted by a blind foreseer. Each time an earth child is born, a special gem falls into her hand, and she knows just the right necklace to bind it to. This gem cannot be broken and can be filled with the greatest secret only known to those that wear one. It can hold extra power, so in times of darkness, when you are all out of strength, you can pull on the power. It refreshes and charges you back to full strength."

Sallisfer was kissing Kal now, and she held tight to him for dear life, her mind spinning. "You want to know how we knew you had been born but not to whom? This necklace you are wearing," Sallisfer breathed, twirling it in his fingers, "Appeared the same day as Valerie and mine did in the pockets of the late Hands. The day you should have started school if your mother hadn't hidden you. We knew then that we must find you. When Valerie became a Master, this necklace appeared in her pocket, and she carried it with her everywhere, hoping it would reveal the chosen one...."

Both Sallisfer and Kal were covered in sweat now, "And it did." Valerie said, making Sallisfer and Kal jump apart as if they had been burned. Kal looked around, astonished, as she recognized that she was no longer at the library but in Sallisfer's room. Then she realized she had no shirt, and neither did Sallisfer, who quickly looked away guilty.

"Your idea to pass the teaching of the chosen one to the Hand of Heaven might not have been the best idea." Valerie spat at him. Kal saw that Valerie was covered in snow. "I figured that at least the idea of Kal being my sister would spare her from your lust, unlike Ava."

"You were going to teach me?"

"Yes, the old hands always teach the new hands. But with you being a member of my family, I didn't want to explain why I was 'playing favorites,' so I argued with the headmaster to swap the necklaces, knowing Sal and I would co-teach you anyway."

Kal blinked, pulling on a shirt she found on the bed. Now it made sense to Kal as she reminisced about the day of the choices. She looked at Valerie, who was still fuming, then to Sallisfer, who would no longer look her in the eye. A question burned in Kal's mind, but she didn't dare share it. "I better be going to bed," Kal said, as she found it was getting harder and harder to stand there in silence with her eyes open.

"Yes, you better. Mother expects us to be home by 5:30 when she wakes us up for school like normal. However, school is closed due to weather which means more work in the barn." Valerie stated. She looked at Kal and said sarcastically, "Welcome to the family." Then she looked at Sallisfer. "I expect you to be ready in half an hour. We have to go, and in this weather, I am flying, so you better be on time, or I am leaving your sorry arse."

Sallisfer stared at Valerie, and all the color drained from his face. Kal could tell he was replaying the time Valerie left without him. She wondered what he had done and longed to dive into his thought. As Valerie turned to leave, Kal realized she had no way home, and Valerie didn't offer to help her. She looked at Sallisfer and saw he was already dressed in a gray jumpsuit with blue goggles on the top of his head. He was packing some things in a bag, "Sooo… where are you going?"

Sallisfer sighed, counting out some bandages. She saw there were canteens, packaged food, and changes of clothes. "We are going on another preventative strike. We are working on prolonging the war as long as possible. The longer we prolong the war, the longer we have to prepare our troops, find, collect, move resources, and train you. You have so much to learn." He stopped and looked at her; his blue eyes shined as he reached out with his hand and stroked her cheek. "I will personally make sure you learn everything you need to become a master."

Kal placed her hand on his; she felt small, and the fact that her hand was so small on his didn't help. "You are destined for greatness. Big things come in small packages." He kissed her slow and sweet, then vanished.

Kal stood there, unsure of what to do next, then a tiny knock was at the door. Kal walked over and opened it a crack; there stood Kris. "Sallisfer just left," she explained.

Kris laughed. "I know. I am here to get you home…. Unless you are going to sleep here tonight, I can come for you in the morning." Kal looked at him and was about to say that was a good idea; then she saw he had bandages on his left arm, which hung in a sling.

"What…"

"It is a long story, and Master Valerie doesn't know yet…I have been avoiding her for a few days now… I don't heal as fast as Sallisfer…. especially when growing new skin and muscles."

Kal was out of the room in a nanosecond and took Kris's good arm in hers, "Tell me what happened?"

"Well, you remember the other day when Valerie went out on her own," Kal nodded, "um…I kind of took things into my own hands to prevent a demon ambush."

Kris said the last part relatively fast and mumbled it together. Kal stopped walking, and Kris came to an immediate halt and looked back at her astonished face.

"You took on a demon ambush by yourself to save Valerie?"

"I' d do anything to save Master Valerie. If I could go with her to fight the demons now, I would, or hell, I'd even trade places… she can be quite a handful and is hard to predict even with my time ability. She takes reckless risks and charges into things head first without think-ing. Still, the amount of fear she hides behind her confidence and cold demeanor," Kris shivered. "She is her hardest critic."

Kal could only stare at him, even more speechless than before. Kris looked back puzzled, his forehead all wrinkled up with his perfectly shaped eyebrows threatened to become a unibrow. "Why are you so surprised? The Hand of Doom needs a guardian angel too."

"What is the Hand of Heaven then?"

"Sallisfer?" The hostility in his voice and the anger that changed his face made him very frightening.

"It should have been me paired with Valerie… but the spirit didn't choose me this go around." He looked at Kal with a new look of interest on his face. "You know we are the next in line, right?"

"The next in line for what?"

"You and me… like, better than Master Sallisfer and Master Valerie. You and I will go off on missions; we will have the power of the universe, life, and death. We will be Doom and Heaven." Kal pulled away from Kris shaking her head and walking away as quickly as she dared backwards. Her head was pounding. Yes, she knew she would be next but didn't realize she would be with Kris. It did make sense, she guessed, but why couldn't she have been paired with Sallisfer. How did she become next? When would that happen…? If Valerie and Sallisfer knew she would take over, why were they so keen on teaching her? They seemed to enjoy what they did… just not each other. Suddenly she tripped over her own feet, slid back into the wall trying to catch herself, and fell down on her bottom.

"Are you ready to go home now?" Kris said with a genuine smile as he looked down at her and offered her a hand up.

"No, you can leave me here to rot."

Kris laughed and grabbed her hand, pulling her up on her feet and brushing her off. Then in a whirlwind, they were standing in the yard of the small yellow house at the Ranch. "I have got to learn how to do that?" Kal breathed as Kris released her hands.

"I can teach you how… if you want."

"Are you allowed?"

Kris laughed again. "We will be learning from each other for a long time. So why not start now, partner?"

***

Kal was replaying the night in her head when the house trembled, and the lights flashed intermittently. She jumped up, thinking the house was under attack. She ran into the living room only to find Valerie standing in the middle of the room, covered in a black fog, her mother and father standing there talking in a calming jumble.

"Valerie darling, you must be exhausted." Ms. Wing said, "Come on, we have some milk, get a shower."

Just then, Ms. Wing saw Kal standing there watching. "Kalea honey, Valerie is just having a moment… go back to bed."

The house shook again, and Koda opened his door slightly to see Kal. "Come on, Kal… Dad will convince Mom to call Sallisfer. It will not be long." He whispered. Kal stepped back a few steps to Koda's room when the darkness deepened and spread throughout the house. Kal stopped and stared. Black wings spread from Valerie's back, and sharp horns protruded from her head. She looked beyond terrifying. Valerie's dad ran at her, speaking in a commanding voice and waving his left hand around. Valerie laughed, and he flew backward into the entertainment center, crashing the television on the floor and crushing him to the ground with a yell.

Valerie laughed again, then white wings wrapped her in a glowing embrace, there was a sigh, and the darkness cleared. Ms. Wing ran to her husband, who was pulling himself up, cussing loudly and looking madder than a hornet. He pushed his wife away with, "I am fine, woman; leave me alone." He snapped his fingers and glowed with a gold sheen; the television and the entertainment center repaired and righted themselves.

He then turned to the Hands. Sallisfer held the sleeping Valerie in his arms and looked as if he was about to pass out himself. "I want an explanation in thirty minutes." Mr. Wing yelled, storming off to the bathroom with his wife staring after him.

CHAPTER 20

Decisions

Since Kris's promotion, Kris took Kal everywhere, letting her know…"You need to learn the aspects of our realm. The ins and outs of the political, social, spiritual, and community of the society you are going to lead."

However, the other masters were not pleased with the unorthodox method of teaching, but they dared not argue with the Hands when they approved the request. So, Kal was shoved from lessons to meetings to the library to be drilled in bookwork, "By the end of the month, you will be ready to take the lower master exam." Kris promised, "You will then get a single star like me."

Kal had learned how to teleport. Although she was not very good at it, she could move from point A to point B down a hallway. Kris had helped her build her animal totem pole, and Kal could transform into a wolf, a lioness, a horse, a small house cat, and a bird. Kris walked her through miner fighting drills while Valerie popped in to guide and instruct while observing.

It became so commonplace that, during Time training with the Master, Valerie appeared smiling in the middle of a lesson; she excused Kal from the Master, who didn't seem surprised. Val took Kal up to the field and ran Kal and Ava through a workout and seemed pleased with the results. Ava, Kal noticed, had significantly improved as well, she stayed at Valerie's heels, and it was rumored she had been accepted into the Cavalry while Kal was stuck in the infantry, at least in practice. The only thing Kal had over Ava was the fact she went to war meetings, but those were not as exciting as riding a horse.

Kal didn't see much of Sallisfer during the day. His double was at school while he manned the infantry. However, at night they would meet in the halls of the Academy. Sallisfer would sweep her off her feet and carry her to her room, where they would cuddle and talk about her magic and school lessons. He would answer any questions she had.

"When will you be able to come back to school? I miss you?" she asked, looking up at him as he smiled down at her in his arms.

Sallisfer squeezed her tight. "I miss seeing you during the day. Tomorrow, we have a meeting to discuss a turning point. I may not be needed once we make this decision. I hope to have your vote on the matter."

Kal was puzzled for a second. "What is the turning point?"

"I can't tell you the details, Valerie, and I will reveal them to everyone," Sallisfer assured her.

***

The next day, Kal entered the meeting late, and it had already begun. "I think this is pointless. We already told you we aren't going to do it," Valerie said to the people gathered. Kal took her seat beside Kris.

"What did I miss?" she whispered.

"Not much. The conference is trying to force Master Valerie and Master Sallisfer to completely merge. They found an old book in the time's hall mentioning it -read this right here," Kris said, pulling an old black leather-bound book turned to a page; it looked like the one Sallisfer had in his desk drawer but considerably older.

She looked at its old yellowed pages and read the hand-printed ink.

March 14, 500 AD

Today Doom and I merged completely. The war still rages on between us and the humans, but we put a dent in them, and I believe they will think twice before trying to attack Castle Starlight again.

Jessy is still very weak from the merge, but they say she'll recover, compared to our son James. I have tried to heal him, we both have, but his heart is broken, he had a secret love with the humans, and now that she knows he's not human and that he's earth, she has doomed him to a slow and painful death.

Write tomorrow,

Inti Dean Sallvers.

Kal swallowed hard; she noticed that the room had grown quiet, and she felt all eyes on her. She looked up from the page.

"What do you think? A little of your past." Master Sing said gruffly, but the humor was in his voice.

"I don't know what to think," Kal admitted.

"Do you think we should completely merge?" Valerie asked carefully. Kal looked at her and could have sworn she saw fear flash across the emerald green surface Valerie had for eyes, but it was gone so fast that even Kal doubted her own senses.

She looked down at the page, desperately wishing she could go back in time to ask this Sallvers guy questions. She closed her eyes, trying to pull on that magic, but it was so unpredictable, and she had not learned to control it yet, although she was getting better at feeling the time pull. Finally, with a sigh, she opened her eyes and looked around at all the awaiting faces of those gathered.

Sallisfer looked eager and almost too willing to do the merge, Kal noted with some inward disgust. She thought *this must be the turning point he was talking about* as she looked at Valerie, who looked cautious and uncertain. "What will you be doing if you completely merge?"

"We will make a dent in demon forces," Sallisfer explained.

Finally, Kal licked her lips and said the only thing she could say; "I don't see anything stopping ya'll. Besides the side effects of being weak, I don't see what's wrong with it."

Sallisfer and Valerie glanced at each other, seeming not to believe her, "So if we were to completely merge, you would support us?" Sallisfer said slowly.

"No matter what?" Valerie added even more slowly as she looked at her with almost a pleading fearful look that, too, disappeared under her mask.

"Yes, why wouldn't I, Masters?" Kal asked.

Relief showed on both of their faces, "I don't know, we just wanted to know. Thank you," Valerie said with an almost forced smile.

"Looks like we're in," Sallisfer grinned, making Kal feel uncomfortable and wonder what she had just agreed to.

"Good, talk to the headmaster, and we'll get the war on its way," Master Masashi said with a smile, standing up to leave.

"We have one more thing to discuss before we end this." Valerie declared.

Master Masashi sat back down, "Sorry, Miss." He apologized. Valerie smiled forgivingly at him as she cleared her throat and stood. She walked to the chalkboard and pulled down a large calendar. "Master Sallisfer and I have been talking, and we wish to stay out of the war if this plan works to slow down the enemy. So, we will join again after Valentine's Day, on the 14th. Today is the 8th, so it isn't that long away." She pointed to the date. The other masters mumbled under their breaths and wiggled uncomfortably in their seats.

"Has the Headmaster cleared this?" Master Masashi asked what the others were thinking.

"Yes, the headmaster has already granted our wish." Sallisfer said, standing up, "He also promoted us; for now on, you will address us as General Valerie and General Sallisfer."

"Congratulations, Generals." Master Tony said, rubbing his long red beard, "When will we all get promotions?"

Valerie laughed, "Well, you can always join the fighters. They give promotions over masters regularly. I am sorry our system does not fit you, Master Tony."

"No, no, it fits fine, Miss. I am still trying to get my gold star to refine the new master's skills and not teach new ones so often. But I also know it will call me out to the fields more, and I'm not too fond of that idea either. I am not a fighting man, Miss. I am a humble farming man."

Valerie smiled, "We also need to talk about promotions with our more experienced students. If your experienced students are ready for the next level, please submit them for testing by this time Wednesday before the ball. The more younger masters we have, the more students can be taught, and the older masters can move on, which means more soldiers we can make. Also, for those students who are not in the power range for combat, we need to discover and refine their true abilities, armor making, weapon construction, farming, resource moving, cooking, medical, and so on." The others nodded around as Kal felt herself go cold with worry. This was a real full-fledged war that was about to take place.

"We would like to start the promotions by naming our top student Master." Valerie smiled, walking over and laying her hands on Kal's shoulders. "We gave Kal the test yesterday, and although Kalea has not been part of our world long, her skills have come in leaps and bounds, and we will continue to train and teach her and her partner. We feel like she is ready to join us as full-fledged Masters."

"Congratulations, Master Kalea," Sallisfer said with a nod to Kal as a blue star appeared on her collar and cuff. She was now a low-rank master, but she was still a master. The alliance members nodded at them in agreement and congratulated her with smiles, handshakes, and pats on the back.

"We have been informed that our next strike will be at the railway," Sallisfer said, pulling a map over the calendar. The map always enraptured Kal's attention. It was rich in color and textures. It could spread out and become a table or expand like wallpaper and cover a wall making it easier to set pawns on or flags. "The railway station is where they are holding all the main troops and equipment."

The railway and its station appeared on the map in great detail. "We scouted the area these last two nights. It houses thousands of Demons." Valerie turned with an unpleasant look on her face. "It is also a breeding ground for hell hounds." A gasp went up among the masters as they understood the threat. "If our strike goes as planned." She looked at Sallisfer. "We will hold off the main war for maybe a month…" she trailed, "…We must use that time wisely no matter how much time it buys us."

The masters nodded. "Are there going to be army backup?" Master Masashi asked, "If not, I would gladly volunteer my division."

Valerie smiled. "There is no need for the army. With our merging, we will be a whole army…."

Master Masashi nodded. "Yes, General."

"Now it is over," General Valerie said with a smile. "You are all dismissed." The members jumped up and filed out of the room.

Valerie sighed and slumped in her chair. She smiled at Kal, who was too shocked to move.

"I must say, Heaven, that you did a good job shutting Kal up," Valerie said. Sallisfer laughed.

"I dare say I did Doom," he said, looking at Valerie with a wry smile. "Think we should wake her?"

"Na, leave her," Valerie said, getting up and walking out of the room, followed by Sallisfer. Who was muttering protests that were echoed by Kris, who had gotten up to go after them but stopped and looked back at Kal.

"Mmmmaster?" Kal said.

"Yes," Kris smiled at her, and she suddenly smiled back as she observed him.

"We are both masters now," Kal said, excitement raising through her veins.

"Finally," Kris smiled, then he suddenly looked at Kal, who was grinning. "You only got a month at being a student. How's that fair?"

"Na' ah, it was a month and seven days as a student," Kal said with the biggest grin on her face that she had ever had in her life.

CHAPTER 21

Last Stand

Valerie stood with Sallisfer facing the railway, "Let's get this over with," she said, trying to stuff the fear she had in a box. Sallisfer nodded, looking grim-faced now that it was time to merge. Sallisfer inwardly was having second thoughts; as he looked into the green eyes that now faced him, he was overwhelmed by emotions. They had only merged in spirit and mind, never into one body. He wasn't even sure how it worked, only what they had read. He looked at Valerie, and knowing his inner turmoil was getting the best of him, he had to be honest with her. His doubt won as he spoke…

"Valerie, if you do not want to do this…" Her finger touched his lips. Valerie had come to terms regardless of the implications. Her resolve solidified his doubt, and the foundation was set, MERGE.

The green in her eyes was gone, replaced by black swirls of power. Valerie was gone, and Doom was in her body. At once, Heaven rushed to meet Doom. With a breath, Doom stood on tiptoes and wrapped her arms around his neck. Their lips touched; they kissed for a moment, then her tongue traced his lips; he allowed entry, and then he was inside her skin within the action of a single heartbeat.

One body was a tight fit for Sallisfer and Valerie, and their struggle to occupy one space created a mini-war almost to the point of separating. However, through understanding and finding their individuality with the merge, Heaven and Doom found the space needed and continued their mission to the railway station.

Doom harnessed the energy of both Heaven and the host that the spirit possessed. As they approached, the station alarms went off, the Demon warriors assembled, and Doom snickered. Then, in a rush, fire laced with Doom's spirit snaked down the line destroying in hungry waves everything in its path. The snake entered the station wiping out the demons before they could even defend themselves. The snake was entangled with Valerie and Sallisfer's spirit, raging its way around the station. The Hell Hound puppies were hairless and barely had their eyes open, but no mercy was shown to them or their parents. Only a few months were needed to make them into killing monsters. The fire rushed around, destroying everything. Then the fire snake hit a door that barely crumbled; it preceded with caution, slowly moving, using the fingers of the flame to kill every living thing in that room.

When they entered, they discovered a horrible sight. Inside the room were small metal tanks. Doom touched the barbaric crafts, and the pain that filled her hand upon contact with the cool mechanical device told her they were remote-controlled. Doom tried to destroy them, but they burned and weakened her. They were the ultimate weapons. Valerie separated from Sallisfer, a plan coming to her head; she pulled a backpack from her mind that she kept just in case. Sallisfer saw the mark on the bag and felt the plan she was forming. Once installed, Valerie was going to send him away in an attempt to save him from being blown apart. He put his hand on hers as she opened the bag of human bombs. "Still fighting fire with fire, he smiled. "I'm in this till the end."

She nodded; Sallisfer put on his gloves and touched the devices as carefully as a child. He helped Valerie place one on each device. Then, for good measure, Valerie pulled a more significant, more dangerous device from the bag, which astonished Sallisfer as she set it up with expert skill. "How often have you done this?" he asked, pointing to the device.

Valerie smiled at him, "I trained myself under the Headmaster's watchful eye. He feared they were up to something like this." Her eyes wandered around the hundreds upon hundreds of deadly metal tanks. She just hoped they had not had the opportunity to ship any out. Finally, with a sigh, she stood and allowed Doom to take back over. They would have to light the room at just the right moment; they had a train to destroy.

Heaven and Doom kissed, and once more, they were inside one body. This time there was no struggle; they knew just what to do. The fire snake formed again, and they were off waiting for the right moment as they listened to the train's distant horn and heard the building rattling as it got closer. Sallisfer and Heaven clung to Doom as she tried to shake them off. "If we go down, we go down together," Heaven said. Doom smiled, and he felt the fight stop and the coil like a cat about to explode. With powers combined, they went in for the kill. Flames engulfed the place, and the bombs went off. A mushroom cloud went up into the sky, held in by a shield created by the Hand's magic to contain the explosion. The force of the blast went upward, with most of the shrapnel and much of the debris being contained within the magic shield. Yet, some of the shrapnel made it over the shield's rim and landed in a field also created by the Hands simultaneously.

Without any means to expand, the powerful yet confined explosion dropped straight to the ground. Its force evaporated any evidence that a train station was ever in existence.

***

The werecat-looking beast stood on the outskirts watching the scenario. When it stopped, Valerie slipped out of Sallisfer and sank to the ground.

Sallisfer stood in shock; there were no more secrets between them, and the wall they had built was gone because of the merging. He knew everything she knew, everything she had tried to keep from him over the past year. Finally, things were starting to click into place. It took him a while to notice that his heart was beating at a slower pace and not because the adrenalin was waning. He looked down and saw Valerie hadn't moved. She lay with her face down in the mud where she had fallen. "No," he whispered, falling to his knees; he rolled her over and checked for breath, pulse, and a heartbeat, but there was nothing. He frantically started CPR, knowing he only had moments to live to save their lives. "Come on," he gasped, waiting for a sign of life. As his heart started to slow, he breathed another breath, and Valerie's heart gave a start, and her breath rushed out with a cough. She lay there, her blond hair streaming out behind her on the ground within a puddle, reflecting the fiery flashing water as it mirrored the scene around them. They had known this would exhaust them, so they had left two trusted people at the rendezvous point to help transport them home. At his current state, Sallisfer would be lucky to make it, but carrying both of them, he may make it halfway. He lay down on the moist, muddy ground beside Valerie's unconscious form and took her into his arms. "We have to try," he said, kissing her cold cheek. "We may die yet, but not here." He closed his eyes and envisioned where they had left Walker and Tema.

He saw himself there safely with Valerie in his arms. He pulled the last of his strength, let a prayer slip from his lips, and allowed himself to fall through space. Sallisfer hit hard on the ground with a loud wet thump and a sickening crack. Lights flashed in his eyes, and it was hard to breathe for a moment. Then, the ringing in his ears quit as he heard shouting and the movements of horses and men. Sallisfer had no idea if this was the enemy or his people; he pulled on his magic, attempting to teleport again, but nothing happened. He was stuck, and panic flooded his inner being as he thought of himself and Valerie. Voices got closer and disappeared just as fast as he heard them. Finally, the grim face of Master Masashi appeared; his slanted eyes stared down at Sallisfer. "I guess you didn't need our help after all," he said.

There was rustling next to him, which alerted his senses- someone was at his side. But his mind negated it as he thought of Valerie. "Valerie," Sallisfer croaked out.

"She is alive… just barely… you two gave us quite a scare being two hours late and then a massive explosion." Walker said, reaching out to take Valerie but recoiled his hand as it became red and blistered with a second-degree burn. "What the?"

Sallisfer held tighter to Valerie, coiling his body protectively around hers.

"You must let go so we can help," Tema said, healing Walker's hand as she stared down at her leader, who was reduced to a shell. Tema doubted that Sallisfer knew that he and Valerie were bleeding from multiple wounds and that although Valerie breathed, it was labored.

"She must go..." blood trickled from his mouth, and he was starting to go into shock. Instincts took over Tema, ignoring the blisters she received, as she uncoiled Sallisfer's snake-like body from Valerie's and called for backup. Walker and Tema performed field medicine on the duo while screams of demon rage could be heard at the railway station and moving closer to their location.

"We are going to have to move." Master Masashi said, arranging his troops into defense mode. "The Demons may have lost a lot tonight, but that makes them more dangerous."

Tema looked at Walker. "Sallisfer has a broken spine. I need a gurney or something to support him."

"We don't have time." Master Masashi said, seeing the flashlights of the enemy searching for them. "Place them into the wagon. Make sure they remain touching. We must get them to Nurse Keasen, who is waiting for them at the ranch."

Tema nodded reluctantly. "If only we had brought someone who could teleport them both to safety at the same time." She hissed as they carefully picked them up, making Sallisfer scream in pain. "Next time, we are bringing another King, or damn, if the Headmaster got off his throne and helped his own people, he could teleport us all out of here."

Walker put his hand on his wife's shoulder as she climbed into the wagon beside the Hands. "We know for next time. Let's get them to the portal."

Once in the wagon, they moved out to find a safer point to stop. Inside the wagon, Tema continued to perform field medicine. She was a healer and the leader of the light cavalry and used all her healing skills and medical swabs to save the Hand's life. Tema started by removing shrapnel and cleaning them with the alcohol she carried in her medical bag. She repeatedly apologized as tears and sweat fell down her face with every scream of agony that bellowed from Sallisfer. His tired body was trying to heal itself. Unfortunately, she was forced to open cuts and clean them before they healed, and when they did, it was with a faster, thicker scab than normal. Tema worried about Valerie, who didn't utter a sound and was not even attempting to heal herself. There was no sign of life besides the uneven breaths and her heart's sporadic, irregular rhythm.

"She is all tapped out." Tema panicked to Walker, who rode beside the wagon leading Tema's mount.

"Merging took too much of her power and energy." Walker speculated, "Instead, focus on stabilizing the breathing. I think I have an idea to stabilize the heartbeat, but it's risky."

Tema looked up at her beloved, guessing at his plan, "You may be a genius, love." She said she worked faster and stabilized Valerie. Then when they found a safe place to rest, she, with Master Masashi, hoisted Valerie's motionless body into the saddle in front of Walker.

Walker wrapped his arms around Valerie and looked down at Tema, "I will meet you at the ranch." He leaned down and kissed her lips, they tethered Tema's mount to the wagon, and Walker rode off with three Cavalrymen as protection.

"This may not be Sorrow." Walker whispered, nudging his bay into the canter, "But old Captain has the smoothest gate around." Holding Valerie stable in front of him, he and his fellow riders aimed for a gate to the next realm. As they rode, he felt Valerie's heartbeat strengthen and align with the horse's gate. Her heart rhythm stabilized, her breath stopped coming out in gasps, and she sighed. A little bit of color returned to her ashen face, and Walker knew it had been worth the risk of separating her from Sallisfer. Finally, they made it to the gate and jumped through, transporting them all to the end of the road that led to the ranch.

Nurse Keasen met them at the driveway. She stepped from a makeshift tent she had occupied while waiting. The dawn lit the sky full of color, and Walker knew they were beyond hours late. Nevertheless, nurse Keasen moved expertly and didn't ask questions. As she followed Walker to the house, Ms. Wing rushed out, followed by Mr. Wing and Kal. Kris ran up the driveway soon after. When he shifted Valerie down to them, Walker was surprised to see burn marks on his armor.

"Be very careful…" he said. Kris moved forward in a surge, took Valerie, not noticing the steam that rose from his hands, and carried her into the house where a bed and Nurse Keasen waited for them. They followed her and discovered that Valerie was now cool to the touch once Kris had put her down and that he was unharmed.

Nurse Krasen had become the Hand's primary caretaker since her little sister had become Valerie's student. Nurse Krasen moved at an astounding speed. She removed and cleaned the rest of the wounds and administered I.V. fluids. Then, with Ms. Wing's help, she replaced the gray jumpsuit Valerie had been wearing with a makeshift hospital gown.

A few hours later, Sallisfer and the rest of Master Masashi's army arrived at the door. Mr. Wing welcomed them in and fed them a meal made for heroes. Sallisfer was relatively conscious when they arrived. He was half man and half snake with no strength to shift back to 'normal.' His clothes hung in tatters, and his broken spine fused wrong, paining him greatly. Kris again seemed to know just what to do. Much to the dazed and silent crowd around them, he smiled at Kal and walked to Sallisfer, who looked just as astonished. "Old friend," he said, "It seems you have found yourself in quite a predicament." He reached out a hand, and Sallisfer hesitantly took it. At once, a white glow formed around them and disappeared. Sallisfer stood looking tired, but his body was whole and radiated with life.

"Thank you," he breathed to Kris, who nodded. Sallisfer walked to her room, and he stood and looked at Valerie, who was now hooked up to monitors. He felt the cold chill of the Headmaster entering the room unseen. The Headmaster had the same question he did, 'with Valerie this weak would Doom take over… was there magic left, or would she have to start a new one on her sixteenth birthday?' Sallisfer reached over and touched Valerie's forehead. Heaven's fingers went in, branched out, and found an empty space; there were no thoughts or emotions, just nothingness.

Frightened, Heaven pulled back and was forced by the eyes of the Headmaster to try again; Heaven reached into the mind once more and traveled the empty halls to three doors. Heaven pressed his hand against each door. Inside one, he felt the purr of Doom, who slumbered with all energy spent. At the second door, he felt the familiar presence that was not Valerie but another she carried inside. Heaven was half tempted to open the door. Knowing that door led to a stronger Heaven, the Headmaster urged him to open that door, but Heaven refused. Now that he knew what Valerie knew, he could not argue with her reasoning for weakening Heaven. Finally, he felt the third door, and there she was, slumbering inside. She was tired his Valerie. She had worked so hard. He took a breath and cracked the door open she did not rush forth; she simply slumbered on. Heaven opened the door fully and left it open. "Let her rest," he told the others when he slipped out of her mind. "She will wake when she is ready." The Headmaster, annoyed, quietly left as he had arrived.

"When will that be?" Kal asked, taking Sallisfer's hand as he looked like he was about to collapse from exhaustion.

"I don't know." He admitted allowing Kal to take him to the couch to sit down.

"A guard and a caretaker will be posted at her side at all times," Walker said. "We will see to the arrangements. We will also post a guard on you… without your other half, you will be vulnerable, General." Sallisfer nodded, and Walker bowed to Mr. and Mrs. Wing and thanked them for the meal. He then left with his crew to the barn to meet and make arrangements.

It irked Kal that Walker had called Valerie Sallisfer's other half, and she wrapped an arm around him as he sipped a cup of cold chocolate milk that Ms. Wing had handed him. He leaned into Kal, and she purred against him, making him smile. He sipped his milk till it was gone, and Ms. Wing handed him a bowl of soup which Sallisfer drank greedily, slurping it down.

"Slow down, or you're going to be sick." Kal chastised, and Sallisfer reluctantly agreed. Once that was done, he rested his head against Kal and closed his eyes.

"You should get home." Mr. Wing said, seeing that Sallisfer had finished the bowl of soup. "Your mother is worried." He reached down and helped Sallisfer up, "I will help you." again, all Sallisfer could do was nod. Mr. Wing helped Sallisfer out the door, down the driveway, and teleport home.

As soon as the army left, Ms. Wing went to Valerie's side and started to weep, "You must wake up. You must."

Kris took Kal's hand and led her numbly out the door, "Let's let her have her moment." he said softly, walking to the barn.

"How did you know what to do back there?" Kal asked.

"I grew up with the Hands. Been with them from the moment they were chosen. I could have easily been in Sallisfer's shoes... the spirit did not choose me. I later learned it is because Hands are supposed to be equal in powers, a time lord and brown sorceress... well, don't mix." He looked at Kal and squeezed her hand, pulling her to him and then away.

"It helps that we are related. We share some of the same power levels."

He then started to dance her around; tension was beginning to unravel in her as she allowed Kris to lead her in a dance. "Kalea Breese?" he asked. "Will you be my date to the Master's Valentine Ball?" Kal smiled at him. She felt the word yes leave her lips before she could even think about his question. Kris grinned and bowed to her. "It will be an honor to be your date."

Kal laughed as he swept her into a dance. There in the growing light of the day. It felt like there was nothing left to worry about now.

CHAPTER 22

Hope Dashed

Valerie opened her senses slowly; the first to respond was hearing; she could listen to the rhythmic beat of a heart monitor. Then touch responded to the cold liquid that dripped into her arm. Next, her mouth was dry, and she craved some chocolate milk. Lastly, her eyes opened and blinked to clear the bright haze of the sunlit room. Someone moved, and a familiar face appeared in her sight, looking down at her with a smile. "You had us all worried, missy," the woman said, her white-blond hair shined with glitter that sparkled and fell with each blink of her hazel eyes.

"Arcy," Valerie croaked. Arcy smiled and opened a carton of chocolate milk they had kept in Blaze's fridge. Arcy put a straw into the carton and allowed Valerie to sip it.

"How long have I been out?" Valerie asked as she finished the carton, feeling a little stronger.

The look in Arcy's eyes belied the calmness of her manner. "Three days," Arcy said. "Three powerless days."

Valerie paused, doing the math in her head. Then, she connected to Sallisfer in rising panic. He rushed mentally, holding her tight with relief, sharing his strength and bringing her up to date with what she had missed.

Valerie opened her eyes again in time to see Nurse Krasen enter the room. Nurse Krasen checked Valerie's vitals and said with a smile, "Let's get you unplugged and in the shower." She started to unhook Valerie from the IV and catheter. "We washed you as much as possible, but you still have mud and blood in your hair. I am sure you will feel worlds better for it too." Valerie nodded.

She allowed Arcy and Nurse Krasen to half lead and carry her to the house's only bathroom. There they sat her on the closed toilet while they put a stool in the shower and warmed the water. When Valerie got into the shower, the shock of the water on her upper shoulders made her gasp as images of what had happened three days ago flooded her mind. Then, as she allowed the water to fall on her and she started to relax, a question began nagging her inner thoughts.

"Did it work?" This question was not answered, even Sallisfer seemed to ignore her, and she was growing suspicious that their plan had gone awry. "Did it work?" She asked once again, power entering her voice.

"Perhaps you should wait to use magic till after you are clean." Nurse Krasen said in a loving commanding voice. "Sallisfer, as I am sure you know, will update you in person. He is bringing Kalea home after school."

Valerie fumed, but considering how tired she was, it kept her from arguing.

Valerie allowed Nurse Krasen to wash her and check her wounds; they were healing remarkably fast now that she was powered, and thanks to the swabs, they were not scarring.

Once out of the bath, Valerie relied on her nurse, who dried, dressed, and brushed her teeth. Finally, dressed in her own night clothes and her teeth clean, Valerie felt better. They walked to the bedroom to discover Arcy had flipped the mattress and changed the sheets. Valerie sunk gratefully back into bed.

A moment seemed to pass, and Valerie was awakened by Sallisfer entering the room. He leaned down and kissed her on the cheek. "How are you feeling?" he asked, searching Valerie's eyes.

"I want to know if our plan worked. Was this all worth it?"

Sallisfer sat on her bed and took her small hand in his, looking longingly at her. "Yes, it worked, but they have to regroup their defenses. They are fighting among themselves, trying to find the traitor who fed us their information."

Fear rushed into Valerie once more as she thought about Holjus; his dark red eyes were almost purple, his sideways smile made her heart flutter, and his shaggy long dark hair that sometimes hid his sexy white ram horns; Sallisfer knew who she was thinking of, for he could see it too in his mind.

"King Krishna has placed his brother, the snotty prince Holjus in charge of the investigation," Sallisfer stated loudly. Then, Arcy entered the room with two cups of chocolate milk, and relief flowed through Valerie like chocolate milk.

"So, what is going on?"

"The same night we destroyed the train station and most of the supplies, they attacked our allies, the Fairy Kingdome. As a result," Sallisfer said, "We are now at war."

"Why do I feel like there is more bad news?" Valerie asked.

"During the attack at the Fairy Kingdome, hundreds of men and women were injured… the master has ordered us to heal them."

Valerie spat out a sip of milk as it suddenly went sour in her mouth. "After he saw what merging did to us?" She asked ragefully, making her milk boil and her cup flame.

"You must control yourself," Sallisfer said soothingly, rubbing his hand over her arm; she took a breath and calmed herself. Sallisfer allowed her to finish his milk. "So, all hope is lost. We are at war?"

"Not all hope, babe." He smiled at her. "We have the chosen one. She will end the war soon enough."

"Where is Kal?"

"Helping your mother feed the horses, your mother was disappointed. She couldn't see you when you were awake earlier. But she was glad to see you charged and alive again… you really had us worried there."

Suddenly Valerie shivered with the cold chill of the Headmaster's arrival.

"You will go tonight." He commanded.

"Why can't Valerie rest?" Sallisfer protested.

"They are starting to die. We have to have soldiers; you will heal them." With that, the chill left, and the Headmaster was gone.

Valerie sagged, and Sallisfer pulled her into his lap. "We will be better prepared this time." Then, he whispered, "Sleep." Valerie allowed the darkness to consume her thoughts once more.

An hour later, Kal walked into the room she had shared with constant beeping and monitoring of her roommate. These last three days, she hadn't rested well, and it didn't help that Sallisfer had been distant and cold to her affections. She walked in and was stunned at once by the room's silence. All the monitors and cords were gone. Valerie sat in Sallisfer's lap, her eyes closed as he collected sparking power trails that were sprouting off Valerie's body like vines.

"Kal." Valerie smiled at her roommate's arrival, "How are you?"

"I was going to ask you the same thing," Kal said, sitting on her bed, not looking at them as Sallisfer started kissing Valerie up and down her neck. But, much to Kal's annoyance, Valerie didn't seem to notice or care.

"I am fine." Valerie said at last, "I should be powered to full soon…." She winced as a power surge flashed up her arm, red horns sprouted on Valerie's head, and her teeth became quite demon-like. "How was school? I bet I have a lot of homework to catch up on."

"I think Jane has done most of it…." Kal disclosed, looking away again. It had been hard these last three days at school too. Jane, Valerie's look alike, had been put into Valerie's place. Kal was under orders to act as naturally as possible to make the Demons think that what Valerie and Sallisfer did to their railway station hadn't affected them. To make the ruse more believable, Jane attended the training of Kal outside of the academy, and Kal had to admit she had learned quite a bit from the changeling.

Kal heard Valerie sigh. "We won't be able to stay here much longer," Sallisfer said. Kal looked over and saw white wings wrapped around Valerie, who now had black swirls in her eyes, and Kal wasn't sure Valerie could see past the smoke.

"Hold it off as long as you can, Sally. I need to talk to Kal." Valerie uttered, clearly in pain.

"I can hear you out later," Kal replied, worried for her friend, who was now shaking in Sallisfer's arms, embraced by wings.

"There may not be a later," Valerie growled through clenched teeth.

"Let Kal walk with us… you can tell her on the go." Sallisfer suggested as he stood cradling Valerie like a child in his arms. Then, with a nod, Sallisfer set a breakneck pace out the door and away from the house.

"Where are you going?" Kal asked, having to shift into a wolf to keep up.

"To the top of puff hill. It should be enough distance so Valerie doesn't hurt anyone."

"Kal," Valerie breathed, "I set you up with Gina to get tested on the next two levels on the 23rd. You have come so far, and I am so proud of you." She reached a thin arm out to Kal, and when it touched Kal, a spark of power shot into Kal, and Kal saw fireworks for a moment.

"All that you need to know on the written test is on the page," Valerie closed her eyes "14 in your book. I know you can do it… run any questions by Kris," again Valerie closed her eyes. "He will know." Sallisfer slowed for just a moment, and Kal transformed into herself. Valerie reached out and kissed Kal's forehead, and another small surge went through Valerie.

"You are powerful, and I have faith in you, Kal. See you at supper." With that, Sallisfer carried Valerie up the trail away from Kal, who stood still for several moments, processing what Valerie had told her.

Kal wasn't sure how long she had stood there, but a breeze that smelled of a mix of Valerie's perfume and Sallisfer's cologne washed past her in a rush. The smell made Kal gag, and then she vomited. Surely Valerie and Sallisfer were not back together again… they just couldn't be.

At supper, Sallisfer had gone home to eat with his parents. After that, it was just the five of them. Because of the instructions to introduce solids slowly, the whole family had Rainy Day Tomato Soup. Mr. Wing, being a gourmet chef, mixed grilled chicken and mushrooms into the soup to give it more zing and served it with grilled cheese sandwiches and sweet tea. Valerie just had soup and water, but she seemed content as she teased her little brother. He told the story of teleporting himself half into a room and half into the wall. His master, Master Kibwe, had to rescue him, and then Koda had to, of course, try again. Valerie laughed. "Did you get it, oh, wall splitter?"

"Yes, but only after I got stuck three more times." Koda laughed with his sister, not at all embarrassed. Valerie beamed at him, "Master Kibwe told me you had become quite a talented shifter when we played cards last week, but he refused to tell me all the things you can shift into."

Koda winked at his sister. "A great master reveals none of his secrets." This sent the whole family into a laughing fit, and Valerie, who had eaten just the top of her soup bowl, got up with a yawn.

"I must retire, oh, secret keeper." She rustled his hair after she bagged her soup. "Just remember there is no greater detective than that of a nosey sister." At that, Valerie smiled and headed to the restroom. When Kal was finished eating, Valerie was asleep in fresh pajamas, her thin leather Handbook with the pen still in it lying at her chin.

Sometime later, Valerie was awoken by Sallisfer, who silently helped her change into her jumper. They walked to the door. Just as they stepped outside, they saw Ms. Wing standing by Sallisfer's car. "Where do you think you are going?" she asked.

"Valerie is too weak to teleport, so I must take the car." Sallisfer said frantic, "We are not going anyplace dangerous."

"Taking my daughter out is dangerous. She is too weak to go anywhere, Sallisfer; she needs rest."

"Mother…" Valerie said, "We are under the Headmaster's orders. We will be back shortly. We have an emergency. People are dying, and we can heal them."

"Y'all are going to merge again?" Ms. Wing said, horrified. "The Headmaster wishes this? This nearly killed you."

"No, the Headmaster doesn't wish it! He demands this." Valerie hollered, "We cannot refuse the order."

"What will happen if you do?"

"We will die, and the spirits will move to the next host. You forget, Mother, that the next host was born roughly around the same time we were born. An occurrence that doesn't happen and has. We have been on borrowed time since Kalea joined the family. Now, Mother, please allow us to do our job. We will check back in with you first."

"Who is going with you?" Ms. Wing asked.

"We are meeting an army; I believe we are healing Master Fisher's and Master Nia's soldiers and perhaps the remaining army. We will be safe."

Ms. Wing sighed, hugged her daughter, and relented, moving away from the car and helping Valerie into it, "Be safe and come back to me in one piece this time."

"Yes, Mother, I love you."

"I love you too." Ms. Wing stepped away from the car and watched it leave, feeling lost and lonely.

"Well, that was different," Sallisfer mused as they drove down the road to the portal into the different realm. "Your mother seems much more caring about this than mine."

"Your mother accepted her only child's fate. Unfortunately, my mother hasn't accepted my fate. Not for the heir to the ranch and the care of all that is on it." Valerie admitted, staring out the window.

"So, neither Koda nor Arcy can do that?"

"They don't have the skills or the love… the horse flows in my blood. It is the beat of my heart, the reason I get out of bed. Koda and Arcy lack that passion; it takes passion to do a job without an end. You can't call out on feeding the horses because you are ill or because you don't feel like getting up and out the door. Taking care of the Ranch means being captive to it to the point of obsession and the land it is on. One must love the captivity of it, or it will go to ruin."

Sallisfer nodded. He knew the ranch and the horses meant so much to Valerie, but having it explained aloud had hit home. He reached over and grasped her hand in his. "What can we do to set your mother's fears aside?"

"Something, neither one of us, will live to see the day," Valerie said, looking at him with tears in her green eyes. It became apparent to Sallisfer as he pulled into the camp that Valerie knew she might not reach age 18 or adorn the white dress and walk up the aisle to marry. She knew that she would never become a mother with children. He felt tears in his eyes as he reached over and embraced her. Sallisfer liked having no wall between them, for he was able to share her fears as she shared his.

CHAPTER 23

Chocolate Milk

The next morning Kal woke up feeling something was wrong. Looking across the room, she noticed Valerie's bed was empty. Kal pulled back her covers and rushed down the hallway, only to be greeted with a smile by Valerie's mom.

"Good morning, Master Kalea," she said, her eyes holding pride in them.

"Do you know where Valerie went?" Kal asked.

"Oh, I thought she told you. Well, it was late. She and Sallisfer were called on an emergency mission around midnight or so last night." Valerie's mother said with a sigh.

"When do you think they will be back?" Kal asked.

"I don't know, it's all classified to me, you know," Valerie's mother said, "I have a family full of classified information. No one can tell me a thing. I feel so out of the loop. I mean, my daughter went off to war at fifteen, and my husband went with her. I don't know what they always seem to know. You would think that I, being the wife of a great sorcerer, would have classification. I didn't even know that Valerie was the hand of doom till she was 4 and was named so."

221

Kal suddenly felt sorry for Valerie's mother, who always had to live with family members who couldn't tell her how they felt, where they were going, or how long they would be out.

"I'm sure..." she was cut off by headlights on the driveway. Valerie's mother jumped up.

"That's Sallisfer's car," she said, opening the front door. Kal stood beside her, looking at a sleek light blue 2007 Convertible. Valerie exited the driver's seat and rushed to the passenger's side. She opened the door, pulled out Sallisfer, placed his arm over her shoulder, and then closed the car door. She walked towards them, talking to Sallisfer as she did so.

"Oh my god!" Valerie's mother gasped, starting to rush towards them.

"No, Mother stay back," Valerie said, holding out her hand. Valerie was paler than a corpse, and her eyes had an eerie glow. She looked deadly and hideous at the same time. It scared Kal, but she tried not to show it.

"Kal, mix two large cups of chocolate milk and find the eye dropper or a baby bottle. I need a bowl of cold water and a cloth as well." Valerie said, hoisting Sallisfer up a little more. He looked awful.

"Come on, Sally, only a little more," Valerie said Sallisfer groaned and shuffled his feet.

Valerie took him to her and Kal's bedroom and laid him on Kal's bed. Kal handed her one of the glasses of chocolate milk and then placed the other one on her bedside table.

"What happened?" she asked.

"We merged completely... again," Valerie said flatly. "The headmaster needed us to heal an entire army, it took both of us to do it, and we did. It was an idiotic thing to do," she said with a grimace.

Sallisfer opened his eyes weakly and then his mouth. Valerie laid her glass down, picked up the eyedropper, and filled it with chocolate milk. She dripped some on his tongue and in his mouth, he liked it, and she did it again. Finally, he closed his eyes, and she continued to drip milk into him.

After about ten minutes, Valerie was falling asleep, so Kal took over. Sallisfer opened his eyes and looked at her weakly. "Horse food," he said.

Valerie sat up, nodded, and walked sleepily into the kitchen. She came back with different greens and other things. Valerie tore some and placed them in his mouth. He could barely chew, so she started to chew them up and put the wad in his mouth, Kal was disgusted, but Sallisfer swallowed gratefully.

"We are never doing that again. I mean, heal that many people at once. That was madness," Valerie said as Sallisfer's color began to return, and he shook his head.

"The next thing we are going to do and continue to do is kill that many demons and twisted humans," he said with a sigh.

"I can do that." Valerie mused, "I mean, merging like that tried to kill me… but I can merge anytime we like to kill." … I can do that."

Sallisfer smiled. "After you become fully powered at 16… it shouldn't try to kill you." he thought out loud… "Look at us now… we are still standing because I am already past 16."

"I guess Sally, we can stick to healing people until after August…." Valerie acknowledged taking a sip of milk. "As long as we find a new way to do it, that was way too awkward," Valerie said with a slight smile. "No offense, but I do not remember it being that way when we destroyed the railway station."

"None taken, little god demon," he said, "No offense… and I remember it was."

Valerie rolled her eyes at him. "Come on, Kal, off to school you go. My dad wrote you an excuse note. I will take you to school and then head to Sallisfer's mother's workplace and tell her everything is okay. I'm sure she is worried sick for this good-for-nothing angel."

"You don't have a driver's license, only a learner," Kal protested.

"So, I have his driving ability, and I'm not taking the main road. I'm taking the back road."

Sallisfer sat up abruptly, groaned, but then laid back down. Valerie shook her head and poured some more chocolate milk down his throat.

"Don't you worry, Sal. I've asked the Earth Children to look after her, and Arcy is going to pick her, Kris, and Koda up at the high school. I got you here safely, didn't I?" Valerie asked hands on her hips.

"Yes, and I'm not worried about that. I'm worried about the back roads," Sallisfer whispered, his voice cracked.

Valerie rolled her eyes again. "I am that damned demon, remember." She grinned, kissed his forehead turned away, and walked out of the room. Sallisfer sighed and shook his head weakly.

"I can't do anything right," he muttered before falling asleep. Kal leaned down and kissed his lips.

"I'll be back as soon as possible," she promised before following Valerie to his car.

"I love this car," Valerie said as they started on the road.

"Are you sure you are safe?" Kal asked, holding on to the edge of the seat.

"Of course, don't you like going fast?" Valerie asked, turning right onto a dirt road; she slowed down in case of a deer, but not much.

The dirt road suddenly led straight to the school's front drive. Valerie pulled up to it, and Kal glanced down at the time, 8:30. She was still in the first block. She sighed, thinking about the green man she was drawing in art. "Here we are," Valerie declared, stopping in front of the office. Kal got out.

"Have a nice day. Meet you at lunch," Valerie waved before driving off. Kal sighed and walked into the building.

"Hey, Kal," Kris called, walking over and smiling with his electric blue hair.

"Hey... Kris."

"What's wrong? You look down...."

"Valerie and Sallisfer had an emergency call last night. They merged completely, whatever that means, but they were calling each other cute little nicknames, and if I didn't know better, I would say they were flirting."

Kris sighed and took her hand in his, it was warm, and Kal's small hand felt like it belonged there. She looked up at him, and he smiled down at her. "It is going to be okay. Okay?"

"Ya..." she couldn't think of much else to say as she stared into his brilliant blue eyes, watching as they swirled lightly with different colors. She did not realize the bell had rung until Kris laughed and released her hand.

"We should get to class." He smiled, walking away. Kal watched slack-jawed, rubbing her hand with the other one.

"Miss. Kalea?" the principal asked, "Is everything okay?"

"Yes, sorry, I must get to my second class." She said quickly, running off to class and trying to explain what she had just felt between her and Kris.

At lunch, Valerie came in and sat beside her with a smile. Sallisfer walked up behind her and sat down weakly.

"You still look sick," Kal expressed, laying a hand on his forehead.

"I am. I'm not staying for a class. I just came to lunch," Sallisfer replied with a smile.

"Same here. Mom is insisting that I get some rest over a minor fever. He's the one that should be yelled at, but no, I am," Valerie growled, opening a lunch box and pulling out an apple. She handed it to Sallisfer, who took it greedily. Then, Valerie pulled out a ham, tomato, and lettuce sandwich and two cartons of chocolate milk, one of which she gave to Sallisfer.

"What's up with this chocolate milk?" Kal asked.

"It's our medication for energy headaches, energy clogs, loss of mind, all of that stuff," Valerie shrugged, shaking the milk before opening it and drinking some of it.

"Oh, I almost forgot. Sallisfer has something to tell you after school."

"I do?" Sallisfer asked, puzzled.

Valerie smiled at him. "You do."

Sallisfer looked at her thinking and still shook his head with a shrug. Valerie sighed deeply. "Men," she muttered, "Got to tell them what to say to a girl."

Kal watched as Valerie's and Sallisfer's eyes met for a moment, and then recognition crossed Sallisfer's face, and he smiled. "I have something very important to tell you during our lessons," he said with a grin.

"It's about time he gets the message," Valerie said, taking a swig of the milk before picking up the remains of her sandwich and walking to the trash can.

Kal shook her head, "So what is the plan for Blaze?" she asked, changing the topic to a lighter conversation.

"Dad and I are going to build him a bigger enclosure and give him a door he can use to come in and out of our room. He hasn't learned about fire yet, and his wings still haven't come in. So, I am pretty sure he'll be okay."

"What's wrong with where he is now?" Kris asked as he came and joined them.

"Ms. Wing thinks that when he starts to learn about fire, he'll burn the house down." Kal laughed with a shake of her head. "I read in Valerie's book that when a dragon is first mastering their element, they can be very unpredictable."

"Blaze is a fire dragon?" Kris asked wide-eyed, "Last time I saw him, he was barely a hatchling, and you had no idea what his power could be. When did you find out?"

"On his second birthday in September, he snorted a smoke ring at Sallisfer. It seems he has a problem with other men around his ladies." Valerie smiled with a toss of her long hair. Kris shook his head with a small laugh.

"Well, I will have to remember that." He said suddenly, tickling Kal, who squealed. Sallisfer grunted, and Kris shot him a grin, daring Sallisfer to say something with his eyes. Valerie swallowed the last of her milk quickly.

"Well, we best be off," Val said, taking Sallisfer's arm. "Come on, Sally. We will see you two after school."

"Okay." Kal smiled.

"Have a good day," Sallisfer said, leaning down and kissing her on the cheek, his eyes never leaving Kris's.

"I will."

Kris ground his teeth together. Valerie quickly dragged Sallisfer from the lunchroom and transported them away.

The rest of the day went by quickly, and soon Kal was headed out to the bus rider line to grab Koda. She found him waiting for her at the double doors. She smiled at him as she led him through the halls to the car rider line to wait for Arcy.

"How was your day?" Kal asked.

Koda shrugged. "Okay, I guess."

"Only, okay? What happened?"

"I missed Valerie this morning. At least you got to talk to her. Unfortunately, she was asleep when I had to get on the bus. I thought I would have to ride it alone, but Allan and Kris picked me up. It was still rather lonely. They have a strange taste in music."

"Who is Allan?" Kal asked.

"One of Kris's brothers… the fourth one, maybe." Koda replied, "I don't know. There are a bunch of them."

"A bunch?" Kal made a mental note to ask Kris. They were passing the two hundred halls and were in the crowd trying to get to the double doors to the car rider line. Kal looked around for Kris and assumed he was already with Arcy.

"I have a bad feeling," Kris suddenly expressed, appearing beside her and making her jump.

"What do you mean?" Kal asked, looking up at Kris's worried face. She saw that he was trembling all over, and she took his hand, trying to steady him.

"I saw," he whispered, his face turning pale and his pupils dilating, "I see." He squeezed her hand, and she gasped at the sudden pain.

"What did you see?"

"I see…I saw…her…Valerie and Sallisfer fighting, and not a little practice fight. There was blood and lots of it!" Kris could barely breathe as he looked at her with his time-shifting eyes.

"There is a fire! I don't know where it is coming from…." He held his head as Kal dragged him along with her to the car rider line. "Oh, I am so confused." He suddenly breathed, letting Kal's hand go when they had stepped outside into the school parking lot as he ran trembling fingers through his hair.

"When do you think it will happen?" Kal finally asked when they were in the car after Arcy picked them up.

"I don't know," Kris whispered, fear filling his eyes along with tears. He refused to look at her as he recovered. Kal laid a hand on his shoulder as they turned and looked at each other while his eyes became misty, "But it will happen soon."

Kal swallowed, "Great."

CHAPTER 24

Hell's Fire

Arcy pulled into the Academy to find everyone being evacuated. Talys ran up to them as they got out of the car. "It is not safe here, my love." He said, "Hell's fire has come down on us."

"What?" Arcy asked.

"The Generals are fighting, and they are using the ancient arts. Unfortunately, Doom seems stronger and better than ever, and Heaven is still weak from the merge. So, the headmaster has ordered an immediate evacuation of all students and a few volunteers to stay with them." Talys shook the headmaster's scroll at them.

"So, you expect us to just pack up and leave?" Arcy asked.

"Ah, Ya." Talys nodded.

Arcy looked at them in the car.

"I think not," Kris said, stepping up. "There has to be something we can do to break them up. They are not enemies!" He teleported off with Talys at his heels.

Arcy looked at Kal. "Are you staying or leaving?" she asked. Kal didn't hesitate as she said. "Staying." Then the sisters turned and looked at their little brother, who stood there with large brown eyes. "Koda," Kal said, guiding him to the bus. "You head home with the others." Arcy interjected, "We will make sure Valerie stays safe." Taking his hand, Kal and Arcy walked him to the bus. Arcy kissed the top of Koda's head before he boarded and told him Mom would meet him at the bus stop.

"I'm scared." Koda whimpered, looking up at her wide-eyed.

"I am too." Kal told him truthfully, "But it's not safe for you." He nodded, and she hugged him before he boarded the bus home. They watched the bus pull away and then quickly joined the others.

She found the volunteers gathered around Heaven and Doom, trying to get them to talk about their troubles, but neither of them was listening. Instead, Valerie was staring at Sallisfer with heat in her eyes.

"Great!" Kal muttered, walking into the middle of the circle. "What did you do to upset her?" Kal asked Sallisfer.

"I... ah...we...ah...merged...and...I... ah...ah..." Sallisfer stuttered.

Valerie laughed, "It looks like the all-mighty one can't talk his way out of this one. Would you like to know what that *thing* did? He tried..." Valerie faltered before she ran up and slammed Sallisfer in the jaw with her fist, and with such force, it sent him backward.

"What did he do?" Kal yelled.

"He nearly ruined everything," Valerie yelled back.

"I said I was sorry," Sallisfer said, gathering himself up.

"Words mean nothing; action does!" Valerie yelled.

"Fine, so be it!" Sallisfer growled, pulling off his shirt and attacking Valerie with a vengeance.

"You're going to get yourself killed," Valerie growled back.

"You're going down with me, so what does it matter?" Sallisfer growled.

A grin washed over Valerie's face. A flash of light engulfed them, transporting them somewhere.

Kal looked at Kris, who started to pace frantically; she then looked at Arcy and Talys, exchanging their own quiet conversation. Then, finally, she looked around and saw that other masters were gathering and putting their heads together.

"WILL SOMEONE TELL ME WHAT THE HELL IS GOING ON HERE?" Kal yelled suddenly, making them all jump and stare at her. Kal felt power coursing through her veins as she looked around at all the masters.

"I am Master Kalea. I might not be as experienced as you are, but I am just like you, a master. Now, before I saturate the ground you stand on with your chopped livers, will someone fill me in?"

At once, Kalea was surrounded by the others and realized that they were just as scared and confused as she was, and now that she had voiced it, Kalea was suddenly being placed in control.

Luckily Kris was there beside her. He organized the masters into teams of four and five. He sent them to different locations to search for the Hands and to keep the damage to a minimum in the human realm.

"You and Arcy stay here in case they show back up. Talys and I will roam, check in with all the teams, and meet you back here. We have to let them fight it out; all we can hope for is the best." Kris hugged Kal with a smile, "It will be okay, Master Kalea." He winked at her before he teleported off with Talys.

Arcy sighed dramatically and fell into a lawn chair that she had conjured up, "You and Kris are cute together. I think I approve of him more than Sallisfer and you." She smiled, motioning to the seat next to her.

"Kris and I are not—you don't think we—oh, I'm so confused," Kal exclaimed, sitting in the chair.

Arcy laughed and took Kal's little hand in her long thin hand. Kal could see she had painted her nails a rainbow of glittery colors to match her rainbow wings and outgoing personality. "As Albert Einstein once said," she lowered her voice to mimic an old man, "Gravitation is not responsible for people falling in love." She squeezed Kal's hand, "All things happen for a reason Sis, and some reasons may not be the right reason, but they all happen. Destiny is a funny thing; throw in a dash of faith, and who knows what the outcome may be."

She gave Kal a breathless smile, "It will be okay. Let things come what they may."

Kal nodded, "Thank you, Arcy. You're the best older sis I could ask for."

They sat silent for a while; a few teams reported and then went out again. Kal shivered from the sudden chill of the darkening air; *what time was it?* She wondered, *what the hell was going on?*

"What do you think this is all about… he almost ruined everything?" Arcy voiced, breaking the silence of Kal's thoughts.

"I don't know. At lunch, Valerie said Sallisfer had something to tell me, and he was confused but then seemed to remember. So now they are fighting?"

"Where is the fire coming from?" Arcy wondered, "I mean, the Hand of Doom is often a wielder of fire because Doom is normally a Demon, but the last two were Earth Children and thus no fire…."

"Wait, Doom can be a demon?"

"Ya… traditionally Doom is a Demon… the mix of earth child and demon creates a powerful bender… who welds magic and fire. A peace-keeper, a leader, the headmaster." Arcy explained, "Now, the last pair of Demon and Earth Child hands happened over fifteen hundred years ago. That is when we started to duel the Demons on our 16th birthday to keep the balance between magic, aka light and darkness. Each demon is paired up with an earth child according to their birthday. So even you have a demon paired up with you to fight next year…."

"I have a demon?"

"Ya… Mom got the letter last month… she hadn't told you yet. The Headmaster checked, and sure enough, a demon was born on the same date and time as you, who was not paired up with an Earth child. Even the demons knew you had been born. For every one of us, there is one of them, until age 16, that is… then the stronger of the two gets to stay."

"So, with this war going on… what if someone's demon or earth child dies before their birthday duel?"

"Then the strongest one has already survived… I don't know. It has never happened before."

Kal pulled down her ponytail and braided her hair absently, thinking of what Arcy had said. "So, the last pair of Demon and Earth Child Hands… What happened to keep the cycle going?"

"They died their last death before the next hands were born… They say Doom died when she was expecting the next headmaster. The baby died with his parents. So, the spirit latched on to the next best thing, a Son of the last set of Hands, the second child maybe, and a full-blooded Earth Child girl. They had children, but they were not powerful enough to become the headmaster."

"So, the Headmaster is…old?"

"Yes, but he is immortal. Very few are gifted with immortality. Purists blame it on too much non-magical blood, but scientists say immortals do not breed. However, it is mentioned that when they try to breed, they realize they can't.

To be immortal means giving up using parts that try to kill you. After a hundred years or so, your body stops aging, which means it stops dying. When that happens, you stop producing and using specific cells and such… at least, that's what scientists say. Most are invulnerable; they do not get cut easily and rarely get sick. The older they get, the tougher their skin becomes, until it is hard and cold like iron. Many vampire stories happen because of immortals. Both Koda and Valerie were born immortal…."

"Wait, Valerie and Koda are immortal?"

"Ya… we think genetics played a role… like magic can be found in all human families because some chromosomes lined up right. We believe that is what happened… Now Valerie's immortality is weakened by the spirit of the Hand of Doom, the Hands die, they get hurt, and she shares with a non-immortal, so it makes matters worse."

"What happens when an immortal dies?"

"According to the fanatics (those who study lore and worship), there is a trial that immortals go through if they are allowed to move on, be reborn, or if they stay on the planet till the end of time. Most immortals that tire of human life go and live with the elves… Elves are believed to have evolved from Earth Children or vice versa… enough women liked pointed ears, and enough women liked rounded ears to make the distinction. The elves, on the other hand, breed, while immortal Earth Kids do not. So, there are more Elves than Earth Children born with immortality."

Kal stared at Arcy, trying to process the information. Arcy allowed a comfortable silence between them and tried to process what she had just learned. Before she could ask another question, The Hands were back and still glaring at one another; Kal saw a bloody hoof print on Sallisfer's shoulder and claw marks, teeth marks, and burns. She looked over at Valerie and saw fire-laced green eyes. Valerie had blood-stained hands, and blood gushed from a shoulder wound, and on her back were two streaks where small teeth went in and tore down her back when she pulled him off. Neither wore much clothing as they ripped at each other with such hatred that Kal shivered as they disappeared into a cloud of smoke.

"I wonder what happened." She whispered once again to herself.

"I do too." Kris said, popping up beside her and wrapping his arm around her shoulders, "Hands are not supposed to act as they do… they are the very balance of good and bad. The very symbol of what the perfect world…." Kris sighed and looked down at Kal with such sorrow that Kal choked up with tears.

"Maybe there is no perfect world." She uttered between sobs, "At least not anymore." Kris held her close to him.

"They will find their balance." He promised into her hair. "They have to, or the world has no hope."

Kal pulled away from him and looked up into his eyes, "At what cost will their balance come?" she asked, feeling weak suddenly.

"Only time can tell." He murmured, "And it is holding that a secret from me."

Kal did not realize that time had passed till the moon rose in the sky, and with a flash of light, they saw them again. Sallisfer was pinning Valerie down with a saber to her throat.

"Oh my," Arcy gasped.

"Shhh!" Kal said.

"NOW LISTEN TO ME, VALERIE!" Sallisfer yelled harshly.

"NO! YOU LISTEN" Valerie yelled, suddenly holding him down. He tried to struggle, but she slit his throat a little, and blood trickled out, much to everyone's shock.

"No, not now, Sally, don't want to end up dead, do you?" Valerie said sarcastically, angry. Sallisfer stopped struggling.

"I'll listen," he spat venomously.

Valerie tightened up and stared at him. She must have been yelling in his mind because those watching didn't hear or see her lips moving, but he winched at everything she said. Then he was back up, holding her down, blood trickling from her neck.

"Your turn!" he yelled as she tried to move, but he tightened his hold, and she gasped for air as he shouted at her with his mind.

They saw tears trickle from Valerie's eyes as she closed them, pain showing on her face as clearly as daylight.

"Stop!" she cried out.

"No, you have got to learn!" Sallisfer hissed.

"I... I," Sallisfer slapped her across the face before getting up and walking away, pulling on a clean shirt, his skin healing quickly but roughly.

Valerie stared up at the sky, tears sliding down her face. Kal walked up to Sallisfer, but he pushed her away, a mixture of feelings in his eyes. Kal stared at his back for a while, then turned when she heard cursing behind her. She turned to look at Valerie just as Valerie slammed her fist on the grass, making them go up in flames.

Kris grabbed Kal and transported them away from the flames to his room in the Academy, quickly closing the window and casting spells around the room that Kal had never heard of. "Are you okay?" he asked as she sat on his bed.

"I.... I think so." She muttered, taking the water bottle that Kris offered, but her hands shook so bad that water spilled everywhere when she went to take a sip.

"Here," Kris took the bottle and helped her take a sip.

"Thank you." He nodded with a sad smile.

"What is wrong?" Kal asked, suddenly concerned for him.

"It's just... I wish I could have done something out there today. I felt compelled to, but...." Kris looked at Kal with apparent confusion.

"But?" Kal prompted, licking her chapped lips, they tasted like charcoal, and Kris quickly helped her take another sip of water.

"I…I heard Valerie in my head… she told me no." He scrunched his eyebrows together and rubbed the arch of his nose. "I don't understand. She held me back… I feel like there is so much more to me that is missing, and I can't put a finger on it. Like a life I lived, but I can't remember."

Kal suddenly found herself hugging him, "There is nothing you could have done. She kept you from getting hurt."

"But, Sallisfer and Valerie are my best friends; we have known each other since they were named…. I don't understand." Kris muttered in her hair.

"It will be okay," Kal assured him, and he nodded, relaxing and hugging her back. Before Kal knew it, she was asleep in his arms. He smiled and healed the burns he was sure she did not even know she had.

He transported her to her room, laid her into her bed, tucked her in as gently as he could, and kissed her forehead. Looking at her starlight hair with black, blue highlights that were starting to form. Kris glided his hand down her cheek to her chin and felt something stirring inside him. He had felt the connection to her when he watched her mumbling to herself while she brushed Raz all those days ago.

Kris had tried to ignore it, blow it off, but as he started to work with her and get to know her, he had fallen for this misfit, clumsy, jumpy witch.

In so many ways, Kal was different, completely the opposite of Valerie. However, Kris had stopped judging and comparing her to his Master. Kal was the best addition to his life, and he knew he would have to fight for her attention as her love for Sallisfer ran deep.

He kissed her cheek. "I will protect you and keep you safe…" he whispered. Then, he stood and looked around the room at the carefully arranged furniture, smiled as he cast some protection spells, and left for his own room. Kris knew he would get very little sleep that night as he tried to find answers to questions he had yet to form.

CHAPTER 25

Doom the Demon

In the morning, charred hoof prints were all that remained of Valerie. Kal was helping the cleanup crew when Sallisfer stumbled out. He ran over to the ashes and sat on his knees, clutching some of the ashes in his hand. He shook his head, mumbling.

"No, no no no." he sobbed.

Kal walked carefully over to him, and he looked at her. "What have I done?" he asked her. "It's consumed her, she's one of them now, and I let it happen," he said, tears sliding down his face. "I let it happen."

Kal shook her head in disbelief; "No," she said, "you couldn't have."

"Yes, I did." he sighed. "I did not understand."

Kal suddenly howled as Sallisfer fell limp. She carefully placed his head in her lap as her body shook in despair. Kris fetched the doctors, who quickly picked him up and carried him inside. Kal slowly followed them as they took Sallisfer down to the medical wing.

She paused at the picture of Valerie and Sallisfer she had seen the first time she walked into the Academy. She stared up at Valerie's green eyes and wondered what had happened to her best friend and if there was any trace left of that bubbly girl Kal had gotten to know and love like a sister. Kal felt Kris's hand on her shoulder. "It will all work out."

He comforted her, "It will, you will see." Kal sighed and continued the walk down to the medical wing.

When Kal could see Sallisfer, he was still unconscious, blankets piled high over him, and a nurse held a cold towel on his forehead.

"He keeps mumbling something, but I can't make out what he's saying," the nurse stated when she saw Kal, "Perhaps you can translate."

Kal leaned down and listened to him. At first, she did not understand him, as if he was speaking gibberish, but slowly she could piece his nonsense babble with actual words.

"Cut off," he muttered, "Can't reach…" she listened some more to the most troubling part. Then, finally, she sat up and looked at the doctor, tears threatening to overflow.

"He is dying." Kal sobbed, "And Valerie completely cut herself off from him, so she is probably dying as well…."

"The Hands can't be separated by mind… they are of one, body, soul, and mind. Take half away, and life is no longer possible…." Kris hugged Kal, who was almost in hysterics. The doctor looked at Kal and sighed.

"We need to find Valerie," the doctor said with authority, his voice calm and clear as he handed them a scroll from the mysterious Headmaster. "We need the two of you to do that." Kris looked over the scroll and sighed as he handed it to Kal.

Kal looked over the almost illegible handwriting that ordered her and Kris to find the Hand of Doom. 'Why me?' she asked herself, but Valerie was her best friend, so she sighed and nodded.

"Okay," she and Kris said with a shrug. They walked out of the hospital part of the Academy and into one of the many common rooms.

"I need to stop by my room and grab some supplies. Why don't you go to the cafeteria and grab some water and food? We don't know how long this could take. General Valerie is just that, a General, and if she does not want to be found, she won't. Also, go to your room and get some travel clothing that can get dirty and is comfortable to wear." He grabbed out of the air a purple silk bag, "Put it all in this bag of holding. I'll meet you on the front steps."

"Um… Kris, I don't have any *Real* clothes here at the Academy yet…" she said, looking down at her outfit. It was one of her training outfits, a now pink halter top and nice fitting jeans.

Kris sighed and rubbed the arch of his nose, "What size do you wear? I'll stop at the Commissary."

"That's not the kind of question you ask a woman… wait, a Commissary? So that's a military thing?" Kal questioned.

"Yes, we have a commissary, and that is a military thing, but this place used to be a military training base, and that's what it looks like to humans. As for your size, I can always look it up in your folder, but I thought asking would be more polite." It took a moment for everything to sync with Kal, and Kris realized just how much Kal did not know about her biological history and how much she had left to learn. He suppressed a sigh and tried to think of all the things he should teach her on their mission, like things about Earth Child's history, the Academy, and things he had learned in kindergarten.

"I'm a size small in ladies, and a size 6 misses petite," Kal muttered grudgingly.

"What?" Kris asked, suddenly out of his thoughts.

"I am not short; I am fun size." Kal finished walking away from him and to the cafeteria. Kris shook his head, sort of dazed, and pulled up her file in embarrassment for missing what she had said.

A few moments later, they stood outside the academy walls staring at the vast forest beyond the training field. "Ready?" Kris asked, grabbing Kal and tickling her. Kal squealed like no other, nearly jumping out of her skin. Kris laughed and laughed. He laughed so hard he snorted and wiped away some tears.

"That was not funny." Kal breathed when her heart had stopped trying to jump out of her throat.

"You're right," Kris breathed, "That was hilarious. When Valerie said you were a scaredy cat, I didn't want to believe it, but you… you…Ow." Kris muttered, rubbing his face where Kal had left a nice red handprint on his cheek.

"I guess I deserve that." He laughed at her grin and nodded.

"Are you ready to get this search and rescue mission started?" Kal asked with a wink handing him the bag, and stared in wonder as Kris made it disappear with a flick of his wrist.

He laughed, kissed her head, and walked down the steps, "Don't just stand there; come on." Kal smiled and ran down the steps after him shifting into a wolf when she got to the bottom. Soon Kris was running beside her, dressed in his red fox form. Kal lifted her nose to the wind, taking a deep breath; she could smell Valerie's faint scent, but it was still clear. "This way," she said to Kris. He nodded and followed her out into the woods.

They followed Valerie's trail for three days. They found trees burned to nothing, white bones cleaned by sharp teeth, and deep pools of black blood.

"I am still puzzled about this fire?" Kris asked as he rubbed his hand over a burned tree. "She shouldn't be able to do fire?"

"Arcy said the spirit of Doom is normally a Demon." Kal recalled she held the information about Holjus and Valerie exchanging powers, "Perhaps with Valerie's power surges, it triggered something in the spirit."

"If that is true, then Valerie could be the next mother of a Headmaster." He stopped and stared briefly, a pink blush on his cheeks. "Yes, Bellona King will be the next Headmaster…" he whispered to himself. Kal stared at him as he shook his head and stared back at her.

"What?" he asked.

"You just predicted the end of the Headmaster…." Kal blurted, "Valerie is going to have a baby?"

"No… I do not think I said that. But if I did… it will not happen any time soon." Kris ran his hand through his greasy hair. He had a light shadow on his chin from not shaving. Kal realized that Kris had not meant to talk aloud, and he was trying to cover his mistake.

Kal felt a pull on her heartstrings; the blush could mean Kris was thinking about his love for Valerie. It seemed all the men Kal cared about had some love for her friend, making Kal more than just a little jealous. But then, a wind blew past Kal, making her forget her thoughts.

As the thick scent of Valerie fragranced the wind, reminding her why they were in the middle of the woods in the first place.

They followed the scent to an old barn. They turned into rats and slipped in. They saw a shadow and heard footprints passing back and forth. "That is a demon." Kris growled under his breath, "They have captured her." Kris went to lunge forward, and Kal held him down with a shake of her rat head.

Kris looked at Kal, they knew who the demon smell was coming from, but they had different ideas about why this demon was guarding Valerie. Kal nodded to the door, and they snuck out of the barn again. "You stand guard. I'm going to get a closer look," she whispered.

Kris shook his head. "It is too risky. That scum has Valerie, if she dies like this, she may not return, and he has won already!" He then sighed and repeated… "The demon has already won if she dies."

"Then let me make sure she is safe… I will let you know. Two of us in there will alert the demon."

Kris reluctantly nodded, "I guess. But I will stand right here, and if he hurts a single hair on your head…."

"I will stay hidden." Kal crawled back into the barn, looking back to ensure Kris was not following her.

"Will you stop that? You're as bad as those wretched animals." Kal heard Valerie say harshly.

"I can't believe you; I told you to tell me if it got too loud, but you didn't listen. This is all my fault. This would have never happened if I hadn't gotten you out of that dungeon, touched your hand, or shared my soul with you…" Holjus stopped pacing as tears were in his violet eyes.

"Well, it did, and I like it. I can live without that retching in my head. I have the freedom to think on my own."

"But it's killing you. You are not the Valerie I fell in love with!" Holjus pleaded.

"People change, dear; by the way, toss me another beer, will you?" Kal poked her head around the corner and saw that Valerie's eyes were nearly red. Holjus pulled a beer out of a cooler and tossed it to her. She pulled the top off with sharp pointed teeth and drank it down. Holjus pulled out his own bottle of cola and sipped at it, looking at Valerie concerned.

"You need help," he said.

"Do not," Valerie said with a smile. "Never needed help in my life."

"Now that's a lie. You needed my help," Holjus growled. "I have hidden you from my kind. You couldn't have done that on your own; now, you can't even walk on that leg or move that arm. You say you don't need help, but you truly need it now, perhaps more than you ever needed." Holjus sighed, taking the half-full bottle from her and then sitting beside her, taking a sip.

Valerie sighed and reached her good hand out to him, and he took it. Their eyes locked for a moment, and softness started to shine in those red-laced green eyes. "I guess you're right, Holjus, but I can't return. I can't. I'll never be able to face Sal or even my old kind again. I might have killed people in my rage. I don't know. it's all a haze." There was fear in her voice, a fear that Kal had never heard before. "But I'm never, and I mean never, going back to the castle. I don't want that slimy snake in my head again."

Holjus sighed and stroked Valerie's cheek, "You must admit that the *snake* had a good point... "

Valerie glared at him but continued as if she did not hear him, "I don't want to answer to no Headmaster! I will find Pegasus and give him my immortality so I can die as the humans do." Valerie said, laying her head on Holjus's arm, tears sliding down her face like a hard rain. Holjus wrapped an arm around her and held her close to him.

"Baby, you are always going to be my other half, but your other half is Sallisfer... he completes you. I know that you know that... And without him, you are going to die." Holjus sighed and kissed Valerie. "Yes, you are a demon but also an earth child of strong blood and power. But you can be better than just a demon. You taught me that there is more to life than rage." Valerie nodded and kissed him back with a smile, some of her color returning.

Kal walked out of the barn and up to Kris, "Tell the Academy that she's alive, don't tell them where she is yet. I'll see if that will be the right thing or not," he stared at Kal, then nodded, changed into a crow, and flew off.

Kal walked back into the barn and saw that Holjus had laid Valerie on a hay bed and covered her with blankets.

"Be back soon, don't try to go anywhere," Holjus warned before leaving the barn. Kal waited till the sound of his wings faded before stepping out of her hiding place in her wolf form.

Valerie's eyes met hers. "I have a message for you, Valerie," Kal said. Valerie looked at her blankly for a second, and then anger flooded her eyes.

"Then spit it out, puppy!" Valerie spat.

Kal refused to let the anger get in the way of her message. "When you're ready to face that you're killing him, come back," Kal said.

"I am never going back to that place again. He can die for all I care!" Valerie yelled.

In the moment it took for Valerie to recognize the fury in Kal's eyes, she was pinned to the ground staring at a snarling golden-eyed pail tooth face. "If that is your final answer, *demon*, you're no better than the rest of them," Kal snarled.

"It is my final answer, and you can kill me. You'll be doing me a favor by taking me out of my miserable existence," Valerie said.

"Miserable! You have no idea how miserable your existence can get." Kal growled.

"You do know what the fight was over, right?" Valerie asked with tears in her eyes, "He wanted to forget you, but I wouldn't have it! He said that Hands should stick together and love one another; I told him I wouldn't let him have me, and by all hells, I still won't! So, kill me, make it fast, and put us both right."

"It was about me?" Kal asked, not wanting to believe Valerie.

"Yes. With this Valentine's Day coming up and merging that cursed way... It finally occurred to him what he did wrong that turned me off from him in the first place. This is why I was afraid to merge, but you said you would support us, so we did it. He's a monster, and one day you'll see that in him; he may seem nice right now, but he's got a serpent heart and a twisted mind." Valerie said, taking a breath, and then she gathered herself up and pushed Kal off her.

"If you don't believe me, you need to go into his mind," Valerie sighed. "See it for yourself. Underneath that clean slate is darkness…. And I know why there is darkness, but it…." Valerie shook her head. "No, Heaven shouldn't be as dark as Doom."

"I… I don't think I can?" Kal said, sitting down and looking at Valerie. "Does he not love me?"

"He does, in his own way, at least. I think love is way out of my league. But I can tell you that he is confused, torn. He feels vulnerable. We both do. It was only a matter of time before we broke down. I hope you and Kris have a better time at this than we did. I hate to have us repeated in more generations," Valerie tried to laugh with a slight smile.

Kal nodded, listening and taking it all in but feeling the pressure of what she was hearing. "I got to go. I'll be back tomorrow," Kal whispered, wanting to escape what she was learning. Valerie nodded to her weakly and then fell asleep.

Kal seeing Valerie asleep left the barn immediately. She ran to the top of a small hill, thinking of the many ways she could try to get into Sallisfer's mind. Not seeing Kris on his way back, Kal returned to the barn only to find Valerie gone, but she found notes. One was addressed to her, along with one for Holjus.

Kal opened the one addressed to her, which only had one word. Book!

Kal found what she had come for. She ran fast back to the Academy. She burst through the doors and pushed people out of her way. Then, she ran up the stairs to Sallisfer's room, finding the door locked; she sighed.

"Need this?" Kris asked, handing her Sallisfer's necklace. It was red, with a serpent wrapped around the stone, its mouth was open, and it looked as if it was about to strike.

"Thanks," she said. Kris nodded. Kal opened the door with the necklace and the drawer she had seen him use that day she had been given clearance. Kal found two books in it, with the same cover and everything. She opened one.

January 1, 1998.

Today Sall and I got promoted to Masters. I don't know if I'm scared or excited. I'm only seven! But I have been Doom since I was age four....

Kal didn't read anymore. It was Valerie's book; she picked up the other and flipped to a page.

August 27, 2003.

Val wore the dress I got her for her birthday, and she looked great in it. I now know why the Hands always fall in love. Being 13 now, I guess I am high and mighty!

write tomorrow,

George Sallisfer King Jr.

Kal, annoyed after reading the content, knowing it was the book, picked it up and closed the drawer. She walked out of the door where Kris was waiting for her. "So, we need to clear the room, so you can get in his mind, right?" he said with a smile.

"Right, I was thinking of saying we need to prepare his soul to go to heaven," Kal said.

"Good idea. I'll help you clear the room and then stand guard outside. After that, you can mess around in his head for as long as you like without being disturbed." Kris said.

"Good then, all set," Kal said. They were transported to the infirmary and worked on getting all the nurses and doctors away. With that done, Kal brought up a wooden chair by Sallisfer's bed and opened his book to where a bookmark was placed. She read and let her mind drift to his. She then slipped into his mind and into the memory.

She was looking through Sallisfer's eyes because she heard his name being called.

"Sall?" Valerie walked up, and his heartbeat went up. It pounded in his chest as he saw what she wore. It was a shiny blue bathing suit-like top and a short matching skirt with no shoes.

"What on earth are you doing here? I told you to stay..." he grabbed her and kissed her then, and when they separated, she looked at him with a blank face.

"Are you okay?" Valerie asked, staring at him with large eyes.

"I am just excited about the show." Sallisfer's voice came out of his mouth.

"Valerie, time to start," came a voice from the back.

"On my way Miss. G," Valerie called back.

"I better go," Sallisfer said with a smile.

"Ya... see you tonight." They hugged and then parted.

The scene changed to looking at the stage. The curtains parted to reveal Valerie in the same short skirt and top. Behind her were two young, muscular men. Valerie laid her hands on each man's shoulders and, using upper body strength, held herself off her feet till she was head level with them. The men then laid their hands palms out; she stepped down on them, and they held her up farther.

She then walked off their hands and on a third man's shoulders, her hands on his head, and she did a headstand. Ohs and ahs went up, along with cheering and clapping. Still in the headstand, Valerie placed her bare feet on her head, again amazed ohs and ahs went up. Valerie smiled, laid her feet on the man's shoulders, and stood up. She then walked onto another man's shoulder and then to another. As soon as her feet left their shoulders, they would bow and leave the stage. Valerie then walked on the hands of one man and did a backward flip, landing on her feet. The crowd erupted with a gasp; even Sallisfer gasped and clapped. Kal rolled her eyes, but she, too, was impressed. Valerie's acrobatic skills were well-placed and practiced as she maneuvered with other performers on the stage. Kal looked around and saw Mr. Wing beaming and boasting to a young lad beside him in the row ahead.

Sallisfer blinked, and the stage went dark; when the light returned, Kal found that Sallisfer was on a battlefield. Kal experienced the memory firsthand through him-found herself walking…as Sallisfer was fighting on foot. Alongside him was Valerie as they sliced with swords at their foe, bouncing arrows off shields. The smell of blood was in the air, dripping off the tip of his blade as he pulled it out of one of his enemies.

"Keep going!" He yelled at the men and women fighting around him as more arrows flew into the air. "Shields up!" And a plank of shields formed at once as they ran after the retreating enemy.

"No one can save us but ourselves!" he yelled over the clatter of armor and shields. "We fight till we win!" Then they charged headstrong into the enemy's reinforcements- tearing threw them like a knife in butter.

Kal lost track of how many lives were lost at the tip of Sallisfer's sword as those who fought with him. As they fought, confidence grew inside of him. *"We can do this!"* he yelled. Looking beside him, he saw that Valerie was getting further ahead of him. Through Sallisfer's eyes, Kal saw that Valerie was aiming for the leader. Val's eyes did not leave the target of a woman who sat on a broad bay watching the battle with a smirk on her face.

Kal then witnessed the most horrible scene in her life, and probably his as well. A saber ripped through Valerie's middle, showing on the other end of her back. She looked at her killer with shock on her face. Then smiled at the wielder of her death and slammed her sword through him before falling to the ground. Pain filled a part of Sallisfer's mind that was not his, and words came in a gasp.

"Bye," Then empty space. Kal flew out of Sallisfer's mind so fast that she flipped the chair over and landed with a crash on the floor.

Kris was at her side in no time. "Are you okay?" he asked.

"I... I think I am," she said, shaking all over by the force of the endless emptiness that she had felt.

"Can you get Valerie's book, please?" she asked.

"Sure, be right back," Kris said, vanishing. A moment later, he handed it to her.

"Thanks," she said, taking it with a quivering hand. She opened the book to the date she was at in Sallisfer's memory.

March 19, 2005

yesterday was the worst day so far of my life!!!!

It all started that morning when I woke up with a headache the size of Starlight Castle.

This war is so pointless; we all know it's going no-where, but that's not why I'm writing. I'm writing because yesterday, March 18, 2005, at 12:30pm. I, Valerie Nicole Wing, died. I was run thru by a saber of the rivals. I can't believe we're having a Civil War over a person that might not even be born yet!!!

We do what we were told to do, bred to do, and we will keep doing it till we die our last death, and then the spirit will continue without us.

Kal stroked the words that ran as a tear that fell ran down the page. Kal sighed as she felt a hand on her shoulder. She looked startled; she had completely forgotten about Kris. He looked just as pale as he read the page over her shoulder.

"Do you remember that day?" Kal asked. Kris's eyes fogged, and pain filled them, and he sighed, holding his head.

"No…" he said. Pain rippled across his face, and Kal took his hand. "Keep reading. I am sure it is important."

Kal nodded and turned back to the page. Unfortunately, she had to skip a few lines as they were smeared.

The one thing I'm worried about now is that when I was struck down, it opened the doors of Sall's heart and let out a terrible monster. He killed more people than anything I ever did.

He didn't just kill the rival's troops. He killed his own! I watched in horror as the hand of Heaven turned into the devil. If he died and I lived, would I suddenly sprout huge white wings and wrap everyone in Heaven's embrace?

He, too, died. By the hands of our own troops! I later read, however, that he would have died anyway.... But now they fear him more than they ever did me! I'm scared if they fear Heaven and love Doom, Hell will be full by the time I get down there. Now I fear I can never give myself entirely to a monster that lurks in his heart. Two monsters are one monster too many.

Hope to have a lighter heart tomorrow,

Val.

Kal sighed and looked at Valerie's drawing on the next page. It looked like a shadow wraith, but she wasn't entirely sure as it was blurry with tears.

"What now?" Kris asked. Kal looked back at Sallisfer's diary, and Kris nodded. He squeezed her hand. "I am here if you need me." With that, Kal allowed herself to be pulled back into Sallisfer's mind.

"What do you mean you won't have me?" Sallisfer hollered at Valerie. He was drunk, and the world spun around Kal, making them both sick.

"I... I can't, Sallisfer," Valerie swallowed, "I can't love a killer like that. That thing that's lurking inside you is something, the only thing that truly frightens me. I can't give myself over to that thing. I'm sorry."

Tears slipped down her face. She walked up to him and lightly kissed him on the lips. "I'm sorry, Sall," she said softly.

"But I have this because of you?" There was pain all over him, both mental and physical. "I have been filtering all your darkness since we were named! Where is it supposed to go?"

"I ...," She walked away from the room they were in and down a hall.

Kal felt pain rip at her heart, forgetting that it was his. Then she opened her eyes to a white ceiling.

"Feeling better?" asked a soft voice.

"Ya...I think," he sat up and looked at Valerie.

"Is she here yet?"

"No, she's not, but the doc says you need to rest and take a class," Valerie said with a smile.

"I didn't mean to, ah...you know," he said.

Valerie raised her eyebrow. "Rest," she said, shaking her head. "What a girl can do to a man," Kal remembered the text message Ava's sister had sent that day. She felt a slight stab at her heart; he had cared enough for his heart to crack. Perhaps he loves me a little bit, after all. Kal blinked, and it changed again. Now she was looking at a tent full of injured masters.

"I guess we get this over with," Sallisfer said, looking at Valerie with a smile. Kal nearly gagged at the sensation of lust that he felt.

"I... I don't want to. But, I mean.... doesn't this feel wrong?" Valerie asked, seeing a glint in his eyes.

"No, we have her support. It's not wrong. Besides, we're under orders," Sallisfer said, taking her in his arms. She snatched them away.

"No, I can't, I won't," she said.

"They're dying," Sallisfer said.

"Yes, I can see that, and I don't want them to die as much as you don't, but I can't allow myself to be pulled into you," Valerie said, "it was one thing when it was vice versa...but now after so soon?"

"Fine, we'll do it the hard way," he said angrily.

Kal pulled out immediately, knowing she would terminate her relationship with him forever. Pain gripped her heart, and she cried out, clutching her chest, trying to rip her heart out.

Kris came taking Kal into his strong arms. Holding her, he allowed Kal to cry on his shoulder. Then led her to her room in the Academy and helped her to bed. Kris sat holding Kal close to him, cuddling her as she cried. He spoke not a word and just rocked her side to side. When the last tear had fallen, Kal felt drained, and she felt Kris shift out from under her and place her head on the pillow. Then she felt her eyelids grow heavy, but her body felt light like she floated just above the bed. For all Kal knew, she was asleep. She blinked heavy eyes as Kris smiled down at her, his blue eyes sparkling with other colors. His lips moved, and she swore he said, "I will love you forever. You can trust I will never hurt you. Can I heal your broken heart?" Kal felt her lips move with a silent Yes before her vision spun and blurred.

She dreamed that Kris held her broken heart in his hand and was slowly mending it back together, singing softly a song she had never heard before. His bright blue eyes were soft with pity and with something she had never seen before. It was a world of color, like a galaxy. She was awakened from that dream just as fast as she had dreamed it. A shrill scream came from the hall.

"Oh, shut up, will ya," came from a very irritated voice. Kal sat up and saw Kris at her door, looking out the hall.

"How is she?" Valerie asked, coming into view; her arm was in a sling, and her leg was wrapped.

"She's better off than you are," Kris said, looking at Valerie up and down.

"Ha, very funny." Valerie gave a tired sigh.

"When she's fully awake, I need to see you both in the infirmary," Valerie ordered.

"Do you need help?" he asked.

"Not as much as she needs you." Valerie smiled and squeezed Kris's hand. "You have come a long way, my friend."

"So, have you."

"I will see you soon." Kris nodded, and Valerie limped away. Kris shut the door and walked back to the bed. He smiled at Kal.

"Sleep," he said. "The night is still young." Kal felt tired again. She laid back down and fell into a dreamless sleep.

CHAPTER 26

Time to Heal

"I'm sorry, General Valerie can't have visitors right now," the nurse said sadly.

"She wished to see us. But unfortunately, we can't have her waiting," Kris replied.

The nurse looked them up and down and nodded reluctantly. "All right then, but don't stay too long; she needs rest," the nurse sighed, opening the door for them. Valerie was in bed reading; she looked mostly restored except for the bags under her eyes.

"Valerie?" Kris asked tentatively. She looked at them with her red-green eyes, and they looked at her.

They stood in silence, staring at each other. Finally, Valerie swallowed and opened her mouth. "I am afraid," she slowly stated as the fire flickered on her fingertips.

"Afraid of what?" Kris spoke just as slowly, taking a hesitant step toward her.

Valerie swallowed again the flames disappeared. "I'm afraid," Valerie repeated. "It's gonna come back."

"What's going to come back?" Kris asked, taking yet another hesitant step closer, Kal caught his hand, and he looked at her.

"The monster," Kal whispered, eyes big.

Valerie nodded weakly, rolling her neck, "I pissed Sallisfer off," she grinned. "We are going to destroy one another."

"Why?" Kris asked, "Is it because of the fire?"

Valerie looked at him wide-eyed "How do you know?"

Kris held back a smile, but Kal could see it on the fringes of his lips, "I have my ways," he answered, walking the rest of the way to the bed confidently.

Kal held tight to Kris's hand and felt his pulse racing in his wrist, yet his hands were not as sweaty with fear as hers. She turned to look at Valerie when she heard her gasp, "It's already here." The door burst open, and the monster's angry gold eyes glared at Kal and Kris.

Kal jumped, and Kris shoved her behind him, a sword and shield appearing in his hands.

"Run," Valerie ordered. "Run as fast as you can and gather as many people as possible. I'll hold him off." A dagger formed in her hand, and she weakly stood on shaking legs in front of Kris and Kal.

"I'm still alive," she growled.

"Not for long," the wraith hissed. Kris tried to get in front of Valerie, but she was powered to full and would not let him pass.

"I have this. Teleport home."

She advanced on the wraith, and with anger, in his eyes, the wraith reached his hand out, and Valerie dropped to the ground, gasping.

"You have taken everything from me!" It yelled with a hiss.

"Me?" Valerie gasped. "I haven't done anything to you. You got what you deserved!"

More anger, if that was possible, flooded Sallisfer's eyes.

"Sal!" Kal burst.

Angry eyes turned to her, and his other hand went out to clutch Kal, but Kris pushed her aside and got caught in Sallisfer's death grip.

"You're supposed to heal, Not Kill!" Kal shouted, hot tears falling down her face. "You are the Hand of Heaven!"

"There is no Heaven." Valerie gasped, holding her throat.

Sallisfer dropped his hands, and a light glow illuminated from him. "There is a Heaven!" He boomed, glowing even more brightly.

"Then stop the darkness." Kal whimpered as she leaned down to help Kris to his feet, who looked ready to jump onto Sallisfer.

"You need to heal the rift," Kris glared at Sallisfer as he tried to shove Kal off his arm. "You must heal the rift between darkness and light."

"I don't know if I can" Sallisfer's words were almost too faint to hear. Kris got away from Kal, and much to her astonishment, he did not strike Sallisfer despite the hot anger in his eyes. Instead, Kris took Sallisfer's shaking hands, Valerie gasped a free breath, and Kal rushed over to her as she lay on the cool floor crying.

"I'll heal," Sallisfer said, letting go of Kris and walking to Valerie. She spooked and huddled in a corner near her bed. Sallisfer stopped and suddenly melted into a blond-haired, brown-eyed boy. Valerie still would not let him near her Sallisfer got into arm's reach when Valerie vanished in a transporter; Sallisfer sighed and disappeared after her.

"We got to find them!" Kris gasped, his eyes wide with fear. "If they start fighting again?"

"You do not think it is over?" Kal asked, scared.

"I believe...well, I know where they are, but not what to call it other than paradise," Kris continued as if he did not hear Kal.

"The Paradise?"

Kris reached out, and Kal took his hand. They found themselves in a lush, warm place. They heard a shill scream, and they ran to the sound. Parting a vine curtain, they peered out to see a gray mare swimming in a beautiful pool. The shrill scream came again, and they saw a paint stallion watching the mare closely on top of the hill behind the lake.

The gray mare, Valerie, walked out of the pool of water and shook the water off, and rolled in the lush grass. They watched Sallisfer descend the hill, trying to come near Valerie, but she stood and shook again, pinning her ears and snaking her neck at him. Finally, Sallisfer backed off in submission.

Valerie snorted and galloped through a field of beautiful green grass and different-colored wildflowers. They could see she still had a slight limp on her right back leg. They heard her laugh as she rolled again and saw Sallisfer shake his head with a smile if horses could smile.

Kal couldn't stand watching any longer, and she left their hiding spot. "What in the world is going on?!" she demanded.

Sallisfer looked at her with bewilderment; he shifted back to his human form and stared at her and Kris. "How did you get here?" he asked.

Kal shrugged. "I'll answer your question if you answer mine."

Sallisfer strolled over as if he thought they were going to jump him or something. He eyed them in utter bewilderment before rubbing his hand down his face in frustration, "We have reached an accord." He spared a glance at Valerie, who was now galloping towards them.

"I got here the same way you did," Kal said, crossing her arms and looking Sallisfer up and down as he moved nervously from foot to foot.

"Hey Kal, hey Kris! How do you like paradise?" Valerie asked, shifting into a human as she walked up to them.

"Okay, where is this place?" Kris said, looking around with awe; however, Kal did not miss the tiny bit of recognition that flashed into his confused but amazed expression.

"Near Starlight castle, only hands can come here, though." Valerie gave a sad smile and glanced at Sallisfer, who nodded at something she must have said in his mind.

"Here is where all our secrets are and where we can or have to live in peace unless one betrays the other....". Valerie trailed off, eying Sallisfer, but her smile didn't fade.

Valerie started to walk, and they followed, "Here is where the heart of the Hands is, our power, our life force... no one can enter, not even the Headmaster. This forest has been growing from generation to generation because of hands." She stopped talking as her eyes took on a look of wonder that enhanced her previous words. Valerie waved her hand around. Kal and Kris watched as her words took effect. They inhaled everything the Hands had created by the fragrance of all they saw; the tall oak, giant redwoods, cottonwoods, maples, and others Kal could not name.

"The past lives here, lingering between the trees, whispering in the wind. As the forest grows, you add yourself to it, and thus when you go...you're never truly gone," Valerie explained, her sad smile landing on

Kal. However, Kal saw that Valerie wasn't back to normal; her eyes were still traced with red flames, her expression pained, and her movements stiff. Valerie was also noticeably slimmer, her blue halter top hanging off her starved frame. Kal thought she couldn't remember the last time she had seen Valerie eat a whole meal, and it was starting to show.

"So, you may want to leave," Sallisfer said, startling Kal out of her thoughts as he wrapped his arm around Valerie, who pushed it away and glared at him with venom.

"Sally, don't be rude," Valerie snapped.

"But..." Sallisfer closed his mouth and took a deep breath. "I mean, they can stay. If they don't, well..." Valerie rolled her eyes.

"That is a problem," she muttered, "I really have to find a way to change that."

"I don't think it's possible...but we can try," Sallisfer griped, looking at his feet and his face slightly red.

Valerie exhaled, replacing her aggravated look with a smile as she gestured for them to follow her farther into the wood. "Let me show you around while he recovers," she smiled as she turned to walk.

"Remember, whatever you see or hear, you're not allowed to share with others, and what is here stays here. Nothing can leave paradise once it has been planted," she glared at Sallisfer, who had a guilty look on his face.

Kal and Kris followed Valerie farther into a forest where between every tree, there was a secret, a story, never to be told to the outside world. Kal could hear them whisper to her and see their wispy forms beckoning her to listen.

"Kal," Valerie called, startling her. Kal hadn't realized she was walking the other way from where they were going.

"Come on, I'll take you to the place where, when Sally and I die, your forest will be."

She led them into a barren desert, with nothing for miles around but sand, wind, and sun. Kal stared at the empty space and turned to look at the lush forest she had just steps from.

"Our place was the same when we first got it. it's up to you to make the trees grow and live." Valerie revealed, seeing Kal's expression.

"How do we do that?" Kris asked.

"We shall answer the question at our deathbed, and the last one is well away, far from now." Valerie glanced at Kal again, and Kal realized that they were measuring their time on her readiness.

"How many lives do hands have?" Kal asked, curious, trying not to think about them leaving forever and her taking up the weight they carried.

"You start out with 4," Valerie smiled, leading them back into the woods.

"So, you have 3?" Kris breathed relief on his face "3 more… if only it was 9."

Valerie smiled at him, took his arm in hers, and leaned on him. "If only." She smiled, giving him a quick squeeze before letting go.

"Do you know how you will die for each one?" Kal inquired, linking arms with Valerie.

"No, but we do know, if I, Doom, die, Heaven will die a slow and painful death. If Heaven dies, I die about one or two seconds after, sometimes instantaneously with him."

"So, if we, being the next level, die when you're still alive, would we come back?" Kal probed.

"No, if you two were to die without being named hands, then you will not, and Sally and I would have to hold out longer than we see passable. So, you two better be careful," she instructed, giving them a stern look.

"Is Sally Sallisfer's name here?" Kris asked, "I have heard you use it in other places too?"

Valerie chuckled and nodded, a sly expression on her face, "Yes, that's what he agreed on when we wrote our names here."

"What's yours?" Kal asked.

"Something I should have never agreed on" Valerie rolled her eyes, but she was now in good spirits and walked lightly down the path back to the creek.

"Like?" Kal pressed. She had to know what he didn't want to say in front of her.

"Baby, are you done with them yet? We have to go?" Came Sallisfer's voice.

"Yes, I'm done!" Valerie said with a disgusted look on her face.

"Baby?" Kal asked wide-eyed.

Valerie grimaced and nodded. "You better not say that for me," Kal said, looking up at Kris with a stern glare.

"Where are you going?" Kris asked, changing the subject and looking Valerie up and down with concern.

"We are going to dinner with the Headmaster," Valerie explained with a sigh.

"Who is this headmaster?" Kal asked, and it wasn't the first time since she had learned about the Headmaster.

"You'll see when the time comes, "Valerie smiled. "For now, you better be off. It is not safe to be here when we are not here. The place comes and goes with us… we carry it with us." She looked dead at Kris, then reached out and took his hand, "I will be okay old friend. Stop worrying about me."

Kris nodded reluctantly. "Take Kal to meet with the Master in the morning. After that, Kris, you, and I have a Cavalry meeting around 11ish to discuss the relocation of the horses to where they need to be. After that, I have shopping with Diana," Valerie stated, then she looked at Kal. "You are to go shopping with my mother around 11ish and have weapons training when I return from shopping. I found something in the storage building the other day that I want you to try." She smiled and trotted off as a gray mare. Kris smiled at Kal, and they teleported to the Ranch.

Kal sighed, "I just want one Saturday to sleep in." She grumbled, "Just one."

CHAPTER 27

Death Number Two

The following morning Ms. Wing, Kal, and Valerie were awake before sunrise to start the daily feeding. Valerie was the first one dressed and grabbed herself a muffin and a carton of chocolate milk as she headed for the door. She looked back at Kal and Ms. Wing as she pulled on her boots. "Kal, don't forget. You have a meeting with the Master today after feeding." Valerie reminded as she stood and pulled on her favorite green hoodie, sticking her breakfast into the large pocket.

Ms. Wing approached Kal and handed her a cup of coffee and a bowl of oatmeal. "I am looking forward to you and I shopping," Ms. Wing smiled at Kal as she sipped her coffee. "I spoke to Master yesterday, and he said he shouldn't keep you long, so we can go early."

"I know." Kal yawned, smiling as she took a bite to eat, still thinking about bed and sleep.

Feeding the horses did not take long between the 3 of them, and Kal helped Valerie brush down Cappy and Sorrow.

When Kris came to get Kal to meet the Master, Valerie was getting on Cappy for a ride with Tema.

The ride in the car with Kris was silent as they rode to the Academy.

"Where are we going?" Kal asked as they passed the meeting rooms where they usually met Master. As Kris led Kal up the stairs into the school. They walked in stride with one another, which was oddly satisfying to Kal. They got a few looks as they walked up the stairs.

"To the meditation rooms. Today we are learning in there." Kris informed. Kal looked at him sideways. "It's a semi-private lesson."

At the second landing, they were on a long window-lit hall. A few steps from the landing, there was a small desk with a petite lady painting her nails.

She looked at them with a bored expression. "The new girl has to sign the contract." she nodded to the clipboard beside her. On the paper were three points

*No food or drink

*Only reasonable indoor voice

*No overnight stays

Kal signed the paper, and with a lazy nod, the girl said, "Master is in room 3."

Kris smiled at Kal and said, "Thank you, Debbie." He led Kal to room 3, and Kris slid the door open. Inside, sitting criss-cross on a matted floor, was an ordinary-looking man with long black hair and a chiseled face, but where his eyes should have been was a galaxy-colored mist. He nodded at them in greeting, holding out his hand. "Welcome," Master said, his voice ringing out deep and full of power. Kal took his hand in hers, hoping it wasn't too sweaty with nerves.

"Greeting," she said in the traditional greeting.

"I look forward to teaching you." Master smiled.

"We look forward to learning from you." Kris nodded as tradition.

The meeting did not last long, and soon Kal was in the car headed to the mall, and Kris was meeting Valerie with the Cavalry. When Kal was done with the mall, Kris met with Kal again, "Want to go for a swim at The Paradise?"

"I thought it was only open when the Hands were there?" Kal asked.

"It is open. Sallisfer is there… he won't mind." Kris had a mischievous look in his eyes that made Kal's cheeks warm.

"Sure," she said. Kris took her hand in his, and they teleported off.

It was the day before Valentine's Day. Sallisfer had picked out the perfect dress for Valerie. He hummed to himself as he imagined her dancing with him in the dress. He smiled as he walked, taking a deep breath of The Paradise air. He was in a good mood as he took an afternoon stroll through the fields. Everything was running smoothly, lessons, meetings, and even schoolwork. In his mind, nothing could go wrong.

He discussed plans and decorations for the Valentine's dance, scheduled for the next day with Valerie as she shopped in the mall with Diana. "What color did you say my dress was again?" Valerie asked in his head.

"Red." Sallisfer smiled back.

"What color do you want the table clothes? Red, white, pink, or violet."

Sallisfer thought it over as he walked, "White and pink, I think." He laughed, making a simple pun that made Valerie roll her eyes.

"Do you think we have enough table decorations from last year? I want this year to be special."

"Baby, we have tons of decorations. Relax; it will all work out."

"Can you think of anything we may need?"

"A soft blanket and a clear night."

Valerie laughed. "I'll see you when I get home."

"Yup," Sallisfer said last, and their thoughts unlinked. He was glad they had ended their hostility with one another, at least for now. They both decided to let bygones be bygones and accept what the other could not change. Valerie loved Holjus. He acknowledged that and stopped making Valerie sick at the thought of her personal feelings. That was amendment number one, which took some time to get used to. Amendment number two, stay on your side of the line unless invited over. This was hard for Valerie and Sallisfer as the spirits of the Hands flowed evenly among their bodies, and they had merged into one, now twice. Lastly, Amendment number three developments toward death was to be as dignified as possible.

Sallisfer stopped and shifted into his horse form, finding it the most relaxing form he had under his hat. He trotted off, thinking of yesterday's discovery that Kal could enter The Paradise.

"This isn't a good sign," the Headmaster said at their appointment. "It is no surprise for Kris as he helped grow the place…but the fact that Kalea could enter…," The Headmaster took Valerie's hand and squeezed it, "Perhaps you have given her too much of an advantage?"

Valerie shook her head, "There is no such thing in times of war."

"There is when it works against your own timeline." The Headmaster snarled, "I demand you to stop increasing her power level. I need you two veterans alive as long as possible."

Valerie was about to protest, but the Headmaster cut her off with a glare and asked, "Have you been able to figure out how to lower the effects of the power surges?"

Valerie looked away, withdrew her hand, stood up from her throne, and walked around the room to avoid eye contact. That's when the Headmaster's changing eyes landed on Sallisfer, cold and emotionless. His thousands of years of living showed in his demeanor but not in his looks. The Headmaster looked like a man in his prime forties, but he was ruthless and cared little for those who would die.

"We have found a way, Headmaster." Sallisfer began, "However, it is not an option."

"What is it?" the Headmaster asked, raising an eyebrow.

"I will continue to have power surges till I am 18." Valerie chimed in, still not looking at the Headmaster. "The power surges are so high and uncontrollable because I am not a woman but a child. A child holding the spirit of a mature adult. Having it inside my body before I could even wipe my own behind properly and sing my ABCs. A child who has walked into Hell and has lived this nightmare since I began to walk. Despite all your careful planning of the "time of my choosing," Valerie stated disapprovingly. Darkness sought for power. The Spirit-Doom is greedy, and it wanted me more than my predecessor. So, it poisoned me, leaking into me the darkness well before you let go of its reins."

Valerie chuckled. "They were released from the bonds you held them in. We were forced to contain them till we could understand what was happening.

Then, finally, when you lost your grip, you gave up and stopped fighting for the innocent children you laid the burden onto. THAT IS WHY I HAVE

POWER SURGES!" *Valerie stated with power, and the room suddenly engulfed in flames. However, the fire was not out of control as they were being held at bay from burning the room. The Headmaster's eyes took in his surroundings, showing his fear briefly before carefully and calmly closing his left hand. Valerie and Doom allowed him to believe he could still control them and calmly eliminated the flames.*

"What do you have to do to lower the surges?" The Headmaster demanded.

"I must become a woman." Something I will be when I become of age."

"So, after 16… so we have to wait 6.5 months or so." The Headmaster sighed and ran his hand through his hair.

Valerie shook her head and turned to leave. "This conversation is over. We will inform you of our progress on the front," Valerie pronounced before saying good night.

Sallisfer sighed, coming back to the present. Tomorrow was his last day of freedom before heading out to war again. *This is not how I imagined my junior year to be, spent away from school while Vinnie gets to have all the fun. Next year… If I make it, I will be a Senior. Will I be able to participate in any events like a typical teen?* He thought as he shook his mane and started to walk again. There were just too many questions fumbling through his mind when he smelled an intruder and pricked his ears. *How could anyone have known that The Paradise was open?* Laughter came from the pool; he shifted into a cat and walked silently to the willow curtains. He peered underneath it.

He saw Kal and Kris swimming, talking, and… holding hands. Anger shot threw him, but he contained it. He and Valerie held hands, and that didn't mean anything. He observed and listened. Kal glanced over at his hiding place and grinned, her gold blue eyes bright, and her usually white colored hair was now blue. Kal cuddled into Kris's arms and seemed to purposefully enrage him as she kissed Kris's cheek.

The gates in Sallisfer's heart burst, and the monster came out. Still, the monster was patient, allowing its anger to grow with each little giggle and slight touch, and when they stepped out of the pool, it attacked the nearest one possible.

Kal watched in horror as Sallisfer attacked Kris. She didn't know how to stop them. As her mind raced with ideas, Valerie transported long sabers in her hands. She handed two to Kal, who looked at them dumbfounded. They had wolf heads carved into the hilt with fierce golden eyes.

"They are yours chosen. You will know how to use them without being taught, and don't be afraid to kill with them," Valerie instructed sternly, but fear was in her green eyes.

Kal tightened her grip on the hilts of her twin sabers, noticing that they felt right in her hands.

Kal and Valerie attacked side by side, separating the monster from Kris. Kal saw in her peripheral Valerie checking on Kris and, realizing he was safe, continued her attack on the monster. Kal didn't think about what she was doing, she just let it happen, and before she knew it, Kal was standing on the bloody ground with Sallisfer's limp and torn body at her feet. She stared at the blood dripping off her blades in utter shock.

"Don't worry," she heard a gasp from behind her. Kal turned and looked over to see Valerie; as she stumbled toward her.

"What have I done?" Kal shrieked as Valerie fell limp over Sallisfer's bloody corps. Kris stared at Kal with an alarmed look as the sky darkened. The crystal-clear pool that had been so tranquil a moment ago suddenly grew violent and dark. Huge waves started to crash upon the shore as the wind began to roar loudly, whipping them back towards the forest, which swayed with creaking trees. Rain turned to hail mixed with sleet poured down on them, leaving welts where they bounced off their exposed skin. Kris pushed his way through the elements over to Kal's side. Kris's face was a mask of horror as he grabbed Kal's hand. The next thing they knew, they were being handed towels as they shivered in a cool dark hallway.

"Strip down and dry yourself off," Valerie's mother said, pulling out a curtain that hid one from the other. Valerie's mother handed them a robe and led them down a torch-lit hall.

"Strange weather we're having, isn't it?" she said, casting a worried look over her shoulder.

"Where are we?" Kal asked, looking around and not meeting Ms. Wing's eyes.

"You're at Starlight Castle, on Mage Hill, in the realm of magic," Ms. Wing said. "This is where all the dances, big meetings, and other things happen." She cast Kal the look that said I know you changed the subject on purpose.

They walked in silence for some time. Kal lost track of how many flights of stairs they took till she had to stop for a breath. The only thing on this flight was a tall hard oak door. The door appeared old and weathered but sturdy and carried an air that chilled Kal to the bone. On the door carved in gold were the strangest letters Kal ever did see. They were not quite pictographs, but they were not letters either.

"What does that say?" Kal asked.

Kris ran a hand over the carvings and shivered. "And what language is it in?" Kris asked, his eyes bright with curiosity.

Ms. Wing sighed; she ran her hand over her eyes and said the words that glowed hot when she pronounced the words in a clear but tired voice, a language neither of them knew.

She then opened her eyes and smiled at the dumbfounded expressions on Kal and Kris's faces. "It's in spell form, well, in the dark spell form. It reads Hands of Doom and Heaven only; on pain of death shall anyone enter." Ms. Wing's smile turned sad. "There once was an incident a few years ago with the last set of hands. A student tried to enter the room…." She paused, "All that was found was a chard resemblance. After that, even the Hands would use the door only from time to time… they keep it well locked. There is a guard who patrols the halls to make sure no one ever tries it again."

"How morbid," Kris muttered, eyeing Kal with anxiety in his eyes.

"Anyway, this way to the hot baths and showers." Ms. Wing led them farther down the hall, up another flight of stairs that led them directly into a large room. The room contained very little but had two doors on either side. A man walked from one door, wrapped in a towel. He smiled, walked to a cabinet, pulled out a blue robe, and pulled it on. Then he walked through the wall. Kris and Kal exchanged a confused look.

"That was Mike; he is a natural...show off," Ms. Wing chuckled.

"That door, as you must have guessed, is the men and the other the women. The robes for unnatural people, like you, Kris, as a Shifter, must come out here. But normal robes are stored in the room. For unnatural, check the tag. It will tell you what they can do."

"Thank you, Ms. Wing," Kris said, walking to the men's room a little faster than necessary, then with a sigh, he stopped before going in and looked back with a grin at Kal.

"What?" she asked, trying to be as natural as possible as Kris was trying.

"Ah, nothing," he said, walking into the room.

"I don't like the look on his face; I wouldn't trust him, Kal," Ms. Wing said, looking down at Kal with a worried but amused look on her face.

Kal had a hard time accepting help from Ms. Wing, as she *thought if she only knew my actions*...then she answered Ms. Wing's concern. "Don't worry, Ms. Wing, I don't," Kal said with a forced grin and walked into the women's room. She walked up to an unoccupied shower room, closed the stall door behind her, and bolted it into place. At that moment, Kal realized the blood on her hands, which left blood on her robe and the door. She quickly turned the water on with a shaking hand and washed her hands with the soap provided.

Kal's body shook, and she felt sobs rising in her throat as tears slid down her face, carried away by the hot water that showered upon her. She had killed her best friend, her sister. She shook as she tried to wash off the blood splashed on her arms. Not only had she killed them out of cold rage, but she had also ripped Sallisfer's body to shreds.

There was no Valerie to yell and then comfort her about almost killing them this time. She had done it; she had killed them. Kal looked at herself in the fogging mirror and found herself even more unrecognizable as the magic left her body.

"When did my normal appearance become a stranger to me?" She whispered, allowing the pain to fade with the magic. Would it be better not to feel anything? She thought.

Kal finished showering and found a clean robe to cover herself once she dried off. She also found a packaged toothbrush and paste in a basket at the sink and brushed her teeth, wondering what time it was, then realized she did not care. She was just ready for bed.

Kal walked out the door to Ms. Wing, who was waiting for her. She looked at Kal and did a double take, "You poor thing. Did Sallisfer and Valerie work you too hard?" she asked, placing her hand on Kal's shoulder. "Let me get you to a guest bedroom. There you can rest." Kal let Ms. Wing lead her down the hall without protesting and helped her into a room. On the bed were Kal's pajamas. She dressed without question and crawled into the big bed. The last thing she saw before she closed her eyes was Valerie's pain-filled green eyes.

CHAPTER 28

Always a Horse Girl

Valerie sat in the barn, her arms around a pony's neck, her fingers deep in his mane as he lay in his stall, letting her cry on his shoulder. "You okay, Val?" Tema asked, looking into the stall, her bay still tacked from their shift on the border.

Valerie nodded, not looking up or moving from where she lay curled around the bay pinto. Tema sighed and looked over at her horse, which flicked its ears, eyeing the scene. "What do you think, Rover?" The horse sighed, and Tema nodded. "I think that too."

"He complained about his breakfast being late." Valerie's voice cracked as she tried not to laugh or reveal how parched her throat was from crying.

"Is that right, Rov… you want your breakfast?" Tema laughed as the horse nodded, and she sighed, "Boys and their stomachs."

She looked at Valerie, who still refused to look at her, before calling to the stable hand who had just walked into the barn for his morning shift. "Good morn Mr. Rengo. Do you mind starting with Rover this morning? I have to attend to my goddaughter." Mr. Rengo smiled as he walked over to them.

"Good morn Ms. Johnson. Did you have a good ride?" He asked, taking the reins with a nod; then he saw Valerie still wrapped into the pony, and his smile faded slightly. "Ms. Valerie, your mother, is worried sick about you up at the house…have you been there with Jack this whole time?"

Valerie nodded, and Mr. Rengo shook his head. "You and that pony go way back. I remember when you and your mother brought him home all those years ago. The wild beast has calmed way down, I see." He looked at Tema and whispered, "Good luck."

"Thank you, Mr. Rengo, for taking the time to untack Rover for me." Tema smiled.

"It is my pleasure." He bowed and led the horse to the cross ties. While he took care of her horse, Tema opened the stall and picked Valerie up. Although Tema wasn't the tallest or strongest, she managed to pull the teen up and into her arms.

"Come now, girl," she said, and Valerie relented, stood up, and walked with Tema to the dock overlooking the lake. There they sat in the marble chairs silently as they watched the sunrise with bright colors painting the sky.

"So…" Tema started as the colors began to fade. "Do you care to tell me why you are covered in blood?"

"I lost another life…." Valerie whispered, "…well Sallisfer is the one who died, but…."

"You die with him." Tema finished at Valerie's nod. She sighed. "How did it happen…you weren't on a mission or anything, were you?"

"No…that is the crazy thing…. we were killed by one of our own." Valerie did not look at Tema as she spoke.

Tema stiffened, "Do we have a traitor in our mix? Did you kill this person back?"

Valerie laughed with a tired sigh, "No, we cannot get revenge that way… I fear it was foretold that the chosen one would kill us."

"So, you knew this would happen, and you *let* it happen…what is wrong with you?" Tema asked.

Valerie sighed, "I didn't know it was going to happen last night, and up until now, I thought The Paradise was safe."

"So, there was no one there to collect your bodies and be there for you when you woke up?" Tema took Valerie's hand. "I remember when you died during the civil war. It was the scariest day of my life. You were 12 years old. You had no right to be out in the battle or die in it….” Tears filled Tema's eyes, and she squeezed Valerie's hand. “Your body had healed itself, and you had been restored to the immortal beauty you were meant to be. An indissoluble breathing shell, Sallisfer wasn't restored till his spirit returned to the body and you.” She looked over the water as they both sat in silence, and a blue heron landed, searching for his breakfast, “You returned to become mortal once more.”

“Is it true I came back crying for my mother and demanding where Pal went?” Valerie asked.

“Yes…” Tema answered, “You have always been a horse girl.”

“Pal has a nice retirement teaching autistic children…As a volunteer at the farm who adopted him, I check on him occasionally.” Valerie stated.

Tema smiled, “Is that why you went to Jack?”

“He was the only horse in the barn… he had his teeth cleaned last night. So, he had to stay in to wake up a bit.” Valerie smiled, “He is also my heart pony and has been here since I was nine.”

Tema nodded. “Yes, he is very special. He put my Jasmine in the water jump his first month on the farm.” They both laughed.

“He has done that to many a girl.” Valerie laughed.

“Not you…” Tema pointed out.

“Well… I have a way with him.” Valerie smiled.

Tema laughed, “You talked him out of it?”

They laughed again, and Tema turned to Valerie. “I am sorry you lost another life…I am even more sorry that I could not be there to guard over you in your weakest moment.”

“You have.” Valerie laughed. “Nothing beats the low I am in now.”

“How is Sallisfer holding up?” Tema asked though the look on her face showed she already knew.

“He is drunk and in a slumber at the moment… he is upset that Kal…Kalea has chosen another.” Valerie looked away, almost ashamed.

“Another? She gave up Sallisfer, as you knew would happen. Who did she choose?” Tema asked, amused.

“Kris.” The name left Valerie's lips in a pained whisper.

Tema smiled. "Does that mean I can have my trooper back whole again? Don't get me wrong, he still can ride, no problem, but darn, he is a total goof."

Valerie sighed, her eyes pained. "He is who he was meant to be if he hadn't been tainted… and I didn't take away everything from him."

"Mental memory may be fixable, but muscle memory is forever." Valerie sighed, and Tema squeezed her hand again. "So, do I get him back or not?"

"Not yet… they are still in the honeymoon phase of love." Valerie rubbed her nose and closed her eyes, "They have to get well attached… as that is happening, he will start to become his old self more and more."

"I see…you wanted him to learn with her, not be above her." Tema realized.

"Kal is very easily intimidated…I did not think she would take to someone who stood with nothing to gain while she was stuck on the sidelines." Valerie leaned back in the chair.

"But…she took to Sallisfer." Tema pointed out.

"I didn't anticipate that twist of event. But unfortunately, it is true, if Sallisfer had minded his own business, it would not have happened at all." Valerie threw her hands up, exasperated.

"How is that the case? She was naturally taken by him as… well, you know." Tema changed her sentence at Valerie's look.

"I know, but still, she was to meet Kris first. Then, Sally, well, Sally had to move in." Valerie leaned her head back over the chair, dirt and shavings came out of her hair as she ran her fingers through the matted mess.

"If either of my girls made half the mess Sallisfer does," Tema sighed and shook her head. "How can his mother just let it happen?"

Valerie watched Tema's conflicted face of thought and made a profound point. "He is her only child and is destined to die…she doesn't want to push him away." Valerie sighed with empathy.

Tema squeezed her shoulder, "You turned out alright. Not an alcoholic by the age of 10."

"Well, he may be smarter than almost everyone, but he has no common sense. I am the brains in that department." Valerie grinned.

They laughed again and then sat silently as the barn became alive with activity. Up the hill traveling at a fast pace, horses came and galloped past them to their stalls for breakfast and grooming. People moved up and down the hill, some to clean water troughs, others to pitch hay or check fencing. Valerie knew her mother had walked by a few times, looking over at them as they had been chatting and wanting to talk but not daring to interrupt.

The dock was a special place. It was respected around the ranch as a place to go for privacy in a place that had no areas for privacy. The dock was also where Tema gave her advice to the young teens. The Lieutenant Generals were the backbone of the cavalry. They advised the young leader and developed the tactics and training needed. So many of those meetings happened on the dock looking out over the lake where a girl could be a girl, and the advisers took the load off her shoulders and made the task easier.

Tema broke the silence first as her eyes never left the girl she had watched grow up. "Is there any way to go back in time and get that life back? Being on the edge of war and losing your second life isn't the best thing you could have done?"

Valerie laughed. "No, it was pre-determined to happen…it moves the timeline a little closer to the end…and gives Kal a major power boost."

"It was worth the thought." Tema shrugged, "I was never good with time stuff."

Valerie sighed and threw a rock she had into the lake, "I hate the shiftiness of it all. The choices of the paths…it is so unpredictable but predictable if you know normal behavior… theory…and probability."

"It sounds like gobbly gunk," Tema declared, standing.

"It is." Valerie stood too and stretched.

"What are you going to do now?" Tema asked as a sly smile spread on Valerie's face.

"I am going to get my revenge on Kal…." Valerie's eyes gleamed.

Tema took a step back. "I thought you said you couldn't kill her?"

"I am not going to kill her…just scare her a little." Valerie grinned.

Tema laughed. "Sounds like a plan. Are you going to be at the ball tonight?"

"Do I have a choice?" Valerie asked, "The Hands are required."

"Just don't take Sallisfer's hangover from him this time… let him suffer for once, and maybe he will learn his lessons."

Valerie looked at her questionably, "But I don't get hangovers."

Tema nodded, "That is why you should let him have it on his own."

Valerie smiled and nodded. "I will try."

"That is all I ask for." Tema gave her a one-armed hug, and they went their separate ways.

CHAPTER 29

Valerie's Revenge

Kal woke with a startled yelp; a huge bang erupted on her door. "KAL! Are you awake?" Valerie hollered from the other side of the door.

"I am now," Kal muttered, sliding out of bed and unlocking the door.

"Good, now come on," Valerie said, dragging her down the hall before she had time to blink.

"Where are we going?" she asked.

"You'll see," Valerie said with a grin. She dragged her to the other end of the hall, into a room.

"Stay here," Valerie stated as she walked out of the room, closed the door behind her, and secured it with a click in the lock.

"How come I have a bad feeling about this?" Kal muttered as she heard the door click to lock.

"I would if I were you," a voice said behind her. Startled to discover she was not alone, Kal flew to the door, screaming. The trauma of the past day terrorized her mind as she pounded her fist on the door and found it useless. Finally, realizing her predicament, she mustered up enough courage in fear as she turned to see who was behind her.

Only to witness Kris rolling on the floor, laughing so hard that tears streamed down his face. Kal pouted, crossing her arms as you stared at Kris.

"It's not my fault you came up behind me," she said as Kris continued to laugh a few more moments before trying to gain his composure.

"Your reaction was priceless," he gasped between each word as he tried to breathe and recover. But when he looked at Kal's face, he broke into laughter again.

Kal scowled and tackled him.

"Hey!" he shouted, using his weight against her and rolling her over on her back.

"Well, you shouldn't have...." she was cut short by him kissing her.

"Love is in the air everywhere I look around," Valerie sang, opening the door. Behind her was a crowd of people.

"Sorry, couldn't help but break into song," she said with a grin. Both Kal and Kris turned uncountable shades of red.

Valerie's grin widened, "Sorry, but I had to do it; you two looked too good together not to *show* it off."

"About that... Can I kill you now? You got a few more lives left, don't you?" Kal asked, glaring at Valerie, and for the first time, Kal noticed that Valerie still had on the blood-stained shirt, she looked pale and worn, and yesterday's events came back to her remembrance.

Kal burst into tears. Overwhelming guilt weighed relentlessly upon her like gravity, pinning her to the floor. "I am so sorry," She cried. Valerie sat down beside her and went to wrap an arm around Kal, who winced away.

"It isn't your fault. It was going to happen eventually." Valerie soothed.

"I used up another life right at the start of a war... when you need them the most."

Valerie wrapped her arm around Kal despite her protest and pulled Kal closer to her side. "Death isn't that bad." Kal looked at her. "It is a nice place. I mean, I have never seen the golden gates or beyond, but the in-between place isn't that bad. They heal the body and mind because the way of death... it can be traumatic... but death is natural."

"Dying because your best friend lost her mind and killed you with strange sabers… natural."

"When your best friend's other half attacks and tries to kill your other half. Yes."

Kal looked at Valerie, who still wore a huge grin on her face, "Just don't kill us again, okay?"

"That's for the first kill, do it again, and you'll find trouble, not embarrassment," Sallisfer said, walking, well not walking, instead stumbling up beside Valerie.

"You had to get yourself sloshed, didn't you?" Valerie muttered, rolling her eyes in annoyance as she looked at him.

"Yes, I did. Having been shredded from limb to limb, I needed something to hold me together," Sallisfer said with a smile. "Unless you care to help?" Disgust crossed Valerie's face as she whirled around to face Sallisfer.

"You…You…" Valerie gave up and kicked him where it hurt. She had moved so fast from sitting beside Kal to standing that it hurt Kal's frazzled mind.

Laughter erupted in the hall as he gurgled and fell to his knees. Valerie turned to her audience and bowed.

"Thank you, thank you very much," she said with a grin before she and Sallisfer vanished in a flash of light.

"Where in the heck did she go off to?" Kal asked, tears now cold on her cheeks.

"I don't know," Kris said, shutting the door and putting a lock spell on it, "And quite frankly, who cares?"

"Do you think they forgive me?" Kal asked.

"Yes," Kris said, reaching out to Kal, who walked to the back of the room. She suddenly had no interest in anything.

Kris sighed, walked to her, and wrapped his arms around her as she began to cry again. He said nothing as he soothed her by gently rubbing her back and holding her as close as he could.

***

Sallisfer spent most of the morning puking his guts out, and let's just say it wasn't all from a hangover.

He couldn't find a way to close the door on his mind to Valerie's… feelings. They overpowered everything else, and the worst part was that he had no clue where Valerie and Holjus were to split them up. He was happy he wasn't near the room where Kal and Kris were, for he had an idea of what was going on in there as well. The thought sent him back to the bathroom. Finally, he crawled into bed and closed his eyes, and by doing so, he could see everything Valerie saw.…

Holjus seeped deep into the cool pond Valerie's parents had on the farm. Sighing as his body cooled down, Valerie laughed as she swam up to him. Pressing her body against him, the water around them began to boil.

Valerie smiled at Holjus, taking his hand and pressing it against her skin; at once, energy seeped from him and into her.

He grinned as her eyes rolled to the back of her head in pleasure. She felt Sallisfer's protest in her mind but totally ignored him. She wasn't going to allow him to ruin this moment in time.

Holjus picked her up and carried her to shore, kissing her slowly.

Sallisfer's fury engulfed her, and she stumbled when Holjus put her down on the ground. She caught herself and forced Sallisfer out of her mind. "I can do what I like," she replied before closing the doors on him. Valerie smiled at Holjus, and he couldn't help but smile back.

***

The next thing Valerie knew, she was opening her eyes to see three hundred Kals looking at her with concerned eyes. Valerie's ears rang, and her head hurt as she tried to recall what had happened. 'How long have I been out? Looks like you and Kris have been busy." Valerie found herself asking as she tried to clear her head of the illusion of multiple Kal's from her mind's eye. Kal looked over at Kris, who was checking Sallisfer's heartbeat. Her emotions split with concerns for her sister and friend.

"Can you help her?" Kal asked, pointing her finger at Valerie, who was grinning.

Kris sighed and walked over to them; he laid a hand on her forehead and said a few words.

The fog cleared from her mind. Valerie got up and looked over at Sallisfer and grinned.

"I am so going to pay for this," she said as she took Sallisfer's arms. She dragged him to the pond, then, much to Kal's and Kris's amazement, she lifted him up and threw him in.

"COLD!" Sallisfer shouted, flying out of the water. The three spectators laughed.

"Bye," Valerie said, transporting off before Sallisfer could get his hands on her.

"Any idea what happened?" Kris asked, "I mean between them?"

Kal shrugged, she knew it had something to do with Holjus, but Kris did not need to know about Holjus and Valerie just yet. "I haven't a clue." She lied, "I just hope it wasn't a reproduction of what I did."

"Hey baby, you did what was right. Don't let Sallisfer tell you otherwise." Kris said, wrapping her into a hug.

"I guess," was the only thing Kal could say.

CHAPTER 30

The Valentine's Dance

That afternoon Kal was walking down the torch-lit hall in Starlight Castle. She stopped at the Hands door; she could hear laughter from the other side and a few words that didn't make sense.

"...got dog?" she heard Valerie ask.

"Mmm...nope, go keep," Sallisfer said.

"You're lying," Valerie said.

"No, I'm not, look," Sallisfer said.

"Ewe, no thanks," Valerie said, and Sallisfer chuckled.

"Come on, it's near one. We have to get ready for the dance," Sallisfer said. Kal heard Valerie sigh.

"Do I *have* to go?" Valerie asked.

"Yes, they are expecting us, so it's a must. I mean, we already RSVP, so we go," Sallisfer laughed.

"Fine, but I'm not wearing that dress you got."

"If you wear it, I'll wear what you got me."

"Deal."

Kal dashed behind the corner and peered around it. She saw Valerie and Sallisfer walk out of the room, wearing robes. They crossed the hall only to stop and face the wall. Which made no sense to Kal until

283

Sallisfer pressed his hand against the wall, and it moved, revealing a secret doorway. Valerie and Sallisfer walked into the hidden room. But right before the door closed, Kal slipped in. Finding it easy to hide, Kal hid behind a cart of towels all colored green and blue, with Sallisfer's and Valerie's initials on them. She almost gasped out loud as maids came into the room threw side doors; they swarmed around, Valerie and Sallisfer.

The next thing Kal saw was them in steaming baths full of bubbles. After that, the room began to smell like Myrtle, the flower that means love.

The maids began to wash both of them, massaging and rinsing. More maids came in with trays. One had two glasses of sparkling grape juice or wine, the other some green grapes. Finally, a man walked in and sat beside Valerie with a string of grapes, and a woman sat beside Sallisfer. Kal's eyes widened as she recognized Hillary. Hillary and the man fed them. It was like they were in Roman times.

Valerie got done first, and the man left. With her last rinse, Valerie was again surrounded by maidens and was dressed in a robe.

Valerie then walked over to Sallisfer's bath. "Leave us," she commanded, taking the grapes out of Hillary's hand. The maids nodded and left. However, Hillary looked jealous, but Kal could tell she was pleased with herself.

Valerie sat on the headboard of the tub, dipping her legs into the hot water by his shoulders. Sallisfer rubbed a hand absentmindedly down her legs, earning him a slight playful slap on the back of the head. He grinned as he kissed her foot.

She laughed, dropped a grape in his mouth, and started to massage his shoulders.

"Alright, what do you want?" he asked, laying his head in her lap and looking up at her.

"Nothing. What makes you think that?" Valerie asked, but a sly grin was coming on her face.

"You only pretend to love me when you want me to do something, give you something, or say something," he said matter of factly.

Valerie sighed, "You know me way too much, old friend." She smiled, feeding him the last grape. "I want you to give the group a show.

I'll play along, I've already asked Holjus, and he thinks it is a good idea…" she trailed off, and Sallisfer rolled over in the tub with a smile.

"What kind of show?" He asked, looking at her like a begging puppy.

"The one that we…. uh, go out."

"Why?" he asked, smiling.

"Rumors are bouncing around out of control, and some of them are true…about me going out with a demon…." Valerie bit her lip, which trembled, and her eyes watered with compressed tears. "I must stop the rumors before the headmaster asks me about them…I can't lie to him, you know that." She looked at him desperately.

"Fine, I can do that, but you have to agree to play along, okay… and I mean fully," he smiled, lifting himself onto his knees, the water falling off his strong, tanned torso.

"Yes, I'll play along….and it better be play," she playfully glared as he stroked her hair out of her face.

"It will be. I have a girlfriend. Even though she hates me, I still love her," he almost whispered as he kissed Valerie's hand that went out to hit him.

Valerie rolled her eyes. "It is for the better, Sally, you know that," she breathed, wrapping her legs around him and pulling him closer.

"I know, baby, but I mean, what does Kris have that I don't?" he asked, nibbling on her ear.

Kal swallowed. They were talking about her and snogging each other.

"He has her mind," Valerie whispered between breaths.

"Yes, but that doesn't make a difference," Sallisfer argued. Valerie pulled back, then took both his hands in hers and held him at a distance.

"But it does. It affects us every day; you know what the prophecy said, I have to choose between my heart and my mind, and one will kill me faster than the other. But, I mean, I…." she trailed off as Sallisfer leaned up and kissed her lightly on the cheek.

"You feel pulled apart, I understand," he said. Then staring into each other's eyes, they drew closer to each other like they were going to make out again but were interrupted by a maid coming into the room.

"Ah....sorry to interrupt?" she said, a blush coming on her cheeks.

Valerie jerked back, raising a hand as if to strike Sallisfer, but waved the maid off instead.

"You're not. Tell the others to come in and get him ready to leave," she said, getting up and walking to the door. "I'll see you in the room," a grin washed over Sallisfer's face, and he nodded.

Valerie giggled and disappeared through the doorway, followed by Kal, who followed Valerie into the Hands' room, not caring what the sign said.

The room wasn't a room at all. It was a door into The Paradise, but not the side she had seen on Valerie's tour.

It had a beautiful canopy bed, a wardrobe, the sky as its roof, and a carpet of grass. Valerie smiled and threw her arms up in the air. The wind rushed around her as if she was the eye of a hurricane. Kal stared from behind the wardrobe, eyes fixed on the scene before her.

When the wind stopped, Valerie was dressed in a long red skirt with a split on the side baring her leg, a one-strap shirt that showed her stomach, and her feet adorned with red sandals. Sallisfer walked in, and he sighed.

"I missed it," he grumbled. Valerie smiled at him.

"What held you up?" she asked.

"Kris was asking me what he should get Kal," he said with a shrug.

"He's just now thinking about that. What kind of guy is he?" Valerie asked.

"I don't know, but he has something for her, but he doesn't know if she'll like it," Sallisfer said as the wind whipped and rushed around him. Valerie stepped into the wind, and Kal exited the room as fast as she could.

She swiftly closed the door behind her and started running down the hall, but she stopped when she realized she had something stuck to her shoe.

She pulled it off and realized it was two playing cards. One was of a rottweiler, the other an overuse cut-ripped-in-half card of a man's upper half, and a handwritten note with an arrow.

Naked Man

"I'm not so sure I want to know about this," she muttered, shaking her head.

"HEY! Hey!" someone called, making Kal jump.

"Sorry, didn't mean to scare the Cat," Kris said as she turned to face him.

"The what?" Kal asked as Kris stood with a goofy smile on his face.

"The scare-dee-cat," Kris said. Kal took a deep breath to calm herself. He was just trying to get her to pounce on him, so he could kiss her again.

"It is not going to work," she said.

A look of disappointment washed over Kris's face to such an extent that Kal sighed, walked up to him, and lightly kissed him on the cheek before walking off down the hall.

Kal laughed as she heard Kris's sigh behind her.

"You want more?" she asked over her shoulder, knowing he was watching her depart.

"Pleeeease," he said.

"Then you're going to have to catch me," she said, throwing a grin over her shoulder. She laughed as Kris took off in pursuit. She took off, racing through the halls of Starlight Castle, dodging whoever was in her way. She glanced behind her to see Kris beginning to gain. It didn't stop her from squeaking when he caught her.

Just as Kal turned to face Kris, Valerie's voice floated up to her.

"I know you two want to be alone, but we have a party to prepare for... So, break it up." She grinned at Kal's and Kris's look of desire for each other.

"Later..." Kal smirked, looking meaningfully at Kris before turning to go to her room.

"Kal! Ava's going to be waiting to do your hair and makeup!" Valerie shouted. Making them depart even faster than they intended.

Valerie then glared at Kris. "Go to your own room and get dressed. I expect you can fix your own hair?" Kris nodded.

He watched as Valerie vanished into thin air before walking down the hall to his room. Kris changed his clothes and fiddled with his hair, trying to get it all to lay down straight before putting on a visor to preserve his manliness from wearing pink.

"Leave it to the generals not to tell you everything when you go shopping," he muttered, looking at himself in the mirror. The day he had gone to the mall to pick something out for Kal, he hadn't known that he would have to wear the color to match. Cringing inwardly, he thought *I picked pink.* Knowing by now that girls take longer and they had almost two hours till the party, Kris sat on his bed and opened his book. Its thick gray-blue leather shined like dragon scales. He turned to a new page that had appeared the night before, "The Mind Meld..." he muttered to himself again. As he read, it had to be Sci-fi Star Trek stuff. Perhaps the book was pulling a trick on him. Maybe Valerie had bewitched it again, like when he had found a spell on how to get rid of pimples. When he performed the spell, his hair turned to spaghetti noodles. The memory made Kris chuckle; he thought of middle school; *what a time to be alive.* Kris tried to conjure more memories of middle school, but his head had begun to hurt again. He rubbed his temple. The headaches were starting to become less and less frequent as these last two months had gone by, his dreams a little more focused, but the days became a little more déjà vu. Valerie had said it was because he could predict the future, but he knew there was more to it, and she wasn't telling him.

"How is this mind meld going to help me any way... I don't think I will be diving into anyone's mind till I am named Hand, and then it is more of sharing it than diving in every once in a while." He closed the book and looked at the time. He still had plenty of time; he got up and paced the room, stopping and closing his eyes. The ache was fading from his head. He conjured up a bottle of water and took a sip to calm his nerves.

A glance at the clock told him it was time to get Kal. He laid the last hair in place and glanced at the basket of flowers, Sallisfer had stated that Kal would like them, but Kris was skeptical.

He sighed, "Might as well get this over with." he picked up the basket and walked out of his room, heading toward Kal's room, which was a short distance and not far from his.

When he reached her door, he heard laughter coming from inside. Kris was unsure of himself, rethinking what he was going to do.

He was about to turn away when Kal's voice came to him from the room. "Come on in, Kris, you're not disturbing anything; we're all done here!" Kris took a deep breath and turned the knob; the door swung open with the force of his push, and what he saw astounded him.

"What do you think?" Kal asked, smiling at him.

Kris stood looking at her, spellbound and near speechless. Regaining his sanity and quickly remembering the question, "You look.... you look breathtakingly wonderful," he answered above a whisper.

Kal loving his reaction, she smiled brilliantly, taking in his admiration, and began spinning around for Kris to see all sides.

Kris's jaw dropped, and his eyes widened. Kal beamed at him as she walked toward him and reached her hand toward his face, and with her index finger, she pushed up his chin, closing his mouth.

"Staring is impolite. Didn't your mother teach you that?" she said.

Laughter erupted from the bed. Ava had sat cross-legged, watching the whole scene. She had been holding back her laughter, but now she was sprawled on the floor laughing.

"It's nice to know my work is appreciated," she gasped as she caught her breath.

Kris looked at her with bewilderment. "You did this?" he asked, pointing at Kal.

"Yep, she did," Kal said, "Even if it might not last long."

Kris smiled weakly, "Don't tempt me," he said, a dizzy look in his eyes.

"You do know those need water, right," Ava said casually, mentioning the flowers.

"...What?" Kris asked, then he looked down at the flowers. He stared at them blankly for a moment, not remembering how they got there. "Oh, yeah," he said, holding out the basket to Kal, "These are for you."

Kal grinned. "I was waiting for you to remember..." she threw her arms around him, kissing him, and...

Valerie walked into the room, "O... obviously, this is a bad time, but the dance party will start in three minutes, and all masters are to be in there, so move it."

Kal pouted at Valerie's interruption but took the flowers out of Kris's hands and placed them on her bedside table. "Then we better be off," she said to Kris, who bowed in agreement. Causing her to giggle.

Valerie was doing a final assessment of their appearance. Then, as they were about to depart, she halted them both. "Wait a minute, Ava, more lipstick, Kris, wash your face," Valerie said, handing Kris a rag out from under her black cloak, along with a mirror, before walking out of the room.

Kris washed his face clean of lipstick; while Ava put more on Kal. Then together, they walked, hand in hand, to the ballroom. When they entered, they noticed that Valerie and Sallisfer weren't in the room.

"They rush us, yet they're late," Kris muttered. Kal nodded in agreement.

They walked toward the group of masters in the center of the room.

"Wine?" a server asked them, holding a tray of wine glasses.

"Ah...no thanks, a little underaged," Kris said. The server looked at them, confused.

"A master is never underaged here. They are all the same, and age does not matter," he said.

"It's okay, Jerry, they are new to the board. They haven't had the chance to be briefed on the ways of the master," Master Masashi said with a smile. He took two wine glasses off the tray and handed them to Kal and Kris. "The Headmaster likes wine to be served with every dinner. He hails from a time water was not safe to drink." He smiled. "Don't worry, it is more like grape juice, not a lot of alcohol if you pace yourself. The real stuff is for the adults."

He nodded to other people mingling around. They varied from very young to old. "Thank you," Kal sipped at the wine, but Kris just held it, looking at it with fear.

Kal looked up at him, "Look, I'm not dying," she said, taking another sip, "See!" She said. Kris groaned at her exclamation.

"I am so going to regret this," he muttered, taking a sip.

"Hey, Kal." Arcy smiled, approaching them while being arm and arm with Talys.

"Hey, Arcy." Kal said, "I love your dress." Arcy smiled as Talys spun her around, allowing the Cinderella-like dress to swirl, leaving rainbow glitter behind.

"I love yours as well. Kris, you did a great job." She gave him a wink. "I also think you look dashing in pink." Kris grimaced and blushed, taking another sip of his drink.

"You all look so beautiful." Ms. Wing smiled as she captured a picture of them. She wore a beautiful green dress that Valerie and Arcy had selected for her.

"Where is Dad?" Arcy asked; just then, Mr. Wing came beaming over with Mr. Wheedle and Master Fisher at his side.

"Love," Ms. Wing said. "I thought you said you would take the night off."

Mr. Wheedle smiled at her and bowed apologetically while Mr. Fisher simply looked bored. "We were just discussing Valerie's progress in her lessons." Mr. Wing said, taking his wife's hand and beaming at Kal and Arcy. "How are you all?"

"I am fine," Kal said.

"Me. Too" Kris said. "Thank you."

Arcy gave Mr. Wing a hug. "I am great, Dad. How are you?"

Mr. Wing laughed and hugged her back. "Hungry, where are the Hands?" He asked 'looking around.

"Fashionably late…as always," said Dona with a shake of her head and checking her watch.

"You must do better." Mr. Wing joked, "Hadn't you talked to them about this."

Dona rolled her eyes. "If they don't show up in a moment, I will send Tema after them." She nodded to Tema and Walker, who were talking to Master Lee by the fire.

"Ladies and Gentlemen! Can I have your attention?" A man called from the top of the steps leading to a double set of doors.

The room grew quiet as everyone focused on the man, "Thank you," he said. "I have the honor to announce the arrival of the Hands!" he said. "I give you the breathtaking, the stunning, the beautiful, Valerie!

And her partner, Sallisfer!" The doors opened, and the Hands stepped out into the room.

Kal could hear every man's heart skip a beat as their eyes landed on Valerie. But she sighed, shaking her head. "This is ridiculous," she muttered.

Kris glanced down at her with a smile, "And just think soon that will be us." Kal smiled and leaned into him, making him purr lightly. After the announcement, Kal walked with Kris.

"You're so nice," she said as they walked to the long tables that held food. The buffet for the special occasion was catered beautifully. The setup was very fancy, Kal thought as she glanced at the food on the table. It was a diverse assortment placed strategically around a giant pig that had been pit-cooked for two days.

Surrounding the centered food item for display were baked potatoes, yams, steamed vegetables of all types, macaroni and cheese- broccoli casserole, and a huge salad. There was so much more that Kal could not identify, and her eyes admired the dessert table. She smiled at the chocolate fountain, the strawberries, and the cookies. She was delighted to see the variety of cakes.

Once their plates were full, they sat down at the next large table. The chairs Kal noted had been carved for people a lot taller than her as she let her feet dangle over the edge of the chair. "I feel like a child in this chair." She smiled as Kris gave her a wink.

Kal watched Valerie and Sallisfer intently as she and Kris ate, wondering if they were acting. If they were, it was a stellar performance. They presented themselves as a couple should. Kris stopped with two glasses of wine and just ate; Kal ate little and didn't stop with the wine till dessert. Kris chose a lovely dessert wine that made Kal wonder if he had ever ordered wine before and when.

After they ate, everyone moved out to the dance floor. Valerie and Sallisfer had the first dance to a song that had the other masters gossiping in quick whispers. Knowingly Kris smiled broadly. "That is the song they first danced to when they were named Doom and Heaven at the age of four. They were against tradition. I see that that has returned." Kris informed Kal.

"What is the tradition?" Kal asked as they watched The Hands dance to an instrumental version of one of her favorite songs. "The Menuet and Gavotte." Kris laughed. "They have been doing that one the last 2 years... it is boring to watch." "He nodded to the Hands. "This is so much more fun.

"How do you know that?" Kal asked. Kris looked at her, a little confused.

"Because the party is for everyone when the Hands are named. Not just for Masters. Everyone must know who's in charge."

Kris said, "Remember, I come from a very magical family." Kal nodded and swallowed the last sip of wine.

Kris shook his head, "Now you are ridiculous," he said, taking the glass from her and making it poof away; then they joined the next dance.

They danced and had a good time till Valerie walked up smiling and making small talk with some of the other masters. She looked at Kal and rolled her eyes with an understanding smile. "You best be getting her to bed," Kris looked down at Kal's elated face and then back at Valerie, a little stunted. "But I want to stay," he whined.

"Bed sounds good to me," Kal said, a huge grin washing over her face as she stared at Kris with lust in her eyes.

"You're right... the bed does sound good..." Kris grinned. Valerie turned an evident shade of green.

"Then go," Sallisfer said, walking up and wrapping an arm around Valerie, who buried her face in his red coat, hiding her sick features.

Kal and Kris vanished in a flash of light, and Sallisfer walked into the back garden with Valerie.

"I believe the party is a success," Valerie said, her arm linked with his as they continued the nightly stroll gazing at the amazing flowers.

"Yes, it is." Sallisfer agreed with a nod. "Thank you for helping it look so amazing."

"Who knew party planning was one of my talents." She laughed, making Sallisfer chuckle.

"I like how you added our song for our dance... caused quite a sensation in there... honestly I thought you had forgotten."

"I almost had, to tell you the truth… But I think the merge, the disappearance of the wall between us…." Valerie paused and squeezed Sallisfer's arm, "I don't know, I just don't hate you that much anymore."

Sallisfer laughed before saying, "Same, back at you."

CHAPTER 31

Love is the Heart of Confusion

Valerie stared out the window watching the rain. Her essay on Alexander the Great laid open on the computer long forgotten. Her mind was far away, racing in the woods of The Paradise, away from this crazy war that was raging not so far away.

March had come upon them fast, and with it came the endless rain showers her southern home knew all too well. March and April were unpredictable months for the weather in any realm and place, but she swore the farm and the rift saw the worst of all the storms. She cast her inner eye on the troops' progress, contacting Tema, who stood guard over the calvary. Tema reporting all was well; everything was going smoothly, and their training was paying off. Valerie felt the tension building behind her eyes and rubbed her temple to lessen the strain. Her mental thoughts gave way to where she wanted to be…. *I should be out there with them, not here, doing homework.* She glanced at the console before she stood and stretched her limbs… Walking around her room, she contemplated heading out despite orders to stay home.

Valerie dismissed her thoughts as she remembered the headmaster's look and statement. "Everyone must have at least two days off the front field." Being headstrong, Valerie reacted to his firm rebuke of her protested days off. And he sealed his demand with a family connection.

"Your mother needs you at home. She has been very worried about you." He waved one of the many scrolls with her mother's handwriting at her. "Besides, it is family dinner night. You should be there for that."

Valerie cleared her head with a physical shake as she pulled at her ponytail holder, freeing her hair; she ran her fingers through it, then recreated a more secure ponytail.

Her walkabout led her back to her study area. She changed the music on the computer to something more upbeat and began to work again. She hadn't gotten far with her studies when her mind started to wander again, and she found herself staring back out the window. The rain was changing to sleet. She glanced at the clock; it revealed it was almost time to feed the horses. She smiled, knowing they were resting in the barn due to the crazy weather.

***

Despite it being a slightly warmer winter, it was a very wet and cold March. The first day of spring had sprung not just two days ago, and Spring break was on the horizon from school. She sighed as she thought about the places she was going to take Kal over the break. "Fire Whip, The Desert, she has to meet the Elves… I wonder if I should take her to the Dwarf mines or if Talys should." She wrote a quick sticky note to give to her brother at supper. She knew she would not take Kal anywhere near the Fairy Kingdom. The last king had died in the Demon attack, and no girl of childbearing age was safe. She looked back at her essay and then back out the window. A soft touch on her shoulder made her jump, and she looked up to see Sallisfer staring down at her. "What?" she asked. He smiled, pulling her from her seat, and she slipped into his arms.

"You are so distracted today." He whispered in her hair as she cuddled up to him as he sat with her in his lap.

"I just don't know what to do." She admitted, with her eyes closed. "About what?"

"About everything… I keep remembering what the oracle said. As Valerie settled into Sallisfer's embrace, her mind wandered, recalling words and saying them once more…

Black glass holds your death in its hands,
Darkness stares into golden eyes,
But love will fulfill any demands
And Life's story is open to rise.

On your soul, there is a path,
One must choose to go with your soul or mind.
Pick carefully. One will lead you to my wrath,
Balance you will never find.
Blood rivers will flow from your veins

Mountains will crumble from your screams.
Your hands will loosen from the reins
Dooming your whole team.

Down to the ashes, you will fall
Rising from the heat, she will succeed."

Sallisfer pulled away from her and shook her a little. "There is no one I would rather be doomed with," he said. "We will figure it all out."

"I am just so confused," Valerie said, her eyes filling with tears. Sallisfer kissed her lips.

"Perhaps I can help," he whispered against her lips.

Kal walked into the house after helping Ms. Wing in the barn. As she hung up her raincoat, Kal pulled out the strange note from Valerie stating she could not help feed. Kal crumpled it up in frustration; lately, she hadn't spent much time with her sister and felt lost not having someone to talk to.

She reached down to peel off her muddy boots and decided that it had to be the weather that had her feeling so upset. Once her boots were off, she stretched and walked to the bathroom, humming a happy tune to offset her mood. It worked as she remembered she didn't have to get up for school the following day. Thoughts filled her mind as she got cleaned up in the restroom, thinking *it is so crazy*. She washed her hands and continued her thought how *it's nearly the end of March.*

She looked at her reflection and smiled at the power sparkling in her blue eyes. "Sorcerous Kalea," she said out loud, only to giggle. As she opened the restroom door, she stopped before exiting passed the door frame. Listening, she heard something but didn't know what. Walking toward the sound, she opened a door; not quite believing what she saw, she blinked. Sure enough, Sallisfer and Valerie were making out on Valerie's bed.

"Ewe! Have you ever heard of the sock on the doorknob," she said. They stopped and looked at her.

"Ah...hey," Sallisfer said, getting up and running his thumb across his lip, extracting the moisture.

"Wait till the *other* one hears what you're doing," Kal said, glaring at Valerie. Valerie looked back with empty eyes, no expression on her face.

"She is away right now." Sallisfer smiled gleefully, his eyes bright with a green fire that flickered in his blue eyes.

"What did you do?" Kal asked, stepping back and staring at him.

"I am simply doing her a favor," he licked his lips to reveal a split tongue.

Kal studied the scene with mounting anger, complete understanding shaping her into a snarling wolf, pure golden eyes staring boldly at Sallisfer.

"To think I trusted you... You are a snake." She grimaced, showing a full array of sharp teeth. "Shall I cut your head off?" She snarled, leaping at him.

He merely sat there as Kal leaped on top of him, rage brightening her eyes.

"Do not pull innocence to take advantage of her..." Kal shook her head, unable to find words to express her fury.

"Fine then, I won't," he snarled, shifting into a snake and trying to wrap himself around her throat. She snapped at his body, scoring a long gash in his side. She pulled away from his coils, letting out an earsplitting howl, calling for Kris.

In an instant, a small fox appeared at her side. Kal growled at the snake growing before her, and then she looked suspiciously at Kris's form.

"I suggest you find something better than that. He wouldn't even have to coil around you to kill you."

Kris glared at her but shifted into a white tiger, hissing menacingly. Kal followed with the cat idea, but she shifted into a black leopard, pale blue eyes filled with rage.

Sallisfer struck out at Kris. His claws deflected the strike from going to his throat, but Sallisfer latched onto Kris's shoulder and began coiling.

Suddenly a giant brown bear rushed into the room and jumped on the snake, biting and clawing at it so much that it let go of Kris and started to strike at the bear. Kal stared at the bear in shock as she realized that the bear belonged to Koda.

"Koda?" she asked, smiling momentarily in wonder that that little boy could transform into something big.

He did not answer as he was in the heart of the fighting.

Sallisfer's blows just grazed off his immortal flesh leaving no trace. Soon all three of them faced the anaconda, fighting and blocking till a shadow fell over the room; they all stopped fighting as a chill crept in. Finally, the anaconda pulled back, shifted into his human form, and bowed so low that his eyes were inches from the floor.

"Master," he said. Kal's eyes widened; the Headmaster was behind them. She fought the urge to look at him, her future master.

"Hand of Heaven," a deep and powerful voice said, "You have once again struck at your own kind."

"I know Master, and I will not ask for your forgiveness," Sallisfer said.

"As you should not," the headmaster said, "But you need to release my right hand."

"Yes, Master," Sallisfer said, getting up and keeping his eyes low. He walked to the bed, where the 'lost' Valerie lay silent and cold.

He slipped over her and kissed her lightly; she blinked and looked at him as her expression returned.

"What in three hells happened to you?" she asked, laying a hand on his bloody side, where there was a fatal wound.

But it stitched and mended as her hand ran over it.

"Some stories are best left untold," the Headmaster said.

Valerie looked up curiously. "Headmaster?" Questioning his presence after looking around the room. "Now, I'm extremely curious," Valerie said, looking at Kal, Koda, and Kris. "Extremely," she muttered again, rolling Sallisfer over. Then she stood up and stretched, not appearing surprised that Sallisfer was on top of her or even seeming to care.

Kal examined her, wondering if it was partly Valerie's fault that this happened in the first place. Valerie stretched again and walked past them.

"Come on, Master, before someone sees you," Valerie said, sounding like a little girl talking to her father, but this was the headmaster she was talking to.

The chill left the room, and Sallisfer looked at them from the bed, "You can move now. He's gone," he said, getting down, "And I am really sorry, guys." Walking out of the room, Kal followed him and watched as he shifted into his horse form and galloped away, leaving behind the sound of hoof beats in the night.

Soon Ms. Wing walked in looking concerned as she placed her coat on the rack and removed her boots. "What is going on?" she asked Kal, sitting in Mr. Wing's chair watching the news while Koda and Kris sat on the couch.

"Sallisfer went bonkers, mama," Koda said with a grin. "I fought him off like a master."

"What?" Ms. Wing asked, staring at her son and looking at Kris and Kal for confirmation.

"We had a bit of a duel with Master Sallisfer….it was all done in fun," Kris said hesitantly.

"Fun?" Ms. Wing looked at Kal, who grimaced and looked away.

"Where is Valerie?"

"He went all snake, and I was unstoppable. I tried to bite his head off." Koda smiled and shifted into a bear in his excitement, filling the whole living room and making the house shake as he acted out some of his mad skills.

"Koda!" his mother almost shrieked, and Koda shifted back into himself, looking sheepish.

"Sorry, mama," he said, "But it was EPIC!"

Ms. Wing looked at Kal. Kal looked to Kris, who stood there, his lips pursed. "Like I said, all good fun," he smiled unconvincingly.

"Hm-um," Ms. Wing grunted. She opened the door and was about to walk outside when Valerie came into view. She walked in with her father, who had his hand on her shoulder.

"Valerie," Ms. Wing expressed in a breath.

"Yes, Ma'am," Valerie asked. Ms. Wing blinked at her, at a loss for words.

"She has had a long day, mama," Mr. Wing said, kissing his wife as he walked in with Valerie. "I will start supper. Arcy and Talys are joining us. Kris?"

"No. Sir." Kris said, jumping up and giving Kal's cheek a kiss. "I have dinner with my grandmother tonight." He rolled his eyes. "I get to tell her all about you." He smiled and turned to the Wings. "Have a great night," Kris said. Then ruffled Koda's hair. "You did good, kid," and he left without a look back.

"His grandmother is going to *love you,*" Valerie laughed at Kal's blush.

"Oh, don't tease," Ms. Wing smiled, gaining her composure. "Go wash up for supper."

Valerie went into her room, and Kal followed, "Are you okay?" she asked.

"Yes." Valerie said as she turned to Kal, tears in her eyes as she prepared Blaze's food and fed him, "I fell into his trap." She whispered. "It won't happen again."

"What did happen?" Kal asked.

"I drifted too far." Valerie smiled then as she wiped tears from her face. "It was beautiful there, so quiet."

Kal pulled Valerie into a hug and got a hug in return. "Thank you," she said in her ear.

"No problem," Kal whispered back. Then they heard the door open and the call for supper. They walked to the bathroom and washed their hands.

Sitting at the small wooden table while Mr. Wing served a simple hamburger helper meal.

"Sorry, I did not get home in time to cook a big meal." He apologized.

"This looks delicious, Dad," Arcy said. "Thank you for preparing it."

"It does look good," Koda said. "I am starving."

"I bet," Mr. Wing laughed. "Is it true that my boy can turn into a bear?" He looked to Valerie and Kal, who both nodded. Then, Mr. Wing laughed again, beaming, "What other things can you do, my son?"

"I am a bear, a giraffe, a falcon, and a Comodo dragon. Also, my master is writing to the Dragon King. He thinks I may be gifted." At this, Mr. Wing choked on his tea and sputtered some noises that Valerie couldn't help but beam over.

"I would be honored to teach you the dragon ways." She smiled.

Koda beamed. "What? You can turn into dragons?" Kal asked, "I mean normal people...not hands."

"Yes." Valerie said, "A few can. Very gifted shifters can with permission." Then, at Kal's look, Valerie continued, "When the time is right, I will take you to see the dragon king. He is part of your training. Perhaps you can ask for the right to change into a dragon then."

Kal swallowed in aww and nodded. After that, the conversation shifted to schoolwork and show plans. Valerie shifted in her seat, gaining Kal's attention. Looking up from her plate and her thoughts, Kal noticed that Valerie had stirred the food around her plate and probably did not eat that much.

"Mother, can I be excused?" Valerie asked.

"Where are you going?" Ms. Wing asked, also recognizing that Valerie did not eat.

"Probably to my tower...or the demon dungeon," Valerie replied, scrapping her plate into Talys's, who grunted his thanks and continued eating.

"Your snoring will probably destroy the whole place if you slept there." Arcy said with a smile, "The whole war would be over before it started."

Valerie laughed halfheartedly. "That is a bad joke," she said.

Arcy shrugged. "Just trying to get you to smile." Valerie beamed at her sister and gave her a kiss on her head.

"I love you." Valerie said as she commenced to kiss her brother's head and said "thank you" in his ear and "I love you." She also kissed her mother and father on the way out the door.

"Be safe," Ms. Wing said. "And remember, school is tomorrow. So, I need you here to get the bus with your brother and Kal."

"Yes, ma'am." Valerie smiled, and she was gone.

"It will be alright, love," Mr. Wing reassured his wife with a squeeze of his hand.

"I just wish I could help." Ms. Wing sighed. "All these secrets…these flares in power? I don't know what to say or do."

"I know, love, I know." Mr. Wing stood and started to gather plates from the table. "All we can do is love and support her."

"What is wrong with her?" Ms. Wing asked, "She has gotten so distant."

"She just has a lot going on. Choices to make that a child her age…" he closed his eyes as the pain showed in his expression. "She shouldn't have to make the choices placed upon her. She is just a baby. Our baby…" Ms. Wing hugged him, and he hugged her back.

"She will be alright, won't she, Dad?" Arcy asked. Mr. Wing smiled at her.

"Time will tell," he said honestly. "It now all depends on her decisions."

Arcy nodded and helped him clean off the table while Talys and Koda went to feed the ranch dogs. Kal started to head to the back of the house to her and Valerie's room when a crash made her look over to see Mr. Wing on the floor, holding his head. "Are you alright?" Ms. Wing asked. Mr. Wing shook his head, gasping.

"I must go." He breathed out raspy, "Something has happened." He used his wife to help him to the door and past the protective barrier, and he was gone with a flash. Ms. Wing stood outside at the tree for a long time while Arcy continued to clean up.

"Do you want to come to my place and meet my new fur baby?" Arcy asked, "You have not been to my house, and I have a few cats that did not make good barn cats. The newest addition is too young to be out in the barn." At the word, cat Kal perked up. She nodded to Arcy with a smile.

"Come on, let's get going while the boys are out." Arcy and Kal hugged Ms. Wing, telling her their plans and leaving. Ms. Wing nodded at their statements and watched them leave. She then continued to stare out across the view in front of her. Her thoughts deeply pondered… Her mind settled upon those she loved. Mr. Wing, Valerie, and she held back tears thinking…*What was going on that she couldn't be a part of?*

CHAPTER 32

Growing Pains

Valerie let herself in the house. She was absolutely spent. The night, which had started out as uncomfortable, had turned into an absolute nightmare. The raid on the outlands just a week outside the castle had not gone as smoothly as they had hoped. The demons had found numbers that were not anticipated. Nevertheless, the battle slowly drew closer to the destination no Earth Child wanted.

"We need a distraction," Valerie whispered as she removed her shoes and hung her cloak and sword behind the door. "Something to throw the Demons off the hunt of war." She rubbed her eyes. "Just to buy us some time."

Exhaling to stifle a yawn, she walked into the bathroom and stripped off her clothing. She looked down at the blood-stained tunic and wondered for a moment- how many lives had been lost last night. She looked at herself in the mirror and saw blood on her face and all in her hair. She wore it like mad war paint, and Valerie was repulsed.

How had a 15-year-old become a war hero? She threw her tunic into the trash and washed her hands, hot tears sliding down her face. She shook with effort as she closed her mind to the images. They flowed like unwelcomed flashes of light, of an action movie that became a horror in her mind. Her emotions overtook her as she remembered; the blank stares of the dead bodies she helped recover, the nameless heroes who waited for loved ones to claim them in the morgue. Loved ones who remained at home, waiting for their family member, only to have a black car drive up with two suited officials to tell them the news. Mothers were learning that sons and daughters would not be joining them for breakfast ever again. Fathers were discovering that their fishing days were over with their buds and that they would never get to walk their little girl down the aisle. Sisters and brothers were going to discover that their best friend was gone forever. As the sobs took hold, Valerie curled up in a ball as the hot water fell on her. Wives and husbands everywhere were finding they would have to become single parents, and the children, oh, the children, their realization they would have to grow up without a parent.

Valerie could feel Sallisfer in her mind, but he was not much comfort as he, too, suffered with the pain of guilt that washed over them both. It did not matter at that moment who was a demon and who was an earth child. The dead were dead, and the deceased had a family and plans. They also had a name that Valerie vowed to learn. She promised to know each person's name that died in this war and carry them with her forever. She stood as the last name came to view, and the hot water had long disappeared, leaving the icy rain of the shower that started to steam off her new resolve.

As she got out of the shower, a light knock at the door told her that her mother was awake, "Valerie dear?" she called, opening the door a crack.

"I am alright, Mother," Valerie found herself saying. Much to her surprise, it felt very true as she wrapped the body towel around her. Her mother walked in with clean clothes.

"You look terrible," her mother said as Valerie accepted the clothes with a thanks. "Are you staying home from school?"

Valerie thought it over, "Yes," she said with a yawn. "I believe I can finally get some rest… and Mama," she hugged her mother- "Dad is fine. He has to make some emotional house calls." Valerie could not contain her inner sorrow and pain from her face. "But he is fine overall."

"What happened?" her mother asked, wiping away tears. "Is it true what the news said… are they getting closer?"

Valerie nodded. "But don't fret; I am doing everything possible to slow them down. I will not let them tear apart our home." She pulled on her clothes. "I just need a better plan to slow them down."

"Perhaps you should cancel today's training." Her mother brushed out Valerie's wet hair as if she was a small child again.

"Last night showed we have to have this training…it is the last one for many of the officers who have not seen the hells of war."

The faces flashed again before Valerie's eyes. "I need a plan."

Ms. Wing cupped her daughter's face in her hand and made her look into her eyes, "Do you remember the story of Alamar?" She asked suddenly. Valerie blinked, trying to pull the memory up in her head. "The reason we have the Dead Falls."

Valerie blinked again, this time with recognition. "Alamar dam the river to make farming land for the village."

"Exactly," her mother smiled a nervous smile, a sparkle in her brown, green eyes that Valerie knew well, for she too had the same gleam of calculations. "Undam the river. Force them to go into the bog."

Valerie closed her eyes, telling Sallisfer, who was also thinking it over, "That will only buy us three days… maybe four if we plan it right."

"It is three more days than you would have had."

Valerie nodded. "I see what you mean." Her mother hugged her, and Valerie hugged her back. "I love you, Mom, and thanks."

Ms. Wing laughed slightly as she kissed her daughter's brow. "I am good for some things." But then, she said, "Don't forget my father was a war hero as well."

Valerie kissed her mother's cheek. "I guess that is where I get it from." And she was off again back out the door into the storm that raged outside. Ms. Wing's smile left as she watched her daughter disappear outside the protective barrier and back into battle.

"Please, lord, hear my prayer." Then, she whispered, "Protect my baby and always let her find her way home."

Ms. Wing then turned from the window, made her coffee, and sat at the table. She looked at her phone planner and noted the day's work that needed to get done. In her weariness, Ms. Wing noticed that Koda had a pediatrician checkup. Ms. Wing glanced out at the storm, "It is going to be a long day," she thought as the aroma from the sip of her drink greeted her. A notification from her phone pinged that Mr. Wing would be home soon.

Thinking of the war, she questioned how many families learned they had lost a loved one last night. The risk of living out in the wild magic realm was well-known to those who chose to do so. Those in Outlander were mostly younger magic welders who wished to live fully in magic and not half and half near the human realm. She wiped her eyes, looked at the time, and took another sip waiting for the time to wake the rest of the house. A noise disturbed her thoughts. A soft shuffling of feet made her look up to see Koda standing with his blanket wrapped around him like a cloak and his stuffed dinosaur wrapped in his arms. His red hair stuck out in odd angles with the beginning of magic highlights of midnight blue so dark that it appeared black. His eyes also bore the sparkling color that came with age and use.

"Mama," he asked, and she reached her arms out to him. He crawled into her lap and rested his head on her shoulder as she pulled him close.

"You're shaking. Are you okay?" Ms. Wing asked.

"I had a bad dream." Then, he whispered, "I don't want to talk about it."

"Then how are you to let the dream go." Ms. Wing asked, "Remember you must let it go; it was just fantasy."

She felt him start to cry, and she held him closer. "I had a dream you…you were caught by the demons, and they ate you alive…. I couldn't stop it."

Ms. Wing looked across the room at nothing particular but thought- this was not the first-time poor Koda dreamt this nightmare- this dream. Since the war started, he has dreamt more about his loved ones falling victim to the Demon slaughter. "It is all better now. I am right here, and nothing will happen to me." She said, "I have your dad and sister remember. Same as you."

"But I can't die," Koda said, his face red and puffy from crying.

"And you better stay that way." Ms. Wing smiled, kissing him, "You are my baby no matter what." He smiled and kissed her back. The watch beeped, and Ms. Wing smiled. "You better get ready for the day. You don't have to rush, though. You have a doctor's appointment this morning with Dr. Roterdice. You are getting so big."

"Is Valerie home?" Koda asked.

"No, she and your father are off. However, your dad should be home soon before we go to the doctor. He said he was on his way. Valerie is out saving the world."

"I am glad we have her," Koda said.

"Me too," Ms. Wing smiled. "Me too." Koda crawled off her lap, and Ms. Wing reluctantly let him go; he smiled and walked away, trailing his blanket behind him.

Ms. Wing watched him until he was out of sight and thought of her new loved one. Time to get Kalea up. She walked to her room to dress, and in her walking, she started to rhyme.

Kal woke to Ms. Wing's rhyming song outside her door. "A little yellow bird sat on my window seal and said, time to get up, sleepy head, a day is ahead."

Kal stretched. Rain battered the world outside her window, pouring in sheets that made it hard to see outside. She groaned as she thought about her muddy walk to the bus stop and pulled herself to her feet to prepare for a day of school. She looked at Valerie's un-slept in bed. She missed her best friend like a sister. She hoped all was well in her absence.

"Good morning, Kal." Koda smiled at her.

"Shouldn't you be getting dressed?" Kal asked, smiling at him.

"I have a doctor's appointment," he grinned, and Kal felt the walls of loneliness closing in…thinking now about her muddy lonely walk to the bus stop.

Kal got dressed in a long-sleeved shirt and blue jean pants. She pulled on her mud boots, slipped her sneakers into her book bag, and walked down the hall to the only bathroom in the house.

She did all her morning chores, sat at the table for a quick bite to eat, and accepted the lunch Ms. Wing handed her. "Is Valerie going to be at school? I thought you said she would be home to go to school?" Kal asked.

Ms. Wing looked at Kal with understanding. "No, she is not going to be at school." She said, "She has to save the world." Kal looked down at her muffin. "You have drill this evening." Ms. Wing reminded her, "Master Phillip requires all infantry and Calvary to attend, which means Valerie will have to be there…." Ms. Wing smiled, but Kal could hear her mutter more under her breath, "*Hopefully. Sorrow was a hellion to get into the barn yesterday. Sure, do miss Valerie's help.*"

"I am sure she will come home." Kal tried to be optimistic. "This place is where she is the happiest. She will come around."

Ms. Wing smiled despite the water in her eyes, "You have added such light to this place, Kalea. Thank you."

Kal smiled, and Ms. Wing's phone alarm went off, reminding Kal she needed to get to the bus stop. Ms. Wing handed her an umbrella, and Kal felt it had a drying charm. She smiled gratefully at her guardian and walked into the rain to meet the bus.

CHAPTER 33

When it Rains, it Storms

The weather got worse as the day progressed. Kal and the other students at the school were directed toward the hallway when the tornado sirens went off. Kris walked to the spot on the wall with her. He smiled at her as they knelt with their hands over their heads. Despite the stern words of the teachers and principal, students still whispered among themselves.

"Do you think we will still have drill today?" Kal asked when they were still in the hallway 20 minutes later.

"Knowing Master Phillip, he coordinated the drill with this weather. I am sure the Master helped. Immortals tend to talk regularly." Kris stated with a bit of amusement. "This will be great fun. When I saw Valerie plugging in the washer and dryer in the barn and Ms. Wing's barn helpers Hue and Kyle cleaning the showers, I did not think it was to prepare for training in bad weather... poor Hawk." Kris shook his head, thinking of his big bay, warm blood, "Hawk loves to work in the rain." He added sarcastically.

"Hold up," Kal stared, forgetting they were in the hall where it was supposed to be silent during potentially life-threatening weather. An update had been issued- a tornado had been confirmed not far from the High School. "You are telling me that Master Phillip and Master… Master are immortal, and they "Talk" about torching us, mere mortals?"

Kris blinked. "You hadn't gotten that far in the book?" he asked, trying to recover the situation as both humans and demons looked at them.

"It is in my book?"

"Uh… Yah…. How far have you read in *Doctor Who*? I didn't mean to spoil it?"

"Doctor Who! Who the hell is Doctor Who?"

"Perhaps you and Master Kalea would like to cower in my office." A familiar voice whispered. Kal's history teacher Mr. Wood winked at them. "I believe your conflict can be settled there." He helped them stand up by their elbows and guided them to a small interior room where a desk with a lamp and an overflowing bookshelf were the only things in the room.

"Thank You, Master Wood." Kris smiled gratefully, plopping down on the floor.

"Your…your…," Kal started to confirm, overwhelmed with realization as she blinked at her teacher. Suddenly becoming aware, she noticed the smallest aura of magic fog that hugged his body. Mr. Wood gave her a knowing smile, his eyes sparkling with magic.

"Yes, Master Kalea, I am a Time Lord as well. I see the past just as you and your mother do… in fact, I was your mother's teacher so long ago." He shook his head. "Such a shame she is in exile. She is quite a Time bender."

Kal and Kris stared at him. No one had told Kal that her mother had been punished to watch a single time period and the Hands would be changing, but she didn't know when.

Valerie felt the time wasn't right to mention- that Kal had unknowingly killed her father in a power surge. She also kept from Kalea the fact that her mother was being charged with murder, along with the failure to educate a minor and the failure to report Kal being the second Doom.

"What did you say about exile?" Kal asked slowly and carefully, keeping her attention on Mr. Wood, but she could see Kris in her peripheral vision to judge if Kris knew anything about her mother being in exile.

"Well… your mother is in charge of handling time changes done to the past, so she is confined to a time period to watch it for changes… you see, it is kind of a gray area that no one can see. So, we know something is about to happen to it, and your mother is in charge of watching it and preventing the change. Since she could not get into the gray area that lasted for about a hundred years or so, she had to jump to the beginning and live it out. Normally it would be a team of Time Lords taking a shift, so the last Time Lord can go home, but in your mother's case, no one can take over for her till the gray area is returned to normal." Mr. Wood rubbed his bald head with a rag. He was sweating like a stuffed pig.

Kal swallowed, choosing her words carefully, "Why was she exiled?"

"Because… because she hid you, of course." Mr. Wood stammered, looking at Kris for support, but Kris, like Kal, was just as shocked as she was. She turned to him.

"What do you know on this matter Kristopher King." She scared herself with how much venom and power she put into those words but tried to mask it, keeping her eyes level and her face set on him as he sat cross-legged on the floor.

"I know it is a crime not to educate a minor on how to use her powers. But unfortunately, she masked yours…you could have died if Valerie hadn't found you in time."

"You make it sound as if Valerie was looking for me." Kal spat, "How does that make my mother a criminal?"

"Well, I was looking for you." Valerie smiled, appearing in the doorway in a lazy, nonchalant way dressed in bell-bottom jeans and a t-shirt topped with a black rain trench coat, her feet adorning black paddock boots. She walked over to Kal, who was seething, and Valerie returned Kal's look with a knowing smile.

"I had been looking for you from the day I entered school. I went to countless schools in this state searching for you. Well, I didn't know it was you at the time, as I was searching for the chosen one. With your necklace in my pocket, I walked to each classroom, searching for a sign that would recognize the one it belonged to. I came close at Woodville Elementary School. I was in second grade and had walked into a first-grade classroom. The necklace went warm, and I knew the Chosen One was in that room. I stayed back a year in the second grade to find the reason why it had warmed, but the trail had gone cold. By middle school, we were growing desperate. We looked into strange human deaths and disappearances, scanned my yearbooks for one recurring photo or name, and found no leads...." Valerie trailed off for a breath and looked at Kal, "Then you sat down next to me in computer class... and I knew it was you. I didn't know how to make contact and wondered what I could say. I saw that your power was blooming, but it was being masked. When I found out we had lunch together, it took all my courage to sit down and say hello to you. After all this time, my search was over, yet I could tell you knew nothing of who and what you were. You kept telling me your mother, MY LEAD detective in time, was a PILOT! I was stunned and sickened until I didn't know what to say or do. Then I fell ill when I saw your birthmark while changing for PE. When I heard what had happened to your father, I was outraged. How could this wonderful Time Lord, THIS WOMAN, cover up her own tracks and child, putting the child's life in danger and all those around her... I did what the Headmaster and I found RIGHT to do. You can visit her when she is locked in, but she cannot leave that time zone until the change is prevented. She must live in that time till then. It was the best punishment for her. She could have received the death penalty."

Kal saw her friend, her legal sister, in a new light. She stared blankly. All the missing parts began to fall into place as her emotional rage radiated from her being. Kalea felt tired and betrayed. She felt the hurt again, remembering the instinctive feeling of being summoned in the first grade. She remembered going home and telling her father, who immediately pulled her out of school. She recalled being homeschooled for two years after and then moving to live with his aunt, who died the following year, and they moved back home. She remembered the day Valerie shyly sat next to her and said hello. Kalea considered the conversations that guided her to discuss her mother and father. Kal sank to the ground and refused to look at Valerie, who sat silently beside her.

"So, your family didn't take me in out of the kindness of your heart, did ya?"

"Oh, my mother insisted. She said no child should or would ever feel unloved. If she had anything to do with it. She doesn't even know you are supposed to be the next hand and replace me. It is going to be okay."

"Okay… okay?" Kal shook all over.

"I want to see my mother now. Is she allowed to call?"

"You must learn proper time travel before meeting her, and she can call? Not sure why she hasn't contacted you. Not that I know how all that works." Valerie smiled a sad, tired smile. "Perhaps Master Wood would be willing to come out of retirement to teach you…."

"I would be honored," Mr. Wood bowed. Kal just grumbled, not knowing what to say or do.

When they were finally released into their classes and allowed to go home early in a lull of the storm, Kal found herself in a makeshift practice trench with the rest of the infantry. She was unsure of the plan because she had not been paying attention.

The rain poured down, and the wind howled. The mud poured into Kalea's boots, and her helmet made so much noise because of the rain she feared she would be deaf. Suddenly the people around her surged forward, pushing her with it. A wild blood-curling war cry could be heard, and much to Kal's astonishment, she heard her voice among them. Then, with her sabers held high, she commenced hand-in-hand combat with the bewitched dummies that were her pretend foe.

All the world faded; the fight, the rain, the mud, and the commotion all left her thoughts except the will to survive. Once one enemy fell, on to the next became a rhythm. Suddenly, the next wave hit, and with it, the Calvary came. After that, things got a little more complicated, like avoiding horses and spears, arrows, and falling bodies. Kal nearly got run over by a riderless horse and then nearly 'killed' by a dummy who had taken advantage of the horse's distraction. More obstacles arrived as mounted dummies road in and started to fight.

Kal started to find a groove again and then was pushed by a mounted dummy into the mud. She rolled quickly, seeing her sabers gone in the muck. She summed her shield charm just in time as the sword bounced off. She scrambled to her feet only to be knocked down again, cursing words she was sure she had no right to say. She jumped up just as light-ning blinded everyone, and the thunder that came with it shook the earth. The dummy recovered faster than Kal and went to strike when a gray horse rammed itself into its horse, knocking the horse and rider away from Kal.

Kal saw Valerie say something but did not know what she said till she felt the hot bar of the enemy sword on her back and found herself at the starting point. Master Phillip looked down at her with disapproving eyes.

"All ways in the back. You never cover your back." He barked. This was true in all the mock fights and battles. It was Kal who got struck down from behind.

"It isn't as if I have eyes on the back of my head. I haven't found a spell to do that yet." Kal pouted.

Master Phillip coughed in disgust. "You have eyes on the back of your head. It is called -you have friends." Kal looked up at him and around at the fellow fighters out of the fighting game. They were talking to one another and shouting encouragement back to the others in the rain. She looked up at the lean-to that protected them from the elements, then back at the others still in the rain. Valerie was still on Sorrow, screaming orders to be heard. They were winning, and the enemy dummies were retreating. The infantry and Calvary had merged nicely like the Hands, the dismounted riders, and the foot soldiers, the horses rushing ahead and the rest catching the enemy running away from them. It was quite a show of teamwork. She looked back at the others, covered in mud like her. She sat beside them, and someone handed her a water bottle.

"It just takes time." Ava said, grumpily glaring at the fight, "At least that is what Master Philip said."

"What happened?" Kal found herself asking, looking at the muddy blob beside her. If she hadn't spoken, she would have never known it was Ava.

"I fell off of Sassy... I landed in a pile of dummies and 'speared' myself." She let out a sigh, the most depressing sigh one could make.

"Was that the horse that tried to run me over?" Kal asked, almost smiling. Ava looked at her and then nodded to the round bail that held several horses grazing.

"Sassy is the cleanest one…" she muttered, "Paint stood in the rain the longest."

Kal could make out the muddy white butt she assumed belonged to Sassy. "I don't think so, but they all look like chestnuts in all that mud."

Ava laughed, "All but Sorrow's white ears." Then, there was a roar of thunderous cheering that was almost as loud as thunder.

"I guess we won." Kal shrugged as whoops and hollers went up from the lean-to, and they all swarmed out to congratulate the 'survivors.' Master Phillip calmed them all down and ushered them all to the barn.

"Great work," Master Phillip barked at them all, walking up and down the barn aisle looking studious with his hands behind his back. He had paired every infantry with cavalry to help cool the horses, clean them, and bed them in their stalls as the storm ranged on.

"Remember, in a real battle," Master Phillip continued as he checked on each of them, "There will be no lean-to if you find yourself struck down. If you are alive, it will be a hospital tent, and if you are dead… you will never know it."

"Such a pep talker." Ava smiled at Kal, who was filling up Sassy's water bucket.

Kal smiled back, "The best."

When Kal filled all the water buckets, she ran to the house while the cavalry cleaned tack. The infantry started to shower in the barn, "If I hurry, I can shower at home before Valerie gets her tack cleaned." Kal burst into the house to the disapproving eyes of her legal little brother and older sister. Kal threw her boots off and sprinted to the bathroom. The door was locked, and Kal heard the shower running, "I'm in here!" Valerie called.

Kal stared at the door, dripping wet, leaving a puddle of mud, and somehow Valerie had beaten her to the shower… "Who is cleaning your saddle?"

"It is a Wintec!" Valerie hollered to answer, "I power washed the mud off, and now it only has to dry."

Kal stared at the door in disbelief, "A Wintec?"

"Ya…" Valerie called, "Is that a problem?"

Anger built up in Kal. She had tried everything to get here first and didn't even see Valerie leave the barn. She knew teleporting was banned on the ranch. Perhaps Valerie had done so, but when Kal looked down the hall, she saw two sets of footprints and wet, muddy clothes in front of the bathroom door. "As if I could have anything first." She muttered, and she started banging on the door.

"What?" Valerie called.

"Hurry up!" Kal hollered.

"Don't you rush me!"

"Well, I am!"

"Ah! You're so annoying!"

"I Don't Care! Now hurry it up!"

"No"

"Yes!"

For no reason, more anger was rising in Kal. She had no reason to be this angry. Yes, she was wet, muddy, tired, and sore. But her anger became more intense the longer she stood staring at the door. She wanted to compress it, hold it down, but she couldn't. It was building up in her.

"Kal, are you okay?" Koda asked.

"No, I feel strange," Kal asked, fighting the anger, "I mean…What do you care!?" It exploded. She put her hand over her mouth, trying to fight it. Suddenly, the bathroom door opened, and Valerie stood staring at Kal while she still had soap in her hair and a towel half wrapped around her.

"Oh my god, what have I done?" Kalea asked, her face fearful.

Sallisfer was suddenly by Kal's side, and Kal directed her anger toward him.

"Kal!" Valerie shouted, grabbing and shaking her, but that only infuriated Kal more.

"God, oh mighty," Sallisfer whispered, looking at Valerie with fogged eyes.

More anger shot through Kal, along with fear and confusion. Images flashed through her mind, some fearful, others irritating, and most were confusing. "Make it stop!" Kal screamed, holding her head.

"I don't know how!" Valerie emitted, and more fear flowed into Kal.

With so much emotion and sight, Kal's heart rate went up so fast that it gave out and stopped.

"KAL!" Valerie hollered, transporting them to the Emergency center in the magic realm.

Sallisfer came along, not concerned for Kal but in calling distance of Valerie, trying desperately to keep the towel around her bare form.

Valerie handed Kal over to Nurse Krasen, who eyed Valerie and Sallisfer. Then darkness filled the room, and they all started to get angry and bicker at one another. Valerie flinched, fled like a frightened rabbit, and disappeared, leaving Sallisfer holding her wet towel. As soon as she had disappeared, the room calmed down, the light returned to normal, and the doctors and nurses got to work on Kal.

"What happened?" Nurse Krasen asked Sallisfer, who stared dumbly at the towel.

"Uh… Power surge?" Sallisfer suggested turning red and shrugging… "She has been reclusive these past days. I thought I found a way to soften them… perhaps I amped them up?"

Nurse Krasen looked at him with a look that spelled out 'amped the power surges are you stupid' but her words were kind "Perhaps you should undo what you did." As she turned to check on Kal, whose heart had started to beat again "and quickly."

Sallisfer nodded and teleported off to find Valerie, who had locked herself in her tower, not allowing anyone to see her. She paced the room, trying to contain herself.

"Let me help?" Sallisfer banged on her door.

"No. Go find Kris and have him heal Kal."

"But I need to heal you."

"Heal Kal first."

Sallisfer sighed and teleported to the ranch to find Kris. When he did, he wasted no time dragging him to the Academy.

"What's wrong with Valerie?" Kris asked, walking with Sallisfer down the hall to Kal's room.

"It's a Doom thing. Soon you'll have to deal with it too… Kal."

"What is it?" Kris asked.

"It is hormones. They happen every year or so, and they get worse the longer you have been named till they get so strong they will overwhelm the whole world, first humans and then earth children. Still, it will dim a little when the Hands have their first." Sallisfer grimaced, "at least that is what we think will happen… Headmaster hasn't a clue… they started when Valerie turned 13…."

Kris smiled dreamily. "I remember that…it was after her first mother flow… we were all still camping with her aunt. Oh, the good old days."

"You remember?" Sallisfer eyed him with a wide smile.

"Yes, I guess this dark rain is jarring the melon," Kris smiled, tapping his head.

Sallisfer's smile widened. "When it first ended. We were back in the barn, and all the boys followed her around for days. You and I had to watch her like a hawk."

Kris laughed and shook his head. "It wasn't easy." But then, he remembered, "Does Heaven have these hormones?"

"Yes, but they filter Dooms. They are good, but you see, you have to be careful. If you wait too long and filter all that doomsday stuff, you'll become a monster, just like me. Gray and foggy colored. It just doesn't go away anymore."

"How long have you been Hands?" Kris squinted up his face, counting on his fingers Sallisfer laughed.

"Almost thirteen years, we were named at ages four and five. Remember, our first merge was at the ages of five and six, big mistake…." Sallisfer trailed off when they passed people in the hall. "It just increased what I have to filter… and despite my pride, Valerie is stronger than I am…. That's why I haven't been able to filter her power as much as I should."

"So, our combining?" Kris asked.

"Don't worry. Combining and merging are two different things. You just have to get Kal out of her shell and back into her head. She is such a flight reflux that she hides inside herself. All you have to do is wake her up. Kiss her, call her, embrace her remind her that she is safe… you are her…her…boyfriend." Sallisfer said the last part with distaste, and Kris eyed his cousin but didn't say anything.

They were silent for the last part of their journey. Finally, when they reached Kal's door, they stopped and reviewed what had to be done.

"All you have to do is kiss her once on the lips, sending an electrical current so she will open her eyes. Look deep into them. They will show you who you are, let your mind go, touch hers, share your strength, heal her, and get out. If you don't, and she heals, you will be trapped, with no way of saving yourself. I cannot help you. You have to help yourself." Sallisfer explained. Kris swallowed and walked slowly into the room. Sallisfer closed the door behind him, staying outside the door.

Valerie sat by the window with tears full of dark power falling from her eyes. They fell onto the brick and dissolved.

Falling from the ceilings to floors, then to ceilings again. Some fell on people who at once fought one another. Others fell on books, and other nonliving living things, making them come alive.

Sallisfer observed all this, trying to contain the power as panic filled the air around him. Then one fell right above his head. He caught it in his hand and absorbed it, smiling darkly.

He checked on Kris and Kal. They were sitting together talking, Kal was still weak, but she was going to live.

Kris saw Sallisfer peer in and put a protective shield over him and Kal because Sallisfer was in the shadow of wrath form.

Sallisfer smiled at him and nodded, "Very good." He said, then disappeared to end the darkness.

CHAPTER 34

Buying the Time

Valerie stood in the shadows of the deserted village now flooded with water from the busted dam. Her team of the best of the best had shoved the enemy troops into the bog, where they were being dampened by elements and insects. She had sent the best shifters to disguise themselves as wildlife to attack the horses that pulled the wagons and trebuchet. A typical three-day journey turned into almost five as they had lost some of their goods. However, with the first troops nearly exiting the bog, they needed to devise a new plan.

Holjus shimmered into view, and they both eyed each other with interest. The tension between them had grown since the desperation to save those Valerie loved and cared about. "How are you?" he asked with a soft purr as she reached out to him, and he fell into her arms.

"I can see as a Demon now." She said, "How do you not go crazy?" He smiled and kissed her, and she returned the action pulling at his clothes. He chuckled, pulling away from her.

"Seeing infra-red and heat now, are you?" He asked. She nodded.

"And I can see inside people, like an x-ray machine." She shivered. "It is creepy."

He laughed and led her over to the deeper shadows, his eyes on the sky.

"I guess being born with this curse, I just don't notice anymore," he said. "Other than that, how are you holding up?"

"Not bad. You?"

He gave a small smile and squeezed her hand. "I am much better now that I am with you." She smiled and then grimaced as Sallisfer flashed in her eyes, reminding them why they were meeting.

With a sigh, Valerie started on the plan. "We have to buy more time…. My people, we are not ready."

"How are y'all not ready?" Holjus asked, "You knew this was coming."

"Not like this… not so fast…your brother has allies we haven't even figured out yet… someone in our ranks is helping him. We just don't know who?"

Holjus sighed and rubbed his eyes, "I can make some inquiries…he is taking me out of school. So, I will start taking a full role in this fight."

Valerie nodded, her eyes starting to shine with tears, but she pushed them back. She was so tired of emotions. "We have found a few weasels… mostly those who fought against us in the civil war."

"Give me a list of those you may suspect. I will start investigating on my end as soon as I can…. I am sorry I can't do more."

"You are not the demon king, my love…his head must be severed before you are crowned." She slid her hands under his shirt, and Holjus laughed nervously and put her hands in his before he started to talk.

Holjus watched her, then took in his surroundings; the dark run-down house they found to hide in, the sound of water underfoot, and the smell of mildew that was already growing in the damaged homes. "At the ravine, General Tine has called for a halt to regroup… he sent a message to my brother that he needs new mules, and he is going to allow the men to rest. But unfortunately, some have fallen ill, and those will have to wait." Holjus dug into his pocket and pulled out a crumpled folded paper and a map. He sipped them both into Valerie's hand.

"He has orders to wait for three days more." He nodded to the path outside the window of the house they had found to hide in. "The fresh forces will come this way… they hope to repair the dam and take the path. Have your people waiting. If you can keep the fresh forces away or ensure they are not fresh when they reach Tine…You may stand a chance."

A howl hummed in the air, and Holjus knew his time with Valerie was ending. "As for your other plan," he breathed, letting go of Valerie and shimmering out of view, "He grows bored of the game…he needs to strike gold soon, or he will focus his whole attention on the war at hand."

Valerie nodded and sighed, knowing this moment was coming and what she had to do. "Thank you," she spoke into the empty air, felt his lips upon hers, and knew he was gone. She slid to the floor, fighting her feelings and trying to get her mind under control.

"I have to get Kal better, and soon," she said. Then, suddenly, Valerie stood and teleported herself home.

CHAPTER 35

Healing Kal

Valerie walked into her and Kal's room with a pile of books and papers. "This is not how I planned on entering April," Valerie commented when she saw her sister reading in bed, propped up by pillows beside the window.

Valerie smiled sadly down at Kal, who had just gotten home from the Academy a few days earlier and was now receiving homebound schooling because she was still weak. It was going to take a little while for Kal to finish healing.

"I am sorry I am not healing very quickly," Kal said for not the first time since she was hospitalized.

"It is fine. You are half human; your human side needs time, and we will give you all the time you need. This is a great time to start your time training, and Master Wood has agreed to be your homebound teacher. He will teach you how to wield and control your past magic and watch over your other studies. You are lucky that this semester you have such easy classes." She put the books on Kal's bedside table.

"How long will this healing take?" Kal asked, eyeing the books.

"Master said you may not obey the doctor's orders, so closer to May?" Valerie laughed. "But if you follow orders, it will be the third weekend of April. So, four weeks at home. The good news is he only saw two possibilities and not your death or something silly like that."

"Ya, nothing silly like that," Kal growled, laying her head back on her pillow. Finally, it seemed that Valerie and the rest of the world were returning to normal. Yet despite Valerie's assurance that it was all a mistake, she could not shake her nightmares of war and darkness that had seeped into her during that frightening exchange.

"What is the plan now for the demon forces? I can smell him on you…. you may want to shower after visiting him," Kal stated. She had learned that the sweet aroma of iron, mixed with the thick spicy smell of smoke lingering on Valerie's skin, belonged to Holjus. It overlapped Valerie's own earthy sent laden with the undertone of woody evergreens and rosemary.

Valerie smelled her shirt and looked at Kal with her eyebrow raised, "Your wolf nose is getting stronger…. I will shower next time if the smell offends you."

Kal laughed. "I just don't want you to get in trouble. What if I am not the only one who can smell it on you."

Valerie laughed and sat next to Kal's bed. "The plan is to keep fresh troops from alleviating the old ones and not let the old ones rest. After that, we have three more days to prepare for a new plan."

Kal looked at her friend, "I am sure you will come up with something."

"Perhaps." Valerie smiled, "But I am not the only genius working on this problem." Kal nodded and picked up the first book of literature.

"I will work on the problem, too," Kal said as she reviewed her literature assignments. Valerie smiled and stood up to leave.

She watched Kal as her attentions went inward then Valerie outspoke thoughts as if affirming herself.

Kal looked up as Valerie spoke. "Following your advice, I think, I should shower, considering I have to report to the Headmaster."

Kal nodded. "Good idea."

Valerie laughed again. "I will check on you daily…I hope."

The next day came and went without much contact from Valerie. Kal learned from Ms. Wing that Valerie was preparing shifts and trying a plan to cut off the Demons within the two days remaining. Kal worked on healing and attacked her schoolwork with vigor.

As the days passed and Kal healed, Ms. Wing tutored her over earth-children history and power-to-strength ratios. Master Wood came by twice a week and helped her learn how to control the past. "The past is set, and when moving into the past, time flies faster than in the present and future." Master Wood explained, "When someone travels to the past, who is not a time lord, they inhabit someone's timeframe and live out what that person is able to do. Timelords create a small space in time. We can be seen and participate or be hidden and observe."

"How do you participate?"

"You have to will it." Master Wood smiled, "You have to really want to be in that moment of time. Only the greatest past benders can do it."

Kal sighed; all her travels to the past had yet to show her that she could make herself live in that time frame. "So those who change time…" she trailed off, looking at her notes and then at Master Wood. His smile had disappeared.

"Those who change time," he sternly prompted, "Are the most powerful and dangerous time benders to ever walked the Earth. Horrible things happen to those who mess with history."

"Can one mess up the future?"

"Yes and no… One can change your timeline. However, it isn't as hard to change what will happen as to what has already happened." He smiled again. "When in the present you have choices that affect each outcome in the future, it is already predicted, but your choice is not always clear. That is why future seers have been unsure and are more confused than those who can live in the past." Kal nodded as she made final notes on what he was saying but in words on her paper, so she could study and remember.

Kris came over often and told long, drawn-out stories of things that might come to be and other fantastic historical tales that always kept Kal on her mental toes. There was never a dull moment. Valerie's mother nurtured and supported her with rehab, and Valerie's father taught her how to cook in his spare time.

It was midmorning on the second week of April. Valerie was returning from her shift at the dam to keep the fresh demon troops from approaching their comrades at the ravine. She was tired and slightly sore from the rough night of flying, but the plan was working so far. As Valerie took the last step toward the entrance, thinking about upcoming events, her body aches became more apparent. Valerie stretched her tired muscles as she walked into the house. With an effort, she pulled off her boots and hung up her cloak; she stood for a moment with her eyes closed, regrouping herself.

Heading toward the bathroom, Valerie was just steps away when Kal came out of the room; Kal's body language and movements expressed pain.

"I am not sure you are ready for a surprise party." Valerie said, eyeing Kal, who was still struggling to walk from the room to the living room the second week of April, "Perhaps I should cancel it."

"Cancel it?!" Kal shook her head violently, dismissing Valerie's statement that she almost fell over from dizziness. She had been looking forward to a night under the stars with fresh air. "I want to do it. You have worked so hard. Your mama will feel so loved."

"Are you sure you can do it?" Valerie watched as Kal lowered herself into a chair, then stood and walked back down the hall.

"Yes," Kal gasped, turning and doing the exercise again.

"Perhaps I can help speed up the healing?" Valerie smiled. "You have been down for 3 weeks. Can I help?"

"No offense Valerie but you have done enough by putting me in this state," Kal grumbled.

"I'm sorry I did not mean to let Doom out." Valerie pleaded, "You know how the Darkness is… Doom just wanted to test you?"

"And I failed." Kal snapped as she continued to do the exercise once more.

"You didn't fail." Valerie corrected as she had done at the hospital. "You simply need more time to prepare. You are, after all, the first Half-Blood chosen to be a Hand."

Kal grumbled under her breath. "I guess that's why I am the chosen one." She rolled her eyes, and Valerie had to bite her lip to keep herself from yelling at her sister.

"Please let me help you." Valerie reached out and touched her sister's arm lightly, power prickling on her fingers, but Kal brushed her off and continued the exercise without a word.

Kal stood, sat down, stood again, and walked back down the hall. Despite all her hard work, Kal had to admit Valerie was right. She was not satisfied with her healing and felt it was progressing too slowly.

"I know what I did was wrong… Sally thought he had fixed the problem, but he made the power surges worse. So, can I please try to fix my mistake?"

Valerie watched Kal struggle with another lap. Her heart hurt for her friend and sister, and it hurt more for the simple fact she had done it to her.

Kal sighed; she stopped midway down the hall and turned to Valerie. Their eyes met, and Kal knew that Valerie was sincere. Kal nodded, "Okay, Valerie, you can try to heal me."

Valerie smiled, took Kal's hand, and closed her eyes. "May the Headmaster never find out."

She breathed so quietly that Kal barely heard her. Valerie thought about health, she thought about being strong, she thought about growing and being brave, and she thought about happiness. Valerie fed those thoughts down her arm into Kal with energy and power. She released it in tiny bits and allowed it to trickle to Kal's fingers, which in turn allowed the energy up her arm and into her body. Valerie focused and tried not to overdo it, so Kal could heal slowly and correctly. When Valerie felt Kal start to quiver and sway, Valerie stopped and opened her eyes. Kal stood there, and her eyes closed. She allowed Valerie to walk her to her bed, and she laid down and rested. Valerie, now beyond exhausted, laid down on her bed with a slight curve of her lips hinting at a smile; she knew Kal would feel much better when she woke for the party.

It felt like she had just closed her eyes when the Headmaster's call came. Valerie growled. She opened her green eyes and looked over at the Headmaster, who stood at the doorway; she glared at him.

"What?" she asked groggily.

"You are needed at this meeting. The plan to hold the Demons in the ravine is coming to an end. We need a new plan." The Headmaster did not yell, nor did he seem angry that she was sleeping on the job, but she could feel his cold gaze, which annoyed her.

Valerie closed her eyes and rolled away from him to face the wall. "I will handle it after the party." Then, lastly, to curb her annoyance with him and the situation." I will make them wait." She heard him grumble but felt the chill air leave the room, and she fell into blackness.

CHAPTER 36

Danger on the Horizon

She stood in the woods alone beside him. This walk had been totally unplanned, just a spontaneous let's go. The early afternoon sun graced them with another beautiful April day.

Valerie's spirits were up as Kal had been cleared to go to school on Monday, new troops were training hard to reinforce the Castle, and the new fresh troops were not arriving at the ravine. If they did come, they were not rested. A slight sniffle had gotten worse around the troops forcing the demons to rest longer than expected. Valerie smiled, thinking about the night before. After the party, she took her book and two of the strongest Sorcerers, and they changed the weather around the ravine to snow and ice. They made it so thick that the Demons would take a while to burn their way through it. It wasn't permanent, but it would buy them a few more days as it prevented the demons from progressing forward.

I'm glad you agreed to show me around," he said with a smile, jarring Valerie out of her thoughts as she observed the human boy who had unexpectedly shown up at the farm.

"Ya, it was getting a little stuffy in the house," Valerie said with a shrug, then stared out into space.

"Who were all those people?" He asked, taking a step towards her.

"Friends of the family," Valerie answered off-hand.

"Why were they all at your house? You didn't tell me Friday that you would have people over." He now only stood a few paces away from the tree she was leaning on.

"Oh, we are getting ready for a horse show. They are all here cleaning trails and fixing up the ranch. I had no idea you were coming at lunchtime, or I would have told you. My dad pays them for their work with good food." That earned a laugh as he sat down on a stump by the stream.

"You know you are positively gorgeous, Valerie." He smiled up at her.

Valerie gave him a sideways look as she leaned on the tree beside him, looking down and calling him by name, "Cert, flattery will not get you anywhere."

She saw his cute human smirk, "But my dark princess flattery gets me everywhere. Isn't that right, Magnoliya?"

She froze and turned a green-rimmed eye at him.

She saw his smirk grow, "Yes, I know your true name, elf, and now you are my slave," Cert said.

Looking at him with a slightly alarming look, Valerie voiced her thoughts. "Cert, you don't know what you are getting yourself into." Valerie almost shuddered as he stood and wrapped his cold hands around her middle.

"Oh… I think I do." Cert breathed on her neck. Doom started to wiggle from its cage, and Valerie was powerless to stop the evil.

"How is it that the sun of God wants the body of the daughter of the devil?" she asked as he pulled off his shirt and started to pull at hers, but she resisted.

"I have always wanted your body Magnoliya; now give it to me!" He demanded, ripping off her shirt and throwing it to the ground. Anger flashed in Valerie's heart. Doom had no true name. Cert could not control the darkness of Doom, and with him holding Valerie by the power of her true name, there was no way to stop the evil. So, Valerie did what any girl in her position would do. She opened the gates to all the sins and malevolence she had kept at bay for so long. Doom was now all the bastard had, and Valerie did not pity him, for he would get what he wanted, but it would cost him dearly.

"A human innocence…." Doom smiled, "This will be a fun experiment." Doom liked its host's chapped lips and allowed a sexier glow to overtake Valerie's form and feminine appearance, which gained Doom the satisfaction of the heightened lust response from the human Cert.

"Come here, boy." Doom flirted, smiling with glee as Cert's primal animal-like instincts kicked in with the help of Dark magic, and he tackled Doom down to the leafy ground.

Abruptly someone yanked Cert upward, and in a Nano-second, Doom was up and glaring daggers filled with flames. "You nasty demon!" Doom cursed, kicking him away from the human Cert.

"Valerie!" The demon called in pain-his violet eyes, making Doom laugh harder as it absorbed the fear that radiated off him.

"Valerie! Can you hear me? Baby, you have to take back control!" The demon yelled. Doom felt its host trying to get it back into its small cage!

"Never!" Doom yelled, kicking the demon again, this time kicking him while standing.

"Doom!" the demon taunted, wiping away the blood that oozed from a cut above his strange eyes.

Doom growled and went to end the demon but got caught off guard and knocked it into the tree. "You cannot give a body what is not yours." The demon spat, trying to stab it with some sort of power compressor.

Doom laughed, and with a flick of a dainty finger, the demon went flying head-first into a big dogwood tree. "My dear demon, this body is MY body. I can give it to who I please." With an evil smile, Doom leaned down and placed a black-lipped kiss on his cheek. "I'll be back for you," Doom whispered, sending needles down the demon's back and replacing anger with pain.

"Please, Valerie, you have to fight. Fight for me! For us!" Doom felt a stronger pull to its tiny cage. But Doom was far stronger than that which tried to fight.

Doom detained the demon like a spider puts its prey in a dark cage. Then commenced taking the seduced human in a beam of light. Doom only cared about gaining another innocent soul.

Holjus was suddenly being shaken. He looked up, "Sallisfer?" he asked, seeing the panicked gold eyes. "Where is Doom! I cannot reach my other half!"

It took Holjus a while to comprehend what had been said. The kick in his head must have been worse than he thought. "I do not know. They vanished." He finally managed to say, which earned a curse from Sallisfer as he dropped Holjus unceremoniously back on the ground. Sallisfer was gone in a flash of bright light.

"Thanks for freeing me… not," Holjus muttered, trying to escape the dark bonds that wrapped him. Suddenly Kal was crouched above him, "Don't move." She instructed, cutting his bonds and healing his wounds.

"Sallisfer and Kris have found Doom." She informed as Holjus caught his breath and gathered his strength; the dark cage had sapped all the air and the vigor out of him.

"Were they too late?" Holjus asked, fearing the answer.

"I don't know." Kal looked off down the creek, "I don't know."

Holjus stood on his shaky legs but did not fall, "Well, let's go find out." He said bravely, but inside, he shook with fear and grief. They teleported to the edge of a clearing where it appeared the fight was taking place between Doom, Heaven, and a friend. Holjus saw the limp form of the human teen who had caused this evil to transpire. 'Is it too late?' he thought. *Had Doom succeeded and taken his innocence and given away the body that was not its body to give away?* Holjus watched as Heaven and Kris were able to pin Doom between them.

"Kalea!" Kris called. Kal laid a reassuring hand on Holjus's shoulder before stepping out from behind the bushes they had been hiding under.

"Yes?" Kal asked.

"Take this boy home. Erase his memory and look for any clue on how he was able to cause this mess." Kris instructed. Kal nodded, casting a spell on the unconscious human. Doom hissed and tried to yank away from them.

As soon as Kal was gone, Sallisfer looked at Kris, "Quick thinking, cousin." He commented.

"I had to get her out of here. She need not see this. Plus, she will be more useful where she is than here waiting." As they spoke, they powered too full. Heaven held Doom equally between them, making Doom scream, holler, and curse, belting out noises that sounded more like an animal on fire.

Anyone understanding magic knew it relied on strength, which was very tiring. All they had to do was hold Doom long enough for Valerie's body to eventually lose its strength. Only then could Doom be placed safely back into its cage, and Valerie could return to the surface.

After twenty minutes or so, Valerie's body shimmered, and then it all happened quite quickly. Heaven took turns kissing and absorbing the darkness, trapping Doom behind bars. Holjus watched as Kris and Sallisfer wrapped Valerie's frail body in their arms.

He could see the dark residue changing from foul to pleasant, and with the two of them, it was one bad thought or deed to two good thoughts and deeds. Valerie came too briefly, taking a breath of freedom before she passed out, leaving a blond-headed young woman lying in the boys' arms.

"It could take years to regain the strength and the power expensed here today." Sallisfer said, "Hell, she could still die...."

Kris shook his head and stood from where they had kneeled, "Be strong, cousin." He smiled, "I will be back with the solution." And he vanished.

"You can come out now, Holjus," Sallisfer called. Holjus stood timidly and walked forward. "I want to thank you for trying," Sallisfer said, looking up at him.

"I am sorry I could not stop her... do you think... do you know... did they..." he could not bring himself to speak it.

"I don't know." Sallisfer admitted, "The boy is alive, so I would think not, but we won't know till Kal returns."

"Will she remember?"

"I don't know that either. No one has ever been this drained before and lived to tell."

Holjus knelt and touched Valerie's cold cheek, "I hope for her sake she does not."

"But Holjus, she hurt you. She could have killed you! You deserve an apology."

"No, she would never have hurt me as Doom did. She had no control. I wish I could have been there sooner and stopped him from getting so far." Sallisfer reached a shaky hand and placed it on Holjus's shoulder.

"Brother, you did what you could. Unfortunately, neither of us knew what was happening until it was too late. The girl has got to learn that her beauty can cause not only us problems if you know what I mean, but others."

Holjus nodded, "She is definitely a dude magnet." He laughed, "That is why I propose a proposition. We must have full contact and/ or visual of her at all times to keep this sh from ever happening again. What do you say, brother?"

Sallisfer thought it over and nodded, "She will not be happy with it, but I do agree Doom could have killed people today or worse, ending all the good in this world… keeping an eye on her is the only option we have right now."

Holjus felt the air cool around them, "Kris is returning." Sallisfer confirmed. Holjus nodded, kissed Valerie's cheek, and disappeared back into the underbrush at the edge of the clearing.

Kristopher appeared, and in his hand, he carried a jar full of chocolate milk, a magic pigment, Valerie's spell book, and a strange necklace; it looked much like Valerie's, but the stone was pale blue, not black. "I took this from the future." Kris told Sallisfer, "Help me pull it over her head."

"Why is it…blue?" Sallisfer asked, gently touching the pendant with awe.

"It is because the time I got it… she wasn't completely pure, but she was pure," Kris explained as he pulled it over her head. "If my calculations are correct, she will not use the magic in the stone for three days after I have replaced it… with any luck, my touch will have worn off.

"So… she does come back." Sallisfer smiled, hugging Valerie close to him. He could feel her strength returning. The magic was already taking effect; her hair had gone from blond to black.

"Sorry to break up the party early, but I have some bad news," Kal said, landing and changing from bird to person. "I wiped his memory and looked around for anything that would have given us a clue on how he got this far… I found this." She brought forth a small black leather-bound book.

"It is a journal. The hand of Doom before us…." Sallisfer said, recognizing it immediately. "The last time I saw the journal. His granddaughter had it in her home library. So how did it get into the hands of the human boy?"

"I don't know the answer to that, and this isn't even the bad news… his mind forgot, but his body did not… they sinned."

All was quiet. Nothing but the wind in the trees could be heard. Sallisfer looked down at the beautiful girl he was holding and felt tears in his eyes. "How did it get that far… How?" he whispered.

"The book contained her true name and a full description of her power. He used her name against her. She no longer had a shield to protect herself from Doom, so Doom took advantage."

"No, Kal… she knew what she was doing," Sallisfer uttered through clenched teeth.

"I don't understand," Kris whispered, grabbing Kal's hand when the wrath flashed before him.

"Don't you see?! She let Doom out because she couldn't defend herself, and I wasn't there to help her! She needed me, and what was I doing! I was taking some stupid test to get into college! I ignored her, she called me, and I ignored her for selfish reasons when I knew… I KNOW! I will NEVER get to go to college because I'll be DEAD! And even if I wasn't …." he looked over to Kris, "even if I wasn't dead… I would still be here… stuck in Trap County because I won't be living if I am not with her." He stood and picked Valerie up in his arms.

"I will merge with her and wipe all that human boy might have left… Kal go back to the house with Kris, wipe his memory of her, and take him back to where he came from… if you have to take his parents there too, I don't care. Then when you come back, Kris, please take my memory of this event. Valerie can't know from me…. If it is with you, cousin, I know I would not have truly forgotten."

Kris looked away, then back at his friend and family member, "No." he said, "I will not take your memory." He defied and stated, "I know what it is like to live without knowing. I will not let you do this. You will find a way, and maybe keeping her from knowing is the wrong thing." He reached up and took the pale blue necklace off Val's neck. "Kal, I will meet you at the human's house." And he vanished.

Sallisfer looked to the bushes where Holjus still watched, "What do you think, brother?" he asked.

"I thought about having you take my memories, too." Holjus smiled a sad smile as he walked over. Kal nodded and smiled back in greeting before going off to meet Kris. "But as much as I hate to admit it, the future boy makes a lot of sense… perhaps we can still keep her from knowing… we must protect her, and to do this… we need to know." Holjus looked Sallisfer straight in the eye, "We have to know so this never happens again." He took the book lying on the ground and set it aflame. "We have to protect her."

Sallisfer nodded, "Yes, but how will I keep her from knowing."

"The same way she kept you from knowing about me… a wall, a locked door, I don't know, hide it in your mind. Don't ever let it come out enough for her to find it just enough so you can remember to protect her."

Sallisfer thought it over, "You make a lot of sense, brother. I will try."

Holjus smiled and kissed Valerie's cheek, "All will be ok, my love. You are in good hands."

Holjus stepped away and watched as Sallisfer absorbed Valerie within him. He purged her completely of the evils she had committed that day. He restored her energy and power to full before they vanished, leaving him alone in the clearing. Holjus looked down at the ashes of the book he had destroyed and thought… *How did a human boy get this? It couldn't be by chance…* Holjus stared at the ashes, vowing he would find out who was responsible and end them!

***

Valerie woke moments later under a tree by the barn. She stood and stretched and then brushed herself off. "How did I get here?" Valerie wondered to herself. She could hear the troops training in the lower barn and those who were running the trail behind the lake. She could see by the sun's tilt that it was almost supper time. Valerie stepped forward away from the tree, and her world went black. The pain flooded her head as she tried to recall what she had done today. As her sight slowly returned, she could feel the stiffness of her joints, and her body ached. Questioning herself, "I feel like I have met the ground... did I fall out of the sky?" She gritted her teeth together and took another step away from the tree; her sight went dark but did not last as long as the first. She could feel her body healing. Magic zipped around her body like little rockets. Valerie took a deep breath to calm herself as she took the last step from the tree toward the rocky driveway. She grew dizzy and nauseous but stabilized herself just in time to see Kristopher's army marching up to the house for supper. Kris saw her and smiled, giving her a salute which she returned with a shaking hand as they marched by her.

"Whatever is wrong with me, he must not know, or he would have asked how I was feeling…." Valerie grumpily mumbled as she walked to the barn where Sallisfer was working with Kal to build her physical and mental strength by training her like a soldier. Valerie slid almost all the way down the hill from the top barn to the bottom as she fought waves of confusion, dizziness, sickness, and blackouts. Sallisfer met her at the bottom of the hill, concern all over his face.

"Are you alright, love?" he asked.

Valerie looked up at him, "What happened to me?" she managed.

"You don't remember?" Sallisfer asked, cupping her face in his hands and staring at her intently. "You fell… we were doing a training exercise with the other masters, and a training sword hit you in the head pretty hard. It must have made you black out because Doom escaped… but don't worry, no one got truly hurt."

Valerie stared at him for a while before she fell into his arms sobbing Sallisfer wrapped his warm arms around her and held her. "I'm… I'm so sorry." She sobbed.

"Don't be my love." Sallisfer soothed, "You had no control over your actions. Heaven was able to do its job, and I was able to keep you safe."

Valerie snuggled deeper into his chest before allowing herself to merge with him. She sat entirely wrapped in love and warmth as Sallisfer carried her to the house. At home, he placed her on her bed, "I will go snag us some food." He went to leave, but Valerie caught his hand.

"Let's go somewhere alone to eat." She pleaded.

Sallisfer nodded, "Ok, I'll be right back with the food."

"No." Valerie pleaded, "Let's go." Sallisfer looked down into her desperate eyes. He felt her confusion as she pushed mentally against his walls. She knew he was hiding something; she knew he was lying, but she was still too weak to get through his defenses, and part of her feared knowing what he feared to tell her.

Sallisfer swallowed the lump in his throat and nodded. He took her hand and helped her to stand, "Where do you want to go?" He asked, feeling like he knew the answer but feared it anyway. He felt her hand tighten around his. The rush of her sudden surge in magic; he could smell the overwhelming scent of magnolias. He could hear the distant roar of her strength, but he could taste her compassion on his tongue. There wasn't a moment to spare. He tightened his grip on her hand, pulled her to him, and transported them away to a mountain in The Paradise. That is when her power hit full-on. No one had ever been as drained as she had and lived, no one had been able to contain their power as long as she had, and no one could have withstood it with her as long as Sallisfer could.

He felt her power rip at him and go through all of his initial defenses, but when it reached the wall and started to make it crumble, he stopped her. Pushing back with all of his power and strength, he powered to full and used their bond to add to his own vigor. Sallisfer closed her from the truth, emphasizing what he had told her, trying to convince her of its worth. Finally, Valerie was in control, her power died down, and she stored the leftovers in the empty black gemstone that hung around her neck. Sallisfer smiled, remembering the pale blue it would become when this was all over with.

"Thank you." Valerie breathed. At last, Sallisfer released his breath with a gust, not realizing that he had been holding it this whole time.

"No, Valerie, thank you." he breathed.

"For what?" Valerie asked, taking his hand. He smiled and took her other one.

"For allowing me to protect you," he murmured. Valerie smiled with her eyes as soft as the colors of the setting sun.

"I have to let you be the man sometimes." He smiled and pulled her close to him, and just as the sun's last light kissed the land, he kissed her soft lips. She felt like a child in his arms; maybe a human's innocent soul could cause hell's blackest pits to lose their grip and allow a little light to shine, 'Perhaps,' Sallisfer secretly thought as he kissed her neck. 'Or maybe the ice is breaking because the magic that restored her was purified.' He caught himself shedding a smile as his lips met back with hers.

"You know." He breathed loudly against her lips, "If you are the second most powerful before your sweet sixteen… how much more powerful do you have to be to top the headmaster."

He felt her smile on his, "Just slightly." she hissed as he pulled at her clothing, as overwhelmed with power as she was.

They teleported into The Paradise and shut all the ways to get there. They hid Paradise from the magic realm and became one, two bodies separated yet connected. Much like they had done the day after Valentine's Day, but with more meaning and understanding. The power of two flowed in one circle, unlike the night after Valentine's Day; however, where it was once strictly out of anger and confusion, this time, it was with a purpose.

They flowed together not because they had to but because they wanted to. This was about devotion and affection. It was not hatred; this was what it was like to be the Hands, harmonized and equal. This is what everyone worshiped. They did not do it out of fear or for tradition. They did it because the Hands stood for balance and equality between good and evil so the world could live peacefully. For, with the Hands, the battle was fought and continues to be fought. But somehow, they always came together enough to meet in the middle. At a state of mind where there can be neither evil nor good, but a place of peace, a place called love.

That is why when the devil played his cards, he chose the two souls that were never destined to be lovers. Little did he know that love can take many shapes and forms, molding and crafting its way around, through, and under any plan.

***

On Monday, Valerie found herself staring down the ravine. Looking at the Demons as they trudged through muddy conditions created by the rain, she and her elite team, including her father, were making. Only the strongest magic welders could change the weather in a remote place without overdoing it. A team of 10 could change the planet rotation if they wanted to; however, they only wanted to make the demon army as miserable as possible without risking more people.

"Whoever sent that platoon in for slaughter was a fool." She said, looking down at the pile of bodies that stood smoldering. 43 more people to add to the death toll and 1 missing lieutenant.

"This isn't going to hold them forever…Gregory was just trying to buy us some more time." Her father said, also looking down at the bodies.

"All he did was lose us some good men that would have aided us in the big fight," Valerie growled, sending a lightning bolt down to hit a nearby rock, causing a small landslide that blocked the path behind the enemy. No more reinforcements would be able to come that way.

She exhaled, "We need a big distraction…."

"How do we do that?" Her father asked, eyeing her with interest.

"I have a plan," she mused, "but I don't have to share it with you."

"You will, to the headmaster," he said, his voice tight with contained annoyance.

"…hmm," Valerie said, pretending to think it over, "I don't think I do."

Before her father could move, she called quits on the magic. "That should hold them at bay," she checked the cloud cover they had produced just over the ravine with one more look checking for any missing parts that would allow sunlight. When she couldn't find any, she nodded to the others, who teleported back to the line to regroup and recover.

"Are you going to the performance tonight?" her father asked.

"I have no choice," Valerie said, "...unless you and Mom changed y'all mind."

"No," he said. "You should be there. It is a family tradition, and this is Kal's first time." Her father said, "It will be interesting to see how Kal takes learning the truth behind her story."

"Well, I don't know if she should know it all just yet," Valerie muttered. "But I guess I have no choice."

"No, you don't." her father said, eyeing the cloud cover. "This was a very clever idea you had."

"I didn't come up with it." Valerie said, "Just as I didn't come up with blowing the dam and sending them into the bog…. Mom is the clever one. I think we need to move her clearance level up. "She smiled and said, "I think The Headmaster would agree."

Her father growled slightly and muttered something, then he looked up with a bright spark in his eye. "Your brother was granted dragon status."

Valerie grinned as she took her father's hand, and they, too, left the ravine in a teleport and started walking up the wooded path to the castle. "I am glad to hear about Koda. When is he getting his wings?"

"Saturday. I trust you will be there." He looked down at his daughter, who smiled up at him.

"Make it Thursday, and yes, I will be there." She laughed. "This rain should hold them off…till the end of the week anyway. I fear we will go into battle again before long to shove them into the forest of the Old Gray King…Some of his old followers will not likely take kindly to the Demon army and will help us keep them away from the Castle. But the regiments are almost ready, and we will meet the Demons on our terms."

Her father nodded. "What are you going to do now?

Valerie laughed and looked down at her outrageous outfit of a now almost ruined blue silk dress with her hiking boots. "Do some laundry. You know Mom only does the clothes in the hamper, and the Sprites in the Castle fuss too much. So, I am going to go to the house and get some clean clothes, especially if I have to go to this thing tonight."

Her father laughed and ruffled her hair, "Get a shower while you are at it... When was the last time you bathed?"

"With soap?" Valerie asked. "I haven't a clue." Her father laughed and sent her on her way.

CHAPTER 37

El Uno Escogido

"Hey, kid-O." Valerie smiled as Kal walked into the house after a riding lesson with Ms. Wing.

Kal had been allowed to roam around the four hundred acres of land that comprised her guardian's ranch. She took care to stay as far away from the arena where the 16-year-olds fought as much as possible.

Kal had ridden all her life but never knew the correct way to sit and carry herself. "Hey, Valerie," Kal laughed, giving Valerie a hug and wrinkling her nose. "You smell like horses." She laughed.

"So do you. Mom says it won't be long till you can move from infantry to cavalry. You have learned a lot in just a few lessons." Kal laughed and looked brightly at the clean clothes that Valerie was sorting out and the pile of dirty ones still waiting to be washed.

"Did you wear everything in your wardrobe?" she laughed.

"And some in Sally's," Valerie stated through laughter.

Kal sat at her desk, beaming outwardly and inwardly about her following statement.

"So, I get to go back to school Monday." She boasted, "Are you coming?"

"No," Valerie said, disappointed while looking downcast, "You are going to have to make friends with Jane." She looked away and then gathered herself up. "Are you up for tonight?"

"Tonight?" Looking up from her human-school work, Kal asked, "What is happening tonight?" Valerie stared at her in disbelief.

"That sun-of-a-betch," She cursed, "he didn't tell you, did he? Oh well, tonight is the dance of the Told or the El Uno Escogido. It is a play about…well you."

"Me?"

"Ya, you are the chosen one…." Valerie stated in a matter-of-fact voice, which suddenly started to annoy Kal.

"Why do I have to be the chosen one! I mean, what does that even matter? How am I special?"

Valerie smiled and took the books from Kal, "Let's go for a ride, and I will explain…ok?"

Kal looked at her apprehensively for a split second, then agreed, "Ok."

They headed out to the barn after a quick change of clothing. At the tack room, both Valerie and Kal were doing *any-mini–miney-moe* on bridles to decide who to ride. In the end, it was Fancy for Kal and Caprice for Valerie. They laughed, grabbed a halter, and headed to the pasture to bring in their mount.

Valerie walked down to the gate. She called for Caprice, no horse. She called again; still, Cappy did not come trotting. Finally, she sighed, "Guess I got to go get you." She muttered, unlatching the gate and walking into the field. She walked, occasionally calling until she saw the big patchy gray mare grazing by the lake with her pasture mates nearby. "I know you heard me." Valerie laughed as the mare raised her large head to look at her with lazy brown eyes.

Valerie gave her the peppermint she carried and pulled the blue and black halter over her head. "Why me?" Cappy asked, "Can't you take out Splash or Rocket? Or how about Willow… maybe…." Valerie gave her a stern look but laughed.

"I picked you today, silly. You should be honored. Besides, Kalea is riding Fancy with us, so it's not like we will do any work."

"Still, I was quite enjoying my grass. Can't you shift or something?" Cappy asked as they started the long walk up to the gate and then to the barn.

"One, we want to talk, and shifting into a horse does not allow much talking… and two, shifting takes up a lot of energy that we can't afford now."

Cappy taking in all Valerie said though still not thrilled knew she had done her best to sway her towards another horse, "Oh well, I tried." Cappy stated and pouted the rest of the way to the gate. Valerie smiled and continued toward the barn. At the gate, they met up with Sallisfer and Sorrow, who had just returned from a long ride to the Rising Hills near the temples of Eden. Sallisfer had been patrolling the shields of the farm. Valerie closed her eyes and could see the lush grass of the rising hills close to where the farm met the break in the realms. This is where they buried their dead companions, the horses whose health fails them or their age takes its toll. Now those lost in the war were buried with honors if the owner wished them to come home. The grass was always greener and thick. The flowers were always more colorful and seemed to grow taller. The trees always provide shade at the right time of day. It was a place where troubled minds could rest and soak in the silence and beauty. Her grandfather had named it The Temples of Eden, a resting ground for four-legged friends who needed a final resting place.

"See Caps, Sorrow never complains." Valerie laughed, kissing Sorrow's black nose and hugging Sallisfer.

Sallisfer seeing her thoughts, asked, "So what will you tell Kal exactly? I mean, you can't tell her everything… it's not Time yet. She isn't ready to know everything…." Sallisfer stated, releasing Sorrow and coming in step with Valerie.

"I don't know exactly… I just know I will tell the truth, but not the whole truth."

"Are you sure I can't come along? Apple Jack could use a good hack." Sallisfer asked, grabbing her and pulling her towards him. They had shared quite a night -when the world had gone dark with Doom's power. It had opened doors of emotion and attachment that they didn't know was possible.

They had learned that they loved each other, but it was not the kind of love that lasted. Instead, it was how a child felt about a blanket or a favorite toy. It was an attachment that would bring back many fond memories when they looked at one another in the future. They knew their love for each other would never go away. And yet stronger and longer-lasting love was going to come between them, such as Valerie's love for Holjus.

So, yes, they needed each other and always will, but when the time came, they would let each other go.

"I love you," Valerie whispered.

"I love you," Sallisfer whispered back, kissing the top of her head. "I will be at your beck and call if you need me."

"I know," Valerie affirmed.

They separated, and Valerie led Cappy up the final hill to the barn.

"What took you so long?" Kal asked, looking at her with a knowing smile.

"Had to go fetch my horse," Valerie said, pointing at Cappy, who seemed to grin.

"Looks like you have your work cut out for you. Good luck getting rid of all that mud." Kal laughed as she placed her saddle on Fancy's red back and tightened the girth.

Valerie laughed, "You were right, Caps; perhaps I should have gotten Daisy."

"Told you so." Cappy smiled, feeling a little satisfaction.

"I will never get used to that," Kal muttered.

"Used to what?"

"You being able to understand animals. It's a wonder you still eat meat."

"Wow, Kal, wow." Valerie laughed, "I get my earth power from Mom. She can talk to animals too. Kind of like Dr. Dolittle.... but not."

"Yet you are not vegetarians."

"No, just because we can understand them doesn't mean we will cut out a huge part of our diet! No, we are omnivores… besides we can understand all living things, including the shrubbery." Valerie explained as she started to curry the hardened mud off of Caprice's gray back.

"You can talk to plants?"

"Yes and no… just like talking to animals, you feed off their energy and body language, but it turns into words in the brain and processes like words and conversation." Valerie used a stiff body brush to remove what she loosened and moved on again with the curry, "With plants, it is mostly the energy they give. The emotion of the energy gives you a wave of information. Not a back-and-forth combo like with animals… for most anyway." Valerie laughed.

"I would not be able to eat at all." Kal declared, staring at Valerie with wide eyes, "I mean, that would just be too cruel. I can hear the spinach crying for help as you place it on your fork… no, I would rather become an autophagy."

Valerie stopped her vigorous brushing to stare at Kal with wide eyes, "You would rather eat yourself?" she asked, shocked. "There is no nutritional value in doing that."

Kal laughed so hard she had tears running down her face and had to run to a stall to pee. The horses exchanged an amused look, and Valerie shook her head. She finished getting the last mud away from Cappy's critical areas and started to tack the large 16' 3 hand mare up.

Kal recovered shortly; as they started to lead the horses out of the barn to mount, Valerie turned to Kal, "Fancy said she agreed with you eating my veggies."

"Really, Fancy?" Kal asked the tall red American Saddlebred. The horse snorted, and Kal squeaked as snot flew all over her hand, making Valerie laugh.

"I guess the main reason I'm not a vegetarian is that someone has to share the taste of steak with poor Sally."

They laughed as they checked girths and mounted. Soon they were out on the trail feeling light-hearted, and Kal began thinking. Although her friend was a demon-earth child, it was like old times between them.

The period before, Kal knew of this wonderful crazy life she was living now.

When they neared the first land bridge, Valerie stopped to allow Fancy and Kal to stand beside her. "Now is the time for you to know what El Uno Escogido is all about." Valerie smiled, "Ride ahead of me and let me tell you the story of The Chosen One."

Kal nodded and nudged Fancy ahead of Cappy on the trail. Fancy sighed and did as her rider instructed, knowing full well that Cappy, with her long legs, would be cussing at her from behind. Cappy pinned her ears back and bobbed her head up and down, but with a quick nudge from Valerie, she backed off and let Fancy come up and pass her. Valerie rolled her eyes and sunk her seat into the saddle, making herself slightly heavier as Cappy began to prance and snap at Fancy's red rear. "Steady," Valerie growled. Then, with a relenting grunt, Cappy settled into a slow walk. Her ears pinned to her head as Fancy swished her tail in almost a taunting way, her ears forward and her eyes gleaming with mischief.

"El Uno Escogido, The Chosen One, is a legend." Valerie started. "There is a legend told by the fates of ancient times. It was found in a Spanish journal well before our generation was even a thought." Valerie licked her lips as she thought about what she was about to say. "It started with the telling of darkness well after the shifting of the blood."

"The what?" Kal asked, looking over at Valerie.

"The shifting of the blood." Valerie stared; she often forgot that Kal wasn't raised like she was. "The shifting of the blood is when humans came to be." Valerie could feel all the history she had learned coming to the surface. "One day a child was born… this child had no ability to work magic… yet it was able to live."

"Had none been born before?" Kal asked.

"They had, but they had died shortly after birth." Valerie said, "This one… a boy named Encio was the first to live without power. Soon more were born, and soon they outnumbered those who could do magic. For a long time, we lived in peace with the non-magic but…" she trailed off feeling her heart start to hammer in her chest as she thought about what had happened all those years ago and who had been responsible.

She pulled Cappy into a slower walk and pulled out a single card she kept hidden in her deck. A tall, muscular man with midnight black hair and vibrant brown eyes. He was dressed in armor and had a sword raised in his hands. The defiant look on his face was etched in Valerie's mind. Ríoghnán Wing, the card read, hummed with magic even now after all these years. Valerie swallowed the lump in her throat as she put the card away and looked back at Kal, reminding herself that she did not start the darkness. "The non-magic…well, they began to fear and outnumber us. We call this time the Shifting of the Blood, as their kind was greater than us… we started to go into hiding. In hiding, we lived in peace and were in balance with everyone…for the most part, anyway. But magic seems to have a mind of its own."

Kal nodded at Valerie. "So, this legend talks about modern times?"

"Yes." Valerie smiled, "May I continue?"

"Yes."

"It started with the telling of darkness well after the shifting of blood, a time when Doom will threaten the very balance of the world." Valerie closed her eyes, allowing the story to flow from her as she saw it in her mind. "However, the fates promised that even in a time of darkness, there will always be light. They said not one set of Hands would be born at the beginning of the darkness but two. They promised that although there was only one set of Hands, the second would pick up right where the other let go…." She paused as she felt hot tears well up in her eyes.

"It was told that the Spirits would choose those of Earth, the firstborn to be Doom, the second to be Heaven… they would come too late… chosen and enlisted innocent and unaware that they would be the downfall of what their ancestors had built." She could see in her mind's eye her own choosing. She watched again as she had a million times before as the last Doom, a shell of a body, turned to dust well over Time to travel beyond… Again, Valerie felt the burn of hate surging through her small four-year-old body. She could see the nightmares that flashed as past lives aligned in her mind and memory. Valerie gasped as she had that day as the cold spirit sucked away her life, pulling on her power. Valerie had been born with power. She did not have to wait as many did for it.

The power inside her bloomed on the day her first cry was heard in the magic realm. So powerful she was at birth it nearly killed her mother, and when it came time to give a few drops of blood, her heel had bent the knife. The mark on her chest, shown red at birth, caused the midwife to drop her, an immortal hadn't been born to a mortal in over two hundred years, and now one was marked with the impending symbol of Doom. Valerie had flown before she had even known what she was, who she was, a perfect green dragon out of the hands of her father, who had to dive to catch her.

Doom had pulled on this natural ability. Although the Headmaster tried to help her learn how to put the spirit at bay, Valerie had just learned about windows and doors in her mind. Her mind was closed as the anklet she had worn, then it shattered as Doom took over. That day, all those years ago, was the day that the darkness had started.

Valerie took a breath and opened her eyes, suddenly aware that Cappy had stopped walking and Kal was watching her from Fancy.

"You had stopped talking… are you okay?" Kal asked. Valerie nodded and motioned that Kal should continue riding ahead of her.

"I was four when the darkness took me." Valerie almost whispered to herself as they started up the trail again. She closed her eyes to compress the anger she felt, knowing her childhood had been ripped away from her. She opened her eyes again, blinking away the tears. "The legend states that the Fates promised that the firstborn Doom would restore the line that was broken when the blood shifted and retires the hidden, forgotten line of the Hands. She of the forgotten born to the forgotten blood." Valerie licked her dry lips and allowed a moment to pass as they walked past a babbling brook; she recalled once more that line and thought it over in her mind. She had always wondered what that line meant. Valerie had figured out years ago while watching the play that the hidden represented the Headmaster. She knew she was the forgotten blood, but how would she retire the hidden?

Receiving a touch on her gift of animal speech, Valerie called out to Kal, "Wait, a doe has given birth ahead; take the path to the left." Then she felt the doe's fear. Valerie jumped from Cappy's back and ran down the path to the doe and her struggling newborn. Valerie calmed the mother and approached. Kal watched as Valerie looked over the newborn, who was born too early. Valerie soothed the grieving mother and healed her body. Valerie looked down at the baby as she contemplated burying it or leaving it as a meal. *Would I one day have children? Would she one day feel the heartache this mother had felt before Valerie had taken it?* She wondered as she walked the cold empty body into the woods.

"What are you doing?" Kal asked. She had tears sliding down her face, and it looked like she was going to jump off Fancy and take the dead fawn.

Valerie rested it in a pile of leaves, "It must return to nature," She stated, her voice flat without emotion that made Kal stare at her like she was some sort of monster. Valerie thought as a smile almost touched her lips. *Perhaps I am a monster*, she thought, but out loud, she said, "This was life and death in one moment. Although it made me sad, I know that even though it was small, it will feed the hungry."

Kal gave her a now thoughtful look, and she nodded in understanding. *No,* Valerie thought *I will not be a monster, and I might have brought the darkness.* She walked away from the doe resting place in profound, meaningful thought.

As she mounted back on Cappy, she reflected on how the day went dark the day she was chosen. Not one hand but both her hands had been clasped as Heaven shared the power of not one but two bodies to smooth over the darkness. *I have also brought back the light.*

They had ridden back down the trail a few feet in silence. "So, is that the end of the story?"

Kal reminded Valerie, "The Fates promised that the firstborn Doom would restore the line that was broken when the blood shifted and retires the hidden, forgotten line of the Hands… What does that even mean?" Kal voiced Valerie's own thoughts, and Valerie wondered in alarm if she had told Kal too much. "What about the second set of born hands… I mean, I am one, right?" Kal asked.

Valerie smiled. The second-born Doom and the firstborn Heaven will be those of Time. They will walk the halls of Time as those who came before walked the halls of the world. Freed of Earthly ties, the second Doom shall combine with the first Heaven and restore the blood-bound child to his place as the true bond to Doom's unholy torrent." Kal turned to see that Valerie's eyes had gone misty, and the next thing Valerie said shook Kal to the core.

"The second-born Doom will be one who walked the Earth before. One who had carried the darkness once before and used it to create peace between those who lurked in the darkness and those who walked in the light. The Chosen One, this Doom was called for when those who lurked became bold and vowed the Chosen One would return to power to finish what had been started -creating ever-lasting peace between all those living." Valerie closed her eyes again. She was now a low-ranking master, carrying the mysterious heavy necklace in her pocket, her fingers memorizing every etching around the stone.

She wondered if Kal had discovered that her spirit animal was not just a wolf, and she studied Kal's back and almost laughed. *"No,"* Sallisfer said in her mind, *"She has not discovered the secret."*

Valerie nodded in agreement and continued the story, "The Fates declared that the Chosen One would be a mighty warrior, one that showed the unique qualities of a wolf and shared the spirit of the regal animal. The Fates confirmed that the one to lead our people to peace through darkness was a kind but ruthless child who would be found by the forgotten spirit when they least sought the other half of what was once whole.

When named, the Chosen will restore the harmony lost by the forgotten and wipe clean all that is not faithful." Valerie opened her eyes and stared at Kal's small frame as she rode in front of her. "It is told that the wolf, which isn't usually a carrier of magic, is the only one Demons shall bow to.

When the Chosen is named, children shall laugh, as joy sings its true song in Heaven's light." Kal glanced at Valerie wide-eyed as parts of what the Told ones had said to her started to make sense.

"I had searched for you so long. In the Spanish opera, we will see that Darkness continued to spread over the land when the forgotten failed to find the chosen. Those who believed in the chosen and those who did not believe clashed. It took 2 years till those who knew better wiped clean those who did not. In the end, the believers won, and the first hands continued to search for the one that could end all wars, the chosen one."

Kal blinked, realizing the story was over, "Why did my mother never tell me? Why did she hide me?"

"I don't know. You will have to ask your mother that one." Valerie replied.

"But—why me?"

"Because you are the wolf, you carry the mark of Doom on your back, and you are my best friend, don't you see? We have a lot of things in common, and we are kind of, in a way, quite drawn to one another. You know what I am thinking, not because you are connected to me, but because you think like me…." Valerie trailed off, "I'm sorry I didn't tell you sooner."

Kal smiled, relieved that she was finally starting to understand her role in this realm, "It's okay. Before now, I probably wouldn't have believed you."

Valerie smiled back, and they continued down the trail, "Will I know how to end all wars when I am named, much like I knew how to use the dual sabers?"

"I don't know."

Finally, Valerie said plainly, "You must have the demons submit to you. If you do not do it right…you could plunge the world into greater darkness."

Kal shivered, "I don't know if I am the right person for the job."

They were out of the woods and stood at the start of a vast field. Valerie stopped beside Kal and looked at her with sad brown eyes, "You are the only person for the job. You will, however, not stand alone. When the Time comes, you will stand with Kris, you and he shall be victorious, or the Fates will be proven wrong, and the world as we know it will end."

With that, Valerie nudged Cappy into a trot that lengthened into a canter, and she was off like a shining silver star. She stopped at the top of a hill looking back at Kal, waiting. Kal nudged Fancy into her rocking horse canter, and when she reached the top, Valerie smiled at her.

"Race you to the dirt warm-up arena." And with that, she was off again.

"Not fair!" Kal yelled after her as Fancy picked up her gentle rocking horse canter again, as Cappy flew ahead at a cross-country gallop with Valerie's laughter flying behind like Super-Man's cape.

After the ride, the girls took care of the horses, then they showered, dressed in their Sunday best, and, with Valerie's parents and siblings, went to the opera. It was in Spanish, as it was initially told. The play was more than Kal could have imagined as she watched what Valerie had told her unfold. She still didn't understand some parts, and when she turned to Valerie for an explanation, Valerie just placed a finger on her lips and whispered, "All will become clear when the time is right."

In the end, Kal had more questions that had yet to be answered, but as she had learned, it was only a matter of *Time*.

EXCERPT

ANGUISH 2

The smell of decay and sickness hung thick in the air as a black bird cawed above the marching dark shadows below the thick cloud cover. Bright red eyes looked the bird over. "Do you think it is one of those shifty earth brats?" The voice was thick with hate. Another set of red eyes looked at the bird as it caught a wind current and started to fly higher and away.

"No, Miltiades you fool." His companion barked, "This ravine is making you see things."

"Keir, I still think we should have blasted it out of the sky… I am sure they taste like chicken." Miltiades grumbled just as his stomach rumbled loudly.

Under their feet in the rocks sat a black lizard who waited for his world to stop shaking as he watched the thunderous feet trudge slowly by. The pack of working animals, which had long been eaten by their owners, forced a few hundred men to be strapped into refitted harnesses to move covered carts while a few men pushed from behind. More men strapped to large, wheeled carts with broken beams grunted with effort as they thundered by. When the ground began to settle, the black lizard took one last cautious look around and started climbing up the ravine walls.

A loan figure sat crisscrossed in the dry grass, waving her hand over it, making it turn green with life with green dancing sparks that slipped from her fingertips. She heard the caw of the black crow and reached out, and the bird landed on her forearm as a lizard crawled onto her palm.

"Report." The girl asked, her green eyes laced with flames shined down at the animals.

"You have two more days at most." The crow answered.

"They are tired and suspicious." The lizard nodded silently, giving his report.

"How many have been able to reach them?" she asked.

Ten thousand strong." The crow and the lizard agreed. Then, with a nervous licking of her lips, the girl nodded.

"And the trebuchets?" The girl asked.

"In parts." The crow and lizard responded together.

"That is at least some good news." The girl admitted. "Thank you." The crow gave a curt nod and flew away, and the lizard disappeared once more. As the girl prepared to stand, a chill took her from behind.

"What have you learned?" The deep voice of her Headmaster commanded.

"They have regrouped and are moving our way, Sir," she answered. "Perhaps we move my brother's ceremony?"

"No." the powerful voice countered, "Our people need the moral boost, and I need you to debrief someone."

"Sir?" She asked, confused. Her worries about a battle on the horizon were almost forgotten, but the chill was gone, and she stood with an aggravated sigh.

"Time to prepare." She thought out loud to no one as she rolled her eyes at the delay of war. But a smile spread across her face as she thought about home, a place she did not see very often. She thought about the honor her little brother was about to receive made her beam. "Koda," she whispered proudly, "You will join the flyers." Then her smile turned into a grin as her mind landed on her adopted younger sister. "Oh, Kalea," she beamed, "Your life is about to be turned even more upside down." She let out a laugh. *Time to go home.*